BOUND BY THE EARL

BOOK TWO IN THE LORDS OF DISCIPLINE SERIES

ALYSON CHASE

Cover image by Dar Albert.

Visit the author website: http://www.alysonchase.com

ISBN-13: 978-1-944802-00-4
ISBN-10: 1-944802-00-2

Chapter One

London, 1814

Julius Blackwell dug his fingers under the mask covering his face. The damn thing itched like the dickens. And smelled like a swamp. He tried to remember the last time he'd worn it. Vauxhall Gardens? That assignation with Godfrey's sister?

His lips scratched the wool as they curved beneath the mask. That had been a lovely evening, notwithstanding his flight along the banks of the Thames with Godfrey's men in pursuit. The man's outrage seemed disproportionate to Julius's offense. His sister was a lovely widow who had more than her fair share of trysts. Her behavior was well known throughout London. In Godfrey's defense, however, it was one thing to know of one's sister's behavior, but quite another to come across it along one of the garden's winding paths.

Julius's escape through the filthy river had been hard won. It also explained the smell.

He readjusted the mask. If only bed sport were the reason he wore it tonight.

The floor board beneath him groaned, and Julius froze. The felt he'd attached to the bottom of his boots was no protection against an ill-constructed house. Blast Lord Liverpool for sending him on this fool's errand. No earl should condescend to sneak through a widow's home in the middle of the night to steal a painting. Not even at the request of the prime minister.

The previous Lords Rothchild would roll over in their graves if they knew what the current one was doing. It had been ingrained in Julius since infancy that honor was the mainstay of the aristocracy. Honor and idleness. Julius was sure none of his ancestors had ever worked a day in their lives, much less worked for the Crown as a spy.

And blast Ashworth for getting blackmailed by Mrs. Abigail Westmont in the first place. Julius always seemed to be the Crown's first choice to clean up the messes the peerage left behind. If Liverpool didn't seek some form of retribution for Viscount Ashworth's latest indiscretion, Julius damn well would.

Easing into another sitting room, Julius examined the walls, but didn't find his object. All that remained to search were the Widow Westmont's own bedchambers. A pulse throbbed behind his temple. Of course, the harlot would keep it close. That painting was worth twenty thousand pounds to her, or a certain disgrace to Viscount Ashworth if he didn't pay.

His footsteps were mere whispers as he crept down the hallway. Julius prayed the widow kept her door well-oiled. Liverpool's instructions were to recover the item at all costs, but violence against women didn't sit well with Julius. Even against conniving blackmailers.

Taking a deep breath, he pressed the door open, the wood hissing over the raised carpet. Moonlight streamed in through the uncovered window, falling on the form beneath the coverlet. Her chest rose and fell smoothly, enjoying the sleep of the innocent.

Julius bit back a snort. Mrs. Abigail Westmont was anything but. Although Julius had never enjoyed the pleasure of her favors, he'd known many men who had. Many, many men. How many of them had she blackmailed, too?

The shadowed walls were bare. He narrowed his eyes. Where would she keep it? He peered over the back of her settee. Nothing. In her wardrobe, Julius pushed aside swathes and swathes of fabric. Julius ground his teeth together and tossed a glance over his shoulder at the sleeping figure. Why did women have so many blasted clothes? It wasn't to impress men. They didn't give their first bollock about current fashions. The less worn, the better. Julius wanted the smallest barrier possible between him and a woman when he bound her wrists to a headboard and bent—

His gaze flew to the bed. On silent feet, he padded close, listening to her even breathing. Dropping to his hands and knees, he lifted the ruffle and stared into the pitch black beneath the mattress and frame. Feeling his way, he searched the floor, finding nothing. He flattened to his stomach and scooted as far underneath as he could, straightening his arm. His fingertips nudged a cloth-wrapped bundle.

Stretching his shoulder, Julius ignored the familiar pain that shot through the joint and grasped the edge of the painting, tugging it towards him. As quietly as possible, he pulled the two-foot square canvas free of the counterpane. Rolling to a crouch, he shot one last look at the Widow Westmont and slipped from her room.

Julius stalked to the window at the end of the hall. Moonlight streamed through the curtains. He unwrapped enough of the canvas to see that it was, indeed, a portrait of Ashworth. Tucking the picture under his arm, he escaped from the house the way he'd entered. He waited for the familiar rush of pleasure and satisfaction that came from evading detection, from gaining entrée where he didn't belong, but tonight he just felt on edge.

Two blocks away, he climbed into his carriage and headed for White's. He found Liverpool where he expected, ensconced in a private room, a stack of papers on the table next to him, smoke curling from the end of his pipe.

"I see you were successful," Liverpool said. Turning a page in *The London Gazette*, he flicked a glance at Julius. The man had only been prime minister for a couple of years, and Julius hadn't yet learned the art of reading him. His predecessor had certainly never communicated with Julius or his friends in person, not when it came to their unofficial government duties. Julius supposed he should appreciate the risk Lord Liverpool took in speaking with him face to face. Either that or the man didn't trust his messengers.

"Did you doubt I would be?" Julius strode to a sideboard, unwrapped the canvas, and propped it against the wall. Taking a step back, he grimaced. "Bloody hell. Ashworth deserves to be blackmailed. He posed for his mistress like this?"

Liverpool peered over the paper, his spectacles glinting in the light. He harrumphed. "I understand the lady painted it from memory. Not very flattering to the man, is it?"

"I'd object more to the girlish pose on the settee than the lack of proportion." Julius cocked his head. "Maybe." Not wanting to look upon it a moment more, he rewrapped the canvas. "I assume the wine-colored birthmark above his groin was the source for the blackmail?"

Liverpool nodded. "Something only his wife and doctor should know."

"A lot of men have affairs."

"Not all of them have the ear of the Prince Regent. Not all of them have built a political platform on family values. The man seems particularly aggressive in wanting to imprison adulterers. Of the lower classes, of course." The prime minister shook his head. "No, Lord Ashworth was a fool to be so indiscrete." He flipped to another page, dismissing Julius.

Another job done. Julius's shoulders sagged. Finishing a job for the Crown usually left Julius in high spirits. Eager for more adventure. Being a spy had given his life purpose. Tonight, he felt drained. He just wanted to get home, go to bed.

With a curt nod, Julius strode for the door.

"Good job, Rothchild." Liverpool's words stopped Julius.

Julius turned and looked once more at the canvas. "You know Mrs. Westmont can paint another picture."

"Yes." Liverpool sucked at his pipe. "It's no longer your concern."

Julius hesitated. "If everyone knew about the birthmark, there could be no recourse to blackmail. A friendly prank among friends that went awry."

Liverpool pursed his lips. "Perhaps. Goodnight, Rothchild."

Crossing the club, Julius ignored the greetings of acquaintances. How tenuously Mrs. Westmont's life hung in the balance. Everything she knew could be taken away from her tomorrow if the prime minister wished it. A scandal created to destroy her reputation. A crime faked to separate her from society. Which path would Liverpool take to eliminate the threat?

The prime minister called upon Julius and his friends in the House of Lords to help the Crown in times of need. But there was a limit to his service. Tasks he wouldn't perform.

Liverpool called upon others less honorable for the jobs Julius refused to do.

It was a messy business keeping an empire together.

Climbing into his carriage, Julius sagged into the velvet seat and called, "Home."

The driver closed the door and poked his head in the open window. "Home, my lord? Or the Duke of Montague's townhouse?"

Julius leaned his head back on the seat and stared at the ceiling. Bugger. That was his home now. At least while Marcus was touring the continent with his new bride. His friend's stifling townhouse with its crush of servants watching his every move.

Its other occupant made him feel just as uncomfortable, but for an entirely different reason.

He sighed. "To Montague's. And don't look so relieved. I know you like staying in the duke's carriage house more than mine."

His driver kept his lips even. "No, my lord."

The carriage shifted as the man took his seat. The flannel-wrapped bricks at Julius's feet had long since cooled, and he tugged his coat tighter about him. Both carriage windows were open, but he made no move to close them. A soft breeze chilled his face and he breathed deep.

His shoulder ached, and he idly rubbed the old hurt. He felt a hundred years old, in both body and soul. He'd seen too much in life. No matter how hard he and his friends worked, nothing would change. The same battles were fought every year. If it wasn't France, it would be the Russian Empire or an internal enemy that threatened the peace. Human nature was set.

The wraith that haunted the halls of Montague's townhouse attested to that fact.

So much pain in one so young. Fire burned in Julius's chest. Each time he saw Miss Amanda Wilcox, he wanted to kill every man that had a part in putting the hollowness in her eyes.

He wanted a lot of things when he saw her. But she was his good friend's sister-in-law and under his care.

He snorted. Marcus had left the chit under Julius's protection while he was away with his new bride. The idiot. Like putting the fox in charge of the henhouse. Or perhaps his friend was brilliant. Believing that if caring for Amanda was Julius's duty, he'd never touch her.

That was putting a lot of faith in Julius. Faith he didn't know was justified.

The carriage rattled to a stop. Julius trudged up the steps to the front door, the damned thing swinging open before he reached it. The butler must have stood sentry by the window watching for him. Always watching.

"Thank you, Carter." Julius handed the man his gloves. "You didn't need to wait up. I've told you that before. Many times."

"Yes, my lord." The man's wig was askew and sleep creased his face, but Julius knew he would have stayed up all night just to open the damn door for him. Next time Julius left the house, he would tell Carter he was staying out till morning so the butler wouldn't wait up.

Carter picked up a candle. "Shall I lead you to your room?"

Julius's scalp prickled. "I know my way. You go on to bed." He waved away the offered candle. "And keep your candle. I can see well enough in the moonlight."

"Yes, my lord." The golden aura faded as the man walked to his quarters. Julius faced the stairs to the second floor and sighed. Too many steps. Instead, he trudged to the duke's library. It was Julius's favorite room in the house, with high ceilings, large windows, and a surprisingly comfortable settee to sleep on.

He pushed the door open and frowned. It was black as pitch, all the curtains drawn. He'd told Carter to keep the drapes open. It wasn't like the man to forget.

Julius crossed the room and pulled back the curtains. The muscles in his shoulders unknotted as the night sky opened up before him. Alone at last. As alone as one could be in a metropolis of one million denizens.

Fabric rustled, and he jerked his head around. Slippered feet disappeared under the hem of a skirt hanging over a bench seat. The body attached to the feet was hidden in shadow, but Julius knew to whom it belonged. Only one woman would be hiding in the dark in this house.

"Miss Wilcox, the hour is late for you to be out of bed."

No answer.

"And sitting in a library without a light seems a bit pointless. Unless you can read in the dark."

She sighed.

Julius moved closer, slowly, careful not to startle her. She moved around the house like smoke, and he didn't want her to slip through his fingers. "Can't you sleep?"

"I'll leave you be if you wish to be alone." Her husky voice surrounded him like a thick fog. The rasp that she'd developed in prison had never truly left.

"I didn't say that." He held out his hand. "But I would like for you to stop hiding in the dark. Let's sit by the window."

He waited, pulse pounding in his ears, until she placed her hand within his own. Satisfaction coursed through him. Amanda shied away from most contact, only stiffly tolerating her sister's embraces. Her hand was cool, and he chafed it as he led her to the settee.

"What are you doing out of bed at this hour?" he asked.

"Waiting for you."

Moonlight fell on Amanda's cheek. A strand of dark hair lay across her neck, and his fingers itched to tuck it back behind her ear. "Was there something you needed? You've only to ask. You know I'm here in Marcus's stead. Anything you would ask of him, you can ask of me."

A smile ghosted across her lips. "I hope not. There's something I wish to ask you that I could never ask my brother by marriage. My sister wouldn't care for it."

He squeezed her hand, hoping to reassure her. "If it is in my power to deliver, it's yours."

Raising her other hand, she laid it atop his so both her hands surrounded his one. Tentatively, she brushed her thumb from his knuckles to his wrist, gently, like he was the one made of porcelain and could be broken.

His skin prickled. The air in the library thickened, grew heavy, and a longing filled him that stole his breath. Its strength had never been matched.

"What I want," she said. "What I've wanted since the moment you moved into this house, is for you to take me to bed and have your way with me."

Chapter Two

Julius's eyes flared, but he betrayed no other indication of surprise at her language. And that surprised Amanda. She thought she'd shock him. What man wouldn't be by such a request?

"Pardon me," he said. "I must have misheard. What is it you wish?"

Amanda's stomach twisted, squeezed. It had taken all her courage to ask him the first time. Now he wished her to repeat her scandalous demand?

"You heard me correctly." She cleared her throat. So much depended upon his answer. The idea had taken root the first week he'd moved into Marcus and Elizabeth's home. He was the first man in whose presence she felt safe since ... forever. Yet she'd had no idea how to implement her desires. How to seduce. Each day she'd watched him leave the house, get swallowed up in the London streets, and leave her behind. Each day she grew more and more desperate.

He narrowed his eyes. They were the first thing she'd noticed about him when he'd saved her those months ago. Not quite brown, not quite green. They'd mesmerized her, given her something to focus on as he'd raced her away from the hangman's noose.

Gleaming in the moonlight, they didn't look as warm and reassuring now as they had that day they'd met.

Laying his arm on the back of the settee, he grimaced slightly. Amanda knew that shoulder troubled him. A past injury he didn't speak of. It usually acted up after a visit to

Gentleman Jack's or a race through the park. Or sometimes after one of his illicit undertakings, which he thought she knew nothing about. On one such occasion he'd favored his right arm for a week. What had he been doing so late tonight to inflame it?

He drummed his fingers on the wood behind her shoulder. "Might I ask why you want me to, as you so quaintly phrased it, have my way with you?"

Amanda smoothed a hand down her skirts. This wasn't going as planned. Weren't most men supposed to jump at the chance to lay between a woman's thighs? Not waste time with interrogations.

"You think men are alone in their needs?" She willed her gaze to remain steady on his face. The dark hid the blush that heated her cheeks. "Much is made of the act. I know my sister enjoys her marital duties. And ... bed sport," she said, tumbling over the words, "is something that all mankind has in common. Nature demands it, regardless of class or race." She worried the fabric of her gown between her fingers and raised one shoulder. "I'm curious. And I want to feel"—*like everyone else*—"something. You are a physically attractive man and I hope I am not unpleasing to your eye. As I will never marry, this solution only seems practical."

"Prettily said, for an act that is far from pretty." Julius crossed one leg over the other, tugging at the knee of his trouser. "When I fuck, there's sweating, moaning, the slap of flesh on flesh. You'll scream from pleasure, but there's not one damn thing pretty about it."

She swallowed, her throat thick. Julius had succeeded where she had failed. He'd managed to shock her senses, just as he'd intended, she was sure. She knew all that the act entailed, but she hadn't thought the earl would put words to the deeds.

It shouldn't have surprised her. The man was intense. Julius Blackwell, Lord Rothchild, was known throughout England as someone it was best not to aggravate. There were whispers about him. About how his time in the East had damaged his mind. Made him unsound.

She didn't believe them. Julius had never been anything but kind to her. A steadying presence she relied upon, especially in her sister's absence. A man she trusted.

She had hoped that the first time she consented to a man touching her, there might be gentleness.

She licked her dry lips. "Does that mean you agree?"

"Hardly." He exhaled loudly through his nose and crossed his arms over his broad chest.

She knew he desired her. She'd learned enough in life to see the signs when a man wanted her body. And Lord Rothchild, for all his kindnesses, for his fraternal protectiveness towards her, was not immune.

"Even if I were in the habit of dallying with unmarried chits, you are the sister-in-law of my friend."

Amanda sank back against the settee. She was prepared for this line of defense. "A friend who left me here. All alone. With you."

"In my care," he amended. "And not all alone. The Lady Mary Cavindish is your chaperone."

She laughed, the sound rusty from disuse. Julius looked as surprised at the noise as she. "Marcus is a smart man. If he were interested in preserving anything but the bare appearance of propriety, he would have called for another one of his aunts to come to London. Lady Mary is ..." simple, sweet, and oblivious, "... inattentive. And Marcus knows that."

"Are you implying that Montague wishes for us to become intimate?" He snorted. "He and I are close, but I don't think he's friend enough to wrap up his wife's sister in a pretty bow for me to take my pleasure in."

"And if he thought it would benefit both of us?" Staring into the darkness of the room, Amanda considered her new brother. He'd been nothing but polite and kind. But he had no illusions about the type of woman she was. He knew there was no reputation to protect. She turned to Julius, her knee brushing his. That brief contact made her skin tingle and her stomach churn. She wanted Julius. But would she have the courage to go through with it? In equal parts, he made her ache and then feel as though she were about to cast up her accounts. If she could take this step with anyone, however, it would be him. "I believe Marcus was giving us the opportunity, if we wish to take it."

Julius cocked his head. "Why do you think you'll never marry?"

Amanda shot to her feet. One hand curled into a fist, and not for the first time she wished she were a man. She hadn't thought he would mock her. "All you had to do was say no. I will look elsewhere."

She turned for the door, ignoring his curse. She couldn't ignore his hand on her wrist.

"I apologize, Miss Wilcox. I'd forgotten—"

"That I'm soiled goods? Has the beau monde stopped whispering about the trollop who killed her father already? Who seduced him with her body, who spread her legs for half the men in prison?" His hand tensed around her wrist, and she shook herself free from his grip. "I've heard how I'm spoken of. My sister, the Duchess of Montague, is given the cut direct by half the ton. I'm treated as though I don't exist. Whom, exactly, do you see me marrying?"

She pressed her palms to her stomach to keep them from shaking but she couldn't control her voice as easily. Julius stepped forward, his face falling into shadow, and she was glad. She couldn't bear to see his expression. The pity. The disgust. Both were equally repellant.

With as much insolence as she could muster, she dipped into a low curtsy. "If you will excuse me, my lord, it is past time for me to retire."

"No."

Amanda hesitated. "Pardon me?"

"I said"— Julius took another step forward—"that I will not excuse you. Not until we've cleared this matter up."

Amanda stumbled back until her shoulder blades hit the

bookcase. Julius rested his hands on the shelves on either side of her. His body was close, close enough to feel the heat of it through her cotton gown. He smelled of bergamot and musk, and her breath caught in her throat. A queer rolling, sliding feeling slipped through her stomach and she didn't know whether to revel in it or try to escape the sensation. Lord Rothchild was like a drug. Intoxicating, stupefying, and thrilling. Her fingers flexed, needing to hold onto something but finding only air.

"Where do you hear these things? You never leave the house." His breath brushed across her lips. It smelled faintly of brandy, and she wondered if she rolled up onto her toes and kissed him, if he would taste of it as well.

He leaned closer, his chest brushing against hers. "Answer me."

She almost moaned. The tips of her breasts tingled and a hollow ache settled low in her belly. What was the question again? Oh, the insults. "If you think only those in society enjoy gossip, you're sorely mistaken."

"The servants." His voice was icy. "Montague's staff talks about you." Julius rocked back, and her body cooled.

"Of course, they do." Turning her head, she blinked at the burn in her eyes. She'd thought shame had been long lost to her. "I overhear them gossip about what is said of me in the other grand homes." Intentionally, Amanda was sure. Her maids did little to hide their words. "And I'm sure if I did anything of interest, that information would be spread among the other houses." Lifting her chin, she said, "It's unfortunate for them that I don't leave the premises."

"I don't know." Julius tucked an errant strand of hair behind her ear. "I find your proposition to me the most interesting event of the night."

"What else happened to you tonight?"

Resting his hand on her shoulder, he brushed his thumb across her collarbone, sending a shiver straight down her spine. "Maybe if you weren't too afraid to have a life outside these walls, you'd find out."

She narrowed her eyes. Well, if that wasn't a challenge to go after what she wanted, she didn't know what was. Grabbing the lapels of his wool coat, she yanked him down.

His grunt of surprise was muffled by her mouth. His lips were firm, unyielding, and warm. With the tip of her tongue she poked at the seam of his mouth until the tip hit his teeth. He did taste of brandy.

And he wasn't kissing her back.

Pulling away, she tried to catch her breath. Her throat was bone dry and her palms were damp. Why wasn't he kissing her back?

"Julius?"

He caressed her cheek with his thumb. "You've never kissed a man before."

Her spine snapped straight. "I beg your pardon! Am I to infer from your comment that my technique was lacking?"

"Yes."

She gaped at him. "You ... scoundrel! A gentleman wouldn't point that out."

"A gentleman also wouldn't fuck you upon request. As you've asked it of me, you must know I'm no gentleman." Putting action to words, he slid his hand off her shoulder and down her body. Slowly, ever so slowly, he cupped her breast and squeezed. His eyes never left her face, assessing.

Moisture pooled between her thighs. Julius's broad shoulders blocked out the moonlight, and darkness blanketed her like a cloak. It seemed like all the major moments of her life happened in the dark. She wanted this, wanted him. Wanted to feel like an ordinary woman, one who could enjoy a man's touch. Bedding Julius would be a healthy first step.

Her body clamored with mixed messages. Desire, yes. But the slight trembling of her hands wasn't only from lust. She leaned into his caress, tried to focus on the sensation, but her throat squeezed more tightly and tightly closed. She slipped away from his grasp fighting back tears of failure.

He raised his hands. "There. You see? You've asked for

something for which you are not prepared."

"Was that a test?"

"Yes." He sighed. "And the outcome was as I expected."

Shame mixed with outrage. She'd been attempting to expand her boundaries, quavering with the effort of it, and he stood there as unaffected as a teacher delivering a lesson. But the disgrace of it was, he was right. She wasn't ready. Not tonight. But soon. Tonight, she would retreat and examine her reactions and try to plot a way forwards.

But she had her pride, and it refused to let him see her run back to her room to lick her wounds. "I wouldn't want you to suffer my inadequate attempts at congress. Perhaps I'll seek a less critical partner elsewhere."

She reached the door before he responded.

"Miss Wilcox, as your temporary protector, I feel beholden to insist that you run the name of any potential scoundrels by me before you commence any affairs." He stalked towards her. "I feel duty bound to investigate their character."

"And you'd allow me that liberty?" Disappointment crashed through her, and tears burned the back of her eyes. She could never put herself through this with another man.

"Of course. As you point out, there is no marriage bed to save yourself for." Pausing next to her, he tugged at the neckline of her gown, straightening the lace trim. "Though I don't think I need worry about it."

Amanda froze. Surely he didn't see that clearly into her mind. See that of all the men she'd known, she held him in an especial regard. Even after this failure, she knew she would try to seduce him again, and the tender feelings he evoked would make giving her body that much easier. That didn't mean she wanted him to know of them.

"And why is that?" she whispered.

"You'd have to leave the house to find yourself a buck. And that, Miss Wilcox, is something we both know you won't do."

Chapter Three

"Lady Mary?" Amanda knocked on her chaperone's door again. "Are you there?" Tugging her wrapper tightly around herself, she hopped from foot to foot, the hall floor cold beneath her bare skin. No Polly this morning with her cup of chocolate, and now no Lady Mary. The house had an empty feel to it. Bleak. Or maybe that was just her own mood.

She looked down at Reggie. The pup tilted his head, and his left ear flopped inside out. Amanda flipped it right and scratched his nose. Reggie was her sister's foxhound, not yet a year old. With Liz away on the Continent, he had become Amanda's companion. His warm body snuggled close to hers in the bed was the only thing that helped her fall asleep at night. His paw nudging her leg when he wanted to play drew her from her waking nightmares, kept her in the present. Amanda was fortunate Liz had left her in such good hands.

"Well," Amanda said, shrugging, "let's go dress and get you breakfast." Reggie yipped, in full agreement. Lifting the hem of her skirts, Amanda tip-toed back to her room, her eyes on the floor. More than once Reggie had tripped her up by darting between her legs.

She didn't see the man standing in her doorway until she'd almost bumped into him. "Julius!" Her heart leapt before she remembered her previous night's embarrassment. She grabbed the collar of her night rail. "What are you doing here?"

He swept his gaze down her body. Her night rail and

wrapper covered as much skin as her day gowns, but with no undergarments constraining her, she felt bare.

"I've come to see if you need assistance dressing. Polly is no longer in the duke's employ."

"Polly left her position?" She leaned against the opposite door jamb and focused on the faint scar crossing his left cheek. It was the only blemish on an otherwise beautiful face, and after Julius's rejection the night before, she needed to see his imperfections. His thin blade of a nose, his high cheekbones, spoke of an elegance that Amanda couldn't match. Even the fact that his skin was several shades darker than any other aristocrat couldn't hide that Julius was a man of breeding, only one who spent much of his time out-of-doors. She was one giant wound, and that scar of his brought them a little closer.

Except, he hadn't quite rejected her. She cleared her throat. "What about Sarah? She can serve as my lady's maid."

"Sarah is gone, as well." Sweeping his hand towards her bed chamber, he guided her inside. Her stomach quivered at the intimacy. He blocked Reggie's entrance with his leg. "Not you, whelp. Off to the kitchen with you. Get some breakfast." He shut the door in the dog's face. Reg gave one indignant yip, but Amanda knew his heart wasn't in it. The dog thought with his stomach and had quickly learned the words 'breakfast' and 'kitchen'. 'Nuncheon' and 'dinner', too. The clatter of toenails on wood confirmed that Reggie was eager to get downstairs to the generous cook.

Julius strode to the window and thrust the curtains apart. He cracked a glass pane open. "I assure you I've had considerable practice helping women dress. I'll do for your needs until Mr. Carter finds replacements for the servants."

"But ... you can't help me dress." Amanda clasped her hands tightly in front of herself. "It would be highly—"

"Improper?" Julius raised one eyebrow. "I thought we'd dispensed with all pretense of propriety last night."

Yes, she supposed they had. Amanda fingered the trim

of her wrapper. There was a growing hole in the lace that Polly had never seen to. Four months ago, Amanda wouldn't have noticed. All she had known was that she no longer wore filthy rags. Prison had stripped her of many things, including her modesty. But a lifetime of breeding crept back. "All the servants have left?"

"Not all." Julius opened the wardrobe and tossed a clean chemise onto her bed. He ran his hands through her dresses. "About half. Enough to keep us fed and bathed. I told Carter there was no rush hiring replacements." He pulled out a forest green gown. "This will do," he said, holding up the dress to Amanda's body. "It brings out your eyes."

Wrapping her arms around her waist, Amanda stared at the carpet. "My eyes are brown." Was the man that oblivious to her existence? She knew every detail about his person, down to the slight crook of his little finger on his right hand. He didn't even know the color of her eyes.

Cupping his fingers under her chin, he tilted her face up. "A beautiful brown, as rich as my morning coffee. And when you become angry or agitated, small flecks of green bubble to the surface." He traced her upper lip with his thumb. "I know what your eyes look like, Amanda."

She stopped breathing. Every swipe of his thumb sent chills racing down her spine. His normal polite reserve was gone, perhaps forever after last night's indecent request. Had he changed his mind?

"You called me by my Christian name. That's the first time you've done so."

Stepping aside, he laid her gown over the back of her dressing chair. "I'm here to help you dress. I think the time for formalities has passed." He raised an eyebrow. "Unless you wish me to ask the cook to assist you?"

"No." Clenching her fists, Amanda tried to dredge up her courage from the night before. She still wanted an affair with Julius. Still needed to prove to herself that her father hadn't broken her, hadn't stolen one of the most basic functions of womanhood from her. And that required allowing Julius access to her body.

She sucked in a deep breath. "No. You will do fine." She grabbed the belt of her wrapper.

Julius made it easy on her, and turned back to the armoire. Picking a crumpled blanket from the bottom of the wardrobe, he folded it into a neat rectangle.

She shucked her wrapper and night rail and slid the cotton chemise down her body. "I'm, uh, I'm covered. Ready for my stays."

Picking up that garment, he turned back to her. His eyes flared but his steps were steady as he approached. She raised her arms, but he made no move to drop the underbodice over her head.

"Julius?" She followed his gaze. Her nipples were hard buds under the thin cotton. She started to lower her arms.

"Keep them up." His voice rasped against her eardrums, sending a spark right to her core. Her breaths became short. Her breasts felt heavy, achy, just from the touch of his gaze. She prayed for him to touch her in earnest.

The gods must have heard her plea. Julius cupped her breast, his thumb circling her nipple.

Amanda shuddered. The chill from Polly's forgotten morning fire a distant memory. The cotton began to abrade her sensitive flesh. It burned. It made her want to coil herself around Julius like a snake.

It made her want to lose control.

Stiffening, she took a step back and dropped her arms. They stared at each other, each breathing heavily.

"Another test?" she whispered.

"No. Perhaps." He ran a hand through his nutmeg hair. "Or perhaps I merely enjoy torturing myself." He gripped the underbodice tightly, his knuckles white. "Have you withdrawn your request?" It gave her a perverse pleasure that his voice was as affected as hers.

She shook her head. "No. I want it. Want you. But ... it was just too much."

He exhaled, long and deep through his nose, his gaze never leaving hers. Holding up the stays, he motioned for her to turn around. He slid the garment over her arms and smoothed it down her body. "I apologize for my behavior. I sometimes forget that you're a green girl."

She couldn't hold back the bitter bark of laughter. "Green girl? You do know my history. I am far from innocent."

The first jerk on her laces jolted her back into his chest.

"You've had experience with abuse, with betrayal. You've no experience with the pleasures a real man can give a woman." Working from the bottom up, he tightened the stays. Each tug stole a bit of her breath.

Julius brushed his lips against her ear. "If I were to give you what you asked"—he yanked the strings tight—"give you a night of pleasure so intense you'll beg for it to end, only to beg for more ..." The strings slid through the next pair of holes, squeezing her ribs, holding her together.

"Yes?" she whispered.

His teeth scraped her neck, and she jumped.

"What would you give me in return?" he asked.

Amanda chewed the inside of her cheek. Wouldn't he be getting what he wanted, what all men wanted, at the same time? "Anything you wish."

"Anything?" With one hand, Julius gripped the laces and tugged her back into his chest. With his other hand, he palmed her belly. Then slid his hand lower to delve between her thighs.

Amanda started and rose to her toes. Sensation flooded her, but she didn't know what to do with it.

"Easy." Julius held her close. He rubbed his palm up and down her most intimate of areas, and sparks danced around her body. It was like she'd walked into a bonfire. It felt so good that it couldn't be right. Amanda gripped his pant leg, not knowing if she should push him away or try to give him the same caress. Not knowing if she should fight or submit. Indecision tore through her, and the back of her eyes burned with the not knowing.

He gave one last squeeze to the apex of her thighs and released her. "How do you expect to give your body to a man when you jump at the first touch?"

Amanda swallowed past the lump in her throat. "I grow tired of your trials."

"Perhaps I am being unfair." He pulled at her stays' strings, the constriction easing her muscles. She could relax into the bindings and not worry about coming apart. He yanked again. "But a woman like you doesn't just offer herself up on a silver platter. I need to know how far you can go, for both our sakes."

He still saw the old Amanda. The woman who, though by no means of his station, had been gently born and bred. A woman who shouldn't even think of such things as laying with a man, much less speak of it. But that woman was gone and buried. Amanda wasn't sure she'd even want her back.

She waited eagerly for the next hiss of string rasping against fabric. For the feel of his strong fingers binding her tight.

"Can women enjoy it?" she whispered. "I've heard some women say so. And ..."

Brushing her hair over her shoulder so it lay heavy on her breast, he rubbed her shoulder. "And?"

She held her breath. She never spoke of this. Of what her father did. Of her time in prison. She might repulse him with her honesty. She stared at the door to her room. Her life was a series of closed doors.

She exhaled slowly. If she was going to disgust him, might as well do it now and move on. There wasn't much left of her heart to break.

"There was a guard at Newgate. He wasn't like the others. He actually asked." She focused on the door handle, not the man standing an inch behind her. It was gold, like everything in Montague's house, with delicate filigree scrollwork around the edges. She'd broken herself of the habit of locking herself in at night, but the key still protruded from the keyhole. A reminder of how uneasy in mind she'd been. Or of how far she'd come.

"I didn't say yes. I didn't say anything. And when he spread my legs, well ..."

Julius dug his fingers into her shoulders. Another binding that made her feel secure.

She turned in his grip and met his eyes. There was no disgust, only kindness. "I didn't enjoy it. But I didn't hate it like I did every other time a man touched me. It gave me hope that maybe, maybe someday I could feel normal."

"There is nothing wrong with you, Amanda. But giving yourself to the first available man won't prove anything." He gathered up the gown and dressed her. "And tempting me can only end badly. I'm not the man for you, whatever I may wish. And I'm not as strong as I'd like." He smoothed the fabric down her back. "Breakfast is ready whenever you wish to come down." With one last squeeze to her shoulder, he turned and strode from the room.

Amanda pressed her palm to her breastbone and rubbed at the ache beneath. He hadn't run away in revulsion, but he'd run just the same. She gathered up her stockings and boots. Liz made it seem so easy with Marcus. Two people in perfect step together. Amanda felt like she was dancing to an entirely different tune than Julius.

She wasn't looking for forever. Marriage truly was out of her reach. But was it wrong to hope for just a bit of that connection between a man and a woman? To experience a touch that brought more than pain?

Perhaps, for her sins, she was destined to always be on the outside looking in.

* * *

Julius tossed the morning paper on the table and stood when Amanda entered the room. With her creamy skin and dark hair, she looked lovely in the simple green morning gown. Not for the first time he wished he had noticed her during her two seasons. Amanda in a ball gown must be a stunning sight. And if he'd known her then, he might have been able to prevent so much of her heartbreak.

It was difficult, but he kept his expression even. So many insults had been laid upon this woman. So much cruelty. Rage coursed through his veins at the injustice of the world. Her father was already dead, nothing could be done there. But the prison guards that had dared touch her, they would be dealt with.

That last one she'd spoken of, the one who'd given her hope. That one he might let live. He'd break all his bones, of course. But hope was a precious gift regardless of its source. It deserved some mercy.

Julius knew what it was to be trapped, subject to the whims of your captors. That Amanda knew it, too, broke his heart. But she didn't need to see his anger, his vengeance. So, he schooled his features into a welcome.

"Good morning, Miss Wilcox," he said. "Breakfast is on the sideboard. Help yourself."

Lady Mary, her ivory hair tucked up under a lace cap, looked up from her egg. She smiled at Amanda and waved her spoon in acknowledgment before focusing back on her breakfast.

Reggie was not so restrained with his greeting. He bounded over and met her at the buffet, slipping on the waxed wood floor. He jumped on her thighs, barking excitedly.

Amanda pointed at the floor. "Down." The pup slouched to the floor. She fed him a bit of ham and stroked his back. "Good boy."

The husky burn of her voice rolled through Julius like whiskey. His cock perked up, and he sat down, scooting his chair under the table. Reggie rolled onto his back, and Amanda rubbed his brown belly. Julius glared at the dog. Lucky bastard.

Julius could have her. He could take her back to her room and be sliding deep inside of her in under ten minutes. The heat between her legs when he'd cupped her had nearly undone him. It had definitely made him doubt his decision. But there had also been fear in her eyes. He wouldn't take her, not when she'd be comparing him to a ghost.

And not when there was a chance he'd endanger his friendship with Marcus. Julius had few close friends. He couldn't afford to lose one.

Amanda placed a few bits on her plate and sat at the table. "Good morning, Lady Mary. I looked for you earlier this morning, but you'd already left your room."

The older woman looked up and adjusted her spectacles. "Good morning, dear. I went for a walk with Jane. If you leave early enough, you can see those newfangled gas lamps still lit."

Lady Mary's maid, Jane, was nearly as old as Marcus's aunt. Julius supposed he could ask her to take over Amanda's dressing duty until a replacement was found. He took a sip of coffee. The thought of giving over that duty didn't hold appeal.

He was a stupid, stupid man. Just when he'd concluded he couldn't have her, he decided to subject himself to a daily vision of Amanda in her undergarments.

Amanda reached for the pot of chocolate and poured herself a cup. "You aren't nervous standing next to one? I've heard stories of grand explosions." She settled her mug at a right angle with her plate and lined her silverware up beneath. Each fork and knife were spaced equally apart, Julius noted. Another reminder of Amanda's need to order her surroundings. Another reason why they wouldn't suit. In his liaisons, Julius needed to be the one in control.

"Stuff and nonsense." The chaperone placed the tip of her knife at the top of her soft-boiled egg. She tapped her spoon onto the knife's handle, as though it were a chisel. "Marvelous inventions," she continued. "Pretty soon, there will be no need for wood for our fireplaces. Gas is like ether; it's everywhere. And then think how tall the forests will grow."

Julius slid his gaze to Amanda. A tiny vee creased her

forehead. Good. She was as confused as he.

"More chocolate, Lady Mary?" he asked. Once the older woman got started on a subject, it could be hours until she finished. And her thoughts were a warren of non-sequiturs and half-formed ideas. Julius paused. Why *had* Marcus sent such a dotty old woman to be Amanda's chaperone? Because he trusted Julius so much that a competent one wasn't needed?

Amanda picked up his paper. "Where are you off to today, Lord Rothchild?" she asked, not lifting her head.

"Off to?"

"You never spend a day within. It's as though you find the duke's home unpleasant." The paper snapped in her hands. "Or its occupants."

He narrowed his eyes. She was not so silly as to think that, was she? But she could hardly know that to him enclosed spaces were their own form of torture.

"I enjoy the fresh air." Craved it. Even now in this open breakfast room with the sun shining through the large windows, his skin itched. That itch was his constant companion until he stepped out of doors and filled his lungs with fresh air. "I would be more than happy to escort you and Lady Mary out of doors. Perhaps a nice drive through Hyde Park?"

Her shoulders turned to stone. "Not today, thank you."

"No." Lady Mary fed Reggie a strip of bacon. "I wouldn't want to go outside when a storm is brewing."

Julius looked at the blinding blue sky and sighed.

"Ju— Lord Rothchild, did you read this article?" Amanda turned the paper and pointed at the front-page story. "About the proposed law eliminating capital punishment for children under ten. It lost a vote in the House of Lords."

He buttered a roll and placed it in her hand. She'd filled out from the emaciated woman he'd rescued from Newgate, but she still tended to eat too little. He'd found it was easiest to feed her when she was distracted. Each morning he added more food to his plate for the purpose.

"I didn't have to read the article," he said. "I was there for the vote."

She paused, the roll inches from her mouth, and glared at him in outrage.

"I voted for the law to pass," he hastily added. "But the opposition led by the Marquess of Hanford was strong. He convinced the assembly that if the law passed the streets of London would run red with blood, violent criminals would take over, and life as we knew it would come to an end."

"The violent ten-year-olds would destroy London?" Amanda tore into the roll and chewed viciously, eyes narrowed. "How many men voted against it?"

He added a bit of beef to her plate, pushed the fork into her hand. "I believe the measure lost by thirty-six votes."

Reggie whined, and Lady Mary fed him another strip of bacon. Julius shook his head. That dog was going to get fat living in this house.

"Thirty-six votes. That's all that was needed." She scooped up a bit of beef and stared at the wall behind Julius, chewing thoughtfully. "Only thirty-six men needed to be persuaded to change their minds."

"Don't fool yourself." He folded his napkin and laid it beside his plate. "Nothing ever changes. This is a brutal world, and we just have to survive it."

She looked at him sharply. "Yes, but the eight-year-olds who get caught stealing a loaf of bread to feed their family aren't surviving it, are they? They're being hanged." She placed a hand on her throat.

His guts turned to lead. She had come too close to that fate. If he and Montague had arrived at Tyburn just minutes later, this sweet woman would have been dead. The good people of London had been deprived of their entertainment that day, but there were many more executions for them to watch. Almost every crime was a capital offense in England, and the reformers voices were faint.

"There's a ball tonight," he said, an idea burgeoning in his mind. "Many in the House of Lords will be in attendance. You should come. Try to persuade those thirty-six men."

Amanda's mouth dropped open. "You can't ... I can't ... what is wrong with you?" she sputtered.

"What seems to be the problem?"

"Do I need to get a ball gown out of my trunk?" Lady Mary asked, her lips turned down. A fly buzzed around her plate, and she pulled a lace handkerchief from her sleeve and waved it at the insect.

Amanda patted her hand. "No. There will be no ball." She turned on Julius. "Every part of what you said is ridiculous. First of all, I would never be allowed into a ball. No one in society will recognize me."

"If you're on my arm, you'll be allowed entry," he growled. Julius was growing frustrated with the strictures of society. Montague seemed to accept that his sister-in-law would remain an outcast for the remainder of her life, but Julius wasn't so disposed. "And no one will dare say a word against you in my presence. Not if they want to keep their teeth."

She ignored that. "Secondly, no member of the House of Lords is going to listen to me, a woman, much less a disgraced woman, on British law."

He leaned back in his chair and crossed his arms over his chest. "There are respected female voices. Not many, I'll grant you, but they do exist. You'll just have to speak louder so the old windbags can hear you over their own sermonizing."

"And thirdly—" She abruptly cut herself off, looking anywhere but at him.

"Thirdly?" he prodded.

Twisting the napkin in her hands, she worried her bottom lip.

"Amanda?"

"Thirdly," she said, her voice so low he had to lean

forward, "you know I can't go out. I. Can't. Go. Out." Her voice broke on the last word.

His chest squeezed as though caught in a vise. Shit, were those tears in her eyes? She needed to be pushed outside her comfortable surroundings. But he couldn't stand it if he made her cry.

"Calm yourself." He covered her hand with his own. "I would never force you to do something you don't wish. But you can't live the rest of your life within these walls. You need to start making some attempts out."

"Not to a ball," she said fiercely.

Julius blew out a deep breath. Yes, a ball would be like throwing a baby into a lake and expecting her to swim. Smaller steps were needed. He rubbed her knuckles, knowing he should pull away. While Lady Mary was an inattentive old woman, she still had eyes. But Amanda's hand was warm beneath his, her skin silky soft. She was breaking his resolve without even trying.

"Any time you wish to venture outside, let me know. I'll be there for you."

Nodding, she dropped her gaze back to the paper. "Do you think some of the lords might be open to persuasion?"

"I do." The House of Lords were like any other group of people. Subject to whim, eager to follow the latest trend. Sheep looking for anyone to follow.

She nodded again, this time with determination. "Then I have some work to do." Rising, she plucked up the paper and tucked it under her arm.

Julius stood. "Where are you going?"

"To Montague's study to write some letters." Reggie padded after her to the door. "As you say, I'm stuck within these walls. I might as well make better use of my time than fumbling around with my needlepoint."

"You intend to start a letter campaign to change the law?" Emotions warred within his breast. Amanda needed a purpose, and she had chosen a worthy cause. But she was in for inevitable defeat. While the men in the House of

Lords were open to suggestion, they wouldn't be persuaded by a letter from Miss Amanda Wilcox. She was too easy to dismiss.

Would she close herself up even more when she finally accepted her defeat?

"I do." Her brown eyes flashed. "It's past time the Crown stopped killing its subjects over petty misdemeanors. As the most advanced nation on earth, it is beyond barbaric."

She strode from the room. Julius remained standing. She was right on all counts. And she'd never win. Man excelled at many things, foremost the ability to annihilate one another.

Bowing stiffly to Montague's aunt, he fled the room. The walls were closing in on him. Reggie yipped at his heels and gave Julius the perfect excuse. He sent a footman for the dog's lead. Reggie spun in dizzying circles when the footman returned carrying the leather strip. After attaching the lead to the dog's collar, Julius grabbed his great coat and escaped from the townhouse. Man and dog strode down the drive at a brisk pace.

Julius sucked in the crisp air and felt his muscles unclench. He may be powerless to protect Amanda from ridicule, but at least he was no longer trapped in doors.

That seemed poor recompense.

Reggie sniffed at a bush. With wide, contrite eyes, the pup backed his rear end under the branches, squatted like a bitch, and took a piss.

Julius sighed. "You can't lift your leg like a real dog?"

Tail low, Reggie slunk ahead.

Julius knew how he felt. He had been charged for caring for his friend's sister-in-law, and he was going to fail. The thought unmanned him.

A soft breeze brushed through his hair. Perhaps he should take Amanda to his country estate. Somewhere with wide open fields and healthful air. Somewhere away from prying eyes, away from the crowds.

Somewhere she wouldn't be able to hear the laughter of the ton as they mocked her attempts to change the world.

Chapter Four

The crush of silk and lace made Julius's temples throb. He hated balls. Hated being swallowed up in a crowd. Cut off from easy access to the exits. They were stifling affairs, tedious, and, in general, a waste of his time. This one, a birthday celebration for Lord Wicking's wife, was no exception.

But this ball he couldn't avoid. Liverpool had sent for him and when the prime minister requested his presence, he had no choice but to attend.

Two girls barely out of their leading strings strolled past, whispering like mad. One shot a coy glance over her shoulder, and Julius huffed. Not bloody likely. What could a chit fresh from her debut know of the world that could interest him? Sheltered, smug, sanctimonious, the lot of them.

Besides, words weren't what he wanted from a woman and conversation was all that society girls had to offer. His body still burned from holding Amanda, and he needed a woman to release the tension. After this meeting, it was time to pay a visit to his favorite club. The one that didn't tolerate artifice but only sought to provide pleasure. The doxies who worked at The Black Rose understood the harsher realities of life. It wasn't pretty, and Julius wished that no woman had knowledge of its cruelties. But at least he had something in common with those women. An understanding that parties and afternoon teas were of no consequence.

Amanda understood that.

Julius grabbed another drink and downed the punch in one swallow. He tugged at his collar. There wasn't nearly enough alcohol in the drink.

Because of her imprisonment, Amanda would understand him better than most. Understand him in a way that not even his closest friends could.

It was also the one reason why he could never have her. Not as he wanted. A person wouldn't consent to being tied up, not if her freedom had previously been stripped.

He remembered the feel of the strings of her stays that morning. The pleasure in lacing her tight. Binding her in such a small way. An itch developed between his shoulder blades just thinking of it.

The band struck up a waltz, and a girl was shoved into his path by her mama. Julius neatly sidestepped the coquette and continued his circuitous route around the room. Liverpool stood with a group of men, laughing uproariously. Catching his eye, Julius nodded and headed out of the ballroom, finding an unoccupied study that he claimed for his own. He opened the window and dragged a chair near it to enjoy the fresh air as he waited.

He didn't wait long.

Liverpool shut the door soundly behind him. "Glad you could make it."

Julius nodded. It wasn't as though he'd had a choice.

The prime minister strode to the desk and plucked a cigar from a humidor like he owned the place. He walked over to a candelabra on the sideboard and lit up. "I wanted to speak with you about Ashworth."

"Oh?" Julius crossed one leg over the other. "Has another painting come to light?"

Liverpool settled in behind the desk. "No, thank God. Although the original painting will be discovered tomorrow in Gentleman Jack's hanging over the ring. A harmless prank by one of the boys who caught sight of the mark in the back rooms of that establishment. That should take away the blackmailer's leverage."

"His embarrassment will be well-deserved." Julius looked out to the dark night sky. The stars were faded, their lights dimmed from smoke. "Then what seems to be the problem?"

Liverpool puffed on the cigar, his cheeks hollowing. "Mrs. Westmont has disappeared."

Julius dug his fingers into the armrests. Liverpool had been known to make people disappear. But if that were the case, there would be no need to display Ashworth's painting. And if Liverpool were behind the disappearance, it wasn't something he would likely discuss with Julius.

"When?" he asked.

"Between midnight and three this morning."

Julius raised an eyebrow. "That's a very defined timeframe."

Liverpool shrugged. "The men I had on her made their rounds every three hours. They saw her in her bed at midnight. She was gone when they came by for their next sweep. Along with her housekeeper, butler, and groom."

"Did she fear prosecution? Retribution?" A blackmailer played a dangerous game. She would have been wise to take precautions.

"Perhaps." Liverpool eyed him through a haze of smoke. "Or perhaps she returned to her employers."

Julius considered the man. Was he suggesting a blackmailing ring? "Have other gentlemen been extorted?"

"Yes." Liverpool lifted the lid on an inkwell and tapped the cigar's ashes into the bowl. "But that's not unusual in itself. People will always seek to control powerful men. But a pattern seems to have developed over the past year. Certain members of the House of Lords have changed their votes most unexpectedly. I believe there is more to it than a group of people seeking to line their pockets. They're looking to control the government."

Julius rose and paced the room. "A crime ring with the intent to infiltrate the House of Lords?"

"Yes."

"That's ambitious."

Liverpool sucked in another lungful of smoke and blew out a line of rings. "Yes," he agreed. "Since the Treaty of Paris has been signed, I don't believe the threat comes from across the channel. I think it internal."

Placing his hands on the back of the settee, Julius leaned forward. "You wish me to investigate?"

Liverpool rose and tossed the cigar out the window. "I need you to find Mrs. Westmont. You are my retrieval expert, after all. And when you find her, find out who she works for. The security of England depends upon it."

Not too grave a task then. Julius pressed his lips tight. "I'll look into it."

"Good." Liverpool held out his hand, and Julius grasped it.

"I might need help," Julius warned.

"Yes, I assumed you'd pull in your friends for aid." The man strolled to the door. "But keep this quiet. No one other than the men who have already worked for the Crown. And Rothchild?"

Liverpool stared at him, his hand on the door's latch. "It wouldn't do to have my investigator succumb to blackmail. You'd do well to avoid your more unsavory haunts."

Julius kept his face impassive. It wasn't a heavily-guarded secret that he was a member of The Black Rose. Nor that he liked practicing his ropework on the women there. He wasn't ashamed of his proclivities. And he damn sure wasn't going to be told where he could or could not visit. "The unsavory haunts might be just the places I need to go in order to uncover a ring of blackmailers."

"Indeed." Liverpool drummed his fingers over the top of the brass door handle, his gaze never wavering. After several seconds, he nodded. "If you get caught up in it, the disgrace will be your own. The government won't be taken down with you."

"I never thought otherwise."

Julius let the other man exit before following him out.

Collecting his greatcoat, he strode from the home.

He stopped on the sidewalk and stared at the night sky, breathing deeply. The tension in his shoulders eased as it always did when he escaped into the fresh air, but that crawling feeling, like ants skittering over his skin, remained. A feeling that was only relieved in one way.

It had been over two months since he'd enjoyed the pleasures The Black Rose had to offer. Over two months since a cable of hemp had slid through his fingers. There had been only one woman he'd fantasized binding of late. One face he'd visualized in the dead of night as he took himself in hand. But Amanda would detest a rope prison as much as he. She could never partner in his rope play. His fantasies would remain in his head.

But, by God's teeth, he could imagine the thick rope crossing Amanda's creamy skin. The positions he could restrain her in, making her open, wanting. His cock thickened, and Julius pressed on his silk pantaloons.

Damn, tight pants. Another reason to dislike the necessity of attending balls.

He should focus on the task at hand, not the woman he would be a right bastard if he bedded. He had his work cut out for him. He and his friends were trained as spies, not investigators, two different skill-sets. And with Marcus gone, their group of five was down a man.

He needed to clear his head if he was going to find the Widow Westmont. Needed to remove Miss Wilcox from his mind for good. Replace the fantasy of her with the reality of a willing woman.

The Black Rose awaited, along with the room he considered a second home. Thick beams, strong enough to hold a person's weight. Lengths of rope hanging on the walls. And the accommodating proprietress, Madame Sable, who was always happy to find him an eager partner.

Climbing into his carriage, he directed the driver to Edward Street. His heart wasn't in it, but the sooner he enjoyed another woman, the sooner he could rid himself of thoughts of his friend's sister-in-law. Laying his head on the seat back, he watched London roll by through the open window.

The carriage stopped in a tidy street where well-painted signs hung over businesses' doors and cheerful planter boxes lined the windows. If the residents knew of the Venus club nestled within their street, they ignored it.

Julius climbed the steps with as much eagerness as if going to see his tailor for a five-hour fitting. He handed his greatcoat and hat to the footman and entered the sitting room. Decorated in rich reds and golds, the room dazzled beneath the crystal chandelier. Julius blinked and looked for the owner. Madame Sable usually held court in this room, accepting praise and presents from the grateful members.

Tonight, she was nowhere to be seen. Of course. Julius slapped his palm against his thigh. That would be his luck.

One of the club's girls, and a regular partner for Julius, stepped close and slid her hand up his arm. "Bonsoir, mon chou. It's been a long time since I've seen that handsome face."

He forced a smile. "Lucy. I hope you've been well?"

She shrugged, her gown slipping off her shoulder. "I've been lonely, with no one to amuse me."

A pretty request if he'd ever heard one. "Care to join me in the Amethyst room?"

Lucy bounced on her toes. "I thought you'd never ask." She linked her arm through his and drew him through the sitting room and down the back hall.

His usual room was empty. It was larger than most of the other chambers and had high ceilings, the only things that made it tolerable when the door closed behind him. That, and the ropes lining the walls, available for his use.

Lucy slipped out of her gown, wearing nothing underneath. She was an attractive woman, plump in all the right places, with a tapered waist and long legs.

Julius felt nothing.

"Which rope would you prefer?" he asked.

She pointed to a thick braid with a rougher fiber.

Julius took it off the wall and uncoiled its length. He didn't usually like the jute. It caused more pain than the hemp or cotton ones. And was nothing like the silk ropes he kept with him at home. But Lucy had tried them all and she liked the bite of pain. He nodded towards the center of the room, ignoring the big bed in the corner. A bed was too soft to match his mood.

Lucy stood under a ceiling beam and positioned her arms behind her in a pose they'd used many times. With more speed than artistry, Julius wove the rope around her wrists and arms. He waited for the familiar prickle. The one that dug under his skin and sent blood pounding to his cock whenever he saw rope cross a woman's body.

And remained waiting.

He tossed the end of the rope over the beam. It swung back and forth, as limp as his member. It wasn't working. He didn't want Lucy; he wanted Amanda. And damn if he could trick his body with a couple of restraints.

Yanking the tail end of the rope back over the beam, he began untying the woman. "My apologies. I have to go."

"But we were just beginning." Lucy shook out her hands.

Julius coiled the rope and hung it on the wall. "I know. Another night."

Leaving her open-mouthed, Julius fled through the club. It used to be a haven. The one building he looked forward to entering. Tonight, it felt more like a tomb.

He told his driver to take him to Montague's, and the carriage bumped across London. They rattled to a halt, and Julius jumped down before the footman could open the door. He handed his coat and gloves to a waiting Carter and trudged up the steps to the second floor. Pausing outside Amanda's door, he pressed his hands on the frame and rested his forehead against the wood.

He wanted inside. Inside her room. Inside her head.

Inside her body. But they wouldn't be compatible. Amanda needed a milksop for a lover, someone who'd hold her hand, let her call the shots. Let her be in control. The need to control the environment for a former prisoner could be overwhelming.

His gut churned at the thought of the pale fop who would be fortunate enough to bed her. Nails digging into the wood frame, Julius took a deep breath. Another. When she did take a lover, Julius would most likely never know.

He pushed away from the door in disgust. Fuck controlling his environment, he needed to control himself. And that started with leaving Miss Wilcox to sleep in peace.

His boot scuffed the hallway floor. Loosening his cravat with one hand, he pushed into his room. He stirred the fire with an iron then went to his window and slid it open. Only when he was leaning halfway out did his mind catch up with his vision.

He whipped his head around. All the curtains on his four-poster bed were drawn. He never slept with the curtains down, never untied them from their posts. The servants knew this. Had Carter already hired a new chamber maid who'd closed them after changing the sheets?

On silent feet, he crept to the bed. Grasping the velvet drape, he flung it back, allowing the moonlight to stream over the counterpane.

And over the naked woman lying beneath.

"What in the devil are you doing here?" His heart pounded. He wished he could say it was from anger.

Amanda propped herself up on her elbows, the sheet sliding down to drape over her breasts. The white silk clung to her nipples like a drowning sailor to a lifeline. Her dark hair lay in loose curls over her shoulders and spilled to the pillow below. "Isn't it obvious?" she asked. "I've come here to seduce you."

Chapter Five

Amanda held her breath. If Julius refused her once more, she ... well, she wasn't certain what she'd do other than scamper back to her room and hide under her pillow. A woman could only take so much rejection.

Her letter writing campaign to members of the House of Lords had given her some confidence. She thought her words actually held a touch of eloquence. She could speak up, perhaps actually be listened to by one or more of the gentlemen.

She'd rediscovered her voice.

So, she'd decided to ask again for what she wanted.

Julius stood over her, his cravat loose around his neck, his chest rising and falling beneath his dark waistcoat. He pressed his full lips into a hard line. "Vixen, you push too far for your own good. A man can only take so much tempting."

"That's what I was hoping." With a deep breath for courage, she pushed up to her hands, letting the buttery-soft silk sheet slip to her waist. The cool air nipped at her breasts, and the peaks hardened.

Julius cursed, loudly and creatively. But his gaze never left her chest. Stretching out a hand, he ran a finger from her collarbone down over the tip of her breast and circled her nipple. His caress was feather-soft, but its impact hit her like a hammer. Her body shuddered, her back instinctively arching into him.

"So pretty." He sat on the bed, the mattress sinking beneath him. "Your nipples look like berries in the moonlight." Leaning forward, his breath whispered over her skin. "Do you taste as good as you look, Amanda?"

She had no words. Excitement and nerves gripped her in equal measure. But she needed this, needed to know she wasn't damaged beyond repair. She pushed the nerves aside and reached for his face. Rubbing her thumb along the scar on his cheek, she pulled him close.

Needing no further invitation, Julius took what she offered. His hot mouth closed around her breast. Amanda's head dropped back and she stared at the tester above. His mouth on her skin was indescribable. He cupped her other breast in his hand. With his thumb and forefinger, he rolled her nipple, sending fire straight to her core.

Arms weak, she sank back onto the bed, and Julius followed her down. His teeth scored her nipple before he lapped at the slight ache. Each stroke of his tongue, every caress of his hand, clouded her mind. Thought drifted away. Only sensation existed.

"God, this isn't right," he muttered. "I shouldn't"—he nibbled on the soft skin on the underside of her breast—"be doing this." Thankfully, his words seemed to be hollow as he didn't cease his attentions. But she gripped his shoulders and held him close to make sure he didn't leave off. Digging her fingers into the fine wool of his coat, one thought became clear.

Julius wore entirely too many clothes.

She shoved at his lapels, pushing his coat over his shoulders. He shrugged out of it and whipped off his cravat. Thumbing the buttons of his waistcoat through their holes, he shed that garment in record time. His shirt easily slid over his head. Julius stood, the light matting of hair across his chest just visible in the dim light. She reached for the buttons on his pantaloons, but he moved to the end of the bed and tied back the bed's curtains.

"No, leave them down."

He hesitated. "You sleep enclosed?"

She nodded.

"Even though you were trapped in a five-by-ten cell for nearly a year?" Confusion laced his voice. Confusion and concern.

"It ..." She didn't know how to express the need she felt to be cocooned. The security she found when she was sealed off from the rest of the world. "It makes me feel safe."

She grew chilled as she waited for his response and she tugged at the sheet, raising it higher.

Grabbing the other end of the sheet, he pulled it back down to her waist. "You can't cover up what you've offered so prettily." He sat beside her on the bed. "I want to understand. You like to be closed up?"

"I need it," she whispered. And she did. If she was allowed into the great wide world, what would the consequences be? Would she control herself? Would she hurt someone, or get hurt herself? Just thinking about all the space that *outside* entailed made her short for breath.

He laid a comforting hand on her knee and stroked up and down the sheet covering her leg. "But ..." He cleared his throat. "You were in the dark for so long. No fresh air. No freedom. Why?"

How could she explain to him what she didn't understand herself? She'd made friends with the dark long ago. In her cell, she'd known that the outside world could no longer hurt her. And she wouldn't be allowed to hurt anyone else. She'd been freer in prison than she had been the first twenty-three years of her life.

Staring at his hand on her leg, she lifted one shoulder. "I like to be enclosed. I can't explain it."

He squeezed her thigh. "All right. Explanations can come later." Rising, he stepped to the end of the bed and released one of the curtains. "A compromise. We'll leave the drapes facing the door closed, but I want to be able to look out the window."

A small sound of distress escaped her lips. She wanted to be as comforted as possible her first time giving herself to a man. And this was a first. Nothing about her previous encounters could be considered giving.

He placed a finger on her lips. "If you like to feel confined, I can help you with that." His fingers danced across her neck before he rested his palm at the base of her throat. He loosely circled his fingers around her neck, and Amanda released a breath. The weight was warm, comforting.

"Do you trust me?" he asked.

She almost laughed. The man had saved her from hanging. Treated her with respect even though she was disgraced. Whatever she had left of trust was his to possess.

"Yes." She moistened her lips with her tongue. "I trust you."

"Then don't move." Bending, he picked his cravat off the floor and folded it into a long strip. "Lift your head," he told her. Placing the silk on her eyes, he tied it behind her, shutting out the world.

He brushed his lips over her ear. "Is it as dark as you like?"

She nodded. Being blindfolded did bring her a measure of comfort. Like she was a frightened horse, needing to be unseeing of danger. The comparison wasn't a happy one, but beggars couldn't be choosers.

With clumsy fingers, she reached for him. Hot flesh met her touch. Hot and hard. She ran her hands over the ridges of his stomach and went higher, stroking his chest. His hair was soft and downy and reminded her of Reggie's belly. Something she was sure was better left unspoken. She liked touching him, but was he enjoying her fumblings?

She frowned. Was she doing this right? He wasn't making any noise. No happy sighs, no grunts of pleasure. She didn't realize she'd have to plot each of her next moves. She'd expected to just spread her legs and let him have his way. Perhaps if she reached lower.

Julius encircled her wrists and lifted her hands. He placed a kiss on each palm. "Don't move. I'll be right back."

The mattress rose. She listened intently, but heard nothing. The door didn't open. No soft footsteps.

She smoothed her palms on the sheet. The waiting was killing her. Finally, a soft rustle met her ears, and she tried to decipher the sound. Fabric against fabric?

The sheet slid down her body to pool at her feet. Her heart pounded. Her mouth dried out. What was he doing? Not knowing whether she should lift the blindfold or not, she clutched the sheets instead. He'd asked for her trust. She would give it to him.

Something soft brushed her ankles, and her body jerked.

"Easy." Julius's voice was husky. The tension in her muscles loosened at the sound. She had a feeling Julius could talk her into most anything with that voice. He dragged something up her leg. It glided smooth as silk but had a weight to it. Her skin came alive wherever it touched.

"Give me your hands, sweetness." His palm followed the path the other object had taken, running up and down her thigh. "I want to make you feel secure."

Unsure, she held her hands up, not knowing what to expect.

She didn't expect her wrists to be tied, a rope encircling her hands and tugging them together in one quick snap.

"Are you all right?" he asked. He rested his palm on her belly, the heat from it soothing the butterflies dancing in her stomach.

"I think so."

"Are you certain? Having your hands bound doesn't bring you any unpleasant memories?"

"I'm ... I'm certain." Her hands had rarely been bound in prison. Only when she was being transported to and from the Old Bailey. Or on her final trip, to the Tyburn Tree. That memory did send a shiver down her spine and she pushed it from her mind. Those recollections didn't belong here in bed with Julius. She focused on what she was feeling. The pressure at her wrists was light, but sure, and there was no bite to the cord. Truly, with a feather mattress beneath her and Julius above her, holding her hands, she was quite comfortable.

She tried to imagine what Julius saw. Did the sight of her, naked and bound, rouse his desire? She hoped the firelight was kind to her form. But with her eyes blindfolded, her worry over whether her appearance was pleasing or not was greatly reduced. What she couldn't see, she couldn't worry about.

"Good." He wound the cord tighter about her wrists, the pressure pulling her elbows close. The material felt like thick cuff bracelets. "Tell me if anything doesn't feel good. If you ever want to stop."

She nodded.

With a tug at her wrists, he raised her arms up over her head. The mattress dipped, and she sensed him leaning over her. She licked her lips. He was close. Close enough that if she raised her head—

"Pull at your wrists," he ordered. She tried to lower her arms, but they didn't leave their perch from the pillow behind her.

"What? Am I tied—"

"To the headboard." He slid his fingertips around the edges of the bindings. "Not too tight?"

"No." She tugged again, but her hands barely moved. She was well and truly stuck. Amanda stilled. The mattress beneath her was soft as a cloud, the chilled air above her as soothing to her flushed skin as a lemon ice on a hot day. Her mind whirled, trying to interpret what it was she was feeling.

Relief. It was relief flooding through her veins. Tears welled behind her eyelids. She didn't understand why, but being tied to Julius's bed felt right.

Placing his hands beneath her knees, he spread her legs wide. "Shh," he soothed, his breath hot on her belly. "You trust me. Yes?"

"Yes."

"Then you've nothing to worry about. No decisions to make. Just lay back and enjoy." He scooped his arms under her thighs and grabbed her hips. His shoulders pressed her legs wide.

The first swipe of his tongue shocked her senses. He was supposed to be rutting into her like a bull. That's what men did. Not touching her with his mouth. Why would anyone even think to do that? Her hips jerked, a futile attempt to evade the sensory overload. His fingers dug into her skin. He licked her again, slowly, leisurely, from her core up to her nub.

"Julius!" Her voice was a strangled cry. His touch was soft, wet, and completely inappropriate. It was the most amazing thing she'd ever felt. Dear Lord in heaven, a mouth on her intimate parts. Whoever thought of this was a genius. It must have been a woman.

Julius alternated between nibbling at her lower lips and lapping at her opening. He blew a cool breath of air over her damp flesh. "You taste amazing. Like honey and spice. Eating you is going to be my favorite dessert."

She merely nodded, the knot at the back of her head tangling in her hair. She needed less talking out of him and more tonguing.

He didn't disappoint. Slowly, he slid his tongue inside her core, and her nerve endings sang. His nose bumped against her clitoris, and she moaned.

Pressing a finger into her, Julius traced a circle around her sensitive nub with his tongue. Her inner muscles clamped down around his thick digit. A whisper of unease, a memory of a past intrusion, tried to invade her mind. She ruthlessly squashed it and concentrated on the here and now. She let her thighs fall wider, enjoying the feeling of being filled. And when he added a second finger, it was even better. She rocked her hips into his thrusts, excitement making her movements jerky.

He stilled his fingers and put firm pressure on her nub

with his thumb. "You look beautiful tied to my bed, Amanda. Like a queen. I can see purple hemp knotted all around your sweet little body. You'll be my canvas." Sucking her clit into his mouth, he pumped his fingers hard.

She writhed beneath him. She wanted to call out, tell him how good it was, but her breath was locked in her throat. She panted for air. A vise closed about her body, squeezing her tighter and tighter. She pulled at her bindings, but she was still secure. Between her tied hands and her pinned hips, she could do little more than squirm.

It was the best kind of freedom.

Julius scraped his teeth over her inflamed flesh, and she was gone. Her neck arched, her mind blanked, and her body shattered. Wave after wave of pleasure crashed through her.

It felt an age before she could catch her breath. But while hers slowed, she realized Julius's had only sped up. A low groan interrupted his heavy breathing.

"Julius?"

"You're beautiful when you're brought to crisis. I almost embarrassed myself just looking at you." His chest brushed her breasts a moment before his lips whispered across her mouth. "I'm stroking myself while watching you. You're so open for me. Just the sight of you brings me pleasure." His teeth tugged on her earlobe before he whispered in her ear, "Do you like the idea of me watching you while I bring myself to completion? Does it make you feel wanton?"

The tips of her breasts tingled. The backs of his fingers drifted up and down her stomach, and she knew that the other side of his fingers were gripping his shaft. He was pleasuring himself mere inches away from her. She bit back a moan.

"You can ... find your pleasure in me." She spread her legs a couple inches wider. "It's what I was expecting."

The heat from his body disappeared, and the mattress dipped between her knees. "I know what you were expecting."

He wasn't touching her, and Amanda felt the full extent of her exposure. He was between her legs, so she couldn't close them. Instead, she pulled them up, tucking her knees to her chest. "If you didn't want to you needn't have gone this far. I don't need your pity."

His laugh was harsh, pained. "The only person I pity right now is myself. Hard as a goddamn pike and too damn guilty to end my pain."

"But I said—"

"I know, sweetness." He pressed a kiss to her knee. "You are quite accommodating. And I am no saint. Another compromise, perhaps."

Stroking his hands up and down her calves, he gripped her ankles and gently pulled her legs apart. Cool air caressed her hot flesh. She started, her arms jerking at their bindings, when his fingers brushed through her slit. He painted her thighs with her own moisture.

"What ...?"

"You wish to bring me pleasure?"

She nodded.

He brought her thighs back together, his hot length trapped in between. Keeping her legs immobile, Julius slowly slid his shaft between her slickened flesh. "This will bring me pleasure." He groaned. "Damn, you feel so good."

Amanda wiggled her bottom, thinking to take a more active part in his gratification. She'd seduced him, after all. It surely should be her responsibility. But his fingers dug into the skin above her knees, his grip firm, unyielding. Her legs were tucked to her abdomen and as confined as her arms. She couldn't see, couldn't move, and a man she trusted was enjoying her body. Her center flooded with warmth. She had no power, no duty. And no fear. It was an intoxicating combination.

The pressure at her knees slackened, and Julius took advantage of the widening of her legs. His next stroke was lower, the ridge of his shaft running right through her folds. A whimper escaped her lips.

He gripped her thighs so tightly she knew she'd bruise. "You're so damn soft. Softer than the finest silk." He pulled back and drove inexorably forward.

And he was so hard. She felt every excruciating inch of his length slip through her lower lips, rub against that hard bundle of nerves. Her core begged to be filled. Her clitoris clamored for equal attention. She didn't know which sensation pleased her more, where she wanted his focus. She arched her back as much as possible. "Please."

"Patience," he said. There was a smile in his voice, a smile she didn't appreciate. If he was going to kill her with wanting, the least the man could do was not laugh at her in the process. She squeezed her thighs together, anything to alleviate the pressure, and was rewarded with a low growl. She clamped down harder.

"Vixen." He thrust faster, and Amanda almost cried with relief. His bollocks slapped against her bottom, and her desire climbed higher. Wrapping one arm around her knees, Julius slid his free hand up her side and cupped her breast. He pinched the tip, hard, and the sharp nip of pain transformed into a craving so intense it stole her breath.

His thrusts became shallow, frenzied. The plush crown of his shaft nudged her clitoris, over and over, and Amanda could climb no higher. She broke for the second time that night, tremors wracking her body.

A long groan tore from Julius's throat, and something hot and wet splashed across her stomach.

They breathed together, their pants the only sound in the room.

A low, "Fuck", broke the silence. The mattress shifted, raised, and Amanda was alone. She was starting to wonder whether she should call out when a damp cloth scraped across her belly. She flinched.

"My apologies." He cupped her cheek, his thumb brushing along the line of the blindfold as he cleaned her.

"I didn't mean to startle you." The towel disappeared, and he gripped her hands, lowering them to her stomach. His fingers tangled with the knots at her wrists.

"Are you all right? Are you sore?" His voice was harsh, almost angry.

When her hands were free, she pushed at the blindfold, confused. The light from the fire, so dim before, made her squint. "I'm fine. Shouldn't I be?"

He reached for her face but dropped his hand before touching her. "The bindings. If you're not accustomed to them, sometimes it can hurt."

"Oh." She rolled her shoulders and flexed her fingers. "No, no pain." Only amazing pleasure. A startling freedom. And now awkwardness. He'd given her what she wanted, in a fashion, and he had enjoyed himself, as well. So why did they both avert their gazes?

She rolled off the bed and plucked her night rail from the floor, slipping into it. She shrugged into her wrapper and cinched the belt. "I'd better go. Reggie will be missing me."

"Of course." He ran a hand through his hair, ruffling the russet locks. Sweat glistened on his bare chest, but that was the only sign on him of what they'd just done. His pantaloons had been quickly reassembled, making her believe he must have only shoved them down his hips in order to free himself. He even still wore his boots.

She'd been completely bare and spread before him, and he hadn't even removed his boots. Her cheeks heated, and she grabbed the collar of her night rail. She sidled around Julius. He made no move to stop her.

She opened his door and heard him mutter, "I'm going to burn in hell."

Him and her both.

She fled to her room.

Chapter Six

The shot to the jaw ripped his head back. Julius's vision darkened around the edges, and he fought to stay conscious. Movement came at him from the left, and he threw his hands up in time to block the next roundhouse. The boxing ring disappeared, and Julius had only one thought. Survival. Stepping close, he threw body shot after body shot into his enemy's gut until the man dropped to one knee.

He grabbed his opponent's ears, preparing to introduce the man's nose to his knee. A shout from the sidelines stopped him.

"Julius!"

Turning his head, Julius blinked through the sweat in his eyes. Maximillian Atwood, Baron of Sutton raised a hand in greeting from the outskirts of the ring. A tall, burly man with an unruly black beard, Sutton was a far cry from the refined elegance of his fellow aristocrats. Next to him, and as different as the sun to the moon, their friend, John Chaucer, Earl of Summerset, sniffed the air and frowned. Whereas Sutton's clothes were made of a dark rough wool, Summerset adorned himself in brightly colored silks and satins. His blond hair was neatly trimmed with the locks artfully coiled about his brow. Both men, however, were unswerving in their loyalty.

Recalling where he was, in a friendly sparring match at Gentleman Jack's, Julius dropped his opponent's head and stumbled from the ring. He gratefully took the mug of water Summerset handed him.

"I don't know why you insist on coming here," Summerset said, pressing a puce silk handkerchief to his nose. "The stench alone would stop any sane man at the doors."

Sutton rubbed his jaw, his fingers tangling in his beard. "You just don't want to work up a sweat in your silk pantaloons. That, and you can't wear your heeled boots into the ring."

"I like working up a sweat just fine," Summerset said. "Only I'm smart enough to do it in a more enjoyable manner."

Julius knew the bickering could go on for ages. He raised a hand. "Gentlemen. And I use that term only in its strictest sense. Why have you come here?"

Summerset turned towards him, all wide-eyed innocence, a look that was pure buggering hogwash but always seemed to have women dropping their pantalets. "Why, because you sent for us. Your most trusted friends. Your closest advisors. Your—"

"I sent a letter stating I had need of your services in the near future," Julius interrupted. "Not to come bother me this evening."

Sutton and Summerset shared a look. A look Julius remembered all too well. When he'd arrived back in England after his imprisonment in the Japanese Empire, it had been his constant companion. Each of his friends had worn it, each man tip-toeing around Julius like he'd shatter into a thousand pieces if they said the wrong thing. Made the wrong move. They hadn't known if Julius's extended imprisonment had weakened his mind.

Julius hadn't known, either.

Grabbing a towel, he wiped the sweat from his bare chest and strode to the chair where his coat and shirt lay folded. He fought against the memories, held them at bay through sheer force of will. Even after all these years, he sometimes still forgot where he was, his mind trapped back in that prison.

Like when he almost beat an opponent to a bloody pulp in a friendly sparring match.

"Why are you here?" he asked, his voice gruff. He gripped the ends of the towel and threw it over his head to pull against his neck.

"We were at The Black Rose last night." Sutton crossed his arms over his barrel chest. "Madame Rose said we just missed you."

Fingers tightening on the cloth, Julius raised an eyebrow. "And what else did she tell you?"

Summerset waved his handkerchief through the air. "Nothing that would be embarrassing to you in the least. Just a conversation she had with sweet Lucy. She, of course, didn't tell us that you fled the club. That you left a woman wet and wanting. That never came up in conversation."

A lick of anger flared before sputtering out. The snide condescension in his friend's voice masked true concern. It was unheard of for Julius to abandon a rope scene. And any act out of the ordinary would be noticed by his friends. Wondered at. Worried over. Like he was a damn hothouse flower, wilting under the smallest bit of heat.

"It's sad when men get to that age where they can no longer perform," Summerset said to Sutton. "Why, if I could no longer please a woman—"

"You've never pleased a woman," Julius growled. "I don't think you can start now." He chugged down more water, his mind turning to the last woman he'd pleased. The one woman that could cost him a friendship if her brother-in-law discovered just what Julius had done to her. How much more he wanted to do.

Bloody hell, she liked to be tied up. How was he to resist her now?

But she was the hothouse flower. Yes, she had deep roots, had survived what no person should have to endure, but she was breakable. Delicate. And she needed a man much better than he.

"Was your usual room taken?" Sutton asked. He laid a

hand on Julius's shoulder. "Did you have to use one of the smaller ones?"

Julius shrugged him off. "I was fine. The woman merely didn't interest me. And there is nothing wrong with my performance." He needed to get that out there. Damn friends. If they'd heard Amanda moaning last night, they'd be in no doubt as to just how well he performed. But then he'd have to rip their ears off. Her moans were only for his hearing.

And the man she chose for her next lover. His stomach twisted, but he ignored it.

Summerset tossed himself down into a vacant chair and crossed one leg over the other. He bobbed an ivory leather boot up and down. "I must sit. A woman, bound before you, restrained just so you could take your pleasure, didn't interest you? Has the earth begun to spin in the opposite direction? Are the French now our bosom friends?"

Sutton dropped down on a chair next to him. "Why does it take you a hundred words to say what needs only a few? And leave the man alone. If a Rose doxy no longer holds his interest, that is no one's business but his own." He shifted about, trying to settle comfortably on the narrow seat. "No matter how unusual that lack of interest might be. Now, why have you sent for us?"

"I didn't—" Julius bit his retort off. It didn't matter what he said to his friends. They'd still be arseholes. Dragging a chair around to face them, he sat. "I've been assigned another task by our mutual friend." He glanced around, but no one was close, and the sound of fists pounding into flesh ensured no one would overhear their conversation.

"I grow tired of our mutual friend and his requests." Sutton rested his elbows on his knees. "Do either of you sometimes wish that we were typical swells, where our biggest concerns were managing our country estates and producing an heir?"

Summerset's mouth opened and closed. He blinked and drew his fair brow down low. "Why would you wish to rusticate on a country estate when London provides so many more diversions?" He tugged on the hem of his waistcoat. "No, I am quite thankful to our friend for relieving us from a life of boredom."

"Of course, you are," Sutton muttered. He slowly straightened his muscular body. "What is the task this time?"

Julius told them of the Widow Westmont, of Liverpool's worry over a larger blackmail ring.

Summerset examined his nails. "Did Liverpool say who else had been blackmailed?"

"When does Liverpool ever say more than he needs to?" Julius scanned the large room, cataloging every man he was acquainted with, and every man he was not.

Sutton leaned forward, his chair creaking. "But you have a name."

"How ...?"

"Because I know you," Sutton said. "It's why you're here, is it not? There's someone you wish to speak with."

Julius narrowed his eyes. He shouldn't be surprised anymore by the baron's intuition. The man had the uncanny ability to read his friends. And his enemies.

Inclining his head towards the far corner of the gymnasium, Julius agreed. "Roswell Audley."

"The Duke of Roxburn's son?" Summerset whistled. "It takes a bold man to blackmail anyone in that family. It is said that the duke single-handedly fought off fifteen men in the Siege of Savannah. That it was only because of his blood-thirsty attacks under the cover of night that the rebels failed."

"His three sons are supposed to be just as deadly," Sutton added. The three friends watched as the young man stepped into the ring with an opponent. Audley was shorter than the other man, but his well-defined muscles more than evened the match. In less than twenty seconds, Audley was standing over his unconscious adversary. "Four blows. Usually takes him less." Sutton turned back to Julius.

"What's he being blackmailed over?"

Julius took a last swig of water. "Don't know." He stood. "That's what I'm here to find out."

His friends trailed him to the ring. "You plan to beat the information out of him?" Summerset asked. "That's not quite your style."

"I would hope that beating the victim of blackmail wouldn't be any of our styles." Sutton placed his hand on Julius's shoulder. "What's your plan?"

"An introduction in the ring. Nothing more for now."

Sutton looked him up and down, eyeing the bruises on his body. "Perhaps I should be the one introducing myself in the ring. You look a bit worse for wear."

"I'm fine." Julius entered the marked-off circle and waited as the unconscious man's body was dragged out. "Ready for another?" he asked the duke's son.

The man lifted a hand, palm up, and curled his fingers. Julius met him in the center of the ring and nodded. "Rothchild."

"Lord Roswell Audley." He bobbed his head and stepped back. "I hope you can give me a better showing than my last opponent." The words were pompous, aggressive, but his tone hinted of despair. His hands shook the slightest bit. Lines, much too deep for his age, bracketed Audley's mouth and the pink tinge to his eyes spoke of sleepless nights. This was a man on the edge, needing to pound out his frustrations.

Julius knew just how he felt.

Audley didn't waste time circling Julius. Springing forward, he threw three jabs in quick succession, then tried to take off Julius's head with a roundhouse.

Julius blocked the jabs and ducked under the wide swing. "Audley?" he said conversationally. "You're Roxburn's son?"

Audley grunted and landed a body shot to Julius's ribs.

Julius retaliated with a right cross. Trying to keep the wheeze from his voice, he said, "I saw your father with

Prinny and the Marquess of Hanford at White's last week, placing some bets. The duke seems to have the ear of the Prince Regent."

Audley clenched his jaw and threw a left hook.

Dropping under the punch, Julius planted his fist in the young man's ribcage. See how he appreciated the treatment. "You must be pleased with the influence your family wields."

Eyes narrowed, the young man came down center line, swinging hard.

Julius ducked. The kid didn't like to be reminded of his relations. A definite sore spot. He needed to see if he could make the sore fester. "Although with that power comes great scrutiny."

Audley halted his approach, his chest heaving. "What in the blazes are you driving at?"

"I've heard rumors." Wiping his forehead with the back of his wrist, Julius took the man's measure. Angry. Combative. Most likely unwilling to reveal his predicament when pressed. But perhaps to commiserate with a fellow victim ...

Julius stepped close and threw a hook. Audley easily blocked it and grabbed the back of Julius's neck. The men grappled, heads locked together. "What rumors?" Audley snarled.

Julius tossed an elbow. "You think you're the only one being drained? There are several of us in the same position. We talk."

Audley pushed away. "I don't know what you're speaking of."

"Of course, you don't." From the corner of his eye, Julius noticed a crowd gathering around their ring. His friends were in the front row, watching him intently. Most likely waiting to see if they'd need to intervene if Julius forgot where he was and began fighting in earnest. He lowered his voice. "But if you did, you should know that not everyone is content to keep paying. Some of us wish to fight back. Remove the threat."

"That's absurd." Audley swung so hard he spun around when he didn't make contact.

"Is it?" Julius ducked his head and rained blows to the man's gut. "You struck me as the type of man to take action. Not passively accept his fate."

"I don't passively accept anything." Audley quick-stepped back and licked at a small trickle of blood from his split lip. "And you have incorrect information."

Julius shrugged. "As you say. But ask yourself why I'm here. I don't need any more money. I've not come to drain you further. I've only come because we share a mutual problem."

Audley furrowed his brow. Stepping close, he wrapped his arms around Julius, and they pretended to wrestle. "It's not only myself I have to think of," he whispered. "My family would become pariahs."

"As long as the blackmailers are out there, the threat will always exist." Julius blocked a knee to his stomach. "Only by finding them and eliminating them is the risk to your family removed."

"Less talking, more fighting!" someone from the crowd yelled.

Julius twisted his lips and pushed off the young man. "The men want a show."

Audley just stared at him, panting. He was torn, Julius could tell.

He needed to make the man's decision easier.

"I have a proposition." Julius circled to the left, shuffling backwards to avoid a jab. "If you win this match, I walk away, never to bother you again. But if I win, we talk."

Audley puffed out his chest. "You think you can beat me, old man?"

Julius was maybe fifteen years his senior. Hardly doddering. His own chest expanded. "Is that a deal?"

A muscle in Audley's forehead twitched. For a moment, Julius thought the kid would turn away. Then, slowly,

Audley nodded and held out a fist.

Julius bumped it with his own and got down to business. He could box with the best of them. The straightforward technique was useful to burn off his frustrations. But boxing wasn't his preferred fighting style. When he fought to win, he turned to the arts he'd learned in the Orient. Their system was ingenious, efficient, and infinitely more dangerous. Men of his station would consider it impolite. It had no place at Gentleman Jack's.

Audley was focused on Julius's hands, so Julius shot out a leg and swept the kid's feet out from under him.

"What the hell?" Audley rolled to his hands and knees, and Julius let him climb to his feet. No need to completely humiliate the boy.

Tucking his chin to his chest, Audley lunged at him, a volley of jabs and crosses aimed for his face. Julius dropped to one knee and grabbed his opponent's front ankle. He pulled it towards him while pressing his shoulder into Audley's hip. For a second time, the man went down.

Using Audley's leg as leverage, Julius flipped him over to his stomach and vaulted up Audley's prone body. Before the man could catch his breath, Julius had one hand at the nape of his neck and one knee on the nerve that ran down the back of his arm.

"Son of a bitch, that hurts." Audley struggled to push himself up, but ended up just increasing the pressure on the nerve. He flopped back down.

"So where should we talk? My house or yours?"

* * *

They'd ended up at Simon's, another club Julius was a member of. The respectable one. The boy had sulked, let Julius know he didn't think his fighting style was proper, but Julius had no doubt the conversation would happen. Lord Audley had made a deal, and the son of the Duke of Roxburn didn't renege on a promise.

Julius had managed to convince his friends that their

presence would only impede Audley's tongue, so it was just the two of them in the corner of the billiards room, snifters of brandy on the side table between them, cigars in their hands. Audley had wanted to go into one of the private rooms in the back, but Julius had told him that nothing looked so suspicious as two men secreted away together.

"What do they have on you?" Audley asked. He stared into his glass as he swirled the brandy. "I'm not discussing my situation unless you do, as well."

Fair enough. Unfortunately for Audley, Julius wouldn't be imparting anything truthful. He had plenty of skeletons in his closet, but, as he wasn't being blackmailed, saw no need to shake their bones. A useful lie would suffice.

"I belong to a club," he began.

Audley stretched his arms wide, brandy sloshing over the rim of his glass. "Who doesn't?"

"Not this type of club. A club that can't be spoken of in polite society."

Audley drew angrily on the cigar and blew out a long stream of smoke. "Again, who doesn't?" he muttered.

"Something unfortunate happened in that club one night," Julius said. "A woman was hurt." That was true enough. Women were hurt there every night. For coin and pleasure.

Audley followed his statement to its logical conclusion. "And you covered it up, but not well enough."

Julius raised his glass in assent.

"How long have you been paying?" Audley asked.

"Long enough." Julius puffed on his cigar. A group of men, old enough to know better, stumbled into the room at the far end, laughing uproariously. A longtime member started, jerked his cue along the felt covering the table, and shot the group a disgusted look.

Dangling his elbow over the armrest of his chair, Julius tipped his glass to the side until the liquid almost spilled over the rim. "They're very good. I've never seen one of my blackmailers. Mysterious notes show up on my doorstep."

"Lucky you. I appear to have a personal representative who is always willing to remind me of the consequences if I don't pay him on time each month." Audley's fingers whitened around the stem of his glass. "Although the man might as well be invisible for all I know of him."

"You know what he looks like," Julius said. "That's a start."

Audley ground out the end of his half-smoked cigar on the bottom of his boot, ash falling to the carpet. "He looks like any other lower-class shit sack. Unkempt. Unwashed. Rude beyond tolerance."

"Of course, he's rude." Julius stared at the ceiling, resting his head back. "He's extorting money from you." And he wondered how 'unkempt' the man truly was. To the son of a duke, Julius most likely looked like a vagabond. Sutton would appear a hardened ruffian. And he didn't even want to consider how Audley would see their friend Sinclair, the Marquess of Dunkeld. Even to Julius's more forgiving eye, that man looked two steps from bedlam.

"Can you give a more specific description?" At this point, anything would be useful. "Hair color, height, weight? Accent?"

"Average size. Brownish hair. Middle-aged. A lower-class accent."

Julius had been wrong. Not everything was useful. "You just described over half the men in London. Anything distinctive about him?"

"No." Audley shifted in his chair. "Except for the scars, of course."

Leaning forward, Julius gripped his fists to keep from throttling the young man. "What scars?"

Audley shrugged. "Little craters that cover his neck and cheeks. Pox I guess." He downed the last gulp of brandy. "He frequents a coffeehouse in Covent Garden. I have my grooms follow him after he leaves my house. The man always loses them after that point."

"Why did you not lead with this information?" Julius

asked, exasperated. This was why he preferred espionage to investigations. People never told him what he wanted to hear when he wanted to hear it. "Anything else? The name of the head blackmailer you've forgotten to tell me? His home address?"

Audley's eyebrows drew together. "No. If I knew that we wouldn't be having this conversation." Before Julius could explain the concept of sarcasm, Audley continued. "But you may want to speak with Martin Dawnley. He was a clerk in the Court of Chancery and another victim of blackmail. He paid even when he had no money, and now England provides his keep in debtor's prison."

Julius rubbed his temple. "How do you know he was blackmailed?"

"I came to know him casually when I helped my aunt with her husband's estate. Dawnley came to me for a loan." Audley snorted. "I refused. Told him he needed to man up and face the consequences of his actions. This was before I was approached by the blackmailer, of course."

"Of course." Julius laid down his brandy and cigar and stood.

"Don't you want to know what they're blackmailing me for?" Audley stared at his boots.

"No." Julius eyed the young man, his lowered shoulders, his tired eyes. If the kid had attained the age of one and twenty, Julius would be surprised. Too young to have to deal with such a threat. At that age, Julius had just joined the military, eager for the adventures life would provide. Still ignorant of life's harsher realities.

He'd learned quickly. In the three years he'd been a prisoner of a local warlord, he'd discovered the depravity of human nature and his own limits on how much suffering he could endure. His two older brothers had died while he'd been captive, and it was their deaths that had saved his life. Their lives for his. It had been a poor trade-off.

Audley looked up, a hint of desperation crossing his face. "They want more than blunt now. They want something I can't give. My father would never—" Leaning forward, he rested his elbows on his knees and dropped his head in his hands. "I don't influence my father."

"And that's what they really want." Julius drummed his fingers against his thigh. He quite wanted to meet these bastards.

Audley dug his fingers into his scalp. "But if I don't get my father to convince Prinny, I'll be hanged. I don't see a way out of this for me."

"You might not see it, but there is always a way out." Julius laid a hand on the man's shoulder and squeezed. "Why would you hang?"

"It's the law. Men like me don't deserve to live apparently."

"Ah." So those were the types of clubs the young lord patronized. It wasn't unheard of for a man to visit a mollyhouse. Most in Polite Society preferred to turn a blind eye. But it was still dangerous, at least for men without Audley's connections. One of England's many capital offenses.

"You are the son of a duke. You wouldn't hang." He'd be shunned. Shipped out of the country. Probably sent to fight on the front lines in the hopes he'd do the decent thing like step in front of a bullet to end his family's disgrace. But not hanged.

"You think not?" Audley stood. "You don't think the government would love to make an example of an aristocrat? To round up the support of the common man by tossing him a bone? And the execution of a titled toff is a very juicy bone." He looked away. "I don't know if my father would fight for me," he said, his voice small.

Julius's gut clenched. That was something he'd never had to experience. He'd always known he had people to count on. His father had left no stone unturned trying to negotiate his release. His friends had exhausted the more disreputable avenues. Julius had come to believe they'd never succeed in their efforts, but he never stopped believing that they'd keep trying to save him. Eventually it had been a combination of his father's efforts, his friends' manipulations, and Julius's own escape efforts that had secured his release.

"You will not hang." Julius stepped close and gripped the man's shoulders. "I will make sure of it." He'd already saved one person from the Tyburn Tree. He could save another if it came to it. But it wouldn't. Liverpool owed him, and Julius was all too ready to collect.

Audley gave him a weak smile. "I almost believe you."

"As well you should." Julius clapped him on the back and turned. Audley fell into step beside him. They gathered their coats and hats and stepped out into the brisk night air.

The bell was tolling midnight, and Julius looked across the street at St. Katherine's church. A candle flickered high in the tower. Julius shivered, thinking of the narrow staircase the ringer had to climb to reach his perch. Poor bastard.

Julius tugged on a glove. "When I have further information, I'll let you know. In the meantime, I wish to speak with your grooms."

Audley nodded. He raised his voice to be heard above the echoing bells and the wheels of several carriages rattling over cobblestone. "I'll tell them to expect you." He stepped to the edge of the curb and waved to his driver parked down the street. The servant nodded and slapped the backs of the horses with the reins.

Audley never saw the man who stole up behind him and shoved him into the street.

A driver yelled. Horses squealed. And the terrible sound of a wheel striking flesh cut through the air.

Julius's core turned to ice. He stumbled to the street. The lad's servant pushed past him, knocking him aside. The driver dropped to his knees by Audley's twisted legs and screamed for a doctor.

A middle-aged man in a long black cloak with a patch on the right shoulder hurried away. Julius changed direction and shot after him, struggling against the crowd flocking to the accident like vultures to a carcass. By the time he reached the corner, the man had disappeared.

Jaw clenched tight, Julius pushed back to Audley. Or what was left of him. Even in the dim light, he could tell the boy was dead. Getting trampled by horses and run over by a carriage would do that to a person.

His body began to shake with rage. Audley had been intentionally pushed, of that there was no doubt. Julius's grand idea of speaking to the lad in the open had been foolish, and had gotten Audley killed. He swallowed, the back of his throat burning.

He'd promised the man that he wouldn't hang.

He should have promised to keep him alive.

Chapter Seven

Reggie whimpered beneath Amanda's hand, and she stilled. The dog had been listless all night and now lay, mewling in pain, on her sister's settee in the morning room. She didn't know what to do. Lady Mary had yet to rise. Julius had been avoiding her the past couple of days, and last night he hadn't bothered to come home. And when she'd asked Carter if he knew anything of canine health, he'd merely curled his lip and turned away.

She couldn't let anything happen to Reggie. Liz would be devastated. The dog had been a gift from her husband when he was just a pup. Although only a member of the family for a couple months, Reggie had wagged his way into everyone's hearts, Amanda's included. With Liz gone, the dog was the only one who was always there for her. She swallowed past the lump in her throat. Nothing could happen to him.

Holding a bowl to his nose, she rubbed a finger gently between his eyes. "How about some cream, boy?"

Reggie closed his eyes and sighed.

Setting the bowl down on the floor, she stood and hurried to the escritoire. When Reggie had first moved into the duke's London house, he'd burned a paw by standing against an oven door. Liz had found an animal doctor in Chelsea who'd made house calls. She found her sister's journal of household accounts, relieved that Liz still maintained her own records instead of relying solely on her servants. She found the entry and noted the doctor's address. Pulling a sheet of paper out of the drawer, she sat at the small desk and wrote a hasty note asking for his immediate services. When she came to the end, she hesitated over her signature.

A request from Miss Amanda Wilcox would receive no response. She was tempted to write her sister's name, but most everyone knew the duke and his new duchess were abroad. Would a note from a member of his staff draw an immediate response? Reggie might not have time to wait.

But if Amanda stood on the man's front step and refused to leave until he agreed to see Reggie, that might do the trick. Her heart pounded at the thought of stepping out of doors. Reggie whined again, and Amanda closed her eyes. She could do this.

Resolved, she folded the note and tucked it up her sleeve. She raced upstairs for her pelisse, grateful that the covering would hide the state of her gown. Without a maid, or Julius, to help her dress, she made a poor showing of it. No stays, and buttons down her back that had found the wrong hole. The doctor would have every right to close the door in her face. If she let him.

She swept down the staircase and rushed for the front door, barely allowing the footman seated beside it time to jump up and open it for her.

The sun's rays dropped on her like a shroud, and she froze at the threshold. She raised a hand to shade her eyes. The half-circle driveway was empty, quiet. A wall stood between the drive and the street, but muted sounds of life could be heard on the other side. Heart pounding, Amanda took a step forward. A group of men stamped along the sidewalk, crossing the entrance to the driveway. They didn't spare her a glance. Amanda looked over her shoulder. The door stood open, inviting. But Reggie was sick. She faced front. Three steps lay before her and the driveway. All she needed to do was climb down the porch and walk to the street.

She took another half-step, the toes of her slippers peeking over the edge of the top stair.

Her heart pounded so hard she could feel her blood pulsing beneath the skin at her temples. She could do this. She'd been outside before, plenty of times. Granted, not since her imprisonment. But nothing had changed. She just had to put one foot in front of the other and she'd make her way to the animal doctor.

She lifted her foot, put it back down. Sweat beaded on her forehead, and she fought to keep back a whimper. There was too much space. Too many directions from which someone could hurt her. Head spinning, she fell back and bumped into a soft body.

"My dear, are we going somewhere?" Lady Mary cupped Amanda's elbow. Faded blue eyes looked out at her from beneath a fringe of white hair. "I would quite like to visit my milliner." She cocked a critical eye at Amanda. "But you aren't wearing a hat. Nor gloves. Your poor skin will burn."

Amanda clutched at the woman's shawl. "Quite." She sucked down a shaky breath. "Quite. Lady Mary, I don't feel well enough to go out today, but I have a very important missive to deliver." She tugged the note from her sleeve and pressed it into the woman's hand. "Would you please deliver this to the animal doctor on Hartford Court? And you can't leave without his promise to come see Reggie at once. Something is wrong with him, and I don't know what."

"Of course, dear." She clucked. "That poor baby. I should have known something was wrong when he refused the bit of beef I offered him last night. Let me go grab my gloves and reticule."

Amanda almost stepped on the woman's heels following her back inside. She wanted to kneel down and kiss the floor. Inside was safe. Inside was where she belonged.

The footman eyed her curiously, and she tried to gather her emotions. "Can you take the Lady Mary to the animal doctor on Hartford? The duke has used him before to attend to Reggie."

"Yes, miss." His gaze travelled down her body before snapping back to the wall with a blank look.

Amanda knew he was only curious about her disheveled appearance, her fright. The man had never acted inappropriately before. But she still shrank back. There were far fewer prying eyes inside than out, but there were still too many. And men looking at her body had never ended well for her.

She waited in the foyer until Lady Mary bustled out, the footman two steps behind. The woman assured her she wouldn't return without the animal doctor in tow. But the duke's aunt was so flighty, she might forget her task as easily as Julius had seemed to forget about Amanda. It should be Amanda going to retrieve the doctor. She was letting Reggie down. She was letting her sister down. Again.

With the front door safely shut, Amanda fled into the morning room and dropped to her knees next to the settee. She stroked Reggie's head, his soft brown fur sliding through her fingers. Sunlight streamed through the window, reflecting off a large mirror on the wall. The ceiling stretched to three times her height. Everything was open and airy, and Amanda hated it. This room wasn't safe, either.

As gently as possible, she slid her hands under Reggie's warm body and cradled him to her chest. He was almost too large now for her to carry, but she managed. After one last whimper, he settled against her and fell back asleep. Feeling as though the walls were watching, she crept swiftly up the stairs and fled to her room, closing the door behind her.

Her bedchamber was dusky behind the drawn curtains, but her step never hesitated. She'd learned well how to navigate in the dark. Heading for her armoire, she pulled open the door and climbed inside. She'd managed to keep herself from succumbing to this weakness for over a month, but her spot in the corner was still open.

Sitting cross-legged, she held Reggie tight, burying her

nose in his fur. With one last shaky breath, she pulled the door closed, sealing herself safely inside.

* * *

Where the bloody hell was she? Julius pressed his fingertips into his skull, hoping the pressure would counteract the pounding from within. Last night he'd gone to his townhouse, surprised the one servant left in residence during Julius's extended absence, and gotten rip-roaring drunk. What else could a man do after getting another man killed? He was paying for it this morning.

Carter had assured him that Miss Wilcox was yet indoors, and of that, Julius had little doubt. She never left. But he'd searched the house high and low and had yet to discover her. His throbbing head couldn't take this.

He strode into her room again. Her chamber smelled faintly of lavender, and he spied the bunch of dried flowers on her bureau. He fingered the faded purple stem, and it broke off in his hand. Desiccated. Dead. There was no life in this room. No spill of colorful gowns an eager chit had been too busy to put away. No half-read book on the low table in front of the fireplace. He ripped open the curtains over the window, letting light in. Amanda existed, but did she truly live?

He tapped his fingers on his thigh. She might not exist for long. If she didn't reveal herself soon, he was going to kill her for scaring him. He didn't even want to consider what Marcus would do to him if he misplaced the man's sister-in-law. He'd start in the attics and make his way down through the house this time. She was within these walls; she had to be.

His hand was on the door's latch when he heard the small whimper. Spinning, he scanned the room. Not wanting to believe it, he dropped to one knee and lifted the long counterpane. He heaved a sigh of relief. No one hiding beneath the bed. That only left one place where a body could fit. He crossed the room and opened the armoire.

Amanda blinked at the light and pulled her knees up close to her chest, causing the pup to whimper again.

It felt like someone had reached inside Julius's chest and ripped out his heart.

He sank into a crouch next to the open door. "Amanda," he said gently. "What are you doing in there?"

She remained silent. Julius remembered the blanket he'd found at the bottom of the wardrobe when he'd dressed Amanda and bit back a curse. How long had this been her hiding place?

"Don't you think it's time to come out?" he asked gently.

She shook her head and hugged the dog close.

Julius ran a finger behind Reggie's ear. "I've heard you've sent for the animal doctor. You'll need to take the dog downstairs to await his arrival."

Closing her eyes, she leaned her head back against the wood paneling. The skin of her neck gleamed like ivory in the sunlight, and she looked as fragile as a snowflake. Such pallor was the height of fashion, but knowing that she only achieved it by hiding herself away turned Julius's stomach. He had to get her out of this house. It bound her like a tomb. He wanted to see her as brown and freckled as a field hand.

She offered up the pup. "You take him down. The animal doctor will be more attentive if you're there anyway."

"I'm not going down without you." His voice was harsher than he'd intended, and Amanda's eyes flew open. He cleared his throat. "We'll go down together."

He could carry her out. Hell, he could toss her in his carriage and force her to walk Hyde Park without a bonnet, something that would put some color on her face. But she needed to break free of her self-imposed prison herself. If anyone understood that, it was he.

What he didn't understand was why she found comfort in close spaces. Just seeing her slight body ensconced in the wardrobe made his skin itch.

His first year of imprisonment had been in a space this small. His cell was a mud pit they covered with a slab of wood. It had almost been a relief when they'd drag him out and bind him. His torture had been their entertainment. The ropes hadn't allowed for even the smallest movements. As his captors had come to understand his rank in British society, the ropes had loosened, his treatment improved. When he'd become the heir to an earldom, the samurai holding him had made the knots so loose they were merely a formality. They'd come to believe that his honor would keep him from running. They'd been wrong.

When it came to life and death, there was no honor. Only survival.

He eyed Amanda, all curled up in a ball, and his muscles hardened to stone. She didn't need his honor, his concern about insulting a friend by having an affair with her. She needed to come out of this exile to the other side, whole. And she wanted to do it, indeed had started the journey, by exploring her sexuality. Who was he to curb her impulses?

But first, she needed to get her lovely arse out of her hiding place.

He offered her his hand, palm up. "Reggie needs you to stop quivering in your wardrobe like a little mouse and take him downstairs." The gold flecks in her brown eyes sparked like fire, and Julius smothered his triumph. Newgate hadn't been able to beat out her pride and that's what would get her through. "So, stop sniveling, take my hand, and get up."

"I do not now, nor have I ever, sniveled." She lifted her chin.

He believed her. "Prove it." He bobbed his hand in front of her and prayed she'd take it soon. His shoulder was starting to ache from holding his arm in front of himself for so long.

"Fine," she bit out. She slapped her palm in his, and even though that jarred his shoulder further, relief coursed through his body. Whatever demons had driven her into hiding were no match for her spirit.

Standing, he pulled her up with him and helped her over the lip of the armoire. Reggie shifted against her chest, and Julius reached for him.

Amanda adjusted her hold on the pup and twisted her hand in Julius's, threading her fingers through his and holding on tight. A dull flush colored her cheeks, but she didn't loosen her grip.

She needn't have worried. Julius leaned close and whispered, "Don't worry, mouse. I wasn't going to let you go."

Her dark eyes flashed at the nickname, and Julius realized just how entertaining it was going to be to tease this woman. Make her so inflamed she had no recourse but to burst out from her shell. He strode for the door, Amanda scampering after him. So very entertaining.

Chapter Eight

Julius shut the door behind the animal doctor and ignored Carter's huff of displeasure at an earl doing a footman's job. He was nearing the limit of his endurance and appeasing a pompous butler would push him over. Standing in the doorway to the morning room, he watched Amanda kneel next to Reggie and stroke his ears. All afternoon Julius had been watching Amanda. First to ensure she'd recovered from her earlier fright. When the color had returned to her cheeks and her hands had stopped trembling, Julius had relaxed. And then his gaze had dropped elsewhere.

He'd watched Amanda's arse as she'd bent over the settee, cooing over the dog. Watched as her breasts, unrestrained by any underbodice, heaved with her sigh of relief when the doctor had declared Reggie's ails temporary. Watched as strand after strand of her lustrous dark hair slipped loose from the messy knot at the back of her head.

He really should hire another maid for her. One to dress her properly and pin up her hair.

She stood, and sunlight turned the thin cotton of her gown semi-transparent. Every soft curve of her body was on display, her breasts shifting naturally against the fabric. The valley between her legs became a tantalizing shadow.

His cock thickened. The maid could wait. An artless Amanda was a sight to behold.

She met him at the door, Reggie in her arms. "I'm going to let him rest in my bed. It's more comfortable than the settee."

He nodded and followed her up the stairs. Her round bottom shifted from side to side in front of his face, and a groan escaped him.

Amanda paused. "Are you in pain? Should we call a doctor for you, as well?"

"I'm fine," he ground out. At least, there was nothing that a doctor could fix.

"Hmm." She continued up the stairs. "I thought perhaps your bruises were ailing you. They look quite painful."

"And yet you've only thought to inquire of them now. Your lack of concern wounds me." His face was a mess, purple staining his skin from his left eye to his lip. His ribs looked worse. Yet he wished he'd let Audley get in a couple more hits. A beating was a sad penance for getting a young man killed, but it was something.

Pushing thoughts of last night away, he followed Amanda to her room and waited at the door as she settled the dog in the middle of her bed. She tucked a pillow behind his back and drew the coverlet up to cover Reggie. Julius would have rolled his eyes over such attentiveness to a dog, but her actions had her bending over the bed, presenting her pert behind for his viewing pleasure yet again.

It was quickly becoming his favorite part of her body.

Sunlight turned her gown translucent once more, and Julius could no longer resist. Striding to the bed, he fitted his body to hers. She froze, her arms planted next to the dog. Julius ran his palms down her arms and encircled her wrists.

"I think Reggie needs uninterrupted rest. We should leave." He pressed a kiss to the back of her neck and gauged her body's reaction. Just because he'd found her in his bed once, he couldn't assume she wanted more.

"Where would you suggest we go?" Was that a hint of flirtation in her voice? The small wriggle of her backside against his groin confirmed it.

He had an idea about that. He only hoped she'd be

willing. "Follow me." Taking one of her hands, he led her out of the room and down the hall.

When they passed his door, she hesitated. "We're not going to your room?"

"Not yet."

They took a back staircase. One maid saw them when they reached the ground floor, her eyes widening at the sight of Julius, and she stumbled over herself trying to curtsy and flee at the same time. Julius's recent firings seemed to have had that effect on the remaining servants.

"Come." Her hand tight in his, he led her down a narrow hallway to the door to the rear garden. He opened the door wide and breathed in the sweet, fresh air.

Amanda cowered behind his back. "What ...?" She cleared her throat. "I wish to return upstairs."

Turning, he took her other hand so he held both of hers in his own, his back to the open rectangle. "I know you do," he said gently. "But it's important for you to go out of doors. This is Marcus's private garden. There will be no one else around. Only you, me, and the sunlight. Won't you come for a stroll with me? Just for a little while?"

Her chest heaved, and she shook her head. "I can't. If you would like a turn about the gardens, you go. I'll wait in your chambers."

Leaning forwards, he brushed his lips over hers. "We'll return to my bedroom soon enough." But first he wanted to see her skin touched by the sun's rays. See whether her sable hair glinted red in the natural light like her sister's did. Watch Amanda break free from her prison. "Let's make it a game. For every five steps you take in the garden, I'll ..." His mind searched for an appropriate reward.

"Take me to my crisis, as you did before?" Her cheeks flushed pink. "I enjoyed that."

As Julius wished for a long walk among the pebbled pathways, that could be quite a large number. But he was always up for a challenge. "All right. The terms are set." He bent his head and whispered in her ear, "How far will you go for pleasure?" And he took a step backwards, onto the gravel path. Their hands were still joined, their arms now outstretched.

Amanda edged forward until finally sunlight broke across her face. She squeezed her eyes tight and grasped his hands even tighter.

"Join me on the garden path and you'll have earned one reward." Pulse pounding, Julius waited while she came to a decision. Her fear and agony were writ across her features, and it tore at his heart. But she needed this push.

She stepped across the threshold, and warmth radiated throughout his body. The first step was always the hardest.

"Marvelous job," he said, keeping his voice light. "You've earned your reward." Coming to her side, he tucked her arm through his and patted her hand. "Just five more steps and you'll have a second. That bed of crocuses looks five steps away. Let's go visit those, shall we?"

She kept her eyes closed for those five steps. She pressed herself so tightly to him that he could feel her heart thumping against his arm. But she reached the flower bed. Such bravery demanded a prize.

Tilting her chin back, he cupped her face. He brushed his thumbs along her cheekbones, across the lids of her eyes. In the full light she didn't look as fragile as she did indoors. Her skin lost some of its translucent quality, for which he was glad. Here was a living, breathing woman, not a delicate bit of porcelain. He traced the bow of her full upper lip, and she sighed. Lowering his head, he joined his mouth to hers.

The kiss was slow, thorough but sweet. When he raised his head, she blinked up at him. A smile tugged at her lips. "That was quite nice, but it doesn't qualify as my reward. I will hold you to account."

Rolling his eyes, he tucked her into his side again. "Let's see how many more rewards you can win." And so they made their way slowly through the garden, kissing every five steps, his body temperature firing higher and higher until

Julius could take it no longer. He bustled her back to the side door and up to his room.

He kicked the door shut and pressed Amanda back against it. Her eyes were wide, dark pools, looking so fathomless he thought he would drown. "That was an amazing showing of fortitude and it is past time I delivered on my end of the bargain."

She licked her bottom lip, her chest heaving. "Yes, please." This woman was so ripe, so passionate. If she was right that she would never marry, it would be a crime to let her body suffer from neglect.

He lowered his head and pressed his lips to hers. She sighed. Tugging at her bottom lip, he swept inside her mouth. At the first slide of his tongue against hers, she clutched the sleeve of his coat and rocked up onto her toes.

The hair on the back of his neck stood on end, and his cock wept against the fall of his trousers. Julius drew back, trying to catch his breath. "Do you want the blindfold?"

She dropped back on her heels. Slowly, she shook her head. "This time, I want to watch."

"Then I'll be sure to put on a good show." He pressed his hands flat against the door above her head. "Turn around."

She complied, but kept her gaze on his face until her neck was twisted sharply over her shoulder. Under watchful eyes, he undid the buttons that ran down her back. Two of them had skipped a hole, but not a poor showing considering she'd dressed herself. She was a resourceful mouse. Pushing the dress down her shoulders, he let it slip to the floor, a puddle of fabric at her feet. Only a thin chemise covered her body and that soon joined the gown.

He clenched his fist. Need pounded through his body. With the back of his knuckles, he traced the line of her spine from her neck to the base of her back. Her skin was so soft. So smooth. And her arse was absolutely delicious.

"Go get on the bed." He strode to a bureau and pulled a box from the bottom drawer. "And no closing the curtains.

I'll allow no retreats after your magnificent foray into the garden."

She sat on her knees in the middle of the huge bed and nibbled on her bottom lip. "I don't want to retreat. But ... I might close my eyes." Her gaze darted to the open window and the curtains billowing in the small breeze. "If it becomes too much."

His heart squeezed, like a rag in the hands of a washerwoman. Life was too short to block it out by closing one's eyes. She should know that. She needed to learn that joy existed in equal measure with despair. And perhaps, if he made her feel secure enough, she would lose all qualms about exploring outside her bounds.

Placing the japanned box on the bed, he lifted the lacquered lid. Under watchful brown eyes, he removed a cable of red silk rope and uncoiled it. The silk slid against his palms, a smooth caress.

He held it out for Amanda's inspection. "This is what I used to tie you before. I also have a hemp rope, and a jute one, but this one is softer and good for novices."

She ran her index finger along the braid, and Julius felt it as though her finger caressed his own skin.

Leaning forward, Amanda peeked into the box and lifted one of three glass bottles. She titled the amber bottle to the side and examined it through a stream of sunlight. "Oil?"

He nodded and wound one end of the rope around his fist.

She replaced it and dug deeper into the velvet lined interior. A wisp of dark hair drifted across her cheek. Brushing it behind her ear, Julius plucked the ineffectual pins from her head, tossing them onto the carpet. Her hair fell in thick waves down her back. It was long enough to serve as its own rope. He could definitely tie her wrists with it. And if she was flexible enough, perhaps even her ankles. He pressed his palm against the front of his trousers. He'd have to think on that.

A deep divot appeared between her eyebrows. She held up a twelve-inch jade column in one hand, and a much smaller one in the other. One end of the columns was softly rounded; the other flared to a wide base. She squinted and brought the objects closer to her face. "There are faces carved at the tops of these. Are they dolls of some sort?"

Biting back a smile, he placed the rope on the bed and pulled out the other three columns. He lined them up in a row before her, from largest to smallest, the pearlescent stones a soft and creamy green against the white counterpane. "Not dolls, my sweet. Tools. Objects to increase our pleasure. When I was in the East, before I was captured, I did a lot of shopping. Sent many toys back home for me and my friends." He took the large one from her and replaced it in the box. "And that's one you won't be using for a while. Not until your body adjusts to the smaller sizes."

"Adjusts ..." Her eyes widened. "Where, exactly, do you plan on placing these *tools*?"

He smiled. "Two guesses." When she continued to frown, he leaned forward and pressed a kiss to her lips. "Trust me. Whatever I do will be for your enjoyment."

Taking what he needed, he put the box on the floor and undressed.

"Why do I think these won't only be for my enjoyment," she grumbled. But the corner of her mouth twitched. The smile faded as the last of his clothes fell away. She looked away from his groin, pink flaring across her cheeks.

He crawled over her, his body forcing hers to lay back. "I promise, if you don't find pleasure in something, I won't either. Now"—he traced the lower curve of her mouth with his tongue and sucked the plump flesh into his mouth—"are you going to stop questioning my every move, or do I need to gag this pretty mouth?"

"You could try." Her eyes glittered darkly. "But I've lived my entire life biting my tongue, never speaking up. I won't let anyone silence me again."

Like an artist before a block of marble, Amanda chipped another piece of Julius's reserve away. If he wasn't careful, she'd carve him into an entirely new man.

"No gags." He settled into the cradle of her hips, his cock nestled against the soft lips of her cunny. Running his nose up her neck, he inhaled deeply. "Besides, I can think of much more interesting things to stick in that mouth than a rag."

Clenching a fistful of her hair, he turned his wrist, each revolution wrapping more strands around his hand until he was tight against her skull. Holding her head immobile, he took her mouth, feasting on her eagerness. Amanda's innocence had long been taken, but Julius would bet that no one had spent any time merely kissing her. It was an intimate act, more intimate than fucking. And Julius loved that he was the one introducing her to that pleasure.

He scraped his teeth along her tongue, exhaled when she inhaled, merging their breaths into one. He made his kisses soft, whispers of a touch, before delving back in and demanding her surrender.

When he finally pulled back, light-headed and out of breath, her lips were swollen and red.

"Julius." She pressed a palm to his chest. "That was lovely, but ..."

"But what?"

Her cheeks flushed red. Julius glanced down. The blush spread to the tops of her breasts, and he couldn't resist taking one of her hard nipples in his mouth and suckling.

"But ... oh, my ..." Her chest heaved with a ragged breath. "But I don't quite know what I'm to do. Should I be touching you? Before, men took what they wanted and left."

Julius dug his fingers into her hip before relaxing. He needed to hear her out. Understand what she needed.

"But with you," she continued, "since we're ..."

"Having carnal relations."

She looked over his shoulder. "Yes, that. Since we're

doing that, I feel like I should do something more or else you'll become disinterested. But I don't know what."

Julius sat back and looked down at the lovely woman laid before him. "First, any time you wish to touch me, you may. It will always be welcome. Unless we're having tea with the prince regent, and even then I think I could make it work."

A smile curved her mouth, but she still chewed her lip like it was made of spun sugar.

"Second, I will never become uninterested in you. Do you know why?" He picked up the rope and eyed the canvas of warm flesh before him. She shook her head, sucking in a sharp breath when he looped the cable over one ankle. "Because even when you do nothing, are unable to move a single, solitary inch, you are the most alluring woman I know." He spoke the truth, and for a minute his gut clenched at the knowledge that their time was temporary. For even though Amanda's prospects for marriage were limited, his were nonexistent. After his time in the East, he'd known he could never take those vows. But that didn't mean he couldn't enjoy the time they did have.

He wound the rope up both legs, pulling them tight together. Julius made sure there was enough give so she could bend at the knees before rolling her onto her side. He crisscrossed the rope around her back and shoulders, weaving a harness. Each inch of silk that slid through his fingers soothed the itch under his skin that was a constant presence. Every coil of rope against her smooth skin settled his nerves.

And inflamed his desire.

He wound and tied, finding peace in the patterns and beauty in the design. Each loop and knot bound Amanda to his bed. To his room. To him. She moved with his unspoken commands, arching her back or lifting an arm to let him work. She made no sound except the soft whisper of her breath. With every foot of rope that encircled her body, her fists relaxed more and more, her eyelids lowering to half-mast. A content Mona Lisa.

Making sure the Carrick Bend knot lay flat between Amanda's shoulder blades, he rolled her onto her back. He adjusted a cable under one arm before he was satisfied. With the remaining tails, he bound her wrists together and tied off the rope.

Her hands were held together at chest level, in prayer pose. Her hips were turned and her legs bent to one side. The rope crossed between her breasts, circling around each plush mound, before disappearing to her back. The harness lightly squeezed the soft skin of her breasts, plumping them, framing them. It was the prettiest picture Julius had ever seen.

Red rope. Creamy skin. Dark hair spilling everywhere. He couldn't stop the groan that tore from his throat.

She was a masterpiece. He trailed his fingers over her skin. "You're beautiful."

Her smile was dreamy. "I'm glad you think so."

"That isn't an opinion." Picking up the linen condom he'd pulled from his box, he tied the contraption around his cock. His fingers fumbled on the bow. He hadn't been this eager to slide into a woman since he'd been a lad.

Gathering up Amanda's legs, he held them against his chest, both of her feet dangling over one of his shoulders. His free hand found her folds. He pressed his thumb between her lips, and slid it up and down, from her entrance to her nub. Her desire slickened his skin, but it wasn't enough. Not for what he wanted. With two fingers, he slowly plunged in and out of her channel.

Her heat almost scalded him, and his cock demanded entry. But he needed her to be completely ready. He gently rubbed the inside of her sheath, searching for that spongy bit of flesh. A breathy moan rewarded him. He added a third finger easily, her body pliant and ready.

Lining his erection up to her entrance, Julius held onto her legs with one hand and gripped the knot between her breasts with his other. Using that as leverage, he pushed his way inside, his mind going white with pleasure.

* * *

It didn't seem possible that anything could invade her peace. Cocooned as she was in silk, her mind had drifted, swept along to a place where she was warm and safe and carefree. But Julius was a force that couldn't be denied. He steadily filled her until she felt the hair on his thighs scrape against her bottom.

She blinked, and all the warmth wrapped around her body arrowed to her core. The hand between her breasts tightened, pulling her chest up, arching her back. Her dreamlike state disappeared and a wonderful reality took its place.

She laced the fingers of her bound hands together and relaxed into his hold. There was nothing else she could do. With excruciating slowness, Julius tunneled in and out, using her harness to pull her body into his thrusts. The bonds cradled her. Every muscle in her body could relax without fear that she'd make a wrong move. The rope held her together. Kept her under control. There was no chance that she'd panic, lash out, and hurt someone.

Her mind clouded briefly with memories but she pushed them away. They were easy to forget with Julius providing an all-consuming distraction.

His eyes were closed, and she watched him without embarrassment. The sunlight caught his hair, and a few strands of gold glinted in the chestnut locks. A reddish tinge dusted his high cheekbones. A bead of sweat rolled from his temple down his bruised eye and across the faint scar on his cheek. Julius dug his teeth into his lower lip as he bottomed out.

Every move he made was deliberate. Every inch of rope lashed across her skin artfully placed. Her only experiences had been with cruel men, usually in their cups, who casually took what they wanted and stumbled away. His focus, his discipline, was intoxicating.

He slammed his body into hers, and she felt a pinch deep inside. He rammed into her again and held himself deep. The nip of pain rolled into need.

He stared down at her through heavy-lidded eyes. "Focus on the moment. I can see your mind going in a hundred different directions when there is only one thought that should be in your head."

She stifled a whimper as he hit that spot again. It felt like he was driving into her womb, and every nerve inside her screamed in delight. "What thought is that?" she whispered.

"How fucking good this feels." He let go of the knot at her chest and circled the tip of one breast with his finger. The hard peak ached, and she tried to arch into his touch. The ropes wouldn't allow it.

Julius retained the power of his thrusts but slackened his pace. He'd plow into her, and then ease back so slowly she thought she would scream.

He toyed with her breasts, pinching the nipples, grabbing a full handful and using that to hold her in place. Fire licked beneath her skin, threatening to consume her from the inside out. It felt like she was about to burst. The ropes held her together.

The slide of his shaft on her inner walls was delicious torture. She needed it to end. She wanted it to go on forever. "Julius," she pleaded, her voice hoarse.

"Need something, mouse?" He traced the seam where rope met flesh as it curved around her side. "If you want something, all you need to do is ask."

Amanda turned her face into the pillow. She'd let Julius do unspeakable things to her body and was enjoying every one of them. Why was voicing her desire so difficult?

She tried again. "Make me feel like you did the other day. Make me come apart. You owe me several rewards."

"That was more of a demand than a request." A lazy smile curled his lips. "But your wish is my command."

He glided his fingertips down her side to her hip and

then around to the apex of her thighs. With her legs tied together, he had to work, but his thumb finally made its way to her bundle of nerves. He circled her clit and thrust into her. Circle and thrust. The friction built to a desperate frenzy, and Amanda clasped her fingers together in earnest supplication. She prayed for the exquisite agony to end.

Julius filled her in a steady pace, keeping her pleasure on his schedule. She coiled tighter, and tighter, until she had nowhere left to go but over.

Arching her neck, she moaned as the pulses of bliss crashed through her body. A sharp nip on her calf brought her back from her stupor.

Julius kissed the reddened bite mark. Staring down at her, his eyes glittered with the hunger of a wolf presented with a fawn. He pulled out of her body, his shaft still hard. "The rope work on your body is one of my favorite patterns. Do you know why?"

Amanda's breath hadn't returned, so she shook her head.

He pressed her knees towards her face, and the ropes around her legs stretched and tightened as her calves met the back of her thighs. "Because it gives me the option for another position."

And before she could even wonder, he rolled her over until she knelt on the bed, her hands pressed tight against her breasts, her forehead resting on the pillow.

"What ....?" She tried to look over her shoulder, but fell off-balance and planted onto her cheek.

"Careful." Julius skimmed his palm over her bottom and found her wet opening. He eased two fingers in and out. "Before we go any further, I want you to tell me if anything is hurting."

"Hurting?" She needed more than his fingers. She didn't know she could want so soon after her crisis, but she did. "Nothing hurts. Now Julius, please."

He chuckled and removed his fingers. "I think we'd better do this without distractions. You can still wiggle your toes?"

She checked and nodded.

"Good. And nothing is pinching at your shoulders?" His fingers slid under the edges of the harness at her back. He tugged gently at different sections, each pull causing the silk to rub against her flesh. It was like hundreds of fingers were caressing her skin at once. She moaned.

"The ropes are fine." She wriggled her backside. "You know where your attention is needed. Stop making sport."

"The mouse might be getting a little too demanding," he said, but there was a note of approval in his voice. "But if you insist, I'll stop making sport, as you say."

The bed shifted, and she sensed him moving behind her. Something cool and smooth prodded at her entrance. Julius pressed, and the object glided smoothly in.

"What is that?" she asked.

"You held it earlier." Julius twisted it and slowly plunged it in and out of her body. "What you thought was a doll. The small one. How does it feel?"

"Too small." She frowned at Julius's chuckle. "And a little cold."

"It will heat up in no time."

The scrape of glass on glass met her ears. Something drizzled on the flat of her lower back before running down between the cheeks of her bottom. The oil.

Julius followed the path of the liquid, his fingers brushing past her tight ring of muscles. Amanda froze.

"Relax." The piece of jade in her channel eased in and out as Julius rimmed her other opening with his thumb. "Has any man ever taken you here?"

She shook her head, her forehead rubbing against the coverlet. Did men take women there? She'd never even thought it a possibility. Why would anyone want to? "Are..." She licked her bottom lip. "Are you going to?"

"Eventually." He drizzled more oil above the crease of her bottom. And this time, after circling her rim, he eased a finger inside.

Every muscle in Amanda's body tensed. The sensation was too foreign, and her mind scattered.

"I promise you will enjoy it. Maybe not at first. Your body needs to become accustomed to it. But it can be very pleasurable for both men and women." Leaving the jade buried in her sheath, he circled her clit with one finger and worked her bottom with the other. "Will you trust me to make this good for you?"

Her body shuddered. "You don't fight fair."

"No, I don't." He added another finger into her back channel and increased the pressure on her clit. She wanted to jump out of her skin. How could her body feel so good and so uncomfortable at the same time? "Well," he said, "do I have your permission?"

"Yes," she said, the word a moan.

"Good girl." His hands left her body, and she whimpered in frustration. When he removed the jade, she felt so empty she wanted to scream.

His finger found its way between her thighs again to circle her clitoris. At the same time, she felt the smooth head of the object press at her rosette.

"Easy now," Julius said. "Just relax."

She tried. She really did. But her body was coiling in anticipation of its coming release. Her flesh burned as Julius pushed the column past the ring of muscles. It hurt, not too badly, and not enough to ask him to stop. She bit the coverlet pressed to her face and clasped her fingers tightly together.

The forward pressure stopped, and Amanda was left with a feeling of fullness, a strangeness to which her body didn't quite know how to adapt.

Julius groaned and ran his hands, slick with oil, over the cheeks of her bottom. He tapped the end of the column, and sensation shot through her.

"Your arse filled with my jade. Your body bound with my rope." He took a deep, shuddering breath. "Absolute perfection."

In one smooth glide, Julius filled her sex. They moaned in unison.

He dug his fingers into her hips and took off like a racehorse. He pounded into her, and Amanda knew he wouldn't be pulling out of her body this time until he'd found his release. She was tied up like a package wrapped in string, and Amanda welcomed the idea that she was his present. His to use. His to enjoy.

Each time he bottomed out he nudged the end of the jade, and it felt like every opening was being taken. Blood pounded at her temples, and her head spun. It was too much sensation, too many nerve endings firing at once. Her brain couldn't process if it was pleasure or pain. But cutting through the muddle was a deep, clawing need. She pressed her thighs together, desperate to relieve the pressure.

Julius grabbed the rope at her back, jerked her body into his hips. The ropes across her breasts tightened. Her skin chafed. Her lungs squeezed. Amanda opened her mouth to scream but no sound emerged.

Julius grunted. The sound of their flesh slapping together filled her ears. He thrust faster, harder, and she broke.

Waves of pleasure came crashing down. Her muscles pulsed around Julius's cock, around the hard jade, and Julius's tempo faltered.

He plunged once, twice, and with a groan held himself deep within.

Amanda wanted to scream, to whimper. She wanted to pound her palms into the bed or claw Julius's back. Her mind was overwhelmed with the glut of emotions, and her body flooded with contradictory sensations. Too breathless to make a sound, unable to move, she did the only action left available. She cried.

Julius slid from her body and eased her to her side. The bed dipped as he crawled off. He returned moments later and untied the knots that held her. The rope at her hands fell away first, and Julius chaffed each palm, rubbed each arm. The harness around her back and chest slipped off, and Amanda sucked in her first deep breath since the silk had touched her skin.

Rolling Amanda to her stomach, Julius drizzled more oil across her back and kneaded her muscles, his fingers smoothing away any lingering soreness.

"Are you all right?" he asked.

She nodded. She turned her face to the side, her cheek resting on the soft pillow.

"It can be quite affecting, being bound." He brushed his thumb under her eye. "But sometimes tears can be a good thing."

She nodded again, feeling as insubstantial as a cloud. Like she could float away. Every inch of her was numb, every inch except the strips of skin the rope had crossed. Those tingled, as though the bonds yet remained. They were invisible marks, ones she hoped wouldn't disappear anytime soon. She drifted, content to merely exist in the moment.

Julius caressed the entire length of her body, every toe receiving the same amount of attention as he'd given her shoulders. She barely noticed when he eased the jade from her body.

Lifting her hand, he pressed his thumbs into her palm, and a moan slipped past her lips.

Julius chuckled. "You like that?"

In response, Amanda threaded her fingers through his, and tugged him down. He settled by her side, his heat seeping into her skin, his breath whispering across her brow.

She rubbed his knuckle with her thumb. She'd never been more connected to another human being. Wrapped up in Julius's arms, in his rope, she'd never felt safer.

But feeling safe was dangerous. That was usually the moment before disaster struck. She needed to keep up her guard.

She yawned. Her heartbeat slowed, like it was pumping

syrup through her veins, making her sluggish and satisfied. Keeping up her guard required energy, and that was difficult to come by at the moment.

Julius wrapped his other arm around her waist and drew her tight to his side, his hand resting on her hip. Amanda buried her nose at his neck and inhaled his scent, as comforting as her favorite cup of tea. She wouldn't worry about any danger now, would allow herself to enjoy the moment. Her eyelids drooped low. Just this once, she'd let herself revel in the feeling of a man caring for her, not just caring what he could take from her.

She knew thinking that Julius cared for her was foolish. Just because they'd lain together didn't mean he had any depth of feeling for her. Men took their pleasure from women and affection had nothing to do with it. If he was a good man, he only took pleasure from willing women and did his best to give pleasure in return.

Which was why, when she woke up alone hours later, it was a good reminder that just because Julius made her feel warm and safe, he wouldn't want to waste his time holding her. His heart, after all, had not been engaged.

Chapter Nine

The afternoon's light was waning, creating grotesque shadows on the walls of Clink Prison. The cell was spacious, as far as they went, with a small bedchamber and a larger living area, but it was still a cell. Even though the door wasn't barred, sweat beaded on Julius's brow.

The past few days had been filled with highs and lows. Standing once more in a prison definitely qualified as a low. As did every time he'd questioned a witness to Audley's murder. Each individual that he'd been able to track down either didn't recognize the man in the patched cloak, or, as in most cases, hadn't even seen him. The lack of progress in his investigation made his fingers itch to pound something. Then he would return home, and there would be Amanda. Sweet Amanda.

The moments with Amanda had been some of the best of his life. Exploring each other's bodies. Luring her into the garden and tasting her lips, warmed from the sun. Learning which rope she favored and which rope she never wanted to cross her body again. He smiled. His jute now lay buried at the bottom of his chest, ne'er to see the light of day until ... well, until Marcus returned and Julius left his house.

Julius held his hands behind his back, the fingers of his right hand digging into his left wrist. He wouldn't lie to his friend about his affair, and he had no doubt there would be a reckoning between the two because of it. He could only hope Marcus would be satisfied with bloodying his nose and not put an end to their friendship. For while he and

Amanda lived under the same roof, Julius knew their intrigue would continue.

Julius loosened the knot of his cravat and fought the urge to check his pocket watch. Again. Amanda would love this debtor's prison. A snug cell she could hide in, with enough creature comforts to live agreeably. Not for the first time he wondered how the horror of captivity could affect two people in such drastically different manners. Him, needing to be free at all costs. Her, relishing being under his control.

He stared out the small square of a window into the prison's central yard, lost in thought. A few of the tenants wandered the grounds. A guard at the front gate kept a watchful eye.

Martin Dawnley shuffled out of his bed chamber, smoothing his hands down a hastily donned waistcoat. "My lord, had I known you were visiting I would have arranged for some tea." The man looked around the cell, blinking rapidly, his cheeks ruddy with shame.

Rousing himself, Julius grabbed two spindly chairs and grouped them together. He dropped into his seat and indicated the other chair. Dawnley lowered down, rubbing his knee.

Julius didn't waste time on pleasantries. "I've come on the recommendation of Lord Audley. You know him?"

Dawnley rubbed his hand across the top of his head, causing his sparse strands of grey hair to stick up straight. "Yes, my lord. But I'd heard the sad news that he'd passed."

Julius arched an eyebrow.

"Even in here we do receive news." Dawnley shrugged. "Especially when that news concerns the son of a duke."

"Of course." Had the news spread that Julius had been with the young lord moments before his death? Had the blackmailers heard of it? If the man who'd pushed Audley was a part of the crime ring, then they already knew of Julius's involvement. His advantage was gone. "He told me that you used to work in the Court of Chancery."

Dawnley nodded. "I was the head clerk."

"And you came in contact with certain individuals who blackmailed you for blunt?"

Licking his lips, the man's eyes darted to every corner of the room.

Julius sought to reassure him. "I, also, have been contacted by the same people."

"Then you know we aren't to discuss it." A bit of haughtiness entered Dawnley's voice, and for the first time Julius could see the civil servant he used to be.

Julius smiled. "I've never been much good at doing what I'm told. And besides"—he spread his hands wide, indicating their surroundings—"what else can they do to you?"

"I have family." Dawnley leaned forward. "These people would have no compunction about hurting any of them to make a point."

"Yes, an unmarried son and a widowed daughter." Julius was nothing if not efficient at obtaining information. "Wouldn't they be better served if their father was out of Clink Prison and earning a decent wage?"

"You mock me."

Julius put out a hand to stop him from rising. "I'm doing nothing of the sort. I have the means to pay off your debt. To assist you in finding employment. But I'll need your help to remove the threat hanging above us like Damocles sword."

Dawnley eased back. "There's nothing to be done. It isn't just one or two individuals you'd be fighting." Resting an elbow on the arm of his chair, he dropped his high forehead into his palm. "There are many people involved. Too many to stop."

"How do you know?" Julius asked. Audley had only seen the one man. Would the clerk have better descriptions?

Dawnley sighed, his shoulders slumping. "There came a

time when I could no longer pay. That's when they approached me for information. They wanted details on the cases passing through the court. And the demand came from an unexpected source."

"Yes?" Julius prodded.

The old man hesitated and dropped his gaze. "There was a woman, one I'd become ..."

"Intimate with?" Julius finished. He didn't understand the man's delicacy. He was a widower. But the lower classes were strange when it came to sexual morality.

"Yes. A widow." Rubbing the back of his neck, Dawnley grimaced. "I'd told her some of my problems. I thought she cared for me." He shook his head. "I was a fool. She was one of them. Had been keeping watch on me for the people she worked for. And she told me they were many."

"And the name of this woman?" The lead ball in his gut told Julius he suspected the culprit, but he wanted confirmation.

"Mrs. Westmont. A very sweet woman." He blushed. "Well, until she wasn't."

Julius rubbed his eyebrow. "So, after you discovered an intimate was among the blackmailers, you gave in to their demands?"

"I refused once." Tugging at his threadbare waistcoat, Dawnley sat up straight. "I told them no more secrets. Mrs. Westmont paid me a visit after that. She took me somewhere, to some sort of private club. I was introduced to a man who handed me a report on every step of my children's days. From when my son left his home, to when he arrived at work, to what he ate that day for lunch. I was told how many pounds of mutton my daughter had purchased. He knew everything. And he pointed out how easy it would be to make one of them disappear. Or one of my daughter's babies." He swallowed, his Adam's apple bobbing. "That is when I gave up any ideas of fighting."

Julius edged forward and rested his forearms on his knees. "This man, what did he look like?"

"Tall and much too skinny. Looked a bit like a scarecrow to tell the truth. With a thin mustache. And before I left that night, I saw him speak to another woman, one with bright red hair. She was wearing a most indecent dress, but then"—he spread his hands—"the club was most indecent itself."

Julius's stomach slowly sank to the floor. "Where was this club?"

"Nowhere you'd want to go. Off Edward Street, I believe."

Of course. It would be the one club Julius had made a second home. He stared at the square of sunlight, breathing heavily through his nose. Dawnley was right. The Black Rose was most indecent. Wonderfully indecent, along with the red-headed Madame Sable who ran the establishment. And now she was implicated in a blackmailing ring.

"And Mrs. Westmont? While you were having this conversation where the man threatened your family, where was she during all of this?"

"I think ..." Dawnley ran a hand through his hair and looked to the corner of the room. "I believe she was in another room. With another man."

Julius stared at the cell's window. It made sense that the madam of a clandestine club would be involved in blackmail. Everything that happened within her walls was of a most private nature. The members trusted that their darkest desires would remain secret. And they paid through the nose to ensure it. The betrayal lanced Julius, and he gritted his teeth.

Julius's need to tie women up wouldn't be enough to ruin his reputation. As desires went, that was tame for The Black Rose. Other members of the ton might snigger behind his back, but no lasting damage would be done. Even if he were shunned, he hardly cared. Julius could live quite happily without the company of society.

But that couldn't be said for all the members. Reputations could be destroyed; lives devastated. Some of his friends might not escape unscathed. He needed to tell them what he'd learned so they could try to control the damage.

But first, he would have a word with the lovely Madame Sable.

Julius thanked Dawnley and fled the prison. He didn't know what the clerk had done to fall prey to blackmail and Julius didn't want to know. He seemed a decent enough man. One who had tried to do the right thing. The tentacles of the shadowy organization were slithering into too many lives. Good lives.

Liverpool was right. They needed to be stopped. By any means necessary.

* * *

Amanda rubbed Reggie's tummy, the repetitive motion soothing her as much as the dog. He flopped his head in her lap and sighed.

"Still not feeling back to your usual self?" She gently tugged at the sheet of paper stuck between her thigh and Reggie's paw. She carefully folded the missive and tucked the square up her sleeve. "I don't feel so well, either."

"Are you ill, dear?" Lady Mary toddled into the room, Carter trailing in her wake, a large basket in his hands. "Did you catch what Reginald has?"

Amanda wrinkled her brow. "I don't know if that's possible." Carter brushed past her and set the basket down by an armchair. Amanda tucked her legs back, digging her fingers into Reggie's thick coat. The butler didn't look at her, didn't say anything untoward, hardly acknowledged her presence at all.

"Do you need anything else, m'lady?" he asked.

"Not at present," her chaperone said.

Without a glance to Amanda, Carter bowed to Lady Mary, and exited the morning room.

The older woman settled into her chair and pulled a square of needlepoint from the basket. "What ails you?

The doctor said your dog will be all right."

"Reggie is my sister's dog." As Amanda had reminded the woman many times before. "And he is feeling much better. Only a little tired."

Lady Mary stabbed a needle through her cloth. "Well, if your pup is doing better, then why are you blue?"

"Nothing of great importance." Fingering the paper tucked in her sleeve, Amanda forced a smile. "I received an answer to a letter I wrote. It wasn't to my liking."

"I often receive letters not to my liking." Lady Mary winced and sucked at the tip of her thumb. "The trick is to ignore what you don't wish to hear until you get the answer you want."

Amanda's hand stilled on Reggie's stomach until he whined in protest. She continued stroking him. "How does ignoring a marquess's dismissal become an acceptance later?"

"Time is as transitive as the human heart." Tugging on a purple thread, the woman grimaced until the string pulled through her square of fabric. "And acceptance and dismissals will both exist only until you decide to choose one."

Amanda bit the inside of her cheek. She ran the words through her head again, but understanding remained elusive. She sighed. For a moment, she'd forgotten that Lady Mary was the one person in the house more cracked than Amanda. She was very sweet, but not someone to look to for advice.

"Who were you writing to, dear?" Licking her thumb and forefinger, Lady Mary rolled her fingers over the end of a green thread. She squinted one eye behind her spectacles and prodded the thread at the eye of her needle. "Maybe I know him and can put in a good word for you."

"This letter is from the Marquess of Hanford."

The bell for dinner sounded, and Reggie's head perked up. He slid down from the settee, a little slower than usual. But if he was in the mood for table scraps, he must be better.

Amanda stood and waited for Lady Mary to rise. "I wrote five letters to the most prominent critics of reforming the law on capital punishment. Only the Marquess was considerate enough to send me a reply."

The women trailed after Reggie to the east dining room. A footman held a chair out for Lady Mary, turned his back on Amanda, and went to his position by the door. Amanda pulled out her own chair.

"Did you explain how unfair the conditions were in prison?" The older woman glanced at the needle still in her hand and blinked. She tucked it into her fichu, the tail of green thread stark against the white linen. "I'm sure if they knew that innocent people were being sent to the noose, and children, they'd change the law very quickly."

Amanda almost envied the woman. She was sweet and simple and assumed everything else in the world would follow the same course. How pleasant it must be to live in that fantasy.

"The Marquess seems to feel that if England lets one guilty man go unpunished, the whole of society will crumble." Amanda watched the footman pour Lady Mary some wine and raised her own glass hopefully. He filled her cup, and Amanda's shoulders relaxed. The servants' rudeness hadn't extended to outright refusal of service, at least not yet. Not where it would be noticed by the duke's aunt or friend. She took a sip, and let the rich plummy flavor soothe some of her irritation over the letter. "Better that a few unfortunates suffer than all of society, he thinks."

The two women sat back, and a second footman placed plates before them, steam still rising from the food.

Lady Mary dug into the beef medallion. "What nonsense. I don't know the Marquess, otherwise I'd give him a right talking to."

Smiling, Amanda fed Reggie a bit of beef. "I would enjoy seeing that." Taking the roll from her plate, she tucked it into the pocket sewn into the skirt of her gown.

"What would you enjoy seeing?" Julius strode into the room and dragged his chair out before the footman could do so. He sank heavily into his seat and draped the white linen napkin across his lap. The fine lines that radiated from his eyes seemed to have sunk deeper into his skin. "I will take you anywhere you wish."

Warmth coursed through Amanda's body at the sight of him. An errant strand of hair crossed in front of his eyes, and her fingers itched to brush it back across his brow. It was rare that he would join her and Lady Mary for dinner, but perhaps he was coming to crave her company as much as she was his. Though lord knows they'd seen quite a lot of each other since their affair began. Day or night, Julius would find any excuse to strip her bare and tie her up. To Amanda's mind, they had done everything together that a man and a woman could. Except for one thing.

She stared down at her plate. They'd never woken up together. Amanda always left his bed alone. Julius would find her soon thereafter to bring her a cup of chocolate and help her dress, but somehow it just wasn't the same.

Lady Mary bounced in her seat and leaned forward, her sleeve knocking a roll to the floor. Reggie ambled away from Amanda, towards greener pastures. "She wants to speak with the Marquess of Hanford. Perhaps you could take her to Parliament so she could have a word with him?"

Julius's eyebrows shot up over the rim of his wine glass. He leaned forwards. "Is that so? And what has the Marquess done to deserve such attention?"

Amanda adjusted the second fork next to her plate, making it even with its brethren. "Lady Mary is mistaken. I have no need to speak with the man. His response to my letter was quite sufficient to lay out his point of view on the issue."

"And, pray tell, what issue was that?" Julius laced his fingers together, his two index fingers extended into a vee, and examined her. It was the type of examination that made Amanda squirm. Julius had done unspeakable things to her just last night, seen her in positions that should make her cheeks flame red with embarrassment, but it was his scrutiny now that made her uncomfortable.

She looked at the row of knives to the right of her plate, but those were all perfectly in line. Picking up a fork, she pushed her peas around. "I wrote to ask him to reconsider his position on that reform bill. He declined. Very politely." The peas formed eight neat rows, with one green ball to spare. She popped the misfit in her mouth, and considered. The Marquess's letter was more condescending than polite. But to a man of that stature, even responding to a disgraced woman was an act of great civility. She should be thankful.

"I see." His eyes glittered darkly. She couldn't read them. He dropped his gaze to her plate with its organized rows of vegetables. "Your beef is growing cold. Eat up."

"Can't you take her to Parliament?" Lady Mary persisted. "He'd have to listen if she explained things to him, face to face."

"I couldn't guarantee her reception, but as I said, I would take her anywhere she desired." Julius sliced into his meat, and Amanda felt a corresponding cut to her heart. He knew as well as she that a trip to Parliament was nowhere in her future. Her jaunts into the garden were one thing. But that was a whole other kettle of fish from venturing into London. Just the thought of the immense buildings, the crowds of people, made her heart pound.

A trickle of sweat started at the nape of her neck and rolled under her collar. She pushed to her feet. Julius hastily stood, as well. "I'm not hungry this evening. I'll bid you all goodnight." The footman opened the door for her. "Come, Reggie." She fled up the stairs, Reggie's toenails slowly clicking behind her. He didn't want to leave the table, but it was for his own good that she stopped him from eating too much. He didn't need another stomach ache.

Shutting her door, she lifted her hand towards the key that rested in the keyhole. No. She stepped back. She wouldn't let one disappointing letter and the thought of being lost inside Parliament make her slip into old habits. She'd already spent too much time in closets and behind locked doors. Being in her own room, the door closed, was enough.

But it wasn't enough to keep out visitors.

Julius stepped into the room without knocking. He carried her dinner plate and a glass of wine. "You ate but two bites. You cannot be full already." Placing the plate on the bed, he shooed Reggie away from the food. He patted the coverlet next to the plate. "Sit."

Reggie's haunches hit the floor, and Julius frowned at him.

"Thank you for your concern, but I truly do not want it." The rich sauces from the duke's cook didn't usually sit well with her.

"I hardly ever see you eat." Placing his hands on his lean hips, Julius narrowed his eyes. "You need food."

"Do I look as though I'm starving?" Stalking to the window, she released the sash. The velvet curtain brushed past her fingertips as it fell closed. "Credit me with some sense. I do understand the importance of food for survival."

"But ..."

She pulled the roll from her pocket and raised it to eye level. "I may not eat in front of you, but I eat." Walking to the escritoire, she lowered the desk lid and added the roll to a bit of cheese wrapped in cloth. She shut the escritoire firmly and turned to face him, arms across her chest.

His face softened. "You stash food away. I should have guessed."

"It isn't anything to concern yourself over. I just like to make sure ..." She swallowed.

"That you don't have to rely on your gaoler to feed you." Julius stepped close and placed his hands on her shoulders. "I know. I did it, too. When I was held by daimyo Muragachi."

That was the first time he'd mentioned his imprisonment to her. She'd heard the rumors, of course.

Even before her world had collapsed, before she'd killed her father in self-defense, she'd heard the stories of the Earl of Rothchild's youngest son. The man who'd been captured while serving his country in the Royal Navy. Of the attempts to secure his release. Of his escape after three long years of imprisonment only for him to come home to find his father and brothers dead of typhus.

An accidental earl, and one that society whispered wasn't right in his head since his capture.

Society was full of idiots. She'd always known that.

"What did he do to you?" She was frightened to hear the answer. Didn't want those images in her head. But, like her, his imprisonment was a part of his being, and she wanted to know all of him.

Julius turned his head. "It's not something a woman should hear."

"Tell me anyway."

His Adam's apple bobbed up and down, and he shook his head.

Amanda pinched her lips together. "Then tell me who daimyo Muragachi was," she said, her tongue tripping over the unfamiliar words. "Why did he hold you?"

Julius closed his eyes, and Amanda didn't think he would respond. Turning away, he pressed his palms flat on the bureau, his head sagging. "Muragachi was a local warlord. The magistrate of Nagasaki sent me to him to serve my sentence after I was captured from the *HMS Phaeton*. We'd sailed into Nagasaki harbor in order to ambush Dutch trading ships that were soon to arrive." His fingers whitened as he dug his nails into the wood. "We had the superior force. The Japanese cannons in the harbor were old, most of them inoperable. Under a Dutch flag, we sailed into the harbor and waited like a spider for its fly as a tender with Dutch and Japanese representatives rowed out to welcome us. We captured the Dutchmen, but in the fight the Japanese jumped into the water and swam back to shore. I was knocked overboard, as well, and nearly senseless. I was taken, the only Englishman captured."

"But if you had superior force, why were you not rescued?" How could he have been left behind? Wasn't the British navy supposed to look out for their own? Her heart burned.

Julius snorted. "Superiority can be fleeting. The magistrate had sent for reinforcements. Eight thousand samurai and forty more ships. Captain Pellew knew he couldn't be in the harbor when they arrived. He couldn't risk the lives of two hundred and eighty men just for mine." He was quiet a moment. "The Dutch trading ships didn't even come that year. It was all for nothing."

Amanda tapped her fist against her lips. She leaned against the desk for support. If he could remain stoic in the telling, she could for the hearing. With an effort. "And your imprisonment? You were there for three years, were you not?"

Pushing off the bureau, Julius turned and paced to the fireplace. "My imprisonment was ... instructive. The samurai have turned ropework into an art form. I learned much by feeling the rope on me, and watching them tie it. Later, as I became more respected, they taught me their techniques." He cocked a hip against an armchair. He smiled but it was twisted and bitter. "You have my gaolers to thank for our intimate pleasures."

Amanda swallowed, tasting bile at the back of her throat. "How can you even look at a rope, much less use one?"

He stalked towards her. "How can you sleep in a wardrobe? How can you tolerate the ropes clinging to your body? If you can tell me that, I'll try to come up with an answer for you."

Holding her hands to her chest, she shook her head. She couldn't explain any of it. She let out a shuddering breath. "If you ever want to talk about—"

"I won't." A muscle twitched in his jaw but otherwise his face was expressionless. She felt the wall he'd erected as though she'd run headlong into it. That didn't mean she had to accept it.

She cupped his cheek, his skin warm and scratchy beneath her palm. "I'm sorry. You must think me so weak when you had to endure much worse."

He stepped back, and her hand fell to her side. "It isn't a competition, who had it worse," he said gruffly.

Amanda nodded, her chest aching. Her heart thudded dully behind her breastbone, and she watched in resignation as he took another step away. As if her presence was a burden.

She was becoming confused again. Mixing up what she felt in his bed with what she felt for the man. Julius didn't owe her his confidences. And he didn't owe her tenderness. He was doing her a favor, teaching her of what was possible between a man and a woman physically, and nothing more.

Rubbing the back of his neck, he turned. "What—" He threw his shoulders back. "Reggie!"

The dog gave one last lick to the now clean plate and jumped off the bed. He kept to the walls as he trotted to the bedroom door and escaped.

Julius slammed the door shut behind him. "I can't believe that animal belongs to Marcus. My friend breathes order and discipline. I would think his dogs would be better trained."

"Reggie is my sister's dog." Amanda wrapped her arms around her sides. "Liz doesn't mind a bit of spirit."

"Yes, I noticed that about your sister." He paced across the room. "But that doesn't—" He froze. "What are you doing?"

Tugging at the shoulder of her dress, she tried to pull the buttons running down the back into reach. "I'm undressing. You are in my room and have closed the door." She might not have his confidences or his love, but she had his body and she was determined to make the most of it. She twisted her arm behind her, her fingers brushing the fabric-covered buttons but not quite able to push them through their holes. Why had she let Julius dress her in such an impractical garment? All dresses should be made with buttons running down the front. It only made sense.

"And is that what you want?" He circled behind her.

Amanda dropped her arms and rolled her shoulders, trying to ease the ache. "Honestly, I am indifferent at the moment. But the world seems clearer when we are in bed together and I am less confused. Everything there is straightforward." Striving to fulfill a physical need was simple, unlike satisfying her emotional state.

"Indifference is a poor argument for bedding someone." He squeezed her shoulders and turned her to face him. "And that isn't why I came to your room tonight. I have a request to make of you."

"And it's not a request for something special in ..." She nodded her head at the bed.

"It is not." Julius tugged at the knot of his cravat. "I want you to accompany me to a club tonight. I need to ask someone questions, and it will look better if I bring a guest with me." He rubbed his earlobe. "As I won't be engaging in my usual activity at this club, you will serve as a distraction of sorts."

"You think it will look less like you're a spy if you have a woman on your arm." Sound reasoning, but they both knew he'd have to find a different woman. A woman who wouldn't shake with terror from stepping out of doors. One who would stand by his side, laugh at his jokes, purr like a cat in heat under his attentions.

Amanda had a feeling she wouldn't like this woman.

His jaw dropped open. "How did you ... why would you...?"

She took pity. "My sister. She knows that her husband and his friends work for the Crown. Did you really think she wouldn't tell me?"

He locked his hands behind his head and stared at the ceiling. "I hope you will be more discreet."

Amanda stepped forward and poked his chest. "Liz isn't running around telling everyone your business. Only me."

National security was important, but sisters didn't keep secrets. Especially her and Liz. They'd agreed they would never keep anything from the other again. Not after Liz had discovered that their father had been abusing Amanda, and Amanda had never told. "And even if I were so inclined to gossip, which I'm not, who would I tell? I have no friends or associates."

Julius looked at her with sad eyes and stroked her hair. She leaned into his touch, her flash of anger burning itself out. With a hand at her lower back, he led her to the bed and prodded her shoulders until she sat. He settled next to her, resting his bent knee on the mattress so he could face her.

"I trust you to keep my secret." He tucked a lock of hair behind her ear. "Will you help me tonight?"

She pulled his hand away from her face and clasped it between her own. "You know I can't."

"You won't. There's a difference."

"Not to me," she whispered. Her chest burned with shame. Her fear had never truly affected her before. She was content to live hidden away. Even her sister's admonitions to leave the house didn't sway her. But Julius had asked for her help, and she couldn't give it.

For the first time, she wished she were brave.

With a finger under her chin, Julius tilted her face up to look at him. "You cannot spend the rest of your life within doors. You need to try to break out of your prison. And you've started. You hardly pause when you leave the house to go into the gardens now. Tonight will be a perfect opportunity to test yourself further. And I don't think it will be as difficult as you imagine."

"Why?" Her mind raced, searching for his angle. "Because my duty to my country will overcome my fears?"

He laughed, throwing his head back and exposing the thick column of his neck. Tapping her nose, Julius shook his head. "No, mouse. After what your country almost did to you, I don't think you owe us anything." Leaning close, he planted his hands on the bed by her hips, caging her in. "I think tonight you will find the courage because it won't really be you leaving the house. It will be a different woman. An intrepid woman. A woman in disguise."

Chapter Ten

A disguise was one word for her outfit. A straight-jacket was another. Yet Amanda couldn't deny that the French corset, binding her all the way from her hips to her breasts, made her feel secure. She might not be able to draw breath, but she was locked up tight, just as she liked. Breathing was overrated anyhow.

Reaching under the hood of her cloak, she fingered the mask Julius had given her to wear. It was crimson, to match the corset, with feathers extending from the edges. It was beautiful, but what earned Amanda's admiration was the fact that it covered half her face, making her anonymous. Her heart had barely raced above a flutter when she'd exited the townhouse, concealed as she was. And even though Julius had opened the windows of the carriage, the darkness outside could almost make her believe she was still safely ensconced in her room, not racing through London to a club Julius belonged to.

A Venus club.

Amanda had thought that nothing could shock her senses any longer. She'd been wrong. Julius had spent the first part of their journey describing The Black Rose as though it was nothing more out of the ordinary than a stroll around the Pump Room.

She'd never known that men's appetites could be so ... varied. And the women's, too, as Julius was quick to point out. Amanda shifted in her seat. For once she'd have news to write to Liz. Her sister's letters from Italy were full of new discoveries, descriptions of art and architecture, admirations over the food. Amanda could only respond that she and Reggie fared well. Her letters were all of three sentences long. Now she would get to tell her sister about a new experience.

The carriage rolled to a stop, and Julius pushed open the door and hopped down. Amanda could hear the footman huff, and she smothered a smile. The duke's household were an unfortunate lot. With their master and mistress gone, they served a woman they didn't want to, and weren't allowed to serve the lord they did.

Julius stretched out a hand, and she grabbed it, holding on tightly. She could do this. Two steps down to exit the carriage. Her feet froze when she saw the cobblestone of the street below. Could she do this? Perhaps it would be better—

Julius yanked on her hand, and she tumbled down the steps, landing heavily against his chest.

His arm banded around her waist. He tugged her hood further down her forehead and leaned close. "No one can recognize you," he whispered. "You can stay wrapped up in your cloak all night, if you wish. Although it would be a shame not to show off how lovely you look in that corset. And"—he traced the ridge of her mask over her nose—"I'll be by your side all night. You are perfectly safe."

Amanda nodded. She hoped he was right. Her palms were damp inside her gloves, and she didn't think her struggle to breathe was entirely due to the tightly-laced bodice. But she had to take the chance.

She held onto his hand like she was drowning and let him lead her past a footman at the door to The Black Rose.

The bright lights of the gas lamps on the walls made her blink. She'd expected dimly lit rooms, with shifty-eyed patrons. Not the tasteful soiree they'd stepped into. The artwork along the walls was elegant, and the plush, embroidered settees scattered about the room fashionable. The walls were covered with hand-painted paper in designs of gold, and candles winked through crystal prisms in the chandeliers hanging from the ceiling.

Two men sitting in the corner glanced up at their entrance. Apparently finding nothing unusual in her cloak and mask, they returned to their conversation. A woman carrying a tray of drinks circulated the room, trading full glasses for empties.

"This isn't what I expected from a ..."

"Venus club?" Julius provided helpfully. "What did you expect?"

"Well ..."

"Women dancing naked? A seething den of iniquity?"

Amanda flapped the hem of her cloak, the crackling fires on both sides of the room making her sweat. "Well, yes. I expected people to be *doing* more than drinking and talking."

Julius placed his palm on her lower back and guided her slowly around the room. "This is the main room. It's like a normal club, where members meet and talk. Sometimes gamble. The amusements begin when you go down that hallway." He pointed to their right, to a corridor papered in muted red-and-gold stripes.

Amanda craned her neck but could see nothing but a row of doors before the hallway ended at a T-junction.

"I'll show you whichever room you'd like." Julius's breath was hot against her neck. He traced the rim of her ear with his finger, and a shiver skittered down her spine. "Just as soon as I speak to someone."

Amanda inhaled slowly through her nose and exhaled through her mouth. If she focused on such minute matters the swirl of people about her wasn't nearly so intimidating. Or so she told herself. "The tall, spindly man you told me about in the carriage? The one who threatened the clerk's family at this club?" Julius had relayed his conversation with Mr. Dawnley, although she suspected he'd kept some key bits of information back. But for a man trained in secrecy, the fact that he told her anything warmed her heart.

"No, it would be too convenient to find that man here

tonight." Julius scanned the room, the flecks of green in his eyes catching the light and making them seem more hazel than brown. He might not think the man was here, but Julius looked like a hunter searching for prey just the same. "It's the proprietress I've come to speak with."

Ah, yes, the beautiful woman with flaming-red hair. Amanda remembered that description, too. She tugged her gloves off, tucking them into her cloak's pocket, and enjoyed the air swirling around her palms.

Julius had a few low words with a man in a service uniform. He nodded, and the man disappeared into a small door in the side of the room. A woman in a diaphanous gown strolled past, carrying her tray of drinks. Julius plucked off two and pressed one into Amanda's hand. "Madame Sable has yet to come down from her rooms. We will wait."

Amanda shifted, placing Julius's body between her and the fireplace. She flapped the hem of her cloak open. "How long must we wait?"

"As long as it takes." Julius stared at the door the servant had gone through, the one that presumably led to Madame Sable's quarters. He had the uncanny ability to hold himself absolutely motionless. He would stand, rooted in place, for as long as it took. It was a stillness she recognized.

But not one she wished to emulate tonight. "Can we find a cooler place in which to wait? Between the corset, cloak, and my hair hanging free, I am hotter than one of Hades' handmaidens."

His lips twitched. "There is a remedy for that." He flicked one side of her cloak back. A cool draught of air swirled across her bare shoulder, and she almost moaned in relief. But the feeling of being open, exposed, caused her skin to itch, and she shrugged the cloak back into place.

She kept her gaze on his chest, not wanting to see the disappointment in his eyes. "The gown you gave me to wear under the corset has no sleeves." Better to let him think she objected on decency grounds.

He stepped close, his chest brushing against hers. "You've left the security of your home. Taken a risk to come here," he murmured. "I am very proud of you."

She drew a triangle in the carpet with the toe of her slipper. Of course, he would see through her deceit. "You must be ashamed of my weakness but are too kind to admit it."

He encircled her waist with his hands and squeezed even tighter than the corset. "You are stronger than you think." He sighed. "And you are also burning up. Perhaps we can find a less heated room to wait in."

Taking her hand, he led her down the red-and-gold hallway, silently opening doors and peering inside rooms, before finding the one he wanted. He pressed his finger to her lips in warning and drew her into a room lit only by a few candles surrounding a low bench. Something shifted, stretched out on the bench, and the figure of a woman lying on her stomach emerged into view.

A naked woman.

Now that was something she could write about to Liz. Julius closed the door and leaned against the wall, drawing her back to rest against his front. As her eyes adjusted to the dark, Amanda made out a few other figures standing around the edges of the room, watching the bench. But much less people than in the main room. Amanda's shoulders began to unclench.

A shadow separated from the darkness and circled the naked woman. The man wore trousers, but no shirt. Squatting by the bench, he lifted a candle from the ground. The light flickered across a broad expanse of bare chest. He moved his hand from the top of the woman's head, along the curve of her back and bottom, and down her long legs, the candle sending flickers of light to illuminate each bronzed inch of her flesh.

Amanda held her breath. She didn't see any rope to bind the woman. No implements to use upon her. As far as peculiar desires went, this seemed rather tame. But the room itself seemed to hold its breath with Amanda, waiting.

It happened quickly. A tip of the candle, a splash of wax. The woman stiffened and gasped. The man repeated his action, this time drawing a long line of candle wax across the woman's back. She writhed under the onslaught, and the man placed a meaty palm on her lower back to keep her still.

Amanda stepped forward, uncertain. Was he burning her?

Wrapping an arm around her stomach, Julius drew her back. "The hurt is only temporary," he whispered in her ear. "And the lady wants it. She comes back for it again and again."

Amanda had a hundred questions, but kept silent, watching intently. The woman's gasps and moans did seem to sound more of pleasure than pain. Putting the candle down, the man ran a hand through his bushy beard before picking up a different candle. With the eye of an artist, he drew patterns on her skin with the liquid wax, holding her down here, shifting her body there. The only sounds in the room were the woman's throaty moans, the crush of skin against velvet as she shifted restlessly against the bench, and the soft drips of wax striking flesh.

The chamber was several degrees cooler than the main room, but Amanda's body temperature rose higher. She pressed her thighs together and tugged at the top of her corset. Through the thin linen of her gown, her breasts scratched against the whalebone.

Tugging her hood back, she gulped down the cool air. Julius gathered her hair and pooled it to one side, over her shoulder. He blew gently on the back of her neck, a soothing breeze.

The tongue he used against her heated flesh was anything but soothing.

With the tip, he traced a pattern from the nape of her neck to her ear, sucking the lobe inside his hot mouth, making her melt. "Do you enjoy watching her struggle against the pain, to see as she surrenders to her pleasure?" His voice was a husky growl, and it sent a shiver from her eardrum to her core. "Do you grow wet seeing her submit? To give her body over to the care of her partner?" He grabbed her skirt at her thighs and began to gather it up. Inch by inch, her legs were revealed to the cool air.

Amanda tugged at the strings of her cloak, loosening the knot. The thick wool shifted down her back, still tied onto her, but exposing more and more. Maybe in the dark room, with Julius at her back, maybe she could remove it.

Her hands froze at the ties when Julius's fingers brushed bare skin. He had her skirt raised to her waist, and only the darkness covered her.

"Do you see how pretty she is in her passion?" He scraped his teeth against her ear, and she sagged against his chest. "Not as pretty as you when you submit. That moment, when you stop struggling against the ropes, stop trying to find comfort, to find satisfaction. When you surrender, and give yourself over to me to pleasure you as I see fit." He shifted behind her, pressing his hard length into the crease of her bottom. "You are the most beautiful thing in the world at that moment."

Her eyes blurred, and the flickering candles turned into dancing spots of lights. His thick finger found its way between her folds, gliding easily. "I knew you'd be wet," he whispered, satisfaction oozing from his voice.

She clutched at his arm, her fingers digging into his coat. Her own gasp was covered by the shriek of the woman on the bench as wax was poured onto her bottom, the candle only inches from her skin. The bearded man sat back on his haunches and appraised his work. With a nod, he licked his thumb and index finger and snuffed out the candles, one by one. Each hiss of the dying flames was echoed in the back of Amanda's throat. Julius's fingers danced along her intimate flesh, making her mind splinter along with her body.

The room went full dark, heavy breathing the only

sound. Leaning her head back on his shoulder, she let Julius's fingers sweep her away. He vee'd two fingers and rubbed back and forth around her clit. He reached his other hand down her corset and pulled out a breast. The tip was aching for attention, and when Julius pinched down, she almost wept with pleasure.

She was almost there. Just—

A gas lamp flared to life, lighting the chamber with amber shadows. The man and woman at the center of the room stood before the small group. He turned the woman so her back faced the audience. Different colors of wax splashed across her body in a lively pattern. The spectators clapped politely.

Julius's hands were otherwise occupied. With one hand he continued his relentless assault, with the other he draped her cloak back over her body, covering her nudity. Amanda struggled to stuff herself back into her corset and rearrange the top of her gown beneath the cloak. She clutched her breast through the stiff fabric. She couldn't let anyone see her like this, red-faced and panting, but her hips had a mind of their own, thrusting into his fingers. She was so close. Rational thought abandoned her, replaced by all-consuming craving.

The bearded man looked up from his human canvas and caught her in his stare.

Heat raced across her skin. Embarrassment. Lust. Need. It was all the same. "Julius," she begged.

Spinning, he nestled her body against the wall, his own blocking her from view. "Do you want me to stop?"

"God, no." She placed her palms flat against the wood, wishing there was something she could grab hold of. "Please..."

With no more teasing strokes, Julius increased the pressure. He thrust two fingers in her channel and circled her clitoris with his thumb. With his other hand, he palmed her mouth and leaned in close. "It's all right. No one can see or hear you. Come for me, Amanda."

She clawed at the wall, ignoring the sharp prick of a splinter. She stood on the edge of the abyss, her heart skipping a beat, before flying off, shattering into a million pieces. His hand muffled her moan, his arms keeping her from slipping to the floor, a boneless mess. He rubbed her slowly, prolonging her crisis.

After her body stopped shuddering, he slipped his hand from between her legs, and her skirts dropped to the floor. He straightened her cloak and pressed a soft kiss to the skin beneath her ear. "There's one more reward I owed you." His lips curved against her skin. "Though I'm still much in your debt."

She took a steadying breath and turned. Everyone in the room was grouped around the naked woman, admiring the streaks of color along her back. No one took notice of what Julius had just done to her in the corner. No one except the bearded man.

He strode across the room, everyone stepping aside for the behemoth. Stopping in front of them, the swarthy man crossed his arms across his broad chest. Amanda shrank into Julius's side under the man's scrutiny.

His fingers disappeared into his beard as he rubbed his jaw. "A new plaything, Julius? She doesn't look much like your usual sort."

Amanda's spine snapped straight. What did he mean? And what was Julius's usual sort?

Draping an arm around her shoulder, Julius pulled her into his side. "Not a plaything. A friend. And someone who will be assisting us tonight, so be nice." He turned to Amanda. "This shaggy fellow is Maximillian Atwood, Baron of Sutton. He rarely has much of import to say, so feel free to ignore him."

Sutton grunted. "Are you sure she wouldn't like a bit of sport?" He eyed her exposed neck and the top of her gown between the folds of her cloak that just barely covered her breasts. "Her skin is delightfully pale. The wax would look wonderful on it."

Julius bared his teeth. "Not. For. You."

Amanda chewed the inside of her cheek. "Assisting you? I thought you only wanted me by your side for appearance's sake."

He squeezed her arm. "Yes, that. And I need you to distract Madame Sable while Sutton and I search her office. A bit of acting, if you will."

Amanda and Sutton were twin images of gaping fish. The baron recovered first. "Julius! What the bloody hell? Who is this woman that you'd speak so freely in front of her?"

"Oh, my apologies," Julius said, sounding anything but contrite. "Did I forget to introduce you? This is Amanda Wilcox, Montague's sister-in-law." Opening the door, Julius led them into the hallway and towards the main room. "And don't worry. She already knows."

"I daresay she didn't know about me." Sutton kept his voice low but his words held plenty of heat.

"Acting?" Amanda squeaked. Her feet took root to the hallway floor. "I am no performer."

Julius swept her hair over her shoulder and squeezed her arm. "I thought the idea might alarm you, so I waited until now to tell you to save you from the worry. But think of it as a bit of entertainment. Just follow my lead."

Turning to his friend, Julius clapped the man's back. "And you, cheer up. She rarely goes out of doors, and speaks to no one but me and Marcus's dotty aunt. Your secret is safe with her."

Sutton didn't look convinced.

Of all the devious, under-handed tricks. Amanda glared at the man who was looking much too pleased with himself by half. Her irritation was so great, she barely noticed as Julius guided her into the main room of the club full of people.

"I don't know what plan you *think* you've devised—" she began.

"You'll do splendidly. Have faith in yourself." Julius

wrapped an arm around her waist. "And in me."

Amanda grumbled to herself, but she didn't have an argument for that. She did have faith in Julius. He always kept her safe.

A flash of red and a tinkling laugh drew their gazes to the center of the room.

"Ah, there's our hostess." Julius's fingers dug into her side. He blew out a breath and relaxed his grip. "Let me introduce you, my dear."

Amanda stumbled forward, her heart rate increasing with each step she took towards the center of the room. All gazes in the room were directed at the red-haired beauty, and Amanda had no desire to stand in the shadow of all those eyes.

"Don't worry," Julius whispered in her ear. "Just let the current take you where it may."

Amanda frowned and tugged the cloak tightly around her body. Julius swept her in a half-circle and presented her to the proprietress, bowing his head. "Madame Sable. How lovely to see you this evening. Might I introduce my guest, and someone most eager to become a member of your esteemed establishment. Mrs. Matthew Walker."

Sutton snorted but covered the sound by clearing his throat. Amanda frowned at him. This was hardly the time to come down with the giggles.

"I'm delighted to make your acquaintance, Mrs. Walker," Madame Sable said, her voice a musical tinkle. "Have you had a chance to enjoy The Black Rose?"

"Indeed, I have." Heat flushed across Amanda's cheeks as she stuttered the words. "Your club is most intriguing."

The redhead laughed, the heavy ruby and diamond necklace she wore shimmering above her breasts. "That is one word for it." She swept a hand towards a closed door. "May I show you to my office? We can discuss membership there."

Julius held the door open and followed the women into a stairwell. "You are most kind. However, Mrs. Walker has a similar complaint as I. Rather worse, actually. And your office, while charming, is most small." The foursome reached the top of the stairs and entered into a large hallway. A window sat at the far end and two doors were on either side of the corridor. Julius swept a hand towards an open door. "Perhaps your interview can be held elsewhere?"

"Of course." Madame Sable grasped the handle of the fan dangling from her wrist and tapped Julius in the chest with the closed end. "But you know my interviews are held alone with the prospect. I demand complete frankness with the candidates, and that rarely occurs when one's friends are in the room."

She extended a hand, to point back down the stairwell Amanda thought, and Julius grabbed it, lightly kissing the skin above her fingers. "Of course. I know your policy well. Sutton and I will wait in your breakfast room." He turned and entered the room across from them, Sutton lumbering behind. Still without his shirt.

Madame Sable eyed the muscled back and bit down on her lip. "There are great benefits to being a member here, as you can see." She turned and entered the sitting room. "But female members remain rare. I am quite interested to learn what piqued your interest." She held her hand out to an empty chair, a smile on her face.

Amanda sidled past the woman and took the seat on the settee that faced the open door with its view of the hallway. She willed her racing heart to slow its pace. "Perhaps"—she licked her lips—"perhaps female membership is rare because men hold women's purse strings. Not because we are so different in our needs."

Madame Sable raised her eyebrows, but settled gracefully in the chair opposite. "Too true. And all too unfortunate. If men only knew what women were capable of they would no longer underestimate our sex."

Amanda shifted. She didn't know of what she was capable. Except for the one moment she'd stood up to her father, the moment she'd lost control and lashed out at him with a knife, she hadn't accomplished anything in her life.

That one horrible deed had achieved her sister's and her own safety from a monster. And that was the grand sum of Amanda's life. It was a depressing thought.

The proprietress loosely clasped her hands together above her knee. "Now, let's get down to business. I take it you heard about our little club from Julius?"

Nodding, Amanda smiled through gritted teeth. Hearing his Christian name roll off the woman's painted lips was as irritating as the scratchy jute rope Julius had tested against her skin.

But it shouldn't be. Julius was a man with a past, and a future that wouldn't include Amanda. He could have as many red-headed harlots screaming his name as he wanted.

A pit opened up in her chest at the thought. She had been fooling herself to think that she could keep her affair from touching her heart. She had been half in love with Julius from the day they'd met and adding physical intimacy had only strengthened her attachment. No, she could no longer fool herself but she prayed Julius would remain unaware of her feelings.

Madame Sable's eyebrows drew together the longer it took her to answer, and Amanda squared her shoulders. She could console herself later. Now, she had a job to do. "Yes." She cleared her throat. "The earl knew we had mutual interests and thought I might enjoy your club."

Said earl poked his head out of the room across the hall and slipped out the door, heading for the office. Sutton tip-toed behind him, his knees slowly raising to his bare stomach with each step. He looked like an extremely large child sneaking out of nursery, and Amanda bit back a smile.

A floorboard in the hallway creaked.

"I was quite impressed with my tour," Amanda said loudly. "You seem to, uh, have something for everyone." A guess, based on the several closed doors downstairs. If dripping wax on a woman was in one of the rooms, she could hardly imagine what the other chambers contained.

Smoothing down her skirts, Madame Sable sent her a satisfied smile. "I do try to cater to everyone's needs. Well, the reasonable ones, at least. The safety of my girls and the other patrons is of paramount importance."

"Of course."

The madam smirked. "If you came with Julius, I can imagine what your need might be."

There was a muffled bang from down the hall, and the proprietress turned to look out the door. "Did you hear something?"

"No." Amanda gulped down a breath. "Nothing at all."

"Maybe I should go check ..." Madame Sable began to rise.

Amanda scooted to the edge of her seat. "Please. I've only ever been tied by Lord Rothchild. But he won't always be available." Especially not if he was thrown in prison for burglary. She swallowed, trying to bring moisture back to her parched mouth. "Can you tell me how your club would handle finding me a partner?"

"Of course." She cast another concerned glance over her shoulder but sank back into her chair. "I can either find another guest whose preferences suit yours, or one of my domestics. They are highly trained, and all interactions would be monitored until you feel comfortable with your partner. Now." She leaned forward, her breasts threatening to spill from the top of her gown. "Let's talk business. It is an annual membership, entitling you to entry any night you wish. Or every night." Her sharp gaze flicked on Amanda's mask. "Anonymity is highly-prized. Each member signs a contract guaranteeing they won't disclose anything that he or she sees at the club to non-club members. You never have to reveal your face, Mrs. Walker, if you don't wish to."

"The members sign contracts." A bead of sweat gathered at Amanda's temple, and she brushed it away. "But what about the workers. As you say, you have many girls." She looked to the empty door and back to the madam. When would Julius be finished? She didn't know how much longer she could maintain the pretense.

"And some men," Madame Sable said. "I provide for every taste. And they, too, are made to sign privacy contracts."

Amanda wiped her damp palms on her skirts. "And you? What guarantees do I have of your discretion?"

The woman opened her mouth, but it was a deep voice that rang out across the room. "Apparently no guarantee at all." Julius stepped into the room, Sutton right behind.

The baron leaned against a side table and tapped a leather-bound book against his thigh.

Madame Sable spun in her seat. She saw the book in Sutton's hand and gasped. She shot to her feet. "How dare you? That is private property."

Amanda pressed her hands to her stomach. Thank the heavens. Her task was done. Rising to her feet, she asked, "What did you find?"

Madame Sable turned her venomous glare on her. Amanda lifted one shoulder.

"We found proof that Madame Sable is as greedy as she is stupid." Julius shook his head. "Keeping the book in your top desk drawer, and with such a flimsy lock?" He tutted. "Did you really think no one would ever come looking?"

Stalking to Sutton, the proprietress tried to grab the book from his hand, but he held it out of reach. "That is proof of nothing. Merely some notes."

Sutton opened the journal. "Aidan, Marquess of Derry. Likes to wear a lead and be made to bark like a dog. Five hundred pounds. Harry Cockburn, second son of the Earl of Manchester. Likes spanking men who are dressed as women. Eight hundred and fifty pounds." He snapped the book shut. "I guess the tupping goes without saying."

"Notes to help me run my business better." Crossing her arms over her chest, Madame Sable stalked back to her seat and sank down.

"And the quid amounts?" Julius asked. "I know the fees

here are much greater than those amounts. But still a nice cut for doling out information to blackmailers." He tapped a crystal dangling from the sconce of a gas lamp and watched it swing. "Did you need the money? I thought this club was more than profitable."

"The Black Rose is extremely profitable. And your accusations couldn't be more wrong."

"I don't think so." Julius came to Amanda and put a hand at her waist. "And unfortunately for you, the men I work with will take my suspicions as fact. Life is about to become very unpleasant for you. Unless you cooperate."

The woman sniffed. "You work for the government, I assume. Those aren't the men who scare me."

"Then you haven't been properly introduced." With firm pressure, Julius guided Amanda to the door. "Sutton will be more than happy to show you just who you're dealing with."

Amanda saw the woman shrink away from Sutton as Julius closed the door. The baron's broad back blocked her view of the proprietress just as the door clicked shut. Gripping her elbow, Julius hustled her down the stairs.

"But we can't just leave them." Amanda turned at the foot of the staircase and tried to push back up. Julius tucked an arm under her cloak and banded her waist. He all but carried her into the main room.

"Sutton won't harm her. Not truly." He found an empty settee along the wall. "But she needs to believe he will, and if we are in the room, the illusion will be harder to sell." He pressed her down into the red silk cushion. "And she doesn't deserve your sympathy. She's responsible for hurting many people."

"So you think. She has yet to be convicted of it in a court." Not that the courts had done Amanda much good. But her sense of justice demanded fair play for those suspected of wrongdoing, even if she was nearly certain they were guilty. Especially then.

The hard lines of Julius's face softened. He crouched

before her. "As I said, no true harm will come to the woman. But she has information we need. Information that could save lives. We need to let Sutton work." He rubbed the skirts above her knee. "And you and Madame Sable are not of a kind."

Amanda laughed, the sound harsh, grating. "I've killed. You accuse her only of selling private information. Her alleged crime doesn't compare."

Frowning, he stood and plucked a column of champagne off the nearest serving girl's tray. He pressed it into her hand. "You're right. There is no comparison. You acted in self-defense. She acts from greed."

"That still doesn't mean she should be ..." Amanda cleared her throat. "Are you certain your friend won't hurt her?"

"I'm certain," he said. "But if it will ease your mind, I'll go back upstairs and ensure the situation hasn't gotten out of hand."

She nodded slowly. She didn't want to be in the club without him, but her worry over the madam's well-being overrode her nerves.

"Any other concerns before I leave?"

"Yes. One." Amanda tilted her head. "Why did Sutton laugh when you introduced me as Mrs. Matthew Walker? Is that another friend of yours?"

"No." The edges of his lips tipped up. He leaned into her space, his breath hot against her lips. "A Matthew Walker is a type of knot. Not of much use for binding a woman, but lovely just the same. He is all too familiar with my predilections. Now"—he tucked her cloak securely about her—"will you be all right sitting here alone?"

Rolling the stem of the wine glass between her fingers, she swallowed. "I'll be fine," she lied.

With a curt nod, he strode for the stairs.

Adjusting her mask, Amanda examined the room. A young woman sat on a man's lap across on an opposite settee, but other than that the scene appeared almost respectable. But very crowded. She fixed her gaze on a chandelier, trying to block out the rest of the room. Julius would be back soon and then they could go home. She'd had quite the adventure, but now she wanted the comfort of her own bed.

Her gaze drifted to the stairwell Julius had entered. Any moment now he'd return. A portly man leaning against the far wall, raised his glass to her, and winked. She tucked her cloak more tightly around her, grateful now for the warmth. Mouth dry, she tossed back a swallow of champagne and looked back at the ceiling. There were an awful lot of candles in the chandelier. Perhaps if she started counting them ...

Raucous laughter made her drop her gaze. The couple across from her had begun a playful tussle on their settee. A man stepped from the hallway to her right, adjusting his cravat. A tall, cadaverous man with light brown hair and a thin mustache. Her heart knocked against the corset. There had to be many men who met Dawnley's description of his blackmailer. Men so slender that they appeared like scarecrows. Men with that unfashionable facial hair. Men who frequented the very club Dawnley had been taken to. The tall man headed for the front door, stopping only when a serving girl put a hand on his arm and gave him a coy smile.

Amanda closed her eyes. What were the odds of all of that being a coincidence? Glancing at the stairs, she willed Julius to appear. He didn't. Downing half of her champagne, she plopped the glass down on a side table and pushed to her feet. She took a step towards the stairs.

The serving girl dipped a curtsy, giving the man a nice view down her dress, and moved on with her tray of drinks. Tall man headed for the door.

Her head throbbed and indecision made her feet feel like lead. Julius wouldn't want her interrupting whatever was happening upstairs, but he wanted this man. And if she did run upstairs, chances were the tall man would have disappeared before Julius could follow.

A party of gentlemen gathered in front of the entrance to Madame Sable's chambers, arms thrown over each other's shoulders, singing drunkenly. And the portly man who had caught her eye earlier fixed her in his sight and headed her way.

Amanda changed direction. The path of least resistance led her to the front door. Her decision was made. Follow the tall man and report back to Julius. But by the time the footman opened the front door for her, the man was nowhere in sight. Despite the cold air swirling around her, sweat rolled down her back. The wide expanse of London surrounded her, crushing in upon her. And at her back was a room full of strangers eager for an intrigue. Both options daunted her, but only one would help Julius. She didn't know if it was her fear, the corset, or the London fog, but knowing what she had to do she suddenly found it quite difficult to breathe.

She forced herself to inhale slowly, the bitter air abrading the back of her throat. She inched her slipper towards the first step. Shuddered when her heel hit the next. There were only two stairs. She could make it.

The swirl of a greatcoat disappearing into shadow made it easier to push through her dread. Her quarry was within sight. She couldn't tell Julius she'd lost him because she'd been too frightened to walk out of doors. She tugged the hood of the cloak over her head. Besides, no one could recognize her.

She scurried up the street, her breaths seeming unnaturally loud in the still night. The cross street a block up was an explosion of carriages and horses, but this side street was a quiet haven. The man strode to a parked coach and waited for the driver to open the door.

Amanda bit her lip in dismay. She was going to lose him. She took in every detail of the coach as it rolled away, its gold coat of arms gleaming under the gas lamps when it hit the main street. She raced after it to the corner, pressing her hand to her side, out of breath. If she could have just—

A shoulder knocked into hers, its owner hustling down the street, not bothering with an apology. As if the contact had knocked off a blindfold, the sights of the rest of the street crashed over Amanda. She lost sight of the gold-crested coach, but twenty other carriages took its place. Pedestrians swirled around her, so fast they made her dizzy. And gas lamps hanging from posts made the street so bright she could have sworn she felt the heat from each flame.

Amanda stepped back, onto someone's foot, and earned a snarl. She spun to apologize, but the man was already twenty paces away. A shout from the street had her twisting back. Two drivers argued from their high perches, one cracking his whip over the other driver, he in turn yelling with indignation. A horse whinnied, and twenty other drivers hollered at the blockage.

Heart pounding in her throat, Amanda grabbed her ears between her palms. The sounds still bled through. She was surrounded, lost in a crush of people, no clear avenue of escape. Bile crept up her throat, burning. Her body was rooted to the spot even as her mind screamed at her to move.

Almost like she was climbing a step, she lifted one slipper high, forced it forward and down. One step closer to her quiet street. One step closer to Julius. Why had she ever left his club?

The sound of wood ramming into wood broke behind her, but Amanda refused to turn. She lifted her other foot. Sweat beaded her skin, and the feathers of her mask stuck to her cheeks. She focused on the mouth of the side street, her vision tunneling to its dark entrance. Everything would be all right if she could just make it back to that street.

She was close. Just a few steps away. Another pedestrian jostled her as he rushed past, knocking her hood back. She blinked, trying to clear her vision. She could see lights from the front of The Black Rose. They seemed a thousand miles away. She focused on those torches, the rest of the world fading to black. As long as she kept lifting her feet and heading towards those lights, everything would be all right.

A man stepped into her path, making her lights disappear. He smiled, opened his mouth to speak, but it was like watching a pantomime. No sounds reached Amanda's ears over the rush of blood. She tried to sidestep around him, to catch sight of her beacons again, but he moved with her, a cocky grin on his face.

It didn't matter. She had nothing left in her. It took all of her energy to merely remain standing. London swirled around her like a cyclone, and she was a fool to think she could withstand the storm.

The man in front of her pointed at her mask, tossing his head back in a soundless laugh. His teeth caught the glow from a gas lamp, and Amanda's gaze fixed on that slight shimmer. If she could just keep one light in focus, perhaps she could keep the encroaching blackness at bay. The man closed his mouth, and her lodestar blinked out.

The world swept sideways. As she fell, Amanda felt each beat of her heart pounding faster and faster until she thought the organ must explode. And when her head hit the sidewalk, blissfully, she thought no more.

Chapter Eleven

Julius left Sutton to wait for Liverpool's men. Where they would stow Madame Sable until their investigation into the blackmail ring concluded, he could only guess. But a trial wasn't in the woman's immediate future. If ever.

Standing at the bottom stair, he looked around the main room at all the members. How many of them were secretly being blackmailed? For how many had this sanctity been turned into a hunting ground? The Black Rose was a refuge for those who couldn't find their tastes met elsewhere. It would be a shame if it closed.

Sutton had said he knew someone who could manage the club while their investigation continued. The proprietress would leave a letter to her attorney explaining the need for her hurried departure and that she'd asked her friend to run the business in her absence.

Julius eyed the constant stream of drinks delivered to the patrons, the skillfully trained lady-birds flirting with the men, the orderly management of the back rooms. Madame Sable's faults notwithstanding, the woman was a brilliant businesswoman. He didn't see how Sutton's replacement could compare.

He straightened his cravat. Not his problem. His problem, his investigation, was now one step closer to being solved since Madame Sable had agreed to cooperate. He was free to take Amanda home, relax, and put off until tomorrow the bother of his duty.

He drummed his fingers against his thigh. The only flaw with that plan was that Amanda was no longer sitting on the settee he'd placed her upon.

With a frown, he searched the room. She wasn't there. Would she have gone into another back room? He knew she was curious but thought her insecurities would have kept her seated. He eyed the long row of closed doors that lined the back hall. Impatient, he grabbed the elbow of a passing serving girl.

"The woman I was with. Did you see her go into any of the rooms?" he asked.

The chit shook her head but raised a finger and brought the footman over. Julius repeated his question.

"Not into one of the rooms, m'lord." The man jerked his chin towards the front. "She left. I held the door open for her."

"You what?" Julius's voice was a low growl. There was no bloody way Amanda would leave on her own accord.

The footman fell back a step. "Yes ..." He cleared his throat. "I believe she was trying to catch up with Mr. Smith. She left right after him."

A Mr. Smith? The Black Rose was fucking littered with Mr. Smiths. "What did this Mr. Smith look like?"

"He's very tall. Well over six feet." The footman scratched his jaw. "And he could stand to eat a few more meals, if you take my meaning."

Yes, Julius thought grimly, he knew what the man meant. And his little mouse was dead. Once he got her safely back home, he was going to kill her. Without another word, Julius pushed across the room and flew out the front door. He took the steps in one leap and landed hard on the sidewalk. Heart pounding, he looked down the street. Empty. Had the tall man grabbed her, smuggled her into his carriage? Left her body lying in an alley?

Sweat beaded his temple, and he swallowed down his panic. Worrying would get him nowhere. Turning away from the darkened end of the street, he jogged towards the busy intersection, stopping at every alley to peer inside. Looking for bodies behind every porch.

A large fight in the middle of the busy cross street drew his attention. A group of five hackney drivers had climbed down from their stations and had come to blows, blocking the street so no other carriages could pass. A crush of pedestrians packed the sidewalk, enjoying the violence.

Julius almost missed the other, smaller crowd clustered not ten feet from him. They faced inward, away from the brawl in the street. Pushing his way through, his heart faltered with his feet when he saw Amanda's still form laying on the ground, her cloak flared out around her body. A man knelt beside her and reached his filthy hands under her knees and shoulders.

Grabbing the back of his collar, Julius threw the bastard into the legs of a man in the crowd. He dropped next to Amanda and felt for a pulse. It throbbed beneath his fingers, and every muscle in his body sagged with relief. He caressed her face and his fingers came away sticky with blood.

The sack of shit Julius had tossed aside pushed to his feet. "Bloody hell. The lady is a ... friend, and I was only going to take her home to recover."

Julius's fingers twitched, and he curled them into the thick velvet of Amanda's cloak to keep them away from the liar's throat. His vision blurred in his anger. "Not yours." He didn't recognize his own voice. "Mine."

The man backed away, palms raised. "I was only trying to help."

Help himself to a defenseless woman more like. Julius's blood boiled, but he refrained from teaching the bastard a lesson. Seeing to Amanda took priority. Gently, he scooped her into his arms and strode back towards The Black Rose and his carriage.

His driver saw him coming and hopped down from his perch, quick to open the carriage's door. Julius climbed inside and winced when he banged Amanda's knee into the bench seat. Her breathing remained even.

He laid her down and untied her cloak. He searched

her body for injury, finding none but the bump on her head. Tearing at the laces of her corset, he peeled it off of her and watched as her chest heaved a deep breath.

He rested his palm on her stomach and sat back on his heels. The slow rise and fall of her belly calmed his racing heartbeat. He pounded on the ceiling of the carriage and yelled, "Home!" Pulling out his handkerchief, he dabbed at the trickles of blood rolling down her cheek and neck and into her hair. The only cut appeared to be at her chin, a deep scrape that held a bit of gravel. He cleaned it as best he could.

Her eyelids fluttered and slid open, her gaze unfocused. Julius hovered over her and cupped her cheek. Her eyes widened. Jerking up, she looked from one open window to the other, chest heaving. "The people—" Her words broke off in a wheeze.

Cursing, Julius closed the windows and drapes. He lengthened the wick on the gas lamp in the carriage only to see Amanda scuttling into the corner, drawing her knees up tight to her chest.

"Amanda," he said, his voice sterner than she deserved. "You're all right. You're safe."

She moaned, burying her head in her arms.

Julius raised her head and ripped off the mask. He gripped her cheeks between his palms. "You're safe."

Digging her fingers into his coat, she closed her eyes. Her breaths remained sharp, ragged. Without thought, Julius dragged her onto his lap, holding her body close. Her tremors spread to him. Her panic became his. The carriage was too fucking small, and he couldn't breathe. Burying his nose in her hair, he closed his eyes and tried to picture them in an open field. On a picnic, perhaps. Amanda lying on a blanket, the wind tousling her dark locks, smiling up at him as the sun kissed her skin.

By God, he would make that happen.

She twisted, and their hearts beat against each other. Rubbing the back of her neck, he tried to force his pulse to slow through sheer force of will. "My God, Amanda, what were you thinking?"

He didn't expect a response, thinking she was too far gone to answer. The shake of her head against his shoulder was encouraging.

"Breathe with me and relax," he told her. He took deep, slow breaths, and was satisfied when she eventually matched his rhythm. "That's it." They sat together, one of his legs going numb under her weight, and simply breathed.

The carriage rattled to a stop. "Keep your eyes closed." Ignoring the pins and needles in his thigh, he lifted Amanda and climbed down the stairs when the footman opened the door. Like a well-oiled machine, the front door of the duke's townhouse opened as he approached. For once, Julius was glad of his friend's servants.

"Shall I send for a doctor, my lord?" Carter sniffed and trailed him to the staircase.

"Not yet." Besides the scrape on her jaw, Julius didn't think Amanda was injured. Not physically. "But stand by."

He took the stairs two at a time, lungs burning, and strode to his room. Reggie scampered out of Amanda's chamber and yipped at his heels. Julius started to close the door in his face, but the pup's mournful whimper stopped him. "Fine. Get in here." Reggie bounded across the room in two leaps and jumped onto the bed, tail wagging. Julius kicked the door closed behind him.

Gently, he lowered Amanda to the bed. She immediately turned onto her side, facing away from him. Reggie lay next to her and licked her face. Throwing her arm over the dog, she pulled him close to her chest.

Julius took a step back, flexing and clenching his fists. The immediate rush for action was over, and his body sagged with lethargy. She was safe. Secure in his care. Pressing his palms into the mattress, Julius slumped over. If anything had happened to her ...

Well, that was something best not thought of. Marcus would have killed him, of course. Letting harm come to his sister-in-law after taking her to The Black Rose. Still might kill him just over taking her to their club. His friend saw the world through a practical lens, however, and knew that his sister-in-law was no untouched virgin. Still, there was no reason to announce the visit.

He placed a hand on her hip, hating the way she flinched. "Would you like some water? Tea?" he asked.

She shook her head. "Can you close the window, please?"

Circling the bed, Julius took one last look at the night sky and pulled the panes shut. He untied the sash around the curtains, letting them fall into place. Concealing his exit. He turned and faced Amanda, her body curled up into a neat ball, almost as small as Reggie's.

He carried the pitcher of water on his dressing table to his nightstand and dipped his handkerchief in it. He cleaned the dried blood from her skin. "What happened out there? Why did you leave the club?" He waited, impatient for answers. She'd taken five years off his life from fright and she owed him that much.

She shook her head, her breaths shallow and quick.

Tossing the handkerchief down next to the pitcher, he crawled onto the bed, nudging Reggie out of the way. He rolled Amanda to her back and straddled her hips. Pinning her wrists to the bed, he bent down until they were nose to nose. "I repeat, why did you leave the club?"

She sighed, and the muscles beneath him relaxed. "Your suspect was getting away. There was no time to find you."

Of course. That made perfect sense. "You little fool! Do you realize how reckless that was? Even for a woman without your complaint it would have been harebrained. Anyone could have taken you. Hurt you." The image of that miscreant bending to pick Amanda up wouldn't leave his head. He squeezed her wrists. "Women don't go strolling through London alone at night."

Her eyes were dark and unfathomable, but at least the fear was gone. "Am I to understand that you don't want to know what I discovered?"

Julius growled and crawled off the bed. He paced around the room, seething with a swirl of emotions. The woman was so damned frustrating. A timid mouse one moment, a teasing minx the next. He fisted his hands. He needed a trip to Gentleman Jack's. Something to do with his hands that didn't involve throttling the woman lying on his bed. He wished he had the same predilection as Marcus. If any woman deserved a spanking, it was Miss Amanda Wilcox for her behavior that night.

He strode for his nightstand and removed his japanned chest, placing it on the bench at the foot of the bed. As soon as his fingers touched rope, the muscles in his shoulders unbunched. He tossed two shorter lengths onto the bed and pulled out the twenty-foot hemp. He dragged the cable through his hands, the movement as soothing as a glass of whiskey before bed.

Amanda raised to one elbow. "What are you doing?"

"Trying my confounded best not to punish you." With a mind of their own, his fingers knotted the rope in even intervals. After each knot, he tugged on the cable, feeling the tension and the give.

"Was that an option?" Amanda tilted her head to the side and narrowed her eyes.

He sighed. "Not for you. Not really." He eyed her form and doubled one of the knots. "But I do need some answers, and I think we'll both be happier if I work while you talk. Take off the rest of your clothes."

Her mouth dropped open. "I just—"

"Scared the life out of me? Yes, I know."

She huffed. "Now is hardly the time—"

He squeezed the rope until the fibers cut into his flesh. "How do you feel when I bind you?"

She blinked and shook her head.

"I can tell you what I see." He leaned over and combed his fingers through her hair. "Your body becomes pliant and your emotions quiet. It brings you peace. For me, it does the same." Laying rope over a woman's body, creating patterns and beauty, bringing pleasure, it all wove together to bring him almost to a state of bliss. "I think if ever we needed this, it would be tonight."

She held his gaze, her dark eyes seeming to hold the answers to every question he didn't know he had. Slowly, she rolled to her knees. She slid the strap of her thin gown off one shoulder, then the other, before pushing it down until it puddled on the counterpane. She wore no chemise beneath it, and her small breasts peaked under his gaze. Rolling to her bottom, she swept the gown down and over her feet. She toed off her slippers and slowly drew her stockings down her legs, tossing them in his direction.

Everything in Julius tightened, and he snapped the rope taut between two hands. Definitely a minx.

"What about your clothes?" she asked.

"They stay on. For now."

She pursed her lips. "How disappointing."

Biting back a smile, he scooped Reggie up with one arm and put him outside the room. The pup yapped, indignant. Julius squatted down and scratched his head. "I don't like to be watched. Not even by dogs. Find your own bed." He shut the door and strode back to Amanda, crawling onto the mattress beside her.

Amanda took his hand and squeezed. He squeezed back, and a world of communication passed between their palms.

Taking his first deep breath since he'd found her in the street, Julius ran the tail end of the rope over her skin. He trailed it over the crease where thigh met abdomen, around her navel, and up between her breasts.

The delicate skin of her chest flushed, and her dusky nipples puckered into hard peaks. Unable to resist, Julius leaned down and kissed her neck, feeling the pounding of her heartbeat beneath his lips. "You frightened me," he whispered.

"Me, too." She threaded her fingers through his hair, the

caress making the base of his spine tingle.

Capturing her hand, he kissed her fingertips before wrapping one of the shorter lengths of rope around her wrist. He hauled her hand above her head and attached the cord to one of the spindles of the headboard. He'd have to remember to compliment Marcus on his choice of beds. For a man like Julius, the four thick posters and slotted headboard were a playground.

Straddling her waist, he sat back on her stomach and gave her a wicked smile. "Now that you can't escape, I have a few questions."

* * *

Each revolution of the rope around her wrist was a tether. A link to the earth that allowed her to float free without the fear of flying away. Her body sank into the feather mattress, and it felt like she was reclining on a cloud. The past hour drifted from memory like a bad dream.

She was safe, at home, with Julius. It had been rare in her life, those moments when she'd felt secure. Her father had robbed her of that when she'd turned thirteen. Newgate had been better. Most days she'd been snug in her little cell, separated from the world. But when the door opened ...

No, she'd never been safe. So many took that feeling for granted. She never would.

He stretched her other arm to another post. No escape now. A tingle started at the base of her skull and shivered down her spine.

Julius misinterpreted its source. Rolling off the bed, he stalked to the fireplace and stacked more coal on the andiron. He prodded the mound with the poker. "There. That should keep you warm. Either that, or I will." His smile was dark and dirty, and she definitely felt the heat.

Julius knelt on the bed and picked up the long length of rope. The purple-dyed hemp scraped across his palms. Amanda loved his hands. Large, with long, tapered fingers. More importantly, she loved the way he used them on her.

Crawling to her feet, Julius raised her ankle and rested it on his thigh. "In the East, I learned the human body is connected by a series of meridian lines. Applying pressure to certain points can cause either great pain or"—he pressed his thumb into the skin below the ball of her foot—"intense pleasure."

Amanda arched her back, swallowing a whimper. Lightning raced up her leg and settled in her core before he eased his grip.

His large hands enveloped her foot, kneading the skin, soothing away tension she didn't even know she'd had. She was putty in his hands. His to mold. Julius hit another spot, one that sent fire racing through her veins, and he smirked. If she wasn't so boneless, she'd want to kick the smug right off of him.

He kissed the pad of her big toe and moved to her other foot. "You can learn the most interesting things, even in the worst of situations. When I was first taken prisoner, my captors delighted in causing me pain." He lifted a shoulder. "That first month, I believe I received first-hand knowledge of every meridian point on my body."

And his captors weren't giving him lovely foot rubs, of that Amanda was sure. She'd known that he'd been tortured and wondered at it. His body was nearly without marks. But his gaolers hadn't needed a blade or a club to break his bones. Her heart broke for the pain he'd endured. No one deserved it, but the kind, determined man in front of her less so than most.

"As time wore on, the daimyo learned of my elevated status in British society. For some reason, that mattered to him." Julius twisted his lips, but his hands never stopped moving. "In their eyes, I became worthier of respect because I was the son of a nobleman. They shared their knowledge with me, and the ropes holding me became looser, the pain ended. Until finally the knot around my wrists was purely a formality."

"Weren't they afraid you'd escape?"

"They followed their own code of honor. As a nobleman, I wasn't supposed to try to escape. *My* honor was supposed to forbid it." Placing her ankle by his thigh, he slithered up her body and took her mouth. His kiss was bruising, possessive. Amanda couldn't get enough.

"They were idiots." He cradled the side of her neck, his eyes darkening to wet moss. "When it comes to survival, there is no honor. Only choosing life or giving up. And there's nothing wrong with choosing life. Do you understand?"

She understood he was trying to reconcile her actions to his personal code. The back of her throat burned, and she swallowed down her pain. There was no comparison between the two of them. Her life hadn't been in danger from her father; only her sanity, and that of her sister's.

"I'm glad you chose life," she whispered. Their faces were so close she felt her breath rebound off his lips and feather across hers. Wrapping her legs around his lean hips, she rocked her pelvis against the hardness trapped behind his trousers. "Most glad."

He groaned. "I'm supposed to be sapping your will, seducing information from you. Not the other way around."

She rolled her eyes. "You know I will tell you everything. That was the entire point of why I chased after the man. To tell you."

One edge of his mouth slid up. "I know. But where would be the entertainment in that?" With one last kiss, he sat back on his haunches and reached for the rope. Her legs were splayed around him, her body open and aching. He gripped her behind the knee, adjusted the position of her leg. He wound the hemp around her upper thigh, one of the knots digging into her flesh.

"Arch your back," he told her. She complied, and he ran the cable across her stomach and around her back before running it down around her other thigh.

Amanda bit the inside of her cheek. This was all very nice. Anytime Julius wound rope about her would be enjoyable. But the ropes at her thighs and waist didn't immobilize her, didn't provide any restraints. Her other experiences, she'd been cradled, her movement, and all responsibility, taken from her. The rope at her hips merely provided a nice scrape.

Scooting down the bed until he lay on his stomach, Julius settled her knees over his shoulders. "Now, for every answer you give me, you'll receive a small reward. If you leave anything out ..."

"What happens then?" Amanda forced her body to remain still. His face was so close to her most intimate parts, his focus completely centered on her body, it was difficult not to be discomfited.

But if she was going to feel abashed, she should darn well yield some benefit, at least. He was so close, his breath stirred her thatch of curls. She lifted her hips, wordlessly trying to demand his attentions.

Julius ran his thumbs down her folds, peeled back her layers. He ducked his head and blew.

Amanda jerked, the ropes tightening on her wrists. She licked her lips. "That feels quite nice. I don't believe that creates a sufficient deterrent."

"Not now," Julius agreed. He blew again, a long, steady stream, his exhalation hot and teasing. "But if that's all that I give you? No more of a touch than that? People have been known to go mad from less."

"You wouldn't dare."

He lowered his head until all she could see were the tops of his tousled locks. Little puffs of air, each one a gossamer kiss, assailed her body. She tried to bring her legs together, supply her own pressure, but was blocked by his broad shoulders.

For the first time in her life, she said a word she'd only heard from the coarsest of men. And from Julius. It felt good rolling off her tongue. Satisfying. So she said it again.

Julius tutted. He lifted his head and threaded one hand under the rope at her waist, tugging her arching hips back to the bed. "Are you certain I wouldn't dare?" He dipped his head.

Wriggling her bottom into the coverlet, Amanda considered. "I don't believe it's possible for you to continue for long. No one can spend all their time merely blowing."

He chuckled, and the late-evening scruff on his jaw tickled the inside of her thigh. "I can breathe for quite some time. Besides, you have no idea what I can endure. The patience I have. I have spent over thirty-six hours hanging from a rafter. I think I have it in me to blow."

And he would. Jerking her head off the pillow, she glared down at him. "Ask your bloody questions already! I said I'd answer."

"Language. You really are becoming quite the gutter-mouth." Shaking his head, he casually slapped his hand down on her folds. The clap of skin striking skin startled her before the sting made itself known. He gusted a breath over the abused flesh. "Just because you are surrounded by barbarians doesn't mean you need speak like one of them."

Amanda squirmed, the heat at her core spreading to the rest of her body until her skin prickled in a low burn. "I saw the man while you were upstairs with Sutton and Madame Sable. I figured it must be the man you wanted. How many tall, skinny, mustached men would be at that club?"

Julius smiled and swiped the tip of his tongue up the seam of her sex. "That's my girl. As long as you continue talking, you'll receive better treatment."

Her thighs fell open, trying to expose as much of her body to him as possible. She'd expose her beating heart if it would bring her more of the same pleasure. He circled her nub and flicked it with his tongue. Her legs quaked. "And, uh ... I followed ..." Coherent thought was dissolving. Her mouth didn't want to form the words. He was a wizard, and his tongue an enchantment.

"Why did you follow?" Julius asked, his voice sharp.

She blinked. Why had she followed? The delicious pressure disappeared, replaced by a weak stream of air.

"No, please!" She jerked hard against her ropes, and the headboard smacked back against the wall. "I need—"

"Then explain to me why you would do something so foolish as to follow a suspect in criminal wrongdoing." He rested his head against her thigh. "I'll keep blowing until I hear an answer I like. And that might take a while."

She twisted her wrist, hoping to slide her hand out of the loop. "I started to go upstairs to tell you, but he was leaving. There wasn't time." She shifted her hips, but Julius was a heavy weight. "You wanted to find him, and I wanted to help you."

He grunted, but Amanda ignored his discontent. He put his mouth back on her and that was all that mattered. She sagged into the mattress. Tracing a figure eight, Julius circled her opening and looped up around her clitoris in one continuous slide. It was exquisite torture, one she wanted repeated every night. Her hips pitched against his mouth, beyond her command. Her body became weightless. The only things that connected her to this earth was the hemp around her wrists and Julius's tongue at her center.

Julius flattened that tongue and increased the pressure. He slid two fingers into her channel.

"Oh, God, yes," she moaned. She swore she could feel his lips curve against her flesh. Clenching her fists, she waited. Waited for the dam to fill, gallon by gallon, until the wall couldn't take the pressure anymore and burst. She was so close to bursting ...

Julius pushed to his knees and slid his cravat off his neck. He licked his lips, his eyes never leaving hers, and wiped the rest of the moisture off his chin with the silk.

The headboard bounced against the wall. "No!" She glared at him as he drew his shirt over his head and tossed it to the floor. "Why did you stop? I was almost there."

"I know." He unbuttoned the falls of his trousers and pushed them down his hips along with his smallclothes. His length sprang free, ruddy and thick. A bead of liquid hovered at the tip, and Amanda's mouth watered. "I want you to come impaled on my cock. Nothing feels better than your sweet cunny clamping down on me." Leaning over, he grabbed a cloth pouch and pulled out a folded piece of linen. His eyes fixed on her core, he slowly stroked his fist from the base of his column to the crown. He rubbed his palm over the head, gathering the moisture beaded there, and eased his hand back down to the root.

She ached to be the one stroking his length. To use her mouth on him as he had on her. His manhood was a thing of beauty, thick and long, and pulsing with restrained power.

"Would it speed this process along if I told you that I didn't follow your man in vain?" She ran her foot along the calf of his trousers, needing to touch him in any way she could. "I saw the carriage he entered. It had a coat of arms on it. One I'd recognize again."

Julius froze. His gaze landed on her face. "Are you certain?"

She nodded and arched her back. "Do I get my reward now?"

"I'd say we both do." With quick motions, Julius slid the linen over his length and tied a knot at the base. He scooped his arms under her legs, and the back of her knees rested on his elbows. Julius crawled forward, his crown nudging her folds.

Amanda nodded to his groin. "Must you wear that? I'd like to feel you, not some paper."

"It keeps us healthy and it prevents against the consequence of offspring." Julius eased in an inch, slipped out. "For me, there is no other alternative."

Amanda tried to widen her legs, but Julius's grip blocked her. The knots he'd tied in the rope pressed into the crease of her legs and hips, and she bit her lip.

Closing his eyes, he pushed into her body, filling the emptiness. "God's teeth, you feel good."

"So do you." Amanda raised her pelvis into his next

slide, felt every inch of him as he drove past her clutching muscles. The linen was stiff, but she could still feel the heat rolling off of Julius. Feel his unyielding power.

Her breath hitched. Without the linen, how much hotter would he feel? What would it be like to have that velvety skin slide into her body? She couldn't help but feel regret.

"We're both about to feel a whole lot better." He shifted her legs higher up his arms, and with his next thrust, leaned forward until his hands were planted near her shoulders and her knees were by her ears.

The rope around her legs went taut, and the knots in the crease of each hip stabbed into her flesh. She jerked, went rigid as stone as fire licked from the source of the knots to every muscle in her body. Her mind couldn't decide if the sensations were painful or not, only knew they were almost too intense to bear. Julius eased his hips back, dragging from her body, and easing the pressure on the knots. Her body collapsed into the bed, relieved. Until he pounded back home and the ropes went taut.

Her mouth opened and closed, not even air able to escape.

Julius leaned down and softly kissed her. "As I said, I know every place on the body that, with the right pressure applied, can bring extreme pleasure."

Pleasure? Was that what she was feeling? She felt each thrust everywhere, from the tips of her breasts to the pads of her toes. That aching, burning sensation flooded her every pore. She didn't know whether she wanted to demand more or beg him to stop.

If her body was made up of meridian lines, then Julius had mapped each and every inch of her. She writhed beneath him, and every time the knots dug into the front of her hips, her body shuddered in ecstasy.

Or was it agony? The shock from the meridian points was too much. His cock tunneling in and out of her body was sensation enough. But with those knots .... The skin under the hemp began to burn. The torment spread, until her hips, her core, her stomach, all became as responsive as her meridian points.

She whimpered. "Please, Julius. Oh God, please."

He pounded harder, faster. He dropped his gaze to where his body tunneled into hers and groaned. His dark hair curled over the top of the linen, shiny from her essence. The muscles of his lower abdomen clenched with each thrust.

Amanda whimpered and yanked at her wrists. The need to touch him was overwhelming.

The pace increased. The knots in her hips sent out short bursts, flaring like lightning. Her breath seized in her lungs. Arching her neck, she tried to suck down air. Black dots swam before her eyes. She wrapped her hands around the rope at her wrists and heaved with all her might, trying to escape the feelings, trying to bring the bed down on top of them, trying to find relief. Sweat beaded across her body, and for the first time in years, she wanted a window open. A cool breeze caressing her skin. Anything to put out the fire.

Skin slapped against skin. Julius's soft grunts filled the room. Jaw tight, Julius lowered himself further and ground his hips into hers. The skin under the knots felt like it was crawling with ants, the pressure never ending. Her body clutched once, twice at the thick length inside.

Bending his head, Julius sucked one aching nipple into his mouth, and pulled.

And like fireworks over Vauxhall Gardens, she exploded into a thousand scorching pieces. His teeth scraping across her breast, his short, prickly hair rubbing against her clit, it all merged with the sparks still shooting from the knots, and her body twisted and bucked beneath Julius, out of her control. Only the ropes held her together.

Julius groaned in her ear, his cock twitching inside her channel. "Sweet Jesus," he whispered and collapsed to her side.

One of her legs was underneath him, but the pressure of

the rope had eased. Amanda managed to catch her breath but could do nothing to stop the tremors wracking her body.

In all her years, she'd felt nothing like that.

After several minutes, her mind cleared enough to form words. "Oh my."

He rolled over and brushed his mouth against hers, nibbling at her lower lip. He tugged on the rope at her waist. "I thought you'd enjoy that." He freed her wrists.

Enjoy didn't even come close. "I don't believe I'll be able to move for a sennight."

"Good. When you move, you get into trouble." They stared at the canopy for moments more, Julius grazing the back of her hand with his finger. "Amanda ..."

"Yes?"

"We should talk."

Why did that not sound promising?

"I don't want there to be any misunderstandings between us," Julius began. "About the future."

Her stomach cramped, and all the muscles that had become so delightfully loose, stiffened. "What future?" Her voice sounded as dead as she felt. She knew where Julius was going with this, and frankly, didn't need to hear it. She was under no misconceptions.

He was quiet a minute. "After ... well, after I became Rothchild, I came to understand things about myself. One of those was the fact that I'll never marry. I'm not suited for it."

She turned her head and stared at him, incredulous. "You're an earl. Of course, you'll marry." It wouldn't be to someone like her, and she understood that.

A muscle in his jaw twitched. "No. The house of Rothchild ends with me. I'll not be eternally bound, not even to save the earldom."

"But"—she rolled up onto one elbow and gazed down at him—"you have to have an heir. You're an earl," she repeated.

He snorted. "And would the world end if I died without issue? Would the walls of my Thornburg Hall crumble to dust?" He picked up a lock of her hair and twisted it around his finger. "When I came back to that estate and learned my brothers were dead, found my father close to it himself, everyone said how fortunate it was that I had lived. At least there was one male left to carry on the name. And I asked, why? Why would it be so bad if a Blackwell no longer carried the title? There must be a second cousin lazing about somewhere who would pick up the mantle."

Amanda chewed on the inside of her cheek. "But isn't it the duty of every gentleman to ..."

"Sire an army of children to propagate the English race?" He shook his head. "I've learned to pick and choose my duties. Babies, a wife, they're all tentacles that strangle a man. I won't be trapped again. Not for anything."

Or anyone, Amanda thought. She lay back. Her heart broke, just a little, for the man beside her. His future looked as bleak and empty as hers. Only Julius was condemning himself to that fate.

She forced a smile on her face. "Thank you for trying to let me down gently, but I assure you, the idea of matrimony never once crossed my mind." And it hadn't. She'd have been a fool to think anything else. "I stand by our original arrangement. A mutually beneficial affair of pleasure. No expectations. No regrets."

Leaning over, he kissed her on the nose. "Good. Glad to hear it."

"Just ... before you leave to sleep wherever it is that you do, could you hold me for a bit?" She'd grown accustomed to falling asleep with Julius by her side. And to waking up alone. Instead of kicking her from his bed, he found another spot to lay his head. She hated that he couldn't even share the bed with her the entire night through. But she was beginning to understand it. Understand him. And she counted herself fortunate that they had this time together.

"Sleep?" One edge of Julius's mouth curled up, a devilish glint shining in his eyes. "Who said anything about sleep? I'm not done with you yet." He rolled over and stretched for the foot of the bed. Digging in his chest, he pulled out a jade and some oil.

Suddenly, parts of Amanda felt wide awake indeed.

Chapter Twelve

"I think you're wrong." Julius frowned at her, his hands on his hips.

Amanda sighed. That seemed to be a recurring theme this morning. "I know. You've said that before. Many times. But you aren't going to change my mind."

"What is the good of arguing with someone if he doesn't even know who he's arguing against?" He paced to the window, and Reggie pounced on his boot. Julius plucked a short bit of rope from the shelf of the library's bookcase and waggled it in front of the dog's nose. Amanda's heart melted. For a man who disclaimed any interest in the pup, Julius seemed most accommodating to Reggie's needs.

Julius looked up at her. "Well?"

Amanda stared at the signature at the bottom of her parchment. It was her handwriting, but not her name. No one would listen to Miss Amanda Wilcox. She was a woman, and a disgraced one at that. But a Mr. A. Wilson? That name sounded strong.

She folded the four pages into three equal sections and tucked the papers into an envelope. "I'm not arguing with anyone. I wrote an opinion piece for *The Times*. I dispute the Marquess of Hanford on several key points regarding his stance on capital punishment. He is free to disagree." Carefully penning the name of the editor on the front of the envelope, Amanda blew on the wet ink.

And her mind flashed back to a very naughty place.

Cheeks warm, she held the envelope out to Julius. "Will you see that this is delivered?"

"If you sign your own name to it." He crossed his arms over his chest. "Obscuring your identity is just another form of hiding."

"I thought you approved of my hiding. Something about it keeping me out of trouble."

"That was last night." He set his jaw. "You'd just scared the dickens out of me."

Amanda kept quiet, and kept her arm out. She had patience, too.

"Fine." Julius blew out a lusty breath. He snatched the envelope from her hand. "But only if you ride with me in the carriage." She opened her mouth to object, but he was faster. "Just ride in the carriage. With the curtains drawn. Most of the way. I will only ride to the newspaper if you are sitting next to me."

"That's blackmail." Amanda rubbed her palms against her skirts. "Earls don't stoop to such lengths."

He snorted. "We're the worst of the bunch. Now, how badly do you want this delivered?"

"I can have Carter send it."

"Not if I tell him not to." Julius raised a dark brow.

He didn't know how right he was. Carter would be only too happy to deny her a service. She looked at the envelope dangling from his fingers, then at the morning paper. How she wanted her voice heard, in a paper she respected. She looked out the window, her heart tripping in her chest.

Did she dare? Her excursion last night hadn't ended well. But if she didn't have to leave the carriage ...

"All right. I'll do it."

Julius beamed, looking much too smug with himself by half. Reggie pounced on his boot, and Julius shook him off.

"But Reggie comes, too." Hearing his name, the dog trotted over to her, and Amanda scooped him up. "He's someone I trust to protect me."

Julius gaped in outrage.

Biting back a smile, Amanda jumped to her feet.

"Shall we go?" If she was going to do something so

foolish, she wanted it done fast. The sooner done, the sooner ended.

"Fine." He slid the envelope into his coat pocket. "Go get a wrap and bonnet, and I'll have the carriage sent around."

She hurried up the stairs, her body a ball of nervous energy. She pulled her spencer from the armoire and stared into the empty space in the corner. She could crawl in there. Curl up. It was quite comfortable. Snug really. Julius wouldn't drag her out of there, kicking and screaming. Probably.

But did she want to be the type of woman who hid among her gowns? She smoothed her hands down the spencer and turned for the hall. Reggie bit the hem of her skirts and waddled backwards, halting her progress. She tugged her gown free. "You're coming, too." She walked to the top of the steps and stared down at the front door. Reggie rushed past her and tumbled down the stairs. His legs slid out from under him on the last step, and he flipped head over paws into the foyer. He popped up at the bottom and trotted to the door, head held high.

Amanda chuckled, and the laughter eased her way down the steps.

Lady Mary clapped her hands together from the entrance of the sitting room. "Marvelous recovery, Reginald." She glanced curiously at Amanda's spencer. "Are you going somewhere, my dear?"

"Julius is driving me to *The Times*." Amanda tugged on a pair of gloves. "If you'd like to accompany us, I'm sure there will be room in the carriage."

"It's too cold for me today." The older woman gave a delicate shiver. "But you two go and enjoy yourselves."

Amanda stared at the footman waiting to open the front door and back at Lady Mary. The woman was supposed to act as chaperone. Would it harm Julius's reputation if he were seen accompanying her unattended? She sniffed, and shook her head at her own folly. It was never the man's reputation that was harmed. And hers couldn't be sullied any further.

There was nothing for it but to gird her loins and venture outside. "Come, Reggie." His solid presence at her side gave her some small solace as she walked through the entry and into the bright afternoon sun. Her feet hardly faltered as she took the steps down to the curb.

Julius opened the carriage door for her, earning a minuscule frown from the footman. Reggie leapt up as if riding in the carriage of a duke was his due. Amanda let Julius hand her in more slowly.

She slid across the seat and made sure the curtain completely covered the window. The carriage rocked as Julius settled in beside her. With a crack of a whip, they jolted forward.

Amanda held her breath, waiting for disaster to strike. Any moment now....

"There's still time to change your signature." Julius picked Reggie up from the seat between them and plopped him down across the way. He slid closer, his thigh nudging hers. "I can have a man bring us a pen when we arrive—"

"No, thank you." Amanda rubbed her cheek and longed for the security of her mask. "My decision stands. But I appreciate your attempt to distract me."

He grumbled. "That wasn't a diversion tactic. I do think you're wrong."

"Yes, we've been over that. Just like you think I'm wrong about the coat of arms on the tall man's coach."

His features were shadowed in the dim interior of the carriage. "You must admit it seems awfully convenient that the family coat of arms you picked out of Edmondson's *Body of Heraldry* just happens to belong to the man who you take to task in your opinion piece." Picking up her hand, he brushed his thumb along her wrist. "It isn't unusual for a strong dislike of someone to cloud one's memory."

"There is nothing wrong with my memory." She was

tempted to pull her hand from his grip, but didn't want to be petty. Besides, it was warm and solid, and she needed something to hold onto. "The coat of arms I saw on the coach last night is the one I picked out of Edmondson's. Just because it belongs to an ignorant buffoon who has no business voting on English law is pure coincidence."

"Yes, you don't sound biased at all."

Amanda frowned. "Are you going to ask Lord Hanford what his coach was doing at The Black Rose? Or does his title allow him the privilege of blackmail?"

His dropped her hand. "No one gets a free pass when it comes to the security of our nation."

Amanda hung her head. "Julius, I apologize. I didn't mean it."

"Didn't you?"

Resting her head on the seat back, Amanda stared into the darkness. There was nothing to say. Julius was a good man, but there was a code, even among good men. By the accident of birth, some men could get away with murder. While she'd been denied a fair trial and evaded a hanging only by a prison escape.

The man next to her had been responsible for her escape. Had saved her life. He was a good man. An honorable one. But if it came down to it, would the Crown look to punish one of its own? Would Julius press the matter?

The coach rattled to a stop, and the silence inside hung heavy. Muffled voices of Londoners strolling past sounded cheerful in comparison.

Julius cleared his throat. "I'll deliver this and be right back."

Laying a hand on his arm, she stopped him. "I truly am sorry."

He nodded and pushed open the carriage door, leaping down, and shutting her in tight.

Reggie snored across from her, giving a little whimper every once in a while. Amanda sighed. She seemed to have the uncanny knack for making those around her unhappy. First Liz, for wasting a year of her life trying to free her sister. Now Julius. Even Reggie suffered from bad dreams.

The air became stifling. Flicking the corner of the curtain back, Amanda lowered the window an inch. A cool breeze wafted through the opening. Men with tall hats strode past. A lady with a lavender parasol and a high-pitched giggle. London teemed with life. And Amanda watched, half-hidden behind the curtain.

Skin itching, she dropped the velvet and smoothed it back into place. She waited for the darkness to soothe her. And waited. It was just her and Reggie, alone in an enclosed box. Her environment was just as she liked it.

So why wasn't she feeling soothed, damn it? Reaching across the carriage, she picked Reggie up and plopped him on her lap. He opened one eye, huffed, and settled back into slumber. His warm body was a comforting weight on her legs, yet the edginess that prickled her skin wouldn't leave her be.

The door was thrown open, and Julius climbed back in. He sat next to her, leaving several inches of bench between them. "It's been delivered. The editor said it would run in the next couple of days."

"He's going to print it?" She clasped her hands together. "Truly?"

"So he said." Pounding the ceiling of the carriage, Julius settled back and stretched his arm along the back of the seat. "Why should that surprise you?"

"I've never been published before." Amanda leaned into his arm. Julius wouldn't understand. For men like him it was taken for granted. If he spoke, people listened. He couldn't understand how voiceless the average woman was.

Thank God she'd written under a pseudonym.

The carriage jolted before turning sharply. It rolled to a stop, and Amanda peeked under the corner of the curtain. "Where are we?"

"I asked the driver to take us across from Hanford's

home. I'm hoping he'll take his coach out today." Julius slid closer to her and draped the curtain over its hold back hook. He looked outside. "I want you to confirm your identification looking at the actual coach and not the picture from a thirty-year-old book."

The back of her eyes burned. He wasn't dismissing her claims. It wasn't absolute trust in her judgment, but it was enough.

She cleared her throat. "So, we just wait and hope?" Amanda leaned forward. Across the street, a short drive led to a four-story brick townhouse. Nothing moved beyond the windows of the house. No footman stood to attention by the front doors. "We could be here forever."

Sliding a pocket watch from his waistcoat, Julius popped open the cover. "It's coming on six o'clock. The time many gentlemen head to the club for a cigar and a drink, maybe read a paper or two before dinner. Be patient."

She sniffed and stared at the drive.

Her neck began to ache from the angle she held it at, and she shifted on the seat. A crush of hackneys clogged the street, the drivers hollering at each other and blocking her view.

She craned her head, unable to see around the blockage. It finally cleared. She sighed. The marquess's front door remained shut. No activity.

Her mind wandered. She wondered where Liz was at that moment. In a museum? Sailing down one of Venice's famed canals? Her eyes lost their focus, the world outside her carriage blurred. As a child, she'd dreamed of travel. India had always held a certain appeal. Did ships have armoires she could barricade herself within? With the great expanse of open sea engulfing the ship, she would need one.

Julius took her hand, stilling the nervous tapping of her fingers against her thigh. "Do you need to return home? Has this been too much for you?"

The worry in his voice carved itself onto her heart. She

cleared her throat. "I'm fine. Merely at a loss of what to do while we wait. Is espionage always this boring?"

He chuckled. "Only if you're fortunate. The alternative is not so pleasant." His thumb stroked hers, sending a tickle to the base of her spine. "Besides, sitting in a carriage with a beautiful woman is not without its enticements."

"Please." Brushing a wayward lock of hair behind her ear, she shook her head. "Beautiful is an overstatement. Especially with my hair in a constant state of disarray. But as you are responsible for the condition of my hair, perhaps you don't notice the disorder."

He trailed his fingers across her nape. "Personally, I like that it looks as though you recently rolled from my bed. But if you want, I'll ask Carter to hire you a new lady's maid."

Amanda angled her head, exposing inches of neck. "As no one sees my hair but you, Lady Mary, and the servants, I don't mind." And she didn't trust Carter to hire her a trustworthy maid. "Do you really keep no"—she shuddered as his lips caressed her collarbone—"no servants at your home?"

"I could only hope." He cupped her breast through her clothes. "At my London townhouse, I keep the bare necessity. A cook. A footman who also is my driver. And two maids come in twice a week to clean. Any more servants than that and they'd be in the way as much as this spencer is." He tried to unbutton it one-handed. "Oh, to hell with this." He hauled her to the edge of the seat, sending Reggie tumbling to the floor with a panicked yip.

Julius cursed. "I forgot about the blasted dog." He picked Reggie up and stroked along his fur, checking for injury. Satisfied, he placed the pup on the seat across from them. "He's fine."

Reggie glared at him, obviously disagreeing. Turning his back, the dog coiled into a ball and heaved a disgruntled sigh.

Amanda bit her lip, smothering her laughter. She couldn't smother her yelp of surprise when Julius dragged her onto his lap.

"Julius, I'm not going to allow you liberties on a public street. It would be—"

A carriage rolled past her window, and she bolted upright. Sliding off Julius's lap, she pressed to the opening, drawing the curtains farther back. "He's not leaving. He's arriving. There it is. The coat of arms on that coach. There's your man." She pointed to the carriage that turned down the drive and stopped before the front doors of Hanford's townhouse. A footman hopped from his perch at the back and disappeared around the side.

Julius nudged her to the side so both of them could see out the window. "Are you certain? It was dark last night, and many family arms can look similar. I can't proceed on intuition."

She narrowed her eyes. "I saw it well enough last night. That is the coat of arms."

An older man with white hair and a cane held loosely in one hand sprang up the steps to the front of the townhouse. He threw his head back and laughed at something his butler said. He patted the man on the arm and strode inside.

"Not the most devilish looking of suspects," Julius muttered.

Amanda frowned. "Looks aren't everything." But she had to admit that the Marquess of Hanford looked more like a doting grandfather than someone involved in a blackmailing ring. Still, that sweet old grandfather had no problem sending ten-year-olds to the noose. She pressed her lips together.

Rubbing his jaw, Julius squinted out the window. "I know he has a son, but I don't think he comes down to London much. I've never met him. I wonder how tall he is."

Amanda settled back into the seat. She thought of the Hanford butler towering over the marquess by several inches. "He might get his height from his mother's side."

"Or it might not be him." He pounded on the ceiling,

and the carriage pulled into the road. "I'm still not convinced you identified the right coat of arms."

"But you'll investigate just the same? You won't let him get away just because he's a marquess?" She didn't know why this was so important to her. It wasn't her task to stop the crime ring. And she'd long since reconciled herself to the fact that the world wasn't fair. Most people were never held to account for their actions. She could only hope justice was served in the afterlife.

Still, she held her breath and waited for his answer. She might not have faith in the world, but she wanted to believe in Julius.

"I'll investigate." Sunlight streaked across his jaw, leaving his eyes in shadow. "But you might not like the outcome. Don't—" He scrubbed his hand across his jaw.

"Don't what?"

"Don't raise your hopes." He laid a hand on her knee and squeezed. "Even if Lord Hanford were no longer a member of Parliament, nothing would change. There are a hundred men who believe just as he does." He shook his head. "The vote won't change if he's arrested."

No, there were thousands of men who supported England's harsh capital punishment laws. But there were also men like Julius, men who wanted reform. And if enough people fought, maybe the minds of people like Lord Hanford could be changed.

She settled back into her seat and gave Julius a reassuring smile. She understood the chances. But with that letter to *The Times* she'd taken a positive step to affect change. She was fighting back.

London rolled past the uncovered window, the slanting sunlight making the stone buildings glow pink. Tradesmen hurried home after their days' labors. Some couples were out for their evening stroll. The city burst with life.

And Amanda didn't once think about closing the curtains.

Chapter Thirteen

Crossing his legs, Julius bobbed the toe of his boot up and down. Liverpool had said to meet him at nine in the evening, but apparently only Julius was expected to be punctual. The dark wood paneling of White's back room made the chamber feel smaller. Oppressive.

Loosening the knot of his cravat, Julius breathed deeply through his nose. Amanda had borne her time out on the streets of London a week ago with admirable fortitude. If she could face her fears so well, he could damn well sit in a small room without breaking into a sweat. Even if the room was windowless. With only one door.

He was fine.

He gripped the armrests of his wingback chair. It had been three years since his return from the East. Would he ever feel natural again?

Liverpool stalked through the door, shutting it with greater energy than necessary. Taking the seat across from Julius, the older statesman crooked his elbow on the armrest and rested his jaw on his knuckles.

The look he sent Julius did nothing to calm his restless nerves.

"I missed my tea because of you." Liverpool plucked a cigar from the silver box on the side table. Not bothering with a knife, he bit off the end and spit it out and dragged a candlestick towards him to light it.

Julius waited until the man was pulling at the flame. "You set the time for our meeting. Though I must say your tea time is extraordinarily late."

Liverpool set the candlestick down on the side table next to his chair. "Cute. But that's not what I meant and you know it." Leaning back in the chair, Liverpool puffed on the cigar and glared at him through the smoke. "I've had a steady stream of peers in my office, gossiping like little old ladies about the debate raging in *The Times* over capital punishment."

"I've had a few of those discussions myself." After Amanda's piece had received the most replies in the paper's history, the editor had requested that Mr. A. Wilson pen another piece. He'd also invited a response from the opposing side. "I hardly understand how I'm responsible for the tumult."

"Don't play the innocent with me," Liverpool said. "I know you delivered the piece by Mr. Wilson."

Of course, he did. Liverpool had informants everywhere. "I'm not the author."

"I never said you were. You don't strike me as a reformer." He coughed and rested the cigar in the ashtray. "But your ward is causing quite the fuss. Perhaps you should put an end to that."

Julius didn't know which claim was more absurd. That Amanda was his ward, or that he had the power to stop her from doing as she wanted. "Miss Wilcox is nobody's ward. She is an unmarried woman who has attained the age of majority. She will do as she wishes." Standing, he strode to the sideboard and poured two fingers of Scotch. "And don't mistake my lack of agitation as a lack of interest in reform. You do know how I voted on the last bill."

"And I respect that vote. But Parliament is the proper place to have the debate. Not in the public papers. And not in my office!" His stern expression softened the slightest bit when Julius put a second tumbler of liquor in his hand. "I hear the chit is a virtual recluse. Don't pretend you couldn't stop her nonsense if you wanted."

Gritting his teeth, Julius turned his back on Liverpool and tramped back to his chair. Slowly, he sank down.

Liverpool didn't know the situation with Amanda. That any nonsense on her part was to be encouraged or risk her withdrawing from life even more than she had. But Liverpool's duty was to protect the empire, at all costs. Individual hardships were of little importance.

"I had an especially galling conversation with Lord Hanford." Liverpool tossed back his Scotch. "The man seemed to take Mr. Wilson's piece as a personal insult. He read me the response he'd written for the paper, word for stumbling word." Running a hand through his greying hair, he huffed out a breath. "Hanford's always been an idiot. Well meaning, but as simple as broth. When I mentioned the true identity of Mr. Wilson, I had to spoon feed him the idea to use that in his response to discredit her."

"You told Hanford that Amanda was the author of the opinion piece?" Heat flushed through Julius's body. If she saw her name in print, read the ridicule and contempt that was sure to come her way, it would strike a blow. A hide-in-the-armoire type of blow that Julius couldn't allow. "She used a pseudonym for a reason."

"And I revealed it for a reason." Minutely shaking his head, Liverpool sighed. "As she can no longer write anonymously, I hope she will stop writing entirely. I will be most unhappy if Lord Hanford finds a reason to come to my office again."

Julius crossed one leg over the other and kept his face calm. He'd have to warn Amanda. Perhaps hide the papers until the scandal blew over. "Well, then, this should make you especially unhappy. Lord Hanford has become the focus of my investigation into the blackmail ring."

Liverpool blinked. "Explain that."

"I have a witness who has identified his carriage as one used by Madame Sable's accomplice." He spared a brief thought as to where The Black Rose's proprietress was now. Liverpool most likely had her secured in a nice set of rooms until the investigation was over. She'd need to be close by for easy access if more questions arose. Although, aside from giving up Mrs. Westmont, Madame Sable claimed to not know the names of any other accomplices. Her information was turning out to be less than useful.

"You can't think—"

"I know her accomplice isn't Hanford himself." Resting his glass on his thigh, Julius cocked his head. "His son?"

"That boy is as bumbling as his father. And about as tall. He doesn't match your description."

"A nephew, perhaps? My witness was most certain." Certain, and biased. He didn't think Amanda would intentionally lie about the coat of arms, but if she were already predisposed not to like Lord Hanford, who knew what her heart would see. After months of solitary confinement, Julius knew the mind could be as deceitful as a Haymarket guttersnipe.

Liverpool slouched. "As stupid as Lord Hanford is, he'd make the perfect pawn. He could be holding meetings for the inner circle of the crime ring in his library without even knowing it." He pointed a finger at Julius and glared at him beneath his bushy brows. "And that's all the more reason to keep your girl out of the papers. If Hanford is a pawn, the crime ring will become nervous if he's made the center of attention. No, in order to keep your investigation running smoothly, this debate over the reform bill needs to be shelved. Understand?"

Julius's stomach dropped. "And how do you suggest I stop it?"

"Confiscate her mail. Tell the chit the paper doesn't want to publish her anymore. Not with her identity revealed." Liverpool narrowed his eyes. "Lie. That is what I've hired you for."

"Last time I checked, I volunteered." Julius gripped his tumbler. "You don't pay me or my friends anything. We do it out of duty. And we can stop anytime we like."

"The government might not pay you in pounds, but don't deny the certain favors you lot have received." Liverpool sat forward. "Most recently, a girl was pardoned after stabbing her father to death."

"After the Crown had denied her rights to a fair trial, she deserved that pardon!" Julius exploded from his chair. "Do not threaten her."

Leaning back, Liverpool laced his fingers together and rested his palms against his round stomach. "Interesting." His gaze was inscrutable. "A pardon can't be taken back. She's safe." He paused for a moment. "Are you?"

"I'm fine." Julius paced the small room, needing this meeting to be over. The walls loomed closer than ever. He jerked on his cravat.

"Are you certain?" Liverpool cocked his head, his eyes not missing anything. "I can have Sutton take point on this investigation. If you need to escape London for a bit, we'll manage. You can take the girl with you."

As if distance from London would bank Amanda's fire for justice. Liverpool might have his finger in every pie, know what every citizen was up to, but he didn't understand the female mind.

Julius gripped the back of the chair and looked the man in the eye. "As I said, I'm fine. And Sutton is busy trying to keep The Black Rose operational. He's placed a supposed friend of Madame Sable's in there as manager to try to divert suspicion."

Liverpool snorted. "That's not likely. I'm certain whoever is in charge of the blackmailing ring already knows she's been picked up. The group is too canny to believe her letter expressing a sudden desire for travel." Picking up his cigar, he tapped off the ash and stuck it between his lips, sucking hard. "I wonder if they'll try to influence the new manager."

"We can only wait and see." Julius gathered his coat. "In the meantime, I've put people on Lord Hanford, see if any of his associates meet the description of Madame Sable's associate. And I'll try to find out if he's been withdrawing large sums recently. He could be a victim, too."

"Thankfully the man isn't on any private committees in

Parliament. He doesn't have much more knowledge than the general public on matters of state." He blew out a long stream of smoke. "Keep his involvement in this as quiet as possible. And let's keep him out of the papers, too. Which means—"

"No more letters to the editor baiting him." Shrugging into his coat, Julius set his mouth in a grim line. That was much easier said than done. Amanda's fight over reform was the only thing to bring a spark back into her eye. That and their nightly romps. But he couldn't keep her tied to his bed permanently. No matter how appealing the idea.

"Tell Montague I know of some men who wouldn't hold Miss Wilcox's past against her." Liverpool shrugged. "As you said, she has no husband to control her. If he wants her married off and out of his hair, have him contact me when he returns from his bridal tour."

Julius bit back a snarl. That wasn't going to happen. Amanda wasn't going to be married off, not to one of Liverpool's yes-men. And any man who wouldn't mind her past could hardly be of the quality that she deserved.

He turned to leave, and Liverpool stopped him. "One last thing, Rothchild. You no longer have to search for Mrs. Westmont."

"You've found her?"

"Her body." Liverpool took a sip of his drink. "She was dragged out of the Thames a week ago. I only received the information today."

Julius swallowed. He knew how difficult it could be to identify a body pulled from the water. The distortions that took place on soft flesh. The bits the fish took away. He could only guess as to who put her there.

With a nod, he stalked from the room, slamming the door behind him. He wanted to slam the whole damn place down. All of London's clubs were filled with smug men and even smugger servants. Knowing they had life by the balls; not caring how the other half lived. A footman leapt to open the front door before him, and Julius growled. How could a class of men who couldn't even open their own doors rule the world?

He stopped on the sidewalk, the cold night air burning his lungs as he sucked it down. He raised his face to the skies and wished the light rain pelting his face could rinse the taint of his meeting away. Liverpool was right. He wasn't a reformer. Julius could see the injustices, but he wasn't the man trying to change them. If he saw a weaker man being beaten, or a woman being abused, he was only too happy to step in. Bloodying his knuckles, breaking noses, those were the fights he was good at. That he enjoyed. But fighting an entire system ...?

He waved his carriage off, not wanting to face the prospect of being cooped up for the ride home. Flipping the collar of his coat up to block out the drizzle, he turned his steps towards Montague's townhouse, letting the wind and rain cool his anger.

But the loathing didn't fade. He wasn't the man to fight the system. But apparently he was the man to block Amanda from her fight. He hated doing it, but Liverpool was right. It was necessary. Change on the scale Amanda wanted would take years, if it ever happened. The threat from the blackmailing ring was immediate. And if they were using Lord Hanford, Julius needed to make sure the man stayed out of the public eye as much as possible.

Amanda's calling him out by name hadn't been helpful. Perhaps Hanford wouldn't have been so quick to take offense if she hadn't. But she was a reasonable woman, he consoled himself. Eager to help him with his task. She'd understand why she had to stop writing her opinion pieces.

And if Julius believed that, he knew as much about the female mind as Liverpool.

Chapter Fourteen

A floorboard creaked, and Amanda called out, "Hullo? Is anybody there?"

It was the second time she'd asked, and like before only silence greeted her. Standing from the small desk in her bedchamber, she picked up her candle and crept to her door. She stretched her hand to the latch, pulse pounding, and jerked it back.

She was being silly. Houses settled. Boards creaked. It didn't mean there was anyone lurking outside her door, peering through the keyhole, ready to burst in on her with a knife in his hand and murder in his eyes.

She twisted the lock in the door and stumbled back. Her imagination was running wild. But with the wind howling outside, rain pounding against her window, and Julius gone out, it was a night for dark inventions. The friendly blaze in her hearth wasn't enough to dispel the gloom.

Reggie snored on her bed, apparently unconcerned of the potential for nighttime intruders. Amanda returned to her desk, ignoring the shadows thrown into the corners from her flickering candle. She was used to the dark. The dark was her friend.

Another squeak, and her shoulder blades slammed together. Just the house settling.

There was a loud thud, and the door rattled in its frame. A curse followed.

Leaving the candle on the desk, she flew to the door and unlocked it, pulling it open. Julius stood in front of her, rubbing his nose. He pushed past her, frowning.

"Why the devil is your door locked? Is someone here?" He paced to each corner, looking behind chairs and curtains.

Amanda scowled. "Who would be here? Mr. Carter?" She shouldn't blame Julius for being suspicious. Since they'd started their affair, she'd never locked her door. "How long were you lurking out there? The creaking floors... concerned me."

"I just arrived home." He flopped into her armchair and stretched his legs out to the fire. His silk waistcoat pulled tight across his chest. "It was probably just one of Marcus's many servants, creeping about. We should go to my house. We'd have more privacy."

"And Lady Mary? She's to join us in such an improper situation?" Amanda wrapped her arms around her body. "We are already skirting the appearance of respectability by you being placed here as my and Lady Mary's protector. A move to your house would lose even that vestige."

"Blast." He scrubbed a hand across his jaw. "Just as well. Marcus would have my hide if I secreted you away. Although he won't be too pleased with the situation here, either."

Amanda stood next to him, her night rail brushing against his thigh. Her fingers itched to tuck the errant lock of hair out of his eyes and smooth the wrinkles from his brow. But something about such an intimate gesture made her shy. She'd opened her body to him. She was being silly. Still, she couldn't make her hand stretch forward. A world of meaning would be in that simple caress. It would tell Julius more than she wanted him to know.

"I won't tell Liz about us, not if it will endanger your friendship with Marcus." Amanda clasped her hands together. "If you don't tell Marcus, he'll never have to know." Which meant their intimacies would have to end upon her sister's and her new husband's return. There would be no sneaking around. Julius wouldn't be climbing through her window at night.

He'd most likely feel their affair had come to its natural conclusion, anyway. That Amanda's fear of being touched had been overcome. That his job was done.

Putting his hands on her hips, he guided her into a straddle across his thighs. "I'll not go out of my way to declare our relationship, but I won't lie to my friend, either. Marcus has a sharp eye. I don't think he'll miss the changes between us." He trailed his fingers across her collarbone and tugged at the tie at her neck. Her night dress loosened and slipped off one shoulder.

Amanda licked her bottom lip. "I don't want to get between you and your friend. Perhaps"—she shuddered under his open-mouthed kiss on her bare skin—"perhaps we should end this now."

It would destroy her if he agreed. But his friendship with Marcus was for life. Their affair would end regardless.

"Don't be an idiot." He slid the other side of her night rail off her other shoulder, his fingers scraping her flesh. The thin cotton pooled at her elbows and waist. He urged her pelvis closer to his. "This isn't ending before it has to." With the flat of his tongue, he swiped across her nipple. Pulling back, he blew a stream of air across her damp skin. Both her nipples hardened to aching peaks.

She started to pull her arms from the sleeves, but Julius stopped her. "Wait," he said. Taking the loose ends of the sleeves, he began tying the ends, pulling the fabric tight and pinning her arms.

"Stop." Her heart warmed at how quickly Julius released her sleeves, the concern in his eyes, even as her arms mourned the loss of their bonds. But her time with him was finite. And she'd entered this arrangement wanting to stretch her limits, needing to explore her sensuality. As much as she adored being restrained, there had to be more.

"Are you all right?" A crease formed in the skin above his nose. "Did it bring back a bad memory?"

"Not at all."

"You no longer like being restrained?" Julius asked, his

voice a monotone.

"Don't be an idiot." She threw his words back at him with a smile. Shrugging out of the sleeves, she placed a palm over his heart, felt the rise and fall of his chest. He cupped her breast in a mirror action, and she arched into him. "I adore it. When you tie me up, it's the only time I feel truly safe."

"You are safe," he said gruffly. "Then why—"

"Because sometimes I want to touch you, too." She unbuttoned his waistcoat, taking her time to caress the ridges of his stomach through each inch of shirt she revealed. She slid the cravat off his neck, frowning at the wet fabric, and tossed it to dry before the fire. "Tupping can't only be about having things done to me. Can it?" she asked, furrowing her brow.

"It can." Julius gathered her hair together and draped it over a shoulder so it covered one breast. "But I understand what you're saying. You want to participate more actively."

Lowering her head, she kissed the bronze vee of skin exposed at his collar. "Not all the time. But tonight, yes." She tugged at his shirt, pulling it free from his trousers, and brushed the back of her fingers across his bare stomach. The muscles tensed beneath her touch. "Is that all right?"

Julius leaned forward and shucked his coat and waistcoat in record time. Grabbing the neck of his shirt, he yanked it over his head and tossed it to the floor. "More than all right. I want you to explore. As long as you're not planning on tying me up, I'm game for anything."

Amanda cocked her head. She glanced at her four-poster bed. She could picture Julius, one limb tied to each post, his body straining against his bonds, her hands roaming his unprotected flesh.

She wriggled against his thighs. She liked that picture. Very much.

Julius narrowed his eyes. "Never going to happen."

Her body cooled, and she dropped her head. That was his worst nightmare and she was fantasizing about it.

She wrapped her arms around him and pressed close. "Of course not. I just want to touch."

The heat from his bare chest warmed her front. The light dusting of his hair tickled her breasts. Burying her nose at the crook of his neck, she inhaled his bergamot scent.

He smelled like home.

It would be so much easier to let Julius take control. Easier, but she'd feel like she'd missed out on an experience. Sitting up, Amanda glided her hands along his shoulders. She found the notch where his collar bone ended at his arm and circled her thumbs into the flesh.

Julius grimaced.

Amanda jerked back. "Are you injured? Did I hurt you?"

"Yes and no." Taking her hands, he put them both on his left shoulder. "The pain was momentary. A light rub is actually good for it."

Tentative, she softly kneaded his skin, examining him for any signs of distress. Julius tipped his head back and rested it on the chair. He sighed, his face relaxing.

She increased the pressure the tiniest bit. "How did you hurt your shoulder?"

"In prison." He rested his palms on her thighs. "Being tied in one position for too long can cause permanent damage. I don't have quite the same range of motion in my left arm as I do my right."

If she could find every last one of his gaolers and hold hot pokers to their feet, she would. With the heel of her hands, she skimmed along his collar bone. The strong column of his throat was exposed, and she couldn't help but lean forward and take a little nibble.

His chest vibrated beneath hers. She slid her hands from his shoulders, down his ribs, and to the buttons of his falls.

He gripped her wrists. "Before we go any further, I need to tell you something."

"All right." Her palms grew damp. He sounded unusually serious.

"Lord Hanford knows you are Mr. Wilson." His jaw hardened. "He will most likely expose your identity in his response to *The Times*."

Amanda opened her mouth. Closed it. She hadn't been expecting that. By tomorrow, everyone could be gossiping about her. Sneering as they said her name. She waited for the panic to come.

And waited. Aside from a slight queasiness in her stomach, the news didn't affect her overmuch. She wouldn't see the sneers. She wouldn't be attending any public event to suffer the cut direct.

All those letters others had written to support her stance, those would stop. And that hurt. She tipped up her chin. "I am sorry that my notoriety will hurt the cause for reform. The laws need to be changed. And I may have just set that movement back."

"You did your best." Julius squeezed her leg. "There are plenty of others who can take up the mantle."

Yes, it would be someone else's cause now. She swallowed past the lump in her throat. It was better this way. Liz didn't need a sister whose shame was constantly paraded through the papers of London.

And Julius didn't need a morose lover. She'd spent too many years dispirited, hollow. She wasn't going to let such a minor thing as her name in the papers bring her low again. She rubbed a hand over the front of his trousers. "Anything else you'd like to discuss?"

He shook his head, his eyes glazing over.

"Good." She pushed his trousers and smallclothes down his hips and gave his hard length a stroke. "Because I, for one, am through talking."

Standing, she let her night rail fall from her hips to the floor and stepped out from the cotton puddle. Her toes curled into the pile carpet. Julius sat before her, legs spread wide, elbows resting on the arms of the chair. Hints of red glittered in his brown hair. His sinewy chest gleamed golden from the firelight. And from the careless sprawl of his trousers, his length rose proudly, ruddy and majestic.

He looked like a dissolute king on his throne, and she didn't know which royal bit of him to worship first.

She swiped her night dress off the floor and folded it into a neat rectangle. Placing it as his feet, she knelt upon it, her shoulders brushing the insides of his knees.

Julius shifted.

The tension rolled off of him in waves, and Amanda's heart tripped with anticipation. Running her hands up his thighs, she felt every inch of his muscle beneath the wool. The power that he held so contained. A power he never used against her.

Amanda dug her fingers into the bunched fabric at his hips. Other men had taken. Her dignity. Her permission. But not the joy that could be found between a man and woman. Julius had shown her that it could still exist, had breathed that part of her into life.

She wasn't broken.

Her hands tingled. Amanda may have been on her knees before Julius, but she felt tall enough to touch the heavens.

Shuffling closer, she circled his navel with her index finger. She traced the fine hairs that arrowed down, down ...

Julius sucked in a sharp breath. Taking pity, she trailed her finger down the base of his length and up to the crown. She fisted him, and slowly pumped up and down. His skin was so soft, so warm, but underneath he was as hard as stone.

Julius released his breath on a groan. He stared at the ceiling. "That feels so good."

"What feels better?" She added her second hand at his base, and gripped him tighter as she eased up to his head. "This? Or when you slide inside of me?"

"I'll not be comparing the pleasures of your body. Everything about you feels good." He lifted his head and stared into her eyes.

She shifted her thighs together. "Hmm. A very

diplomatic answer. Perhaps you need more information to compare." Tilting her head, she licked the underside of his shaft, following the course of a thick vein than ran its length. She'd heard enough bawdy talk at the prison to know men could derive pleasure from a woman's mouth. She could only hope she'd please Julius. His crown peeked out from the surrounding skin, glistening with moisture. She suckled at the tip. He tasted of salt and musk, and she drew harder.

Julius groaned. He pushed her hair back from her face and gripped her head in his hands. Chest heaving, he stared at where her lips touched his flesh. "Amanda, you don't have to do this. I don't expect reciprocity."

"I know I don't have to." She held his throbbing flesh to her cheek. This man demanded nothing from her, took nothing. "And that's why I want to." Sliding her hand down, she tightened the skin of his shaft and licked his length again. She rolled her tongue around the crown, dug the tip into the small crevice.

He moaned.

"As this is my first time," she said, swiping her tongue across the soft sac of his bollocks, "I welcome any instruction."

"You're doing marvelously." He watched her under heavy-lidded eyes as she stroked and licked his cock, pausing to suckle the tip from time to time.

His legs shifted. "Can you ...?"

She lifted her head but kept her hand moving, from his base to the crown and back again. "Yes?"

"Take me deeper." He covered her hand with his and tightened her grip. "When you suck, take me as deep as you're able."

Rising up on her knees, she enclosed her lips around him and sucked him into her mouth as far as was comfortable. He moaned, gripping her head but letting her maintain her pace. She looked into his eyes intently, loving the pleasure she saw there.

He tightened his right hand in her hair and dropped his

left to her breast. He rolled her nipple and pinched hard to match the deep draw she took. She whimpered, the sound muffled as he drew her head closer.

The apex of her thighs grew slick. Her core ached. She sucked harder. She let his shaft slide over her tongue until it nudged the back of her throat. Her body involuntarily swallowed.

His hand jerked in her hair, making her eyes sting, before he relaxed his hold. "Do that again," he breathed.

She tried. Her body rebelled, and she had to pull back for some deep breaths, before going in again. A bead of liquid oozed from his tip, and she licked it away. She wanted to taste all of him. Swallowing his head, she bobbed up and down, gripping his base with both hands. She squeezed her thighs together and whimpered.

With his hand guiding her movements, she took him deeper each slide until she developed a pattern. Her mind blanked as her body focused on this one act. Her throat loosened, and she inched him deeper.

His scent filled her nose. His taste was imprinted on her tongue. In that moment, he was her world.

Her whispered name roused her from her stupor.

"Touch yourself," he demanded. "Put your hand between your legs, and stroke yourself, just like this." He caressed the side of her breast. "I want to watch your face as you come, feel the vibration of your moans around my cock as you break apart."

He took control of her head, smoothing out the up and down motion, slowing the pace. Leaving her free to concentrate on her own pleasure. Slowly, she eased her fingers between her thighs. Touching herself in front of Julius, felt ... wicked. Wanton. Like something one of Madame Sable's girls would do.

At the first glide of her fingers against her clit, she stopped thinking about propriety. She widened her legs and rubbed harder.

"Easy." Licking his thumb, Julius circled her nipple.

"Slow, like this." He shifted his hips. "Brush your fingers down your lips and ease two into that sweet cunny. Get them good and wet. Then glide them in circles around your little bud."

Amanda obeyed. Somehow, her foray into taking control had rebounded. From the hand at her head to the commands he gave, Julius was directing the show.

If her body wasn't on fire, and her mouth hadn't been full, she would have one or two choice things to say about that.

Her fingers slipped through her folds, circling her clit faster and faster. With her other hand, she pressed Julius's hand tight to her breast. He got the message and tugged on her nipple, rolling it to a hard point. Sensation shot from her breast to her core. Her fingers faltered, gave one last swirl, and her body pulsed with pleasure.

She moaned, and Julius twitched in her mouth.

"Mother of God." Threading his fingers through the hair at her scalp, he brushed her cheek with his thumb. "That was beautiful." After she recovered her breath, he urged her head lower. "I'm going to come in that pretty mouth, and you're going to take it all down. Isn't that right, mouse?"

Yes. She wanted that, too. She clutched at his trousers, and let the feel of him rolling against her tongue, scraping against the roof of her mouth, subsume her. She wanted his release, as much as he'd wanted hers.

He thrust his hips to meet her mouth. His heaving breaths melded with the crackling of the fire. "I'm going to..."

Amanda sucked him as deep as she could, felt him jerk, and liquid heat coated the back of her throat. She swallowed and watched his eyes slide close, saw his cheeks stain the color of brick. He groaned, loud and long, and satisfaction oozed through her body.

When he sagged back into the chair, a boneless heap, she eased her mouth up his length. She licked around the crown, cleaning him up, and he made a sound of protest.

"No more. I beg of you."

Laying her head on his thigh, she calmed her own breathing. As far as educations went, Julius had turned out to be an outstanding teacher. Never in her life had she thought that she'd be capable of doing so much with a man. Of feeling so much.

When Liz and Marcus returned, would he ...?

She slammed the doors shut in her mind on that thought. No use hurting herself today on what was sure to come tomorrow. Enjoy the moment. If her past life had taught her anything, it was finding the joys in the seconds between.

Julius stroked her hair, a soothing caress. She closed her eyes, fatigue digging in its claws. She blinked back awake as Julius scooped her onto his lap. He picked his coat up from the floor and draped it over her.

"There is a very nice bed not five feet away," she mumbled. "Why don't we move over there?"

"We will. When I have recovered." He tucked a lock of hair behind her ear. "Although Reggie seems to be taking up half the thing. He pretends to sleep, but I know he was watching." His chest rose and sank with his sigh. "Debauched dog."

She threaded her fingers through the hair on his chest and smiled.

"The next couple of days in the papers are going to be rough." Resting a hand on her rump, he pulled her closer. "Perhaps you shouldn't read them. I can tell Carter to keep them out of the morning room."

"Don't bother. I can handle rough."

He hesitated. "You don't know how vicious the ton can be. Even the Cits love nothing more than to moralize. A woman who killed her father lecturing about capital punishment? They will eat you alive."

She rubbed his shoulder and tried to sound more confident than she felt. "It isn't people's words that frighten me. A little public mockery is nothing I can't handle."

"Fine." His voice was resigned. "It should all die down in a couple of days, now that Mr. Wilson has stopped writing."

Amanda nodded, her heart thumping painfully, and braced for the storm.

* * *

The storm arrived in the form of five bluestockings on her doorstep the very next day.

Her morning had started out badly. Waking up with cold sheets beside her and nothing to keep her warm but a banked fire. She should be accustomed to it. No matter how entwined her body was with Julius's when she fell asleep, she always awoke alone.

Julius couldn't stand to be trapped with her until the morning.

She shouldn't take it personally. She suspected he had been more open with her than with any of his past lovers. But when she stared at the expanse of empty bed, her foolish heart couldn't help but twist.

Breakfast hadn't fared much better. Julius was absent, leaving her alone with the Lady Mary. Her companion felt the need to read each and every word written about the scandalous Mr. Wilson and his secret identity. She read them with relish, as if expecting Amanda to find the same joy at each insult to her person as her chaperone seemed to feel.

She had taken a book from the library and was about to scurry upstairs and hide away in her bedroom when she heard Carter speaking to someone at the front door. And informing her that Amanda was not receiving visitors.

She paused, foot on the bottom step. Did she receive visitors? For the past two years the question had never arisen. Liz had visited her in prison, but that hardly counted. Did she want to receive visitors?

She squared her shoulders. As Carter seemed set against the idea it seemed only right that she engaged in the pastime.

She hurried forward as the butler began to shut the door. "Wait! I'm here." She ignored Carter's sniff of disapproval and peered onto the porch. Five sets of owlish eyes stared back.

One of the woman, wearing a patchwork gown of colors so garish it made Amanda dizzy, stepped forward. "You are Miss Amanda Wilcox? The Amanda Wilcox who wrote under the pseudonym Mr. A. Wilson?"

Amanda's shoulders drooped. They were an unusual looking group for a morality league, with their abundance of spectacles and sturdy boots. But she supposed indignation came in all shapes and styles.

"Yes. I wrote the pieces." She clasped her hands before her. "If you have any responses, I know *The Times* is only too happy to publish them." Each and every last excoriating letter.

The woman clasped a parasol to her stomach. "I am Mrs. Elizabeth Fry. We are the Ladies' Society for Prison Reform, and we'd like to discuss the next steps of your plan."

A woman with a small nosegay of violets pinned to her bonnet poked the speaker in the back. "I thought we'd agreed to call ourselves Women Standing Together Can Break the Chains of Bondage."

Mrs. Fry rolled her eyes. "A bit wordy, don't you think? May we come in? There is much to discuss and little time."

Amanda's gaze darted between the women and she snapped her mouth shut. She cleared her throat. "Yes. Of course." Throwing open the door, she stepped to the side. "We can adjourn to the ... uh ..."

"Perhaps your guests would be most comfortable in the bronze sitting room," Carter suggested. Amanda almost sent him a grateful smile before she remembered that sitting room was at the rear of the townhouse, its windows only facing into the backyard. Less chance of anyone seeing the motley group in the duke's home.

Still, it was a comfortable room. "Yes." She turned to lead the women back. "Please have refreshments sent up," she told Carter, her voice airy, as though she gave orders to servants every day of the year. She could feel his disgust burning into her back.

The Ladies' Society settled themselves on the settees. Mrs. Fry sat on the armrest, her leg swinging. "We didn't expect to find a fellow reformer in the home of a duke." Leaning forward, she picked up a Venetian glass bowl and turned it in her hands. When she casually flipped it over, Amanda's heart lodged in her throat. She didn't know how valuable the bowl was, but knowing the duke's tastes, she could guess it was worth more than she was.

She gently pried the bowl from Mrs. Fry and placed it back on the table. Out of the woman's reach. "What was it you wanted to discuss? I believe I laid out all my views in the two pieces *The Times* published. I don't think I have much more to say on the matter."

The woman with the flowers in her hat scooted to the end of her seat. "Nothing more needs to be said. It's action that is called for."

Mrs. Fry sighed. "Perhaps we should start with introductions. The firebrand over there is Miss Bernice Shaw. The one next to her is Mrs. Jane Smuthers." The redhead nodded a greeting. "And the two sisters"—Mrs. Fry pointed to the two women with strikingly similar features on the other settee—"are Gladys McGuire and Gwyneth Bartlett." She poked her parasol into the floor. "The six of us are going to end capital punishment in England."

Amanda counted, and counted again. "Do you have another member?"

"Of course."

Amanda's shoulders sagged with relief.

The parasol poked at the air by Amanda's chest. "You are the sixth member of the Ladies' Society for Prison Reform," Mrs. Fry said.

"Women Standing Together Can Break the Chains of

Bondage," Miss Shaw muttered.

Amanda blinked rapidly. "I'm really not one for joining groups."

"Nonsense. The cause needs you."

"Then the cause is in trouble." Perching on the edge of an armchair, Amanda linked her fingers together, the tips turning white. "In case you haven't yet read the morning papers, I am the last spokeswoman your cause needs."

"Rubbish." Mrs. Fry slashed her parasol through the air, the tip knocking a brass box off a side table. Cigars spilled across the Aubusson carpet.

One of the sisters popped up and put it all to rights. She tucked a lock of her short ash blond hair behind her ear and gave Amanda a small smile.

"You are exactly what we need." Mrs. Fry leaned forward. "A woman who's faced the devil. Who's felt the burn of the noose against her neck, only for the government to later realize its mistake."

Amanda laid her hand on her throat. Rope had never encircled it, thank goodness, but after Mrs. Fry's impassioned statement she could almost feel the sting. She'd have to tell Julius her neck was off limits to his rope.

"Only a person who has escaped the Tyburn Tree has the true authority borne of experience to speak of reform." Mrs. Fry stabbed the air. "You are exactly what we need."

Amanda shrank back from the make-shift rapier. The reformer would be wicked in a duel.

"And you've already brought such consciousness to the issue," Mrs. Smuthers said. "All of our efforts combined haven't garnered as much attention as your two pieces. And you've even made that despicable Lord Hanford try to defend himself."

"Exactly." Mrs. Fry stood and paced the room, a bundle of bright colors and contained energy. Grey was just beginning to encroach on the hair at her temples, and Amanda was surprised the woman didn't demand its retreat. She seemed much too indomitable to submit to anything, even time. "By responding to you, Lord Hanford has given you credibility. People have to listen. I think we should call for a public debate."

One of the sisters, Gladys perhaps, clapped her hands. "Ooh, that's a lovely idea. Where should we hold it? On the front steps of Parliament? Or perhaps The Queen's Palace?"

Amanda curled back into her chair. She shot a longing glance at the door. Why had she contradicted Carter and let these women in the door? She licked her lips. "I'm sure a debate would be most informative. And I think you should do it. You. Not me. Never me."

Five rounded sets of eyes landed on her. "Of course, you must do it," Miss Shaw said. "You against Lord Hanford. It's the only partnering that makes sense."

Amanda smothered a hysterical chuckle and pressed her fingers against her lips. Ever since she'd awoken this morning, nothing had made sense. The idea of her, in public, debating a marquess .... That was the exact opposite of sense.

She gripped her skirts. "I'm sorry you've come all this way, but that just isn't possible. You've wasted your time."

"Hogwash." Mrs. Fry had as many colorful interjections as patches on her dress. "We can help you prepare, of course. And we'll advertise it in other papers to ensure a large audience. But it must be you to debate. Surely you see that."

What Amanda saw were five dotty women who actually thought they had a chance at getting a debate with a member of the House of Lords. Who thought that Amanda was as mad as they were, that she'd join in their insanity.

Amanda firmed her voice. "It's not possible," she repeated. The back of her throat burned with restrained emotion. Had she a typical childhood, a loving parent, would her answer have been different? If she'd never set foot in Newgate Prison, would she have had the courage of these women? Stood in front of hundreds of people and spoken her mind?

Perhaps. But if all those circumstances had been met, she most likely wouldn't have given the topic of capital punishment a second thought. She would have been married off to a country vicar, or a man of business, and taken the views of her husband.

She pursed her lips. Either way, these women expected too much. But she did want to help their cause. "I can't debate Lord Hanford in public, but I will respond to his article in the paper. If the editor will publish it, now that my identity is known."

Mrs. Fry scoffed. "Of course, he will publish it. Do you know how many people will buy his paper now that an admitted murderess is writing for it? You should demand a percentage of his profits."

Amanda's eyes widened. "I admitted to killing my father, but murderess goes a bit far. I was defending—"

Swishing the parasol inches from Amanda's face, the reformer cut her silent. "Irrelevant. The point is that capital punishment shouldn't exist for anyone. Getting the law passed eliminating it for children is merely a start." She sat on the coffee table, her knees bumping Amanda's. "Your letters are all very well and good. As a first step. But the next step is confronting the men responsible for that archaic policy. You simply must agree to the debate."

Amanda freed the Venetian glass bowl from under the woman's skirts. She ground her jaw. Her admiration for the Ladies' Society for Prison Reform was swiftly declining. "The debate that doesn't exist? Lord Hanford would never debate any of us. There is no benefit to him. And I will say for the last time that my leaving this house to enter into any debate is impossible."

Gladys, or perhaps Gwyneth, piped up. "You've already engaged his interest enough to respond to your letter. Is it really so outrageous to think you might lead him to a debate?"

"Very well said, Gwyneth. Now"—Mrs. Fry tapped the

ground between her feet with the tip of the parasol—"about your debate."

"There. Is. No. Debate." Amanda breathed deeply through her nose, trying to calm her irritation. "I will send another letter to the editor, and that is all I'll agree to." And she was beginning to regret even that commitment. "Now, if you ladies will excuse me, I should get started on my response to Lord Hanford." She stood and strode to the door.

Mrs. Fry flattened her mouth into a hard line. Using the handle of her parasol, she pushed to standing, and the rest of the women followed suit. "Very well. I look forward to reading your next piece."

Miss Shaw pressed a folded piece of paper into Amanda's hand as she passed. "We meet every Tuesday evening at Gwynnie's house. Her husband is bedridden, so doesn't mind us in his sitting room. Come if you're able."

"Thank you." She led the group to the front door and waited as the footman pulled it open. "I wish your group much success." But she wouldn't be part of it. Lord, was that how she sounded to Julius when she discussed her ideas? Like a zealot? Mrs. Fry's passion, while admirable, was also highly provoking.

She should refrain from discussing her next piece with Julius. He could wait to hear her ideas when they were published, like everyone else.

Mrs. Fry halted on the top step and thrust open the parasol. As it was neither raining at the moment, nor sunny, Amanda didn't quite see the point. The reformer tilted up her chin. "If we can get Lord Hanford to accede to a public debate, will you agree?"

Clutching the door frame, Amanda shook her head.

"You will agree to at least think about it," Mrs. Smuthers said. She tossed the end of her shawl over her shoulder. "Reasonable people at least think of all the possibilities before refusing. And I know from your writing that you're reasonable."

"Well, of course I'm reasonable—"

"Good. It's settled." Mrs. Fry took the steps at a parade march. "We'll let you know what we hear from Lord Hanford."

Amanda watched their backs as they filed down to the sidewalk and turned left at the street. It was several moments after they'd disappeared from sight that Amanda stepped back inside the house. "You can tell Mr. Carter to cancel the refreshments for my guests," she told the footman.

He twisted his lips before giving her a quick nod, and Amanda knew that no tea service had been prepared. Not for her and her irregular company. The disrespect was rising to intolerable levels, and she pondered telling Julius. But he'd just dismiss all the servants, and then where would she and Lady Mary be? Amanda didn't know how to cook and she doubted the aunt of a duke did, either.

Sighing, she strolled back to the breakfast room and poked her head inside. Empty of the older woman. But *The Times* still lay on the table. Amanda scooped it up and carried it back to her room. She would need to reread Lord Hanford's arguments now that she'd agreed to try to refute them.

Pulling open the drapes of her bedroom window to let in the grey light, she leaned against the sill and gathered her nerve. Reading the attacks, the insults to her person wasn't easy. But considering she refused to debate in person, it was the least she could do.

She might not be a firebrand, but she could still help the cause. She opened her window for some fresh air, then settled at her small escritoire and began to write.

Chapter Fifteen

Julius tapped the folded papers against his thigh and waited for his horse to be brought around. Glancing back at the closed front door, he swore he could feel Amanda's presence behind it. Leaning against the barrier, yearning to come out.

He'd thought after their trip to the newspaper office, she'd be eager to leave the house again, but she'd flatly refused his invitation. She didn't seem any closer to ending her exile than before.

She'd written again. Under her own name this time. If he weren't so worried he'd have been proud. He'd tried to blackmail her again, threatening not to deliver the letter unless she accompanied him. But the attempt had been half-hearted, and they'd both known it. Amanda needed to want to come out on her own.

Tucking the missive into the inside pocket of his coat, he grabbed the saddle of the horse a stable boy led before him and swung himself up. He tugged the thoroughbred's head around and dug his heels into its flanks.

And pulled up short.

He should burn the letter. Tell Amanda he'd delivered it to the paper, and they refused to publish it. That's what was best for his assignment.

"Damn and blast." He kicked the horse's flanks and sped off. Towards the offices of *The Times*. It wasn't Amanda's fault she'd riled up Lord Hanford. Julius had plans to speak with him and he'd just add in the suggestion that he stay out of the papers for the time being. It was the marquess's letters that were the problem for his investigation, not Amanda's.

How could he take away the one thing that renewed her interest in the world?

The editor nearly ripped the papers from his hands when he arrived at the newspaper's office. "'Bout time she wrote something more."

"Lord Hanford's response was published only yesterday." Julius sucked at a papercut on his thumb.

"And this morning I got five hundred new letters to the editor weighing in about this controversy." The man flipped through the pages Amanda had written. "The papers have been selling faster than a harbor whore on payday this past week."

Julius raised an eyebrow. "Does that mean you'll publish Miss Wilcox, even under her true name?"

"Damn right it does." The editor rubbed his jaw, leaving a smear of ink. "With this new steam printing method, we can now print a thousand sheets an hour. You tell her to keep 'em coming as fast as she can. We'll keep up." He chortled. "Old Tobias down at *The London Chronicle* never had an escaped prisoner writing for his pages."

Julius clenched his hands. "Her conviction was overturned."

"Sure, sure." The man waved him off. "I've got to go give this to the typesetter." And without a farewell, he hurried into the bowels of the office.

"Well." Julius tugged at the hem of his waistcoat. "I guess that settles that." One task done, he left the newspaper and climbed back on his horse. His next chore wouldn't be nearly so effortless.

Across town, he was shown into a tidy study decorated in brown leather and hunter greens. Julius guessed this was the one room that Lady Hanford did not control.

"Lord Rothchild." The marquess clapped his hands together. "What a delight to have you call. Just wonderful."

Tufts of silver hair threaded through with snow white

threads stuck up in a wind-tossed halo around Hanford's head. Light blue eyes twinkled from under bushy eyebrows. He rocked onto the balls of his feet, the top of his head just reaching Julius's chin. "Shall we sit?"

Julius settled across from the older man. "Thank you for seeing me. It's been some time since we've last spoken."

Hanford clasped his hands at his belly and leaned back. A button on his waistcoat struggled valiantly to cling to its hole. "We had quite the debate about government pensions during session when that funding bill came up. '02 wasn't it?" The marquess pursed his lips, his gaze losing focus.

"You have a good memory." That bill had come up for vote in '12. Julius hadn't even been a member of the House of Lords in '02. But they had thrown a couple of volleys back and forth when the bill had been up for debate. On that point, the marquess was correct.

Hanford tapped his forehead. "The cranium might have a few wrinkles on it, but it's still in tip-top shape." He glanced around and frowned. "Boy!" he hollered.

A footman melted away from his position by the wall. "My lord?"

Hanford started. "Oh. Didn't see you there. Pour me and my guest a drink. Brandy?" he asked Julius.

"Thank you." Julius took the glass and lifted the snifter to his nose. Smelled good. He took a sip. Tasted even better. The marquess knew his brandy. He rested the glass on his armrest. "I read your piece in the paper yesterday. You seemed to have knocked over a hornet's nest."

"Have you come about that?" Resting his snifter on his belly, Hanford sighed. "Reforms to that law were discussed and rejected. No need to bring it up again."

"Reforms can be raised every year," Julius said dryly. "Besides, I thought Miss Wilcox made some good points."

Hanford grumbled. "Miss Wilcox. Tried to pass herself off as a man, did you know that?" He tapped a finger to the side of his nose. "But I was on to her. Can't get much past me."

"Indeed." Crossing one leg over the other, Julius plotted his attack. "I was at Simon's and heard talk of it. It seems that having her identity revealed has made her a more sympathetic mouthpiece. Viscount Ashworth was saying no woman should have to go through what she has."

The marquess snorted. "Viscount Ashworth is a blockhead."

Julius shrugged. There really was no arguing that point. Although in a competition between Viscount Ashworth and the marquess, it was anyone's guess whose mental capabilities would come out on top.

"By responding to the article you've only fanned the flames of the debate higher." Julius swirled the amber liquid, trying to look as nonchalant as possible.

"And why shouldn't I?" Leaning forward, Hanford punched at the air, brandy slopping over the rim of his glass and falling onto the carpet below. "She mentioned me and others by name. Accused us of being unfeeling." He sniffed. "I can only do what I feel is right for our country."

"Of course," Julius said as soothingly as possible. "Your many years of service do you credit. But perhaps if you didn't respond to Miss Wilcox's next letter, if you just let the furor die down naturally ..."

Hanford scrunched up his face. "I can't let her have the last word. The public is fickle. They'll believe whatever anyone tells them to."

Due to the diversity of letters to the editor, Julius could hardly credit that sentiment. "You must do what you feel is right, of course." And Liverpool would have to accept it. If the prime minister made one move to silence Amanda, all bets were off. There were limits to how much duty Julius owed the Crown.

Perhaps Julius could turn this to their favor. If Hanford became a target, he might draw out the crime ring. Julius could capitalize on their mistake. And hope his treating the marquess as bait didn't get the man killed.

The old man sparred with a fly, deep lines creasing his

brow.

Julius hated to put a man like that in the line of fire. But he saw little alternative. Holding his tumbler by the tips of his fingers, Julius said, "I believe I saw your son at Gentleman Jack's the other day. A tall, slender man. With a slim mustache."

"No, that's not my boy." Hanford tossed back the rest of his brandy. "Gilbert isn't much taller than I am, and he likes his puddings a little too much if you understand what I mean." He patted his stomach.

"Of course."

"But that sounds like my attorney, Mr. Eustace Allan. He looks a bit like a spider, that one." The marquess shivered. "He was here when you called. I sent him to the kitchen for some tea."

"You what?"

Hanford blinked. "Well, as you said, he is a spindly fellow. I figure my chef might fatten him up."

Julius buried his face in his glass. "As you say." Family attorneys weren't accorded the same status as gentlemen, it was true, although it wasn't unheard of for one to be knighted if he was of service to a particularly noteworthy family. But sending one to the kitchen for a meal like a tradesperson could only be seen as an insult. Or that the marquess was completely lacking in knowledge of social niceties.

"Do you think he's still here?" Julius couldn't be this fortunate. Investigations for the Crown were never that easy. He—

"I would imagine so," Hanford said. "We haven't finished discussing changes to my will." He stared into his empty glass, licking his bottom lip. At Julius's silence, he raised his head. "Oh. Did you want me to call for him?"

Pushing to his feet, Julius stalked to the door. "Why don't I go down to see him? He can't afford to miss any meals." Julius forced joviality into his voice. "If it is the man I saw, he dropped a watch at Gentleman Jack's."

"All right." Hanford toddled after him. "Though I can't imagine Allan at Gentleman Jack's. Do they even let attorneys through the door?"

"The members are fairly egalitarian when it comes to bloodying noses. Is it through here?" He pointed down a stairwell.

Hanford nodded. He trod heavily on each step, his breathing becoming labored. "I can't remember the last time I've been down here. It's quite"—he panted—"the adventure."

Julius quickened his pace, trying to leave the wheezing man behind. The element of surprise was one of Julius's best tools, and the marquess was ruining it. Following his nose, he strode for the end of the hall and through the open door.

A maid glanced up from the ovens. "Can I help you, sir?"

A plate with half a serving of mutton and a thick slice of bread lay on a slab wooden table, a mug to its right.

"Where did he go?" Julius demanded. He poked his head into the hallway and looked back towards the stairs.

Hanford toddled next to him and looked at the empty kitchen. "Allan left? But we weren't finished."

The maid pointed to the kitchen door that led outside. "He went that way."

Julius rushed to the exit. "Thanks for the drink," he shouted back to Hanford and fled into the garden. He took the corner to the front of the marquess's house at a sprint. Hanford's house was in Westminster, a block from St. James Street, and the afternoon crowds filled the street.

One man stood a head above everyone else. Mr. Allan weaved through the pedestrians on the sidewalk, and Julius's gaze focused on the bobbing top hat.

"My lord, do you want your horse?" One of Hanford's groomsmen held his thoroughbred by the bridle at Hanford's front steps.

With one last glance at Allan, Julius raced back and

leapt on his mount. "Yah!" The horse galloped into the street, nearly knocking over a street sweep.

Julius ignored the shouts behind him. He stood in his stirrups and peered down the street but no top hat stood above the rest. Julius hit the cross street and looked left. There. Digging his heels into the horse's flanks, he took off, only to pull up as a hackney cut in front of his path.

"Get out of my way!" But everyone had decided now was the time to leave work and travel down St. James Street. Maneuvering his horse through the crowded street was slow going, and Allan's long legs ate up the ground faster than Julius could keep up. Not without knocking pedestrians to the ground.

"Damn it." He drew his horse behind a carriage moving at a tepid but steady clip, and let the other conveyance forge the path. The pace was marginally faster. He stood again in his stirrups and checked that Allan was still on the street. He followed the man until he ducked into a coffeehouse.

Julius stopped in an alley across the street. He waved a street sweep over, a boy who couldn't have been over the age of twelve. "Will you take a message for me?" He showed the boy a sovereign, and the lad nodded eagerly. He gave the sweep directions to Sutton's house and the message. The boy raced off, dust kicking back from his heels.

Julius settled in to wait. Several patrons entered the coffeehouse. One portly man exited, a wrapped meat pie in each hand. But Allan remained within.

It began to rain. Huddling between his horse and the wall of the building next to him, Julius tugged the collar of his coat upward and turtled his head down. A little bit of damp didn't bother him. He could outwait anyone.

Although the man must surely be in his third cup of coffee by now. Or had decided to stop for a meal. The delay gave Sutton time to arrive, his own horse stamping and pawing the ground, mist billowing from its nostrils.

The large man dropped to the ground, mud splashing

from under his boots. "What have we here? The boy you sent was noticeably short on details."

Julius dipped his head. "Max. Did you send a note to Summerset and Dunkeld?" His gaze never left the front door of the coffeehouse.

Sutton grunted. "They're both in Scotland. The Dowager Marchioness has found another potential bride for Dunkeld, and Summerset agreed to help rid him of the female."

"So, neither is available to help." Julius had other men he could turn to. Men who worked for the right amount of blunt. But none that he trusted as he did his friends. With Marcus still away on the continent, and John and Sinclair off doing God knew what to some poor, unsuspecting chit in the north, all that remained were Max and himself.

Not enough pairs of eyes to keep watch on the suspect as Julius had hoped.

Max shifted, mud squelching beneath his feet. "Do you need someone removed from the coffeehouse? I could start a distraction—"

"No fires." Christ. And Julius's friends thought he was the one with issues. Sutton's obsession with fire had gotten the man into trouble more than once. Julius didn't need even more attention drawn to this investigation.

"Fine." Max shrugged. "I'm always happy to drag someone out by their ankles if that's what you wish."

"We're here to observe. See where my suspect leads us." Julius gave Sutton a description of Allan. "Can you go inside the coffeehouse, see if he's meeting with anyone? Maybe get me a meat pie while you're at it?"

Max handed him the reins to his horse and looked both ways down the street before crossing.

"And be discreet about it," Julius said to his back.

Max tossed a rude hand gesture over his shoulder, and Julius smiled. Thank God at least one of his friends was still in town.

The grey sky had darkened to purple before Sutton

emerged. He trotted across the street and pulled two small apples from the pockets of his great coat. He gave one to each horse. "Your man is sitting alone. Eating enough to feed a family of four for a week." He rubbed the nose of his horse. "I don't know how he stays such skin and bones."

Julius's stomach rumbled. It had been a long time since he'd grabbed a roll from Marcus's kitchen for his breakfast. "Back exits?" he asked.

Sutton shook his head.

Small crumbs dusted Max's bushy black beard, and Julius narrowed his eyes. "Did you remember my meat pie?"

"They looked truly disgusting in there. I did you a favor." Max licked at the corner of his mouth.

"Greedy bastard," Julius grumbled.

They waited another twenty minutes, watching the customers come and go, before Allan skittered out. Julius mounted. "Here we go."

Sutton heaved himself onto his horse, and the men turned their mounts' noses down the street, following the attorney at a sedate pace. The man obviously thought he had lost Julius. The rain began to come down harder, and Allan bought a paper to hold over his head. He scurried along the sidewalk.

Sutton squeezed the tail end of his cravat, wringing out water. "I love the jobs you have us do, Rothchild. It's never in a pub in front of a roaring fire with you."

"You got to amuse yourself at The Black Rose before the unpleasantness with Madame Sable. That's cozy enough."

Sutton grunted.

"Is your friend installed there as manager?" Julius asked. "Is the club still operating?"

"For now."

Julius glanced at Max from the corner of his eye. "Problem?"

The big man heaved a sigh. "Let's just say Mrs. Bonner

was none too happy when she discovered the nature of the business I asked her to run. But she's pragmatic. She'll get past her qualms." He tucked his chin, and rain rolled from the brim of his hat onto his chest.

"I see." Julius filed that tidbit away for future reference. Something about the name Bonner pulled at the strings of his memory, but there wasn't time to delve into it now. Pulling back on the reins, Julius nudged his horse into the shadows. "Allan entered that building."

Sutton dropped to the ground. "We're in a business district. I don't think it's his private rooms."

"The man's supposed to be an attorney. His office, perhaps?" Julius dismounted and tied his reins to a porch rail. "Let's go find out."

The bells of St. Katherine's tolled, and Max bumped Julius with his shoulder. "What say we get a drink at Simon's after we question the man? We're awfully close to the club and it's a miserable night."

Julius grunted. It depended on how the interrogation went whether he would need that drink or not. Otherwise, Amanda would warm him up better than alcohol.

They pushed through the narrow door and faced a short hallway with one door on either side, a rear exit at the end, and a steep staircase leading to the second floor. Julius checked the doors on the first level. One held a sign reading: *Caritas, An Association for Benevolent Aid*; the other, *Feathered Friends, An Ornithological Society.*

Sutton climbed the stairs, silent for such a large man, while Julius pressed his ear against the bird watchers' door, listening for any movement.

The back door creaked open. Allan stood on the threshold, one foot hovering above the ground, eyes rounding in surprise as he caught sight of Julius. He turned tail and ran back into the rain.

Hollering for Max, Julius raced down the hall and burst out the back door into a small yard where the privy stood. A side gate slammed shut, and Julius ran for it, kicking it open.

Max pushed out the front door and fell into step beside Julius. They ran down alleys, darted through cross-streets, slowly gaining on their quarry. Allan had the leg length for sprinting, but no stamina.

The attorney raced across the steps of St. Katherine's and around its side. Sutton and Julius pounded into the narrow alley and drew up short. Two strange men stood in their path. The door in the side of the church squeaked shut. Julius took a step towards it, and one of the men got in his way. The ruffian wore a cloak with a patch on its right shoulder. Small craters marked his face.

Julius clenched his fists. So the man who had blackmailed young Audley was also his murderer. He would pay dearly for both crimes tonight.

"More company," Max murmured.

Keeping his back pressed to Max's, Julius turned his head, saw two more men block off their exit from the alley. The gas lamps from the street made the men's shadows stretch long against the side of the church.

Sutton cracked his neck. "Four to two. It could be worse."

Julius smiled grimly. It had been worse. Many times. Something glinted in one of the men's hands, and Julius's smile dimmed. He shrugged out of his coat.

"I don't suppose you gentlemen would care to introduce yourselves?" Julius asked. "No? Unmarked graves for all, then."

The man with the knife lunged forward. Julius threw his coat at him, and the man stumbled, batting it away. Grabbing the hand holding the knife, Julius twisted the wrist until the man shrieked and dropped the blade. He sensed movement behind him and tossed the man to the ground before spinning to face the next attack.

Audley's killer swung at his head, and Julius ducked. Quick as a snake, he swept the man's legs out from under him. A desire to toy with the animal, to inflict as much pain as possible, took root in Julius's mind. But when his opponent picked up the knife of his confederate, Julius's thoughts focused on survival.

He jumped back when the man swung the blade in a wide arc. It caught the edge of Julius's coat. Blood pounded through his body and he steeled himself to wait for the man's next move.

Following the same path, the attacker brought his arm back across his body, slicing the blade through the air. And leaving his center exposed. Julius seized his opportunity. He leapt forward and struck the heel of his palm into the man's throat, watching him crumble to the ground while clawing uselessly at his neck. It didn't take long for him to suffocate.

Max sighed. "Did you have to do that? Now we only have three to interrogate."

The other men pounced, and Sutton was too busy fighting for further recriminations. Julius blocked a punch, grabbed the man's wrist and twisted it behind his back. With a yank, the man's arm popped twice, broken in two places, and he fell to his knees screaming.

Julius kicked him in the back and moved on to his next victim. Sutton had one man by the throat and was covering his head to deflect the blows from another. Julius grabbed his friend's attacker from behind and wrapped his arm around his neck. He squeezed.

The man struggled, arms flailing, making glancing contact with Julius's head. He clawed at Julius's arm, his blows growing weaker. The man tapped once, twice, on Julius's elbow, then sagged in his arms. Julius maintained his grip as he brought the man to the ground.

After fifteen seconds of zero movement, Julius released him and let the man flop to his back. Julius pushed to his feet and headed for the door Allan had disappeared into.

Max shook his hand and stepped over the body of the man he'd laid out. "Interrogations usually work better when people are left conscious."

Julius jerked his head at the man with the broken arm.

He lay curled in a ball, cradling his elbow and moaning. "I left one awake. Besides, who are you to talk?' Pointing at Max's victim, he tugged the door open and strode inside. Only to pull up short.

Max ran into his back and cursed. "It's blacker than pitch in here."

Reaching his hands out, Julius felt the rough stone walls close on either side of him. Too close. Sweat beaded at his temples. He tried to suck down a deep breath, but the air was thick. Heavy.

He was in a very tight space. He could always tell by the air. But Allan had fled this way. Julius took a step forward, and the temperature climbed a degree.

Max dropped a meaty hand on his shoulder and squeezed. "I'll go. You go back and question our attackers."

Julius shook his head. It was a useless movement in the dark, but his throat was clogged. He took another step, his legs turning to jelly beneath him. He couldn't leave this to his friend. It was his task. His suspect.

"I think there's a light up ahead." Max's breath was hot on the back of his neck, and Julius wanted to elbow him back. But he kept inching forward.

The ground dropped beneath his searching boot, and Julius swayed. He cleared his throat. "Steps down," he warned Max.

"We're in the catacombs," Sutton said quietly. "It's going to get even tighter."

Mind swirling, Julius sagged against the stairwell wall. The catacombs. A prison to hundreds of lost souls. He'd never make it.

Self-loathing ate at his insides. "Go." He crowded next to the wall, giving Max space to pass. "I'll go talk to our other friends." Max's cloak brushed past him, and Julius's knees gave out. He sat hard on the stairs. He'd go talk to their friends just as soon as he could take a decent breath. Just as soon as his hands stopped trembling.

He clawed at his cravat, pulling open the collar of his

shirt. He thought he'd moved past these episodes. Overcome his weakness. But he was as pathetic as ever.

The back of his eyes burned, and he squeezed them tight. His ragged breaths were loud in the stone vault. He concentrated on smoothing them out, forcing the air through his nose in steady exhalations. His heartbeat slowed from its frantic race.

Well, if he couldn't move forward, he'd have to go back and see what he could learn from the fuckwits in the alley.

Digging his fingers into the crevices between the rough blocks in the wall, Julius pulled himself to standing and headed back. He dragged a hand along the stone, relishing the bite to his flesh as much as using the wall as a prop against the dizziness that swamped him. A rectangle a shade lighter than the black tunnel beckoned to him, and he stumbled to the opening.

He stepped outside and leaned against the church's wall, chest heaving. Rain pelted his upturned face. He only wished it could wash away his shame.

He opened his eyes. The alley was empty of bodies. Perfect. He'd even failed at his pity task. Forcing his legs to move, he walked both ends of the narrow lane. But no one jumped out. No clue was conveniently left upon the muddy ground. Shoulders slumped, he stood across from the door and waited for Sutton. If nothing else, at least Audley's death had been avenged. But that thought was a poor comfort.

Five minutes later, his friend's bulky frame appeared in the doorway. Alone.

"You didn't find him." Julius's voice was flat. It was more statement than question. His weakness had delayed his friend. Obstructed the mission.

"I found him." Sutton rubbed his jaw, his fingers getting lost in his beard. He blew out a long breath. "But he won't be talking.

"His throat was slit from ear to ear."

Chapter Sixteen

"'A woman as excitable as a child, too afraid to leave her home, yet daring to lecture England on its proper management.'" Amanda snapped the paper she held straighter and angled it towards the light streaming through the window. The response from Lord Hanford had appeared in today's paper, and Amanda was still fuming. She read more highlights to Lady Mary. "'While her histrionics might suffice to send ill-informed women into a fit of the vapors, we must not let it sway the rest of society. A woman like Miss Wilcox is not to be encouraged with her nonsense. Should not be listened to. By lending such a woman your support, you do neither England, nor her person, any favors.'"

Lady Mary stabbed a needle through the pillowtop she worked on. "Hogwash. I can't believe *The Times* let him have the entire second page for that. Men." She shook her head. "They can never speak their minds in one sentence when a lengthy exposition is available."

It wasn't the length of Lord Hanford's diatribe that bothered Amanda so much as its content, but she appreciated the woman's indignation on her behalf. With Liz gone, and Julius nowhere to be seen the past two days, any friend was appreciated.

She rubbed the heel of her hand along her skirts. The personal attack had shocked her, but that wasn't what had her worried. How had Lord Hanford known she didn't leave the house? Her movements, or lack thereof, weren't common knowledge. They had no mutual acquaintances.

She glanced at the older woman. "My Lady, do you spend much time visiting your friends here in London? Surely your position in this house must be dull, yet you have no guests come to pay a call. Have a cup of tea and chat. It was really most unfair of Marcus to ask you to be my companion."

"Why is that, dear?"

Amanda spread her hands. "Because your charge doesn't do anything. Go anywhere." She swallowed. "Because I'm a recluse." The breath shuddered from her lungs. She'd finally admitted it aloud. Julius and Liz knew it and now so did the rest of London.

She looked at the paper again. She seemed so pathetic. The woman too frightened of her own shadow to ever step into the sunlight.

What would the Ladies' Society think of her now? At least they would understand why she couldn't publicly debate Lord Hanford.

"It isn't as though you are keeping me from a glittering social life," Lady Mary said dryly. "And you aren't the only one shunned from polite society."

Amanda wrenched her gaze from the newspaper. The normally vapid expression on the older woman's face had disappeared.

"Now don't mistake me. I am in just the position I'd like to be in life, my dear." Her chaperone tossed the needlepoint onto the settee cushion next to her. "I correspond with the close confidants that I do have, and the subject matter is much more thought-provoking than the typical parlor-room talk. And infinitely more entertaining than gossiping about your comings and goings. No offense intended."

Reggie pawed at her knee, and Amanda let him jump into her lap. "No offense taken," she said faintly. "But how did you know ...?"

"That you were wondering how the marquess knew of your predicament? Based upon the timing of your inquiry into my social life, it was the logical conclusion."

Amanda's cheeks heated. She had shown a boorish lack of interest in the woman's life, except as it pertained to Amanda's own concerns. And she was beginning to realize that Marcus's aunt was infinitely more compelling than the woman let on.

"Would you like a drink?" Lady Mary asked.

It seemed like the perfect time for a drink. Amanda reached behind her for the bell pull, but her chaperone waved her down. "Don't bother the domestics. I can pour a bottle just as well as they."

The older woman stood and sauntered to the sideboard. She uncapped a bottle of sherry and poured them each a full glass.

Amanda didn't know how to phrase her next question. "Lady Mary, you aren't quite as ..."

"Addlepated as you'd thought?" She handed Amanda her drink. "I know, dear. And you aren't as meek as you think, either." She resettled herself on the settee and took a large swallow of sherry.

"But why do you act so distracted?"

"Have you ever wondered why I never married?" Lady Mary patted the settee, and Reggie abandoned Amanda's lap and raced to the older woman. She pulled something small from her sleeve and fed it to the dog. "It was entirely by choice, I assure you. My father was quite a wealthy earl. His daughters were esteemed commodities."

Amanda cocked her head. "Your father didn't force the issue? Arrange a marriage?"

"He would have, had I left the matter up to him alone." Lady Mary pinned Amanda with a look. "To most of society, status is all that matters. I learned very early on that what I thought or cared about was of little account to my father or the suitors he placed before me. Even my sister couldn't understand my reluctance. Once she'd married Marcus's father, she tried to throw me together with eligible gentleman. I swear, by the end, my family was hoping I'd be caught in an indelicate situation with a gentleman so we'd be forced to marry."

"Then how did you remain unwed?" If an earl had wanted to marry his daughter off, her objections would have been of little account.

A small smile danced around the older woman's lips. "A woman's intelligence might not be a desirable trait to men, but her soundness of mind is. I learned to act in a manner that most gentlemen found unsuitable for the prospective mother of their sons. As my father never truly needed a marital alliance to improve his finances, he didn't press the matter too greatly. Especially after my sister's grand success in landing a duke. My father's reputation could withstand a spinster daughter."

"You don't appear crazy." Absent-minded and simple, yes. But Amanda had seen men marry much stupider and for much less incentive. "Not so as to scare men off an earl's daughter."

"You didn't know me when I was of marriageable age." She scratched Reggie under the chin. "I could put on quite a show," she cooed to Reggie. "Yes, I could." She straightened and resumed her normal voice. "I only tell you this because you've shown yourself as a woman with a brain in her head. Your letters to the editor are quite astute. And I don't want you to be too hard on yourself, no matter what Lord Hanford says. We all have our ways of coping, dear. My father, bless his soul, thought all women were good for was to be wives and mothers. I rebelled by being so foolish that no man wanted me. I thumbed my nose at his narrow-minded view of women by remaining happily unwed."

Lady Mary took a sip of her sherry. "And, of course, by taking many lovers."

Amanda swallowed her sherry down the wrong pipe, and her body went into paroxysms of coughing.

"Are you all right, dear?" Lady Mary gave her a smile of old, vapid and sweet, and Amanda coughed harder. She nodded and held up a hand, asking for time to recover.

When her body calmed, she sagged back into her seat. Her new brother-in-law's choice in chaperone was shockingly subversive. And absolutely marvelous. She wondered how much Marcus knew about his aunt. He was a man who didn't seem to miss much. But who would suspect the spinster had a hidden life?

Amanda carefully took another sip of sherry.

"I haven't seen your Lord Rothchild for a while." Lady Mary picked up her needlepoint. "Has he left our company?"

"No." Julius wouldn't leave without telling Amanda. She was nearly certain. "He is kept busy with his duties in Parliament."

"Will he champion your cause in the House of Lords?"

Amanda rolled her glass between her hands. "I don't know." Julius was busy with his own cause. He agreed with her stance, and if the reform law came up again, she was sure he would vote yea. But his duty lay in his intelligence work. She chewed on her lower lip. Julius was investigating Lord Hanford. Would *he* have told the man of her fears? She didn't want to believe it, but Julius was a determined man. If it would help to insinuate himself with Hanford ...

Her heart squeezed. It shouldn't matter whether Julius had spoken of her to Hanford or not. They had made no promises. Had made no pledges to the other.

But it did matter.

She stood. "I'm going to retire early. I'm not feeling well."

Lady Mary blinked. "Before dinner?"

"I'm not hungry." And she had a roll and some fruit in her room for a private meal. She paused at the doorway. "Thank you. For sharing your true self with me. I'm glad you trusted me."

"Of course, dear. Feel better." She looked up from her stitches. "Oh, and as a word of caution, my room is adjacent to yours, yet down the hall from Lord Rothchild's. The wall between your room and mine isn't as thick as one could hope."

Amanda pressed a hand to her throat. "Lord Rothchild's room from now on," she promised and made her escape.

Reggie stayed with Lady Mary and her sleeve full of treats.

Shutting herself in her room, Amanda strode to the window and flicked the edge of the curtain up. The sun was just beginning to set, and Julius still wasn't home.

She dropped the curtain in disgust. This townhouse wasn't his home. She could have no expectation that he would return to her each night. That he would care that she worried about his disappearances. She paced between the window and the empty fireplace. She had told him she expected nothing more than a few educational and diverting nights, a safe place to explore her limitations. She needed to honor that promise. Julius was nothing more to her than a restorative aid.

She flopped face first on the bed. She was the biggest liar in England. She may have intended for Julius to be nothing more than a means to an end, but he hadn't remained such. The thought of him walking away when Marcus and Liz returned ...

She drew her knees up and hugged her pillow. The thought of that physically hurt. In such a short time, Julius had come to mean the world to her. That he could discard her so easily was not to be borne.

She pushed up to sitting. But would he discard her? Perhaps, while he'd been working his way into her heart, she might have done likewise? Circumstances changed. Just because Julius had once said he could give her nothing more than his nights, that didn't mean he still felt the same.

Lady Mary had shown courage by telling Amanda who she really was. Amanda could do no less. She needed to tell Julius her desires had changed.

Marching from her room, she ensconced herself in the wide chair in front of his fireplace and waited.

And waited.

She jerked awake when an unfamiliar step fell in the hallway outside Julius's door.

Amanda jumped from the chair and raced to his bed. She untied one of the tester curtains, covering her side of the bed, just as the door opened. Frozen like a stag before a hunter, Amanda listened as the floorboards creaked. It definitely wasn't Julius. She would recognize his step. His breathing. The man on the other side of the curtain was a stranger.

Something dropped to the floor. There was a whoosh, a hiss, and Amanda recognized the sound of a fire crackling to life. She dropped her head. It was just a servant getting the room warmed. No one was after her.

The door snicked shut, and Amanda peered around the curtain. All clear. She clambered off the bed. The heat from the fire leeched through her clothes, and she stepped closer to the flames. With the room warming up, there was no reason she couldn't greet Julius in a more seductive manner. If she was to convince him of a future with her as his mistress, it was best to showcase all that she had to offer.

Without his aid to dress that morning, she was back to wearing a shapeless gown that buttoned down the front. It was easily shed. She removed her slippers and stockings and contemplated her chemise.

Leave it on and retain some modesty? Or greet him as a new-born babe enters the world? She drew the thin cotton over her head. She would be baring her soul to Julius tonight. Might as well do it while baring her body.

She picked up her clothes, folding them neatly, and placing them on the bench at the foot of the bed. The slippers went underneath. She tied the bed's curtain back up and climbed onto the mattress, lying back on the crushed velvet coverlet.

She turned one way, and tried to picture what Julius would see when he walked through the door. She twisted the other way, shifting her knee. Perhaps totally nude was a mistake.

She thought of Lady Mary with all her lovers and girded her courage. She could be a seductress, too, damn it. Finding a position she liked, she rested her head on her arm and waited. She would not fall asleep again.

She blinked awake to find Julius standing beside the bed, gazing down at her. She rubbed her face. "Julius. When did you get back?"

"Just now."

"What time is it?"

"After midnight." Julius picked up a lock of her hair and rubbed it between his fingers. "You should go back to sleep."

Remembering all the mornings she'd woken up alone, she asked, her voice tart, "But then where would you sleep?"

His eyebrows drew together. "What?"

"Never mind it." Amanda shook off her irritation. His leaving before dawn only bothered her because she didn't know if it meant anything deeper – that he didn't want to stay. With her. She took a deep breath. Pushing to her hands and knees, she crawled to the edge of the bed. "I missed you. You've been gone awhile."

"Yes."

Amanda pursed her lips. That was all the explanation she'd get?

Julius held himself rigidly. Fatigue had etched itself around his eyes. She bit her lip. He didn't need an interrogation. She ran her hands up his chest and untied his cravat. She drew it off, and the scent of stale whiskey wafted across her nose.

"Would you like some tea?" she asked, forcing herself not to shrink away. But there was something different about Julius that night. The smell, the hard look in his eyes, reminded her of her father. Which was foolish. The men were without compare.

"I don't need tea." He grabbed her hands before she

could push his coat from his shoulders.

She tried to find the answer in his expression, but it eluded her. She had to ask. "What do you need?"

"I've had a bad couple of days, mouse." He traced the line of her throat with his finger. "I need to fuck. Hard. So hard I can forget, just for a little while." His tongue followed the path of his finger. "I need to hear you scream my name. Feel your tight little body squeezing around me."

Amanda shuddered. Each filthy word that fell from his lips brought more heat than the fire. His lips found her nipple and pulled. She arched her back, grateful for the arm he wrapped around her waist, giving her support. She moaned in protest when he raised his head.

"And tonight, I need you to tie me to the bed." His voice was hoarse and unsteady.

Amanda straightened and saw the desperation in his eyes. "But ..."

"I need to conquer my fears. And you're going to help me." Julius stepped back and pulled his japanned chest from the bedside table. He pulled out various lengths of rope and laid them on the bed.

Amanda picked one up while he stripped. The hemp felt heavy in her hands. Rougher than she remembered against her own skin. She'd wanted the chance to control their encounters. The chance to own his body as he did hers. And maybe, when he was unable to flee, she'd find the courage to open her heart to him. All good things.

But something about this felt wrong.

"Are you certain?"

He flashed her the same smile he'd given Madame Sable, all careless charm. It chilled her to the bone. "Why not? It's just a little rope. Nothing I haven't dealt with before."

He climbed on the bed and lay on his back. The cords of his neck flexed as he watched her pick up a second rope.

"Yes," she said slowly. "But when we're in bed together we're supposed to be enjoying ourselves. Notwithstanding torture. Why would you want to put yourself through it?"

"Not all of us are content to let our fears control us."

Amanda snapped her head back, as though slapped. The ropes fell from her hand.

Julius cupped her thigh. "I didn't mean it like that. Just... I want to do this." He gave her that smile again. Even though Amanda saw through it, it still had the power to soften her. "And trust me, if you are touching me, I will be enjoying myself immensely."

That Amanda could understand. She crawled up his body and straddled his waist. She rested her hands on his chest. His heartbeat leapt beneath her touch. "That is all very well and good, but you haven't considered one problem."

"What's that?"

She bent down, touching the tip of his nose with her own. "I don't know how to tie your knots."

She kissed the corner of his mouth as he pondered that. The patterns he created on her body with his rope were works of art. She wasn't quite sure what he expected from her.

One of his hands fell to her hip as he rocked his pelvis into hers. She broke off the kiss and dropped her forehead to his shoulder.

"Take one of the shorter ropes," he told her. She picked it up. "Make a loop and wrap it around my wrist." He waited for her to comply. "Then thread the end through the loop and pull it tight."

The rope slid taut around his wrist. A fine sheen of sweat broke out across his brow, and Amanda hesitated.

"Tie the end to the headboard." His voice was encouraging even as a tremor ran through it. He tugged lightly at the bond. "Good. Now the other hand."

She picked up the rope. His whole body tensed between her thighs. Julius gritted his teeth, and a little piece of Amanda's heart broke away. He was so willing to face his fears. She was surrounded by strong, courageous people.

And inspiring. Rubbing a soothing circle on his chest, Amanda felt her own fears slipping away. She was ready to tell him how she felt.

But this wasn't the time for him to hear it. If he didn't reciprocate, it would only add pressure when his nerves were worn thin. After he experimented with the rope. Then she'd tell him.

Right now, she needed to make this experience as good for him as possible. She looped the rope around his other wrist but made no move to attach the end to the headboard. Instead, she slid down his body, kissing a new spot on his chest and stomach every inch she lowered.

The muscles of his stomach tensed beneath her lips, and she hoped it was from an entirely different cause than the rope. Her hair trailed over his skin. It brushed over his hardening length, and Julius groaned. So, she did it again.

"Jesus. Have I ever told you how much I love your hair?" he asked.

Amanda shook her head and blew a light stream of air across his crown. She liked hearing the word 'love' come from his mouth. Hopefully she'd hear it again that night. A bead of moisture pooled at the tip of his cock, and she licked him dry. Gripping his base, she slowly ran her fist up and down. "Do you still have that oil in your chest?"

"Yes. I bought more since we began our affair. I'd almost used it all up on you." With his free hand, Julius clenched the coverlet. His breath was coming heavier, and Amanda didn't know if it was from anticipation or discomfort. She hoped the former. Crawling to the side of the bed, she leaned over and rustled through the lacquered chest, pulling out an amber bottle. She drizzled a small amount of oil onto her palm and rubbed her hands together.

"The rope around your wrist, does it make you feel linked to the earth? A connection that keeps you from disappearing?"

He huffed out a laugh. "Sure. Let's go with that."

Amanda's mouth went dry. He wasn't enjoying the experience like she did. Well, if he was determined to continue, she would distract him from the bonds. She wrapped both hands around his cock and stroked. The oil on her hands made the glide easy. His skin warmed the oil, and the oil, in turn, heated his skin.

He groaned. "You found the ginger oil."

She remembered that oil. The slight burn that accompanied the slickness. If she lowered herself onto his length, they could burn together.

Her core clenched. She wanted to feel him, skin to skin, so badly. She wanted that final bit of separation removed. Maybe she could convince him, just this once.

Gently, she cupped his bollocks and rubbed the oil into the downy soft sac.

Julius shuddered. "My other hand. You need to tie it."

"Are you sure?" He was already so tense. "I think we have enough to give you a taste."

"I don't need you to think. I need you to tie my fucking hand."

Amanda froze. He was distressed and lashing out. She knew that, but it still hurt.

"I apologize." He cleared his throat. "Please. Just do it. I need to know I can handle it."

She crawled up the bed and took his hand. Threading her fingers through his, she eased his arm into position. His biceps bulged, and she squeezed his hand. "Whenever you want me to take off the ropes, just tell me."

He nodded, his breath shallow. When she tied the rope to the bed, he turned his head away.

This wasn't the tender evening she'd anticipated. Something was disturbing Julius. Something he didn't want to share. But he trusted her enough to have her bind him, and that had to mean something.

Lying next to him, she stroked his length and softly kissed his chest. "Relax. You're safe here. I'm going to take care of you."

His laugh was bitter. "Do I sound as trite as that when I say those words to you?"

The back of Amanda's throat burned. "No." She blinked away tears. "You sound wonderful. I believed every word you said."

Pushing up to kneeling, she grabbed the bottle of oil. Focus. This moment was about Julius. She drizzled the oil across his thighs and tried to stroke his worries away. His muscles bunched and released, the tension retreating only to reappear when she moved to another spot.

She worked the oil down his legs and concentrated on his feet. She dug her thumbs into his arches, remembering how good that had felt on her body. She looked up the long length of his body stretched out across the bed. Julius looked like a man on the rack. Not one about to enjoy the pleasures of a woman.

Smoothing her hand up his legs, she circled her fingers around his cock, stroking until it was throbbing with need. A slow smile curled her lips. He might not be fully enjoying this, but she still had the power to satisfy parts of him. She straddled his hips, and caressed the hard planes of his stomach. Bending over, she circled the flat buttons of his nipples with her tongue.

His chest heaved beneath her mouth.

"I can't wait to take you in my mouth." She kissed his stomach. "Suck you until you beg for release." Dipping her tongue into his navel, she swirled it around. "Then stop, let your need ebb, before beginning all over again."

"Turnabout is fair play." Julius shifted beneath her. He pulled the ropes taut before sagging back into the mattress.

"I'm glad you understand this is an act of redress. Delaying your satisfaction as you have mine so many times before." Opening her mouth wide, she took him deep. The ginger burned hot on her tongue, and she wanted that feeling everywhere. She swallowed when he hit the back of her throat. Aside from a grunt, Julius remained silent.

She worked him with her mouth for a few moments,

and raised her head. She circled her palm over his crown. "I could do all that, but I want something else."

Julius stared up at the canopy. "What's that?"

"I want to feel you, deep inside me." Positioning herself, she rubbed the head of his cock along her folds. She shuddered from the luxuriousness of the sensation. "We can do that from this position, can't we?"

"This is a very good position." His eyes met hers, dark brown orbs surrounded by a circle of green, like moss crawling across wet earth. He jerked his head towards the side of the bed. "The linen pockets are in the chest. I'll tell you how to tie that knot, too."

She laid his length against his stomach, and slid her folds against the velvety ridge. She was so wet, and she didn't know if it was her or the oil. "I want to feel *you.*" She let the pleading enter her voice, even though she was supposed to be the one taking what she wanted. But she couldn't take this. "You. Not a piece of treated linen. Can't we just this once—"

"It just takes once." He shook his head. "I will not get you with child."

Amanda's cheeks heated. "But other men have ... I have never come down with that condition. I don't know that it's possible for me." She'd never voiced that particular fear before. The fact that no children had come from her previous encounters had always been blessings. As it should still be now. She would never marry, and if she wanted to have lovers, her inability to carry a child was a benefit.

But she couldn't deny there was a small part of her that would love to carry Julius's child.

"And you don't know that it isn't." His voice hardened. "I can't take that chance."

The chance that he would be burdened with her. A flicker of pain fluttered to life behind her breastbone. "What about if you tell me when you're close?" She eased just the head of his cock into her body, wanting to slam down and take him whole. She wouldn't, but the want remained, bone deep. "You tell me, and I'll—"

"I said no!" Julius roared. With two turns of his wrist, he pulled his right hand free. Jackknifing up, he pushed Amanda off of him and twisted around to untie his other hand.

Amanda widened her eyes. "How did you get out?"

"You tie knots like a two-year-old." Pushing off the bed, Julius paced around the bed. He rubbed his wrists, breathing heavily. "What were you thinking? You know I won't enter a woman without protection."

"I said I'd pull off of you. I just want to feel you skin to skin." Amanda rolled off the bed and looked for her chemise.

"If you want nothing between us then bend over the bed. Your training with my jades is about to bear fruit."

Amanda's jaw dropped open. "Are you suggesting ..." She couldn't even finish her thought. Yes, he'd been preparing her body. But she'd be damned if she let him take out his anger in that way. Picking the shift from the bench in front of his bed, she dropped it over her head.

"Changing your mind?" Julius stepped close, his muscles coiled tight. "Is that something you're not comfortable with yet?"

"I understand your point," she said coldly. "All you had to say was no."

"From my position, it didn't look like you were taking no for an answer." Sweat glistened on his shoulders. Heat rolled off his body. "Are you trying to trap me? Tying me to the headboard wasn't enough for you?"

Amanda rubbed her chest. The flutter of pain had turned into a flock of birds all beating their wings in unison. "What are you saying?" He couldn't possibly think she'd tried to deceive him into marriage. He knew her better than that.

"I don't know, Amanda." He ran a hand through his hair. "You see your sister making a conquest of a duke. You think you can secure a title, as well?"

"No," she whispered. The room spun around her, and she blinked, trying to find her center. She licked her lips. "I have no hopes of ever marrying, much less marrying a gentleman." Picking up her dress, she looked for the right end of it. She gave up and held it to her chest. "Even were I to become with child, I have no expectations of you. I'm sure Marcus would settle me comfortably abroad, so you needn't have worried."

Julius narrowed his eyes dangerously. "No expectations? You don't think I would take responsibility?"

Amanda turned her back. He didn't believe her. Didn't know her at all. "I think we've said all that needs to be said." She picked up her slippers and cradled the whole mess to her stomach. She hoped no one was about, because she wasn't going to waste time in dressing.

He let her leave without another word. She ran for her room, tears streaming down her face. She locked her door and leaned back against it. Her pile of clothes tumbled to the floor.

She was a fool. Thinking that Julius could ever develop feelings for someone like her. She was a fallen woman, a disgrace. And it was time she remembered her place.

Throwing herself in her bed, she pulled the covers over her head and cried. She couldn't remember ever wanting anything so badly as she wanted Julius's affection. Not even her freedom when she'd been imprisoned.

Hope was a demanding mistress. Amanda could at least thank Julius for ridding her of that burden.

Chapter Seventeen

Julius kicked his friend's leg. "Wake up. I didn't ask you here so you could get your beauty sleep."

Sutton jerked awake and wiped the back of his hand over his mouth. He stretched, and the carriage they were sitting in rocked from side to side. "What? I was just resting my eyes."

"Uh huh." Julius stared out the mesh curtain into the grey morning light. He and Max had been parked across the street from the headquarters of Feathered Friends since four that morning. After finding Allan's body, they had searched the offices of the building they'd chased him from.

They hadn't found one mention of birds in the office of the ornithological society. They had, however, found a cabinet full of racing slips.

England's revenue department listed both the Feathered Friends society and the Caritas benevolent aid society as subsidiaries of an Ariadne Corporation. The government showed its business office address as a townhouse in Chelsea. Julius wanted to see who entered the building.

Max cleared his throat. "As I remember, you didn't ask me to come. You pounded on my door and dragged me out of bed to accompany you on this arse-crack of dawn adventure." He yawned. "The office wasn't going to go anywhere. We could have waited until morning."

"It is morning." Julius narrowed his eyes, but the tramp limping down the sidewalk passed by the office.

"Sure, now." Max tilted his head. "What got you up so early. I would have thought with that lovely bit of flesh warming your bed, I would have to be the one dragging you out."

"Shut your mouth about her." Julius shifted. "And she wasn't in my bed."

"Ah." Max nodded. "Still kicking them out when you're done."

Julius jerked his head around and glared at his friend. "What in the blazes are you talking about? I don't kick women out of bed."

Max crossed his arms over his chest and dipped his chin. "When's the last time you woke up next to a woman? Shared breakfast with her?"

"I eat breakfast with Amanda all the time." Along with Lady Mary, and a footman or two lurking about. But Julius could see that Sutton might have a point. "So, I don't like to linger. Nothing wrong with that."

Max flipped the edge of the curtain up and peered out the window. "Your problems go well beyond lingering, and you know it. You don't even want a woman's arms wrapped around you." He turned back to Julius and gave him a sympathetic smile. "Staying in the same bed with someone isn't a promise to spend the rest of your life together. It just means you regard the woman well enough to greet her in the morning."

Dropping his gaze, Julius ground his back teeth. Amanda didn't think he didn't respect her. She couldn't. Although, he'd been such a right sot last night, who knew what she thought. Aside from thinking he was a fuckwit. That had been fairly clear.

And he was. He'd overreacted to Amanda's request. Lost his temper. And it was all because of those damn ropes around his wrists.

He tugged at the cuffs of his sleeves. He could still feel the hemp scraping his skin. Embedding in his wrists. Sweat broke out on his forehead. It was something he never wanted to feel again. But if he didn't overcome his fears, he could let his friend down a second time.

He never should have let Max go into the catacombs alone, not when they were chasing men who didn't hesitate to kill. The shame of that was crushing. Drinking himself senseless hadn't helped. And making Amanda use his ropes on his body damn sure hadn't been the answer.

If something didn't change, he would have to resign from the Crown's service. He was a liability.

"This woman of yours," Max began.

"Careful." He wouldn't let anyone talk about her as though she were a light-skirt. Not even his friend.

Max rolled his eyes. "She means something to you."

Something that wasn't meant to be. The bitterness of the situation almost choked him. A woman like Amanda needed a man by her side. Someone who wouldn't run scared when things became serious.

Waggling his eyebrows, Julius tried to inject levity into his voice. "They all mean *something*."

Max leaned forward and got in Julius's face. "Do not make light of this. You roused me from bed so now you get to listen to me. Tell me, how many times in your life have you cared for a woman? Someone who has actually meant something to you? And don't give me some bullshit joke."

Julius remained silent.

"That's what I thought." Max settled back. He picked up the flannel-wrapped brick at his feet and tucked it under his coat. "You of all people should know how short life can be. How easily someone you love can be ripped away." Max stared out the window, his eyes unseeing. "Don't let what happened in Japan consume you so much that you can't take the happiness that is offered."

Julius hesitated. "I never knew you lost anyone."

"I didn't." Max stared bleakly into the distance. "I was the one doing the ripping."

They sat in silence and watched London come to life. Julius turned his friend's words over in his mind. He knew they were logical. But fear wasn't logical.

"There." Max scooted forward on the bench seat.

"Someone's opening the office."

Julius leaned forward and peered through the mesh curtain. An unassuming man in a wrinkled coat fumbled with a large brass key at the front door. "They never look like criminal masterminds, do they?"

Max was already halfway down the carriage's steps. "It doesn't matter what they look like. They all bleed the same."

Julius hurried to catch up to his friend. He didn't want the bleeding to start too early. Not if it wasn't necessary.

Max pushed through the door to the office, not bothering to knock. The man they'd seen opening the door stood at a row of shelves, a stack of papers in one hand. He spun around, his breath whooshing out in a hiss when he saw them.

He held a hand over his heart. "Gentlemen, you surprised me." He stepped to a large desk in the middle of the room and laid the papers down. He tugged at the middle of his coat, but the ends didn't meet across his round stomach. "What can I do for you?"

Julius circled the room. The door they'd come through, one near the back that appeared to lead to a small kitchen, and two windows. No other means of entry or egress. "I am the Earl of Rothchild and this is the Baron of Sutton. We'd like to ask you a few questions."

The man's eyes bulged. He clawed his fingers through his hair and tugged at his neckcloth. "Of course, of course. What can I do for such esteemed callers?"

"For starters, you can tell us who you are and who you work for?" Max placed his hands on the desk and leaned forward into the man's space.

Julius stepped to his side and patted Max's shoulder. "My friend here is a little tired, so you'll have to excuse his manners. But an introduction would be appreciated." He gave the little man a wide smile.

"Uh, sure. Faulkner." The cotton of his neckcloth stretched under all the tugging. "Lawrence Faulkner. And

I'm the clerk for the Ariadne Corporation."

"A pleasure to meet you, Mr. Faulkner." Cocking a hip on the desk, Julius casually swung his leg back and forth. "And what is it exactly that you do here at Ariadne?"

The man shrugged. "I pay the bills. Manage the correspondence. Like I said, I'm the clerk."

Max prowled around the desk and poked his finger into a shelf. Faulkner started to turn around.

"But what does Ariadne do?" Julius brought the man's attention back around. "The records office lists it as the parent company to twenty-six organizations. From bird watching, to a charity for war widows, and a hospital for the poor. You can understand our confusion."

Faulkner pressed his lips into a white slash. "Are you interested in ornithology?" He shook his head and muttered, "I get more crazy letters from your lot than regarding all the other businesses combined."

"Do we look like bird-watchers,' Max growled in the man's ear.

Faulkner squeaked and skittered to the side. His hip banged into the desk.

"Max, be nice," Julius warned.

"What?" Max cracked the knuckles of his right hand. "As you said, I'm tired. And I haven't yet broken my fast. And three nights ago, I slipped in a pool of a man's blood." He leaned towards Faulkner. "Have you ever seen a man with his throat slit? It isn't pretty. So, forgive me if I forget the niceties."

Faulkner opened and closed his mouth, no sound emerging.

Julius sighed. The longer this investigation continued, the less finesse it was conducted with. "Just tell us about the Ariadne Corporation. Who do you work with? Who hired you?"

"I work alone here." Faulkner flapped his hand at the office. "It's just me. I answered an advertisement in the paper and was hired by the company's attorney. A Mr.

Allan. I pay the rents each month for the various offices and respond to correspondence. That's it."

"What type of correspondence?" Max asked.

"Questions from the public. There aren't many." Faulkner scratched his head. "I don't think the business and charities do much promotion. But occasionally I'll get a letter, asking if the Feathered Friends is doing anything to save the Whooper swan, or something like that. It's a really good job."

Julius was sure. Minimal work for a full paycheck. "Besides from Mr. Allan, who else have you met in the company?"

"No one," Faulkner said. His eyes grew wide as Max crowded into him, and the clerk fell back. "I'm the only one who ever comes here. I swear."

Perfect. Another dead end. "Let's go get you some breakfast," he told Max.

Sutton lowered his head and glared at Faulkner. "Hmmm." The sound rumbled from his chest. Faulkner scrambled back until he was wedged between the wall and the shelves.

"Stop having a lark." Julius stomped to the front door and slammed out. He hated dead ends. He strode for the carriage and threw himself in.

"What now?" Max clambered in beside him.

"The London for a coffee and a pastry?"

"I didn't mean breakfast." Max rolled his eyes. "But that sounds good." He shouted directions to the driver, and the carriage rocked to life.

Julius rubbed his temple. "I'll tell Liverpool to put men on him, of course. But his story rings true. It would be smart of the organization to hire a legitimate front man."

"Tell the men to look out for the poor sot, as well, during their watch," Max said. "This crime ring seems to cut their losses quickly when their men have been discovered. Those four men in the alley, five if you count the one who slit Allan's throat, must have followed the attorney from the coffeehouse as we did. He told someone he'd been discovered, and they killed him."

Julius had the same thought. Human life meant nothing to these people.

"I don't understand." Max scratched his cheek. "Why have all these sham organizations? I can't imagine a bird watching society being lucrative for a crime ring."

Julius kicked his foot up on the opposite seat. "No, but ever since the income tax was created to pay for these bloody wars, people have been looking for ways to avoid paying it. Setting up a series of false charities would be a good way to go about that. People want to keep their coin in a bank for security reasons, but with the new law, banks are reporting deposits to the Crown. If they make it look like donations ...."

"Very clever." Max drummed his fingers on his thigh. "What about the subsidiaries? Are we going to sit on their offices?"

"Men are looking into them." Shaking his head, Julius blew out a breath. "But whoever filed all the paperwork, Allan I presume, did a superb job of muddying the trail. Nonexistent shareholders, investors with addresses outside England. Liverpool's men are going through the documents trying to untangle the mess."

"Poor bastards. I prefer our way of getting information." Max cracked his knuckles, and Julius nodded. His friend stretched his mouth into a smile. "Well, now that our part is done, let's talk about your girl some more, and how you're ruining your life by acting like a right git."

Julius rested his head on the back of the bench seat and stared at the ceiling. He changed his mind. Drowning in paperwork didn't sound so bad.

Chapter Eighteen

Elizabeth Fry marched back and forth in front of the fire, her skirts swishing dangerously close to the flames with each pivot. "But don't you see? After his latest attack, you must debate Lord Hanford. It's the only way."

Perching on the edge of her seat, Amanda prepared to stomp on the woman's skirts should they burst into flame. Really, the reformer was exhausting just to watch. A raging bundle of energy trapped in a diminutive frame. Resisting her entreaties was increasingly tiresome.

"You read his letter in the paper," Amanda said. "You know the reason that isn't possible." Amanda had been repeating the same thing ever since Mrs. Fry and Miss Shaw had pounded on her front door. Resigned to the confrontation, Amanda had led the women to the morning room and attempted to state her case.

The women didn't listen to reason. They were like Reggie when he got a good grip on his rope. Determined to hold onto their idea at any cost.

Lady Mary glided into the room, two footmen behind her. "I heard we had guests, dear, and thought they might want a spot of tea."

Amanda smiled at the woman gratefully. Mrs. Fry might be a persuasive and forceful speaker, but no one could talk in circles like her companion. "Thank you, My Lady. This is Mrs. Fry and Miss Shaw. They're members of the Ladies' Society for Prison Reform. And this is the Lady Mary Cavindish."

Lady Mary clapped her small hands together. "How

exciting. I've heard of your ministry in Newgate Prison, Mrs. Fry. It's all quite noble." She sat on the edge of a settee. Reggie trotted into the room and went right to the older woman's side, waiting for his treat. Lady Mary pulled something from her sleeve and tossed it into his open mouth. "Amanda, did you never see Mrs. Fry while you were there?"

Heat clawed up Amanda's cheeks. Yes, everyone knew she'd been a resident in that hellhole, but it wasn't something that was discussed in polite society. She glared at her chaperone. Amanda had needed the dotty woman who left everyone around her in a muddle. Not the interested, intelligent one. Plus, the woman had stolen her dog. Well, her sister's dog, but still.

"No," she gritted out between clenched teeth. "I never saw her there."

"I didn't start my ministry until after your incarceration." Mrs. Fry poked around a tray a footman had settled on the table. She came up with a scone studded with cranberries. "Horrid place. I'm not quite sure how you stood it."

Amanda hadn't had a choice. It was amazing what a person could stand when she had to.

She would have thought Julius's rejection of her last night would have been more than she could bear. It had carved out her heart, left her hollow inside. But after the initial pain, all she'd felt was numb. This morning she'd dressed herself, read the papers, played with Reggie, all without feeling a thing. She'd survive, because there was no other choice.

But she didn't know how to face Julius again. She and her chaperone didn't really need a male presence for security. There were the servants, after all. Perhaps Julius would understand and return to his own home.

Leaving her bed just as empty as her heart.

Miss Shaw leaned forward. "What was it like? Being in Newgate?"

Amanda poured herself some tea, ignoring the tremble

in her hand. A drop of the hot liquid splashed onto the fingers holding the cup, and she pressed them into her skirts. "About what you'd expect." She sipped the tea, not minding the burn along her throat. She'd been cold for all those months. She could never complain over scalding tea.

"But what did you do with yourself?" Miss Shaw nibbled on a sweetmeat, her eyes wide. "Were the guards—"

"I would think if you are so curious, Mrs. Fry could take you along for her ministries." Lady Mary tapped her fingers on the rim of her teacup. "No need for you to only imagine it. Or ask Amanda."

The woman's shoulders sagged. "Elizabeth won't take me."

"For your own good." Mrs. Fry broke open her second scone. "You wouldn't last two seconds," she said around her mouthful. She swallowed and turned to Amanda. "Now, since you do understand the horrors of that prison, how can you refuse to try to change it? Prison reform is needed *now*. We don't have time to wait for you to get comfortable."

"You have ambitions beyond eliminating capital punishment." Lady Mary pulled out another treat. She pointed to the floor, and Reggie slid to his belly. As soon as the morsel was in his mouth, he popped back up to his haunches.

Mrs. Fry nodded. "Capital punishment is just the first step. Every reasonable person should understand the injustice of executing children and adults for petty crimes. But so much more needs to be done."

"Then you debate Lord Hanford!" Amanda stood. "You have the passion and the knowledge of the subject. Why come to me?"

"Hanford has already engaged with you." Mrs. Fry flattened her lips. "He's responded to you when he never has to me. I think it is because of your unique position. Someone who was nearly executed by mistake, without the benefit of a fair trial. And the sister of a duchess. That gives you leverage. A voice most people do not have. You need to use it."

Pounding her fist into her thigh, Amanda spun away from the women. It all sounded so easy coming from Mrs. Fry's mouth. But the reformer was confident. She couldn't understand the way Amanda's throat closed up just thinking about facing a crowd.

Lady Mary tried to be the voice of reason. "Perhaps we should look into a way to make Hanford take notice of you, Mrs. Fry. If you co-wrote a piece with Amanda, that would bring you to the marquess's attention."

"Miss Wilcox is the one with the notoriety," Mrs. Fry insisted. "All the letters to the editor are directed to her. She is the obvious choice."

"Well, I have every confidence that Amanda will do what she feels is right." Lady Mary stirred a lump of sugar into her tea with a decided manner. Her spoon clinked heavily against the china, and each strike of the teacup felt like a blow to Amanda's body. Everyone thought she could be stronger than she was. Had faith in her. And she was going to let them all down.

The walls that had always felt so safe loomed close. Amanda's stomach heaved, and she clenched her hands together. For so long, safety had been her goal. Going to bed without fear had been a luxury, one she wouldn't take for granted. But safety was no longer enough. She wanted to be free.

Something tugged on her skirt. She looked down, and Reggie whined, pawing at her leg. He needed to go out.

She sucked down a large breath, forced her shoulders to unclench.

And she was going to be the one to take him.

Resolved, she turned to face her guests. "Reggie needs a walk. I'll leave you with Lady Mary. Enjoy your afternoon, ladies."

She strode from the room, tapping her thigh. "Come, Reggie." His nails clicked on the wood floor behind her.

When she asked the footman to fetch his lead, Reggie spun in paroxysms of delight. Or confusion. He'd never seen Amanda with the lead before.

She attached it to his collar and faced the door the footman swung open.

The young man eyed her curiously and raised an insolent eyebrow as the seconds ticked by and she didn't move. "Shall I take the dog for his walk?"

"I can do it." Her voice wheezed through her throat, thin and thready.

"I don't suppose you need an attendant."

Amanda didn't know if that was a question or a statement. Either way, she wouldn't make it if a footman followed ten steps behind, watching her every stumbling step.

"I don't suppose I do." She took a step forwards. Another. Her forward momentum was made easier as Reggie tugged at the lead, eager for the out-of-doors. The slanting afternoon sun caught her across the face, and she squinted. The glare made it easier to step across the threshold. She didn't see the barrier. But she felt the change in the air as soon as she crossed it.

Reggie yipped and strained for the steps down to the drive. The lead slid through her fingers, and she readjusted her grip, holding the loop firmly between her cold hands.

Three steps until she reached the top of the stairs. Reggie stared up at her from the bottom, prancing in a circle, encouraging her on. Two steps down, and she stood on the curb. If she broke her journey down into small segments, it would be possible. It would be roughly fifty paces until she reached the street. She could walk fifty paces.

Bringing her hands to her mouth, she blew on the stinging skin. She'd forgotten her gloves. And a coat. She looked over her shoulder at the open rectangle of the front door. The footman stood to the side, watching her like she was a monkey in a menagerie.

If she went back for her gloves, she wouldn't come back out.

Setting her shoulders, she forced her feet forward. She counted each step, staring at the pavement in front of her. When she hit fifty, she started counting up from one again. Any number higher than fifty made her throat close and her lungs burn.

She reached the street at thirty-four paces, and shied back when a man hurried past. Reggie sniffed at a bush, squatting to pee, and Amanda let him take his time. She stared at the ground and tried to block the world out. She couldn't look back at the house. If she saw the distance between herself and safety ...

The sounds from the street were strangely deadened. All she heard clearly were the ragged breaths clawing in and out of her throat. She kept her elbows pressed tight to her sides and tried to take up as little room as possible on the sidewalk.

Reggie tugged her ahead and she stumbled, losing count of her first few steps. The sound of her heartbeat thrashed in her ears, blocking out even her pants. Her legs trembled, went soft, and she had to grab onto the fence next to her to stay upright.

Reggie danced around her, tangling the lead.

She couldn't catch her breath. It was like she was wearing ten corsets at once, each one pulled tighter than the next. Little black spots swam in front of her eyes.

A hand landed on her shoulder, and she jumped. A man stood next to her, eyebrows lowered. His mouth moved, but Amanda didn't hear him. She uncoiled the lead from around her feet and skittered away. She reached the corner and took a left.

She would start again at one. She quickened her pace so each count matched her heartbeat. One hand gripped Reggie's lead so tightly the leather imprinted in her skin. The other opened and closed uselessly by her side.

She reached the next corner and whimpered. She was

now as far from the house as her walk around the block would take her. She should take comfort. Each step would be bringing her closer to home.

Reggie tugged again, and she stumbled after him. Twenty-one, twenty-two .... Someone else bumped into her, and she lost count. She fisted her left hand, digging her nails into her palm. Start over. One, two .... Tears scalded her eyes. It was no use. Her whole body shook. In a lifetime of reckless decisions, this one had topped them all. She swayed to a stop, her head spinning.

She wasn't going to make it back home. Blinking, she tried to fight back the encroaching darkness, but she was losing this battle like all the others.

A tear rolled down her cheek. Why was she so weak? She'd thought she'd found some confidence these past weeks, but it had only existed when Julius stood beside her.

As though wishing made it happen, a warm hand slid around hers and squeezed.

Amanda looked to her side and tried to bring Julius into focus. The instant his fingers had touched her, she'd known it was him. Warm. Strong. Comforting. Her shoulders sagged with relief. She'd make it home.

A slightly hysterical laugh burst from her lips. "I thought I could take Reggie for a walk."

The skin around his eyes crinkled. He cupped her cheek and leaned close. "And you have. Now it's time to go home." Julius bundled her into his side. He unbuttoned his great coat and wrapped one flap of it around her body. With one side of her pressed against him and the other covered in the heavy coat, she quickly warmed up. His arm around her waist gave her strength. With a shuddering breath, she nodded and stepped forward.

Julius took the lead from her hand and matched her pace. His breath blew hot against her cheek. "When I arrived at Marcus's and the footman told me you were out, I almost had a fit. I'm going to throttle the man for not accompanying you."

"I didn't want him to." Although had she fainted, it would have been nice to have someone to carry her home.

Julius brushed his lips over her brow. "I'm so proud of you for facing your fears."

She'd been a terrified puddle of mush, about to collapse on a public street. She didn't see how that qualified her for accolade. But her voice was still too unsteady to argue.

"I need to apologize for what I said last night. Having ropes on me again ..." He shook his head. "I didn't handle it as well as I'd hoped. And I took my wretchedness out at you, which was unforgivable." Stopping at the corner, he tilted her chin up with his finger. "But I hope you'll forgive me, just the same."

The sincerity in his eyes slayed her. She looked away and wrestled with her expectations. Nothing had changed. He was the same man he'd always been: kind, decent, and temporary.

The pedestrians walking past gave them shocked looks. Snuggled up against a man, sharing his coat on a public street, was positively indecent. If anyone recognized Julius, his reputation would suffer.

She pushed against his chest and stepped back. "I wasn't trying to trap you into a commitment."

He pulled her back close. "I know. You had no expectations." He pinched his lips. "In fact, if ever a woman presumed too little, it is you." Shaking his head, he pressed her hand to his chest. "But we can discuss that later. I need to know if you forgive me?"

A woman strode by, bumping Amanda's shoulder. "Disgusting," she hissed.

Amanda shifted. "Julius, we're standing too close. People are judging us."

"I don't care about their opinions." Resting his forehead on hers, he sighed. "I care about yours."

Amanda closed her eyes and gave into the pain she knew was to come. She would take whatever scraps of attention Julius would give to her, for as long as he was interested. And then he would leave. Leave her to become the spinster aunt to Liz's children. Leave her and take on other lovers, ones he could escort to balls and the theatre. Leave her to ache in the half-life she would have without him.

He was a good man. He'd want to see her happy and healthy before he moved on. And that would be her gift to him. She'd present him with someone strong. Someone who didn't need Julius's arms wrapped around her in order to fall asleep. Someone who didn't have a fit of the vapors stepping out of doors. She would show him a woman who was happy, so he could leave with no regrets.

"Of course, I forgive you." She knew better than anyone how close together fear and anger lie in the human heart. She'd jumped, heart racing, whenever her father had entered a room. It had taken less than a second for the terror to transform into a blinding rage when her father had implied he'd turn his attentions to Elizabeth. That rage had taken her senses. It had given her the strength to overcome a man twice her size and drive a steak knife deep between his ribs.

It had left her stone-faced as she'd watched the man who'd raised her gasp for life, only to drown in his own blood.

Julius saying a few harsh words couldn't compare. His not loving her enough was merely a fact of life. Nothing that needed forgiveness.

She tugged at the sides of his coat. "Now, can we get back home? I think I've used up my daily allotment of courage."

They hurried down the street, pausing only to let Reggie sniff another dog. When they reached their drive, Julius slid the hand at her waist around to her stomach. "Will you wait for me in my room?"

Amanda turned at the foot of the porch. Did he truly think she would deny herself the pleasure of his bed? That her forgiveness had a limit? "Of course."

Nodding, he bustled her up the steps and knocked on the front door. He tossed his hat to the footman who opened it. "I'll take Reggie down to the kitchen for his dinner," Julius said. He nodded his chin towards the stairs, and Amanda took that as her cue to make for his room.

She took the steps two at a time. Out of breath, she held her hand to her side and made her way down the hall at a more dignified pace.

The evening fire had already been laid in Julius's room. Amanda kicked off her slippers and sat on the edge of the chair in front of it, rubbing her hands together before the flames.

Julius pushed through the door, holding a tray in his hands, and kicked it shut. He set the tray on the low table next to her. "I got our dinners, as well as the dog's." Shucking his coat, he sank into the chair next to her. He stretched his legs out and sighed.

Amanda fixed a small plate and handed it to Julius. "You seem happy."

"I will concede content." He turned his head to look at her. "It is a great burden off my mind to know you forgive me."

Amanda nibbled on a bit of beef pie. "I, too, am glad we're no longer in a quarrel."

Julius slid his cravat off and unbuttoned his vest, getting comfortable. The white silk shirt beneath clung to his chest, and Amanda tried not to stare. He dove into his meal. A bit of sauce pooled at the corner of his mouth. He wiped it away, and stuck the tip of his thumb in his mouth, sucking it off.

The tips of her breasts tingled with heat. Her body remembered how good his mouth felt. She undid the top two buttons at her neck and gulped down some wine. The chairs were positioned too close to the fire.

Julius narrowed his gaze on her throat. Setting his plate down on the table, he asked, "Hot?"

She nodded.

"There's a solution to that." Crossing one leg over the other, Julius rested his elbow on the armrest, and his chin on his fist. "Stand up."

She stood.

"Take off your dress. Slowly." Julius swirled the wine around in his glass and took a sip, his gaze never leaving hers.

Wanting to tear the heavy cotton from her body, Amanda forced herself to ease the buttons through their holes. When she reached the waist of her gown, she shrugged the sleeves off her shoulders. The material fell to her waist, and she pushed the dress over her hips and to the floor. She plucked it from the ground and began to fold it.

Julius took it from her hands. "Later." He tossed the garment over his shoulder and sat up. "With the firelight behind you, I can see every line of your body beneath your shift."

Amanda twisted, trying to see what he did.

He growled. "I can see how hard your nipples are for me. Hard and tight and begging for my mouth." Grabbing a fistful of the skirt of her chemise, he pulled her between his legs. He rubbed his thumbs over the tips of her breasts. "Your skin must be so sensitive right now. Is your shift scraping against your skin? Driving you crazy?"

Her chest rose and fell beneath his hands. "Yes."

He slid his hands down her sides and tugged her closer. Close enough that when he stretched his neck, he could take one of her hard peaks in his mouth.

She fisted the shoulders of his shirt. Arching her back, she tried to press more of her flesh into his hot mouth. The first pull sent a bolt of desire straight to her core. "Julius," she moaned.

"Shhh." He blew against the wet fabric, and her knees buckled. Only his hands kept her upright. He moved to her other breast, lavishing the same attention on it.

Dazed, she glanced down. The thin cotton had become translucent where his tongue had laved. Her nipple stood dark and erect beneath the clinging shift.

Setting her back a step, Julius cupped her breasts. Then he grabbed the neck of the chemise and tore it down the middle.

Amanda gaped at him.

"Get on the bed." Julius toed off his boots. He tugged the ruined garment from her body and then smacked her lightly on the bottom to get her moving.

She scampered to the four-poster. Her skin felt tight, itchy, as though it didn't quite stretch properly around her frame. Running her palms down her thighs, she sucked in a deep breath and devoured Julius with her eyes. He removed his clothes with a ruthless efficiency, his shirt tearing at the shoulder when he ripped it over his head. Every inch of skin he exposed made Amanda ache. She loved the feel of his body pressed against hers, slick with sweat, hot from exertion. She clenched the coverlet.

She wanted to feel every inch of him.

He prowled towards her, his eyelids at half-mast. He raised a knee on the bed, and she pressed her hand against his chest to stop him. She held her breath. The last time she'd expressed this desire, things had gone very wrong. "Julius, I want ...."

"Tell me."

She dug her fingers into the dusting of dark hair across his chest. "You said you'd go without the linen if we ... you know." How did people normally talk of this? *Did* people talk about it, or did men just take what they wanted without the conversation? She wished she could be more direct, but her upbringing didn't allow the words to pass her lips. She was sure she wasn't alone. And if it wasn't talked about, and men dove right in, there must be a lot of confused women in England.

His eyes glittered darkly. "Are you offering me your arse tonight, Amanda?"

Cheeks burning, she nodded. Perhaps directness was overrated. A euphemism never hurt anyone.

He skimmed his palm from her hip to her breast. "Are you certain? Because I would love nothing more than to feel you wrapped around me, skin to skin. To empty myself deep within you."

She dug her nails into him and shuddered. "Yes," she whispered.

He took her lips, his kiss gentle, slow. His tongue found hers and met it stroke for stroke. He placed one hand at her nape and one hand on her bum, and pulled her into his body. His cock pressed against her belly, heat rolling off of it in waves. The kiss turned feral. He nipped at her tongue and swallowed her moans down as though he needed them to survive. The tips of his fingers dug into her bottom, and each point of pressure sent a twinge of desire to her core.

She gripped his hip and tried to keep up. Each plunge of his tongue was demanding, possessive. His heartbeat pounded against her chest, and excitement slid through her veins.

She might not mean forever to him, but in that moment, he wanted her as badly as she wanted him.

Reaching between them, she took hold of his length and stroked. The hand at the nape of her neck tightened. Pushing his chest into hers, Julius eased her back until she was lying on the bed.

He pulled his mouth from hers, breathing heavy. "Roll over. On your hands and knees." He arranged a pillow under her and pushed her down so her belly rested on it, her knees spread. Placing a hot open-mouthed kiss on each vertebrae of her spine, Julius slid down her body. "Don't move," he told her when he reached the base.

Amanda hugged the top of the pillow and waited for his return. Turning her head, she tried to follow his movements but only heard rustling behind her. The mattress sagged under his weight, and he crawled beside her.

Hemp scraped across the delicate skin on the inside of her elbow. The slight abrasion sent a shiver down her back. Tapping her hip, he urged her up an inch, far enough for him to slide the rope around her knee. He pulled the end tight, and Amanda's elbow and knee were tugged together.

She rolled her shoulder, settling into the feeling of her unusual freedom.

Julius kissed her back. "All right?"

"Yes." Already she felt coddled. Protected. Cool air licked between her folds, and her ache turned into throbbing need.

Binding her other arm and leg together, Julius ran a finger between the ropes and her skin. The cables were snug, but not tight. They did their job, keeping her immobile, and unaccountable. She could raise her head but nothing more.

"Have I told you how beautiful your skin looks against the purple hemp?" Julius asked. "Like I've captured my very own queen." He trailed his fingers along the rope, from her elbows to her knees, and Amanda felt every faint vibration deep in her bones. He traced at the seam where cable met skin, around her thigh and up to the crease where her sex met her leg. He teased at her lower lips.

Amanda lifted her hips as far as the ropes allowed, trying to get him to touch her in the right place. He chuckled and kept his finger feather-light. "Julius," she said, a note of warning in her voice.

"Why do you think I love tying you up, Amanda?" He grazed his fingers over her clit, so gently it felt like the kiss of butterfly wings dancing over her skin. "You look beautiful, yes. But when I have you secured as I want, you're defenseless against me. I can torment you, toy with you as much as I want, with you unable to stop me. You're completely open to me."

He circled the tip of one finger at her opening, and she whimpered. She wanted to sink down on him so badly, force the contact.

"So damn wet." He spread her slickness down her folds, and circled her nub. "But let's get you a little bit wetter."

Oil trickled over her lower back, rolling down her

bottom. Julius smoothed his hands across her skin, rubbing the slickness in. He skimmed around her upper thigh and scissored his fingers around her clit with his left hand. Laying his right hand on her lower back, Julius slid his thumb between her cheeks and circled her opening.

The twin sensations made her shudder. She rocked her hips back and forth, settling into his rhythm. The pressure on her nub increased and waves of pleasure built, one on top of the other until she was about to break.

Julius removed his hand.

More oil drizzled across her back. Julius rubbed her thighs and calves and worked his way up to knead her bottom. Her muscles slowly released, and she sagged against her bonds.

He slid his left hand down between her thighs and flicked her clit. His thumb danced around her back entrance, never penetrating, only succeeding in making her body scream to be filled.

Julius eased his right thumb between her cheeks. He slicked the oil around the ring of muscles, over and over, and all of her nerve endings sparked. For a feeling that had started out so strange when Julius first touched her there, the sensation was quickly becoming one of her favorites. She climbed towards the crest of her wave, panting with need, and Julius dropped his left hand. Again.

She almost cried. "Why?"

He didn't pretend to misunderstand. He also hadn't stopped circling her back ring with his thumb. "When I press into you, I want you so desperate for relief that you'll beg me to take you, any which way." The tip of his thumb pushed past her muscles, and she tensed. He flicked a finger against her nub. "I know why you like being bound. Once you're in my hands, at my mercy, you know there's no use fighting. You don't have to worry whether something is right or proper. Sensible or wanton. It just is. So, relax into my touch, and accept."

The taps against her nub quickened in pace. Sweat

rolled from her hairline down into the coverlet. Amanda's whole body felt as though it were shaking apart. Only the ropes held her together. She was so close, but she'd never felt so empty. Her core clenched at nothing, weeping with frustration.

"Julius, please." She wasn't above begging. Not if it would get her relief.

His finger slid inside her, oil making the passage easy. A second finger joined it, and Julius slickened her inside and out.

He slowed the finger at her clit, and Amanda used the coverlet to muffle her scream. Julius pulled his fingers from her opening. Just as slowly, he pushed back in, but this time the intrusion was much larger.

"Easy," Julius murmured. He reached around her hip and stroked her clit again. "Just relax. Don't fight it."

Amanda bit the inside of her cheek. It burned. And not in the pleasant way like when Julius dragged the rope across her skin or when the ginger oil met her sensitive flesh.

Thank God he hadn't used that oil tonight.

Just as slowly, Julius pulled out until only the tip of his cock remained lodged inside her. Only to start the process again.

She writhed in pleasure from his finger at her clit, even as she shied from his invasion.

The next stroke Julius burrowed deep, and she felt so full she thought she might burst. When he bottomed out, she couldn't help the squeak of distress that escaped her lips.

He dug his fingers into the flesh at her hip. "Relax, my sweet. Trust me. This will feel good."

He retreated. He pressed in. Each time she tried to keep from crying out. Did this feel good to Julius? Because it certainly wasn't doing anything for her. It was too much. He was too big.

But he'd asked her to trust him. The bindings at her elbows and knees kept her secure. For that alone she was thankful. And she'd received her wish. She could feel every excruciating inch of him. His cock was hot and slick and so smooth it felt like he was covered in satin instead of that horrid linen. She tried to imagine him in her other channel, how good his bare length would feel there.

Anything to keep her mind off the fact that she was being torn in two.

Buried deep inside of her, Julius paused. He kept his hips still and circled her clit. It helped, but she couldn't ignore the pain.

So, she focused on the good. The tingles bubbling to life with each pass of his fingers. How close she felt to Julius in that moment. There was nothing between them. All their cards had been laid out. She knew where she stood with him, what she could expect. And he understood her better than anyone. Cared for her, in his own way, more than anyone else ever had, barring her sister.

So, if this one act—she ground her teeth together as he started to move again—if this one act gave him pleasure, she'd bear through it. She was accustomed to suffering in silence. She could do it again, now, for this man.

He pulled out, and she reveled in the reprieve. It was temporary. He'd be driving back in, steady and relentless. But the absence of pressure became its own pleasure.

He groaned as he slid back in. Amanda tensed her shoulders, waiting for the burn. It came, but more muted than before. A small tingle slipped into the place of that missing pain.

On the next slow plunge, the tingle dominated. Nerve endings she hadn't even known existed flared with pleasure.

She tried to wiggle into it, to chase the feeling deeper. Her bindings wouldn't allow it, so she sagged into the bed. Her only obligation at the moment was to feel. She didn't have to worry about anything more.

Julius moved both hands to her hips, controlling her movements completely. She'd allowed this man to wrap her up like a bow, and each slow stroke unraveled her piece by piece.

The last bit of tension seeped from her body. She gave up the final illusion of control. When he bottomed out again, she couldn't contain the small cry of pleasure.

* * *

Amanda wasn't enjoying this. A bead of sweat gathered at Julius's temple and trickled to his jaw. It landed on her upturned rump.

Julius bit back a groan. By the gods, her arse was magnificent. Pert, with padding in just the right places. And bound as she was, it was offered up perfectly for his fucking pleasure.

He'd dreamed of tupping this arse. And now he was there, sliding through the tight, erotic channel. He almost cried like a babe at the exquisite pleasure. His body screamed at him to pound into her, find its release.

But she wasn't enjoying it.

So, he kept the pace slow, gentle, knowing he could do damage to her sensitive flesh. The turtle's pace was killing him, but not as much as the tight bunching of her shoulders, her tiny mewls of distress.

If he didn't care for her so damn much, those little squeaks would be cute. As it was, he didn't know how much more he could take. He knew women could enjoy this act with some training, but Amanda had already had so much pain in her life. He couldn't take being the cause of more of it.

Burrowing his fingers into the soft skin at her hips, he grunted and pulled out until only his crown remained snug in her arse. He would stop.

He eased back in, and fire raced along his cock. Right after this stroke, he would pull out. His balls pressed against her arse, and a small sound from Amanda caused his head to snap up. That hadn't sounded like pain.

Slowly, too slowly for his demanding cock, he withdrew to his tip then slid his way back into heaven. He watched

Amanda's reactions all the while.

And there it was. That moment when a woman's whimper of distress transformed into a moan of pleasure. The best fucking moment in the world.

A little faster, he retreated and plunged. Her body went completely limp and a throaty little groan escaped those pink lips.

Halle-fucking-lulah. She was there with him. He trembled in relief. He didn't have to stop. His shoulders tensed, and the need to piston his way to oblivion almost overwhelmed him. But he could still hurt her, tear her delicate skin, so he clamped down on his control.

Julius focused his gaze on the pucker where his cock disappeared into her body. The sight alone almost made him come. Her creamy skin was flushed pink and looking as dewy as a rose in the morning's mist. He ran his fingers around the ropes, making sure her skin wasn't pinched. The tips of his fingers scraped along the hemp and then were soothed by the silky softness of her skin. Grabbing the cables at her knees, he jerked her onto his cock.

They moaned together.

Dropping his head back, he stared at the canopy, his eyes glazing over. Nothing had ever felt so good. And no one had ever submitted so sweetly to his ropes. After all that Amanda had borne, the fact that she trusted him with her body, with her pleasure, would have brought him to his knees if he hadn't already been there.

He pulled out to his head and looked back to where they joined. His cock was dark purple and thick with veins, and he knew he wouldn't last long. He pounded harder, and his balls knocked against her lower lips.

She mewled and dug her fingers into the counterpane. Tension gathered between her shoulder blades, but Julius knew this time it was from anticipation. Each slap of skin on skin dragged a whimper from her mouth. She strained against the rope, trying to match his pace.

"Don't fight it." The words were strained, and he forced

them out of his parched throat. "I'll get you there. Don't worry." Bending, he kissed the nape of her neck, tasting the salty sweetness of her skin.

His thrusts became jerky, his body past control. Instinct took over, and he drove into her, over and over. One hand at her shoulder and one at her hip, he took and gave in equal measure.

Amanda's arse twitched around his cock. Her skin flushed and heat rolled off of her. Her crisis was nearing, but he needed her to get there now. He was so close and couldn't leave her behind. He slipped his hand around her hip and circled the spot she needed.

She arched her back and the ropes snapped taut. "Julius," she pleaded. "Don't stop. Please God, don't stop."

His throat tightened along with the rest of his muscles and he couldn't reassure her. Words were beyond him. But there was no way in hell he would stop. His balls pulled close to his body. A tingle started low at the base of his spine, and he resisted the spiral towards oblivion.

He tried to loosen his grip at her shoulder, knowing his fingers bit into her skin, but his hand wasn't obeying his mind. He yanked her into his thrusting hips, shaking with denied need.

His finger faltered at her nub, the circular motion too complex for a brain that had gone black. He pinched down, hard, and prayed.

Amanda opened her mouth on a silent scream. Her whole body convulsed. The muscles surrounding him clamped down, and Julius could hold out no more.

A sound he didn't recognize tore from his throat, something primitive, elemental. Her arse gripped him so tightly he couldn't thrust through his orgasm. Could only rock into her channel. Pulse after pulse of his seed was ripped from his cock until he thought he'd never be able to come again. With one last twitch, he collapsed over her, completely spent.

Their chests rose and fell as one. The skin of her back

was hot and damp against his stomach and chest. He buried his nose in her hair and let the scent of her heat and lavender soap flood his senses.

"Are we still alive?" Amanda asked, a shaky laugh in her voice.

Julius didn't know and didn't care. As long as he was with her, he was happy.

His muscles felt like dough, and there were other parts of him he didn't feel at all. But rope still bound Amanda, so he forced himself up. With one hand on her lower back and the other gripping the base of his cock, he eased from her channel.

Her arsehole winked at him, his come slipping from the opening and rolling down to her cunny. The sight was almost enough to make him hard again.

Untying his ropes, he stretched Amanda out, making sure her skin pinked, rubbing away any soreness. He went to the pitcher of water on his nightstand, wet a rag, and cleaned them both. She was boneless beneath his hands, her eyes closed to narrow slits.

"I love your hands on me." Her words were slurred with fatigue. "And I loved feeling you release inside of me."

Was that all she loved? Julius pulled the coverlet over her and tugged her into his side. He held her tight, knowing that made it easier for her to drift off.

He watched as her breathing evened out, as her head fell to the side. He watched her until the fire sputtered in its grate and burned out.

Something had changed between them, and life had just become complicated. He knew this, but his mind was blank when it came to what needed to be done about it.

Marriage was the obvious solution. Sweat beaded on his forehead. Being bound to one woman, even one as wonderful as Amanda, wasn't something he could bear. And children he would need to protect from harm? There was a war going on with those upstart Americans. Two wars really, if one considered that the cessation of hostilities with

France was likely to end at any moment. How was a man supposed to ensure his family's safety in wartime?

His own father hadn't been able to save Julius. Not with all his money or his diplomatic connections. Julius had been left to rot. His pulse raced, and Julius tried to rein in his anger.

And it was anger. He'd never realized how much he'd blamed his father for not rescuing him. His friends had traveled to Japan, risking their lives and readying to break him free from his prison while his father had sat behind his desk and written letters.

Julius knew his father had loved him. The man must have been desperate. But the idea of leaving England to go search for his son wouldn't have crossed his mind. By the time Julius had returned, his father was too sick to confront.

Sleep tugged at his eyelids, making them heavy. In a minute, he'd get up and go to the library to catch a couple hours sleep on the settee. In a minute, the feel of Amanda's arms wrapping around him would make his skin itch. But he wanted a few more moments of holding her.

His last thought before drifting to sleep was that if he ever did have children, there would be no land too far that he wouldn't travel to save them.

Chapter Nineteen

Julius balled the newspaper and chucked it at the fireplace. It fell short by several feet. The bloody bastard. He had no right to say such things about Amanda. The Marquess of Hanford was in sore need of a lesson in manners.

Lacing his fingers behind his head, he leaned back in his chair and stared at the ceiling of the library. Amanda was a floor above, snuggled up in his bed. He didn't know if she was tired, or if she were coming down ill, but she'd shown no interest in rising that morning. He'd thought of calling for the doctor, but knew there was a chance he'd exhausted her the night before. He'd used her in ways in which she wasn't accustomed, and she needed rest.

Now he almost hoped she did come down with a slight cold. Anything to keep her safely tucked in bed and away from the papers.

Someone scratched at the library's door, and it swung wide. A footman stepped through, followed by Max. The footman bowed. "My lord. You said to show the Baron of Sutton in when he arrived."

"I know what I said."

Max arched an eyebrow before thanking the servant and shutting the door. He tossed his hat onto the settee and followed it down. "Working on your charming personality again?"

"This house is infested with indolent servants." Julius clenched his fists. "I had to relieve a footman of his duties just yesterday. If I'm to be surrounded by the snooping lot of them, the least they could do is their job."

Max stretched his legs out. "I hope you didn't call me out on this miserable afternoon just to grumble. I was in the middle of a good book when I received your note."

"Your fascination with the works of the anonymous "By A Lady" continues to surprise me. Real men don't read *Pride and Prejudice*, so consider yourself delivered from shame." Julius dodged the hat Max threw at his head and settled back into his chair. "Have you read *The Times* today?"

Max shook his head. "I was too enthralled with Walpole's *Castle of Otranto*." He narrowed his eyes. "You know I only picked up that other novel by mistake."

Julius pushed himself out of the chair and stalked to the fireplace. He bent and picked up the crumpled newspaper. Dropping it in Max's lap, he went back to his seat. "Page two. Above the fold. Where everyone will see it."

Max scanned the article, his lips pinching into a tight line within the circle of his dark beard. "Has she seen this yet?"

"No. But I'll have to tell her eventually." If Amanda was starting to poke her toe outside, she would have to be prepared for this new source of scorn. As much as Julius would love to hide the papers, he couldn't hide her from the venom people would spew.

Max tossed the paper aside. "Is Marcus getting copies of *The Times* sent to him?"

Julius's body went slack. "Bloody hell. I didn't even think about him." Acid churned in his gut. "He's going to kill me."

"Yep," Max said, altogether too cheerfully. "It's printed in the largest paper in England, hell, maybe the world, that you're tupping his sister-in-law. I would definitely make sure that your affairs are in order."

Julius returned to staring at the ceiling. His good friend would kill him. And then drag him to the altar to make sure he did right by Amanda. Which Julius couldn't, in good conscience, refuse to do anymore. Circumstances had changed because of Hanford's article. He would deny his relationship with Amanda, of course. But the only honorable course left was to marry her.

He loosened the knot of his cravat. The idea didn't send him into cold sweats, but it still set his pulse to pounding. And what would it do to Amanda? He could hide her away in the country, but there were still societal obligations that couldn't be ignored. A countess had duties.

And he was still thinking of his marriage in customary terms. He had to remember who Amanda was. There would be no callers. No invitations. No balls for her to host. No guests would attend.

Perhaps her life as his wife would carry on much the same.

Max poked through the cigar box on the table next to him and came up with a fat roll. He went to the fireplace and picked up a piece of coal with a pair of tongs. He placed it against his cigar and puffed it to life. "How did Hanford know about your dalliance? It isn't even common knowledge that you're here as the ladies' protector." Returning to his chair, he plopped down and crossed his legs.

"It has to be one of Marcus's bloody servants." Julius glared at the door the footman had come through. "Why he keeps so many of them underfoot I can't understand. Always spying and gossiping."

Max tilted his head and blew out a stream of smoke. "But he pays them very well. He'll be disappointed to learn one of them betrayed him."

"I should just fire the lot of them."

Sutton rolled his eyes. "That wouldn't look improper at all. Now isn't the time to flaunt your disregard of societal expectations." He blew a delicate ring of smoke into the air. "Did you call me here to figure out who the informant is?"

"No." Julius tapped his fingers along his thigh. "Let's go for a walk." He scooped Sutton's hat off the floor and handed it to him.

Sutton looked at his hat, looked at his cigar. "A walk?

It's drizzling outside. You know I don't like rain."

"Yes, you're like a large, annoying cat." Julius poked his head out the door and called for Reggie. A scrabbling of nails on the stairs was followed by the dog's black and brown face charging straight at him. Julius held up a hand, and Reg sat down, his body sliding across the waxed wood floor with his momentum. Julius rolled his eyes and looked back at his friend. "Now, find your balls, put your hat on, and let's get out of here. The walls have ears."

Clamping the cigar between his teeth, Max tugged his hat down but it insisted on tilting askew. His thick crop of wild black curls didn't allow for fashion. He grumbled the entire way out to the portico, frowning when Julius attached Reggie's lead. "Now we're dog-walkers?"

"Reggie is a fine dog. You should be proud to walk him," Julius said.

Reggie found the first shrub on the drive and dropped into a low squat. Steam hissed where piss met cold earth. Sutton raised a bushy eyebrow.

"Never mind that." Reaching into his waistcoat pocket, Julius withdrew a folded missive and tossed it at his friend.

Snatching it from the air, Max rested the cigar on the brim of his hat and unfolded the letter. His eyebrows shot to the sky. "You've become one of the blackmailer's victims."

"In essence, yes." Julius tugged on Reggie's lead, and they turned onto the main street. The word victim had never sat well with him. "I'm to cease and desist all investigations or else my predilections will be revealed to the world."

Max flipped the page over. He jabbed a thick finger at a line. "Is that one true? I don't remember you and the dowager duchess ever playing."

"You were in Prussia. That lady was very inventive." And sweet. "A lot of innocents could get hurt if those stories are revealed."

"And you."

Julius shrugged. "You know I don't care what the ton thinks of me. Hell, in some circles this would only improve my reputation."

Max carefully refolded the note. "What will you do?"

"Carry on and deal with the consequences as they arise." He gazed steadily at his friend. "These people must be stopped."

Max nodded. "Agreed. What next?"

"There are some more offices we can search." Julius stood. "But first I want to pay a visit to Hanford."

"And you want me to go with you as an additional sign of force?"

"I want you to stop me from throttling the man," Julius said. They reached the corner and turned back. "Hanford has irrevocably changed the path of Amanda's life, without her consent or desire. He's insulted her and made her a target for contempt. For that, he must pay."

Grabbing his arm, Max pulled him to a stop. "He's an old man fighting for his way of life. As doddering as he is, Hanford might not have even realized the consequences of what he wrote."

Julius wasn't so sure. The methodical and vicious argument in the man's article made Julius question the image of Hanford as a mutton-headed fool. And if Julius was mistaken about Hanford's character, he might have been mistaken about the man being merely an unconscious dupe to the crime ring.

Unless Hanford was cleared of all wrongdoing, Julius wouldn't underestimate the marquess again.

A hackney lurched past, and Reggie skittered sideways, threading himself through Sutton's legs.

His friend glared down at the pup. "This beast is an insult to the name dog. Where did you get him?"

"He's Amanda's." Technically her sister's, but Reggie was a great solace to Amanda. And if that's all the dog was ever good for, he would be an admirable animal. One to whom Julius would be eternally grateful.

The pup tilted his head, a soft brown ear flipping inside out. Tentatively, he stretched his hind leg up, taking aim.

With a roar, Sutton leapt to the side, the stream just missing his leg. A rhododendron bush wasn't so fortunate.

Julius beamed proudly. "Look at that. Our Reginald has become a man."

"He was an inch away from becoming dead." Sutton grumbled deep in his throat, but the dog ignored him, obviously not taking the man as a threat. Reggie pranced back to the house, Julius in tow.

With a scratch to the dog's head, Julius handed the lead off to the footman, and he and Max made for the stables.

Finding Hanford proved more difficult than Julius had anticipated. His butler said his master was at White's. The doorman at White's said the marquess had moved on to Boodles. And the manager at Boodles had no idea where Hanford had gone.

"Back to his house?" Max asked. They collected their horses from the stable and swung into the saddles. Steam billowed from their mounts' nostrils, and the saddle blankets were as soaked through as Julius's greatcoat. The rain was only a light drizzle, but the air was heavy with mist.

"Not today." Kicking the flanks of his horse, Julius trotted up the street. "Let's check out one of the offices under the Ariadne Corporation before it becomes too dark to see."

Max rode beside him, the shoes of their horses clopping against the cobblestone. He tucked his chin, and his bushy beard covered his neck and chest like a scarf.

Julius tugged the collar of his greatcoat closer. Beads of water dripped off the brim of his hat. What he wouldn't give to be warm in bed with Amanda. He regretted leaving her side so early, before she awoke. Usually it felt like an escape slipping out from between the sheets before a woman opened her eyes. That morning he'd had to drag himself from sheer force of habit. The feather bed had been soft and inviting, the woman next to him more so.

He'd waited for the usual tendrils of anxiety to coil around him as he'd watched the light in the room soften from pitch black to a soft charcoal. And the agitation had never come.

He'd left anyway.

They arrived at the office of the Society for the Health of London's Chimney Boys, and tied their horses in front of the stables across the street. The office was a small standalone building on one of the grottier streets of Chelsea. The windows were boarded over, and no one answered their knock.

Max stroked his beard. "No one here to take my donation. You'd think they didn't care what happened to the lads who risk life and limb to clean our chimneys."

Julius tried the door. It wasn't locked, and he pulled it open. Slipping inside, he waited for his eyes to adjust. The only light came from the open door.

A light sparked. Max stood next to an oil lamp attached to the wall, working his flint over a small tinderbox. He lit the lamp and a dull glow fought for dominance with the shadows. Max shut the door and looked around. "This could take a while."

He wasn't joking. Towers of documents circled around them. Papers littered the floor. The office was just the one room, no other exits led out. The boarded over windows sent a chill down Julius's spine, but he wouldn't turn tail and run like he had in the catacombs. He swallowed. "It looks like whoever was here left in a hurry." He stepped forward and his boot slipped on a piece of parchment. "Do you think they used this office for storage?"

"I can't imagine they'd leave incriminating documents lying about." Max picked a piece of paper off the nearest stack and held it to the light.

The wood porch creaked from the other side of the door. Julius and Max froze, then melted into position on either side of the entrance. Muted voices. A thump. The door eased open.

Julius grabbed the fist on the handle and twisted,

throwing the man to the floor inside the office.

"Oi! I know his jacket is hideous, but it hardly deserves a tumble on the floor."

Max peered around the doorjamb. "Dunkeld? What the hell are you doing here?"

A behemoth of a man filled the entrance. Sinclair Archer, the Marquess of Dunkeld, looked down at the floor. He shook his head, his auburn hair swinging in the low tail tied at his nape. "What I'm not doing is letting someone catch me off guard. How many times have I told you to look to the side before entering a room?"

The Earl of Summerset glared at him from the ground. "I did look. But Rothchild is a shifty bastard. We all know that." He took the hand Julius held out and hauled himself up. Brushing the dust from his clothes, he turned on his friends. "A fine welcome to Sin and me, and after coming all that way to save your pathetic arses."

Dunkeld shut the door and leaned back against it, crossing his arms. "I, for one, was glad to escape Scotland. My mother came too close this time to marrying me off. That woman could run Rothchild neck for neck when it comes to craftiness."

"What are you doing here?" Julius asked. He loved his friends, but Dunkeld and Summerset could bicker for hours like two old hens. It was an art form keeping them on point.

Pulling a lavender handkerchief from his pocket, Summerset rubbed at a spot on his pantaloons. "We got word of the attack on you at St. Katherine's and came straightaway."

"Not straightaway. I had to put an end to the engagement my mother arranged for me." Dunkeld lumbered around the room, peering around every stack of paper. "The foolish woman is convinced I am in dire need of a wife, and she managed to convince my neighbor's daughter that she was the woman to tame me."

A wide smile spread across Summerset's face. "I had a

delightful time convincing the chit otherwise."

"You're fortunate her father never caught on to your midnight liaisons," Dunkeld grumbled. "Or there would have been a wedding for sure, and—"

"That wasn't what I meant," Julius interrupted. "I mean, what are you doing *here*." He waved his hands about the office. "And now. How did you find us?"

"Oh." Dunkeld cleared his throat and looked at Summerset. He, in turn, busied himself straightening the elaborate knot on his cravat. "Well," Dunkeld said, "after you two were almost killed—"

"Hardly that," Max said, looking offended.

"—I thought it prudent to put some of my men on you. You know, just to watch and step in if needed." Dunkeld scratched his jaw. "They've kept me updated of your whereabouts."

"We almost caught up with you at Boodles," Summerset added. "But then Sin said he had to have a drink and we fell behind."

"You've had men watching me." Julius breathed out through his nose, trying to keep his temper in check. His friends were only trying to help.

He wanted to plant his fist in their faces.

Sutton stepped forward. "Gentlemen, it's cold and wet, and I have a book I'd like to finish tonight. Not"—he narrowed his eyes at Julius—"*Pride and Prejudice*. Can we leave off the bickering and search the office?"

"Fine." Julius gritted his teeth.

Dunkeld merely grunted.

Picking a piece of paper off the floor, Summerset held it between the tips of two fingers. "What, exactly, are we looking for? A signed confession from the ring leader?"

"How droll." Dunkeld walked past, bumping his shoulder into Summerset's.

"And this is blank." Holding it up to the light, Summerset flipped the paper over. "A lot of the papers on the floor are blank." He rubbed his fingers together. "And oily."

Sutton scanned the paper in his hand. "And this looks like racing scores. From eight years ago."

Julius poked his tongue into his cheek. Grabbing a handful of papers, he examined them. "I don't even know what these are. They read like a diary."

"Ooh, anything naughty?" Summerset peeked over his shoulder.

"Will you grow up?" Dunkeld slowly turned in the center of the room. "What is going on here?"

The door rattled in its frame. Julius rushed to the exit and depressed the handle. It didn't open. He threw his shoulder into it. A harsh chuckle came through the door, followed by several loud bangs.

"Allow me." Dunkeld pulled him aside and kicked the door with a leg the size of a tree trunk. The wood vibrated but remained shut. He kicked it a few more times. "They must have barricaded it with a boulder."

"Or you're not as strong as you think you are," Summerset said.

"Can the two of you please shut up?" Sweat rolled down his back, and Julius's shirt clung to his skin. They were trapped. His pulse pounded in his ears, and he didn't hear if anyone responded.

Striding to one of the boarded-over windows, Julius pulled open the pane. He tested the strength of the planks nailed to the outside wall. There was no give. He pounded his fist against the wood. Whoever had closed up the window had the skill of a carpenter.

"Shh. Everyone be quiet." Sutton pressed his ear against the door. They all listened to the slight creaks on the porch, the hushed whispers. Something hissed, sounding like a colossus sucking in a deep breath.

"Fuck." Clenching his fists, Sutton backed up. "Everyone get away from the walls. They've set the building on fire."

"That would explain the oil poured over the floor."

Summerset strode to the corner of the room, his heels clicking on the wood planks. He picked up a rickety chair, tossed it aside. "The papers and furniture make nice kindling."

Smoke coiled under the edge of the door. It snaked a leisurely path around a stack of papers before drifting towards the ceiling.

"Ideas anyone?" Sutton felt the side wall, and shook his head. "The fire's been set on multiple sides."

Dunkeld propped his foot on the desk and unsheathed a large knife from inside his boot. "I'll work on a window."

Sutton nodded at Summerset. "Help me with the desk." They each picked up a side and used it as a battering ram on the door. Sutton yelled over his shoulder, "How'd they know we'd be here?"

Julius ran a hand through his hair, his gaze darting around the small room. The smoke was becoming thicker, scratching his throat, and the walls seemed to sway ever closer. He needed to focus. "They didn't. Or not us in particular. They know Liverpool's men are searching all the offices. I think they picked one that would make a good trap and waited. We just happened to be the lucky bastards who walked in." But would they ever walk out?

Dunkeld was chiseling at the edge of the window where board met wall. Sutton and Summerset had found a rhythm trying to pummel down the door. And Julius was standing like a lackwit in the middle of the room.

He needed to help his friends, get out of here, and get back to Amanda.

And he had nothing.

The blade snapped in Dunkeld's grip. Coughing, he kept his fist wrapped around the handle and punched at the boards.

Julius covered his mouth and nose with the elbow of his sleeve. His eyes watered. He stumbled forward, thinking to help at the door, and tripped over a chair. The back snapped off. Julius blinked down at it, an idea forming.

Grabbing the legs, he smashed it against the wall until the seat broke off and he held one leg. The end of it narrowed to the slot that had inserted into the seat. Striding across the room, he nudged Dunkeld aside. "Stop. You'll break your hand."

"Better than burning to death."

Sutton doubled over, wheezing. "Oh, the smoke will kill us first."

Placing the slotted end of the leg at the edge where window met plank, Julius shoved with all his might.

Dunkeld grunted and took the leg from him. With the handle of his broken knife, he hammered on the blunt end. The slot wedged under the board a millimeter. Julius hoped. But tears were running down his cheeks, his eyes were burning, and it was hard to see.

"Hit harder," Julius yelled.

One watery blue eye rolled Julius's way, glaring. Dunkeld's blows shook the walls. The leg slid another inch, the board arching around it.

"A little further in and we can use the leg as a lever." Julius bent and gripped his knees, coughing. His head started to spin.

"Got it." Dropping the knife handle, Dunkeld wiggled the leg until he was satisfied, then pressed the side of it against the wall and pushed. One of the boards snapped away from its nail. Cool air wafted in through the opening, and Julius greedily sucked it down.

"Over here," Dunkeld called to Sutton and Summerset. He tore away the remaining boards.

Sutton poked his head through the window. "There are flames climbing the wall about two feet over. We have to move quickly."

As one, Dunkeld and Sutton linked hands and bent low. Summerset planted his jeweled boot onto the makeshift step, and they heaved him up and out.

"You should go next, Sutton." Julius didn't want to leave any of his friends behind.

"We don't have time to argue," Dunkeld growled. "Get your arse out of here."

Grinding his jaw, Julius obeyed. He couldn't deny he was desperate to escape the prison. And arguing further would only put them all in more danger.

He gripped the windowsill and stepped into their hands. They heaved him through the opening, and Julius landed in a heap on the other side. Summerset dragged him away.

Sutton rolled out next. He held a handkerchief to his mouth and stumbled back a step.

Dunkeld's head appeared in the window. Reaching his arms through, he jumped. His chest got wedged in the opening, and he swore.

Sutton and Julius each grabbed an arm and heaved backwards. Dunkeld's massive body inched forward, then popped free like a cork from a bottle of champagne. The three of them tumbled to the ground.

"Move," Sutton croaked. He crawled away from the fire, and Julius and Dunkeld followed. Summerset stood in the middle of the street, a small pistol in his hand. Firelight glittered off its pearl grip.

Neighbors had begun to gather. A bucket brigade formed and they attacked the fire. It hadn't yet spread to the surrounding buildings.

Dunkeld staggered to his feet. He pointed at Summerset. "You had a gun in your pocket this whole time? Why didn't you use it?"

"I don't think shooting at a fire kills it." Summerset surveyed the crowd like a hawk eyes a hare. "They're probably watching. Saw that we escaped."

Julius placed a hand in the mud and pushed himself to his feet. "It doesn't matter. They would have known by morning that they'd failed."

"They meant the attack to stop the investigation," Sutton said. "Trying to intimidate us."

"Anyone feeling intimidated?" Julius looked each of his friends in the eye, saw the same resolve he felt. The dirtier these people played, the harder he would come for them.

Sutton held out his hands, palm up. He turned his face to the skies. "I won't complain about bad weather ever again. The damp slowed the spread of the fire. The rain just saved our lives."

Chapter Twenty

Amanda extracted the hem of her gown from Reggie's teeth. "Bad dog. Clothing is not a toy." She looked around the morning room but didn't see his rope anywhere. She'd already hunted for it in the other rooms of the ground floor to no avail. Julius would have to get him another.

She didn't bother to ask the footmen to search. She'd found the latest edition of *The Times* on her bed that afternoon, after she'd crawled out of Julius's. It was folded neatly to the second page, her indiscretions front and center.

One of the servants had placed it there, a deliberate taunt. The smirks of the footmen had grown more pronounced. Mr. Carter outright ignored her.

She strode into the library, Reggie at her heels, and pulled up short when she saw the figure seated behind the desk. "Julius! I didn't hear you return." She rocked onto her toes, her feet wanting to hurry to his side. Propriety, and a lingering sense of irritation, stopped her. Reggie leapt onto the settee, circling three times before dropping down on his side.

"I've only been back a couple of minutes." Pushing back from the desk, Julius stretched out an arm. No amount of irritation could stop her from accepting that invitation. She went to his side, and Julius pulled her down onto his lap. "I have some correspondence to respond to and then I'll be up."

This close, she couldn't not touch him. She tucked a damp lock of hair behind his ear. "Julius, is there something you neglected to tell me?"

His eyes widened, the picture of innocence. "Whatever do you mean?"

"I don't think my question could be any clearer."

He twirled a lock of her hair around his finger. "Do you refer to the fact that our Reginald has finally become a man? It is big news, but I thought you'd want to congratulate him for yourself when you see him relieve himself against a tree."

"What? No." She wrinkled her nose. "That's not what I'm talking about, as you well know."

His shoulders slumped. "Is this about the paper? I was going to tell you, I just hadn't found the right time."

"Wrong again." She smacked his chest. "You dismissed another servant. That poor footman who didn't accompany me for my walk."

"Of course." Julius firmed his lips. "He didn't do his job."

"I told you I wished to walk alone." Even though she had to admit that had been a foolish idea. "No wonder all the servants detest me if you fire everyone who slights me in the least."

"What do you mean they detest you?" Julius's chest vibrated against her shoulder with his growl. "Do they insult you?"

The house would be empty before Liz and Marcus's return. She pasted on a bright smile. "Of course not. You're damp. We should get your coat off of you before you catch cold." Sliding her hand under his chilled coat, she pushed it down his shoulder.

Julius trapped her hand. "You can take my clothes off in a minute." Turning the wick up on the oil lamp on the desk, Julius picked up a letter and squinted at it. Three or four others were tossed carelessly on the desk before him.

She'd managed to distract him from dismissing the entire domestic staff, but now she was the one distracted. Amanda wrinkled her nose and sniffed. She pushed back his coat, and the smell of smoke intensified. "Were you at a bonfire?"

He arched an eyebrow. "In the rain?"

"Then why do you smell like the inside of a char pit?"

His eyes scanned from left to right, not looking at her. "Hmm? Oh. My friends and I were inside a building that was set afire. I'll burn the clothes if they smell that bad to you."

Amanda pushed off his lap. "You what?" She examined him from head to toe but saw no injuries. "Are your friends all right?"

"Dunkeld has some nasty scratches on his stomach and fist, but he's seen worse." His voice trailed off, and he turned the letter over to read the back.

Amanda snatched it from his hand.

Startled, Julius looked up and finally seemed to realize her agitation. His brow knit together. "We all survived unscathed. It is nothing to concern yourself over."

She poked him in the chest. "You may not think I have the right to care, that I'm just one of your bits of muslin, but I do care. A great deal. And when you say you were in a burning building, I think I deserve a little more information."

"Now just a minute." Julius shot up. "I've never said you were a bit of muslin. And don't insult me, or you, by claiming such."

"Tell me about the fire." Amanda could be as tenacious as Reggie with his rope. Sweet words wouldn't turn her from her course. "Is this about your investigation?"

He ran a hand through his thick hair, and a damp lock stuck straight up. "The blackmailers don't appreciate my snooping. The fire was an attempt to intimidate us." He shuffled through the papers on his desk and came up with a tan piece of parchment covered in a looping scrawl. "I also received this note, threatening to expose my unusual preferences."

Amanda took it from his hand and skimmed its

contents. She pursed her lips. "What would happen to you if this information came out? You can't lose your title, can you?"

"No. Very little would happen to me." Julius plodded to the large globe in the corner of the room and lifted the lid. He pulled out an amber bottle, and poured himself a drink. "Want one?" he asked.

Amanda shook her head.

"My income would remain the same. I would lose no society that I care about." Sitting on the desk, Julius stretched out his legs. He swirled the dark liquid around in its glass. "It isn't myself that I'm worried for."

"Yes, the women mentioned would face scandal." Amanda pressed a hand to her uneasy stomach. She placed the letter on the desk, something elusive tugging at the edge of her mind.

"I will have to warn them, of course." He sighed. "Normally, I'd be most concerned about how such information would affect my betrothed. Frankly, however, there is nothing the blackmailers could say about me that would affect you more than what has already been said."

Her heart stumbled to a stop. "Betrothed?"

Julius drew her to stand between his legs, resting his hands at her hips. "Hanford wrote another piece in today's paper. He accuses us of having an affair. No matter how much I deny it, the damage is done. I'm sorry."

"Yes, I saw it." She filled her lungs, trying to breathe through the pain. Her happiness was so close. She never thought Julius would offer for her. It was monstrously idiotic. And wonderfully kind. And she could never accept. Not when he was pressured into it. She wouldn't be another prison.

"You did?" Running his hands up and down her arms, he pulled her closer.

"Yes. As did Lady Mary. She congratulates us on our nonconformist lifestyle, by the way." Amanda rested her hands on his shoulders and stretched her lips wide. "And nothing in that paper means we must wed. As you say, my reputation could go no lower. There is nothing to preserve."

She kissed his cheek and tried not to cry. "Now stop being silly and tell me what you're going to do about the men who tried to kill you."

A spark of hope flared to life in his eyes and slowly faded. "This isn't something you can dismiss so easily. Besides"—his Adam's apple bobbed—"marriage wouldn't be so bad. It can't be much different than as we are now, living together, in the same house. Only it would be forever." A bead of sweat rolled down his hairline.

Was he trying to convince her, or himself? Either way, he wasn't doing a very good job. She patted his cheek. "There is no need for us to be swayed by public pressure."

"Forget public pressure. Your brother-in-law will insist."

"And I will refuse." She stepped away from his warmth. This conversation was a dagger to the heart. She remembered the desperate look in Julius's eyes when she'd tied him to the bed. The anger and loathing. If she gave in to her heart's dream, she would face that look every day of her life. She cleared her throat. "But I won't inflict my reputation on my sister and brother. I've been thinking that when they return I should travel abroad. Take up residence in a foreign country where no one knows me. I'm sure Marcus would be more than happy to pay for my upkeep outside of England." Liz's reputation was already tarnished by having such a sister, but the distance would help. Marcus was too pragmatic not to acknowledge and want that.

Unable to look at Julius, she shuffled through the other letters on his desk. She returned to the blackmail letter, wondering what about it struck her. Something gave her a feeling of familiarity. And if she focused on that, she wouldn't have to think about everything she'd just given up.

"Amanda—"

"What's this? It mentions my name." She held up a creased missive, cutting off whatever argument Julius's honor felt it necessary to pursue.

He grunted and, with a sigh, took the paper from her hand. "One of my fellow members at Simon's. He has an idea for a bit of sport, as he calls it. He wants the infamous and revolutionary Miss Wilcox to come speak about reform tomorrow night. He's reserved the main meeting hall and had the rules prohibiting women from entering the premises suspended." Julius cocked his head. "I know Bertie thinks it would be a scandalous lark to have you speak to the members, but I was thinking it might do your agenda good. The members are influential in politics. You might convince some of them."

"You want me to go to your club?" The back of her throat shriveled to dust, and she swallowed. "To speak in front of a large group of unfriendly men? Men who now know that I've been intimate with you?"

"When you put it that way, it sounds unreasonable."

"What other way is there to put it?" Amanda's voice squeaked on the last word. "This isn't going to happen."

"But you've started going out of doors ..."

"And I will keep trying." She reclaimed the letter, folded it, and stuck it down the front of her bodice. Out of Julius's sight, hopefully out of his mind. What on earth was he thinking? "But I'm going to get my feet wet by wading into the ocean, not jumping off a dock."

His eyes tracked her movements and centered on the covered bundle at her breasts. "Fair enough." He reached for her and drew her back close. "You were talking of removing my wet, smoke-ridden clothes before, yes?"

Tucking her hair back behind an ear, Julius leaned in and took her lobe into his mouth. He bit down lightly.

Amanda swayed closer. Sliding her hands under his coat, she rubbed his firm chest. His clothes had pretty well dried by now, and Julius had warmed up nicely. Still didn't mean she wasn't going to take his clothes off. She loved the contrast of his hard muscle covered by the softest of linen shirts.

Her gaze drifted to the desk. And the blackmailer's letter.

No. Julius was doing unspeakable things to her ear, tingles were lighting up all over her body, and she wasn't going to waste this moment wondering why that letter had caught her attention. Besides, that was Julius's concern. Her concern was to eke out as much pleasure as possible from what remained of their relationship.

He traced the rim of her ear with his tongue, then plunged inside, the moist caress making her shudder. She tilted her head, offering him a long expanse of neck.

He accepted the invitation. He pressed soft lips down her throat as he undid the top two buttons of her dress. When he reached a particularly sensitive patch of skin, Julius scraped his teeth across it and sucked lightly.

Amanda dug her fingers into his shirt. His mouth. Julius had the most amazing mouth. She let her eyes slit open, and her gaze fell on the letter. The haze that had wound its way around her mind dissipated. What was it about that damn letter? It was like there was an itch on her brain that she couldn't scratch.

"I want to lay you out on this desk"—Julius gripped her bottom and pulled her flush to his body—"lift up your skirts, inch by inch, and make you scream so loud the servants in the neighboring houses hear you. There are some benefits to our secret being out."

"Uh huh. Sounds delightful." She dragged the letter closer with the tip of one finger.

"Then you're going to unbutton my falls, take my cock out, and take it so far—"

"Eureka!" Amanda pushed out of his arms and raced from the room. She left Julius standing, mouth agape, his hands opening and closing on nothing.

Reggie followed at her heels, barking at the chase. She reached the top of the stairs, out of breath, and hurried for her room. She pressed a hand to her side. All those months of remaining inactive indoors were catching up with her.

She went to her escritoire and pulled the top down. A short length of rope lay on the desk. "Sorry, Reggie. I'd forgotten it was here." She tossed the toy to him, and he settled down before the fire, gnawing on the jute.

Only two of the slots held correspondence. One was reserved for letters from Liz. The other held the one missive she'd received directly from Lord Hanford. She pulled it out and hurried back down to the library.

Julius was fixed in the same spot. "What the bloody hell just happened?"

"I know who your blackmailer is." Excitement made her voice shake. She brushed the other letters to the corner of the desk and arranged her letter and Julius's blackmail one side by side. "Hanford wrote both of these."

Julius placed his palms flat on either side of the letters and bent close. "Hanford wrote this to you? The condescending prick."

She flapped a hand. "It didn't matter. Ignore the words. Just look at the writing."

He turned his head from letter to letter. Eyebrows lowered, he met her gaze. "I don't see it. Hanford's letter to you is a neat script. The blackmailer's hand is loose and much larger."

"Well, of course, he wouldn't make it obvious." She bent next to him and pointed at a line. "Do you see the 'T's in your letter. The cross line in almost all of them is a nice straight bar. But in the word 'must' here, and"—she flipped over the page—"the word 'investigation' here, the bars are angled upwards. Significantly so. And the little curly cue on the end is distinctive. It's as though the author were trying to conceal his natural style of writing, but forgot in those two instances."

Julius held the letter up to the oil lamp. "There's a discrepancy with his 'h's, as well." He picked up her letter. This time when he looked at her, he smiled. "It wouldn't hold up in a court of law, but it's enough for Liverpool to authorize a private search of his home. The noose draws tighter."

"You don't seem surprised."

"I suspected his bumbling old man air was merely a ruse." Folding up both letters, Julius tucked them into his coat pocket. "And Hanford was the only one who knew I was investigating Allan. He must have sent the order for him to be killed so the attorney couldn't betray them."

Amanda shivered. "And this is what you do? Spend your time chasing killers? Escaping from burning buildings?" How did he stand it? It was a good thing he didn't want to marry. What wife could survive spending every night wondering if he would come home?

He rested a hand on her shoulder and rubbed his thumb along her collarbone. "Investigating crime rings and killers isn't my usual task. The Crown uses me more as a recovery agent. I retrieve lost or stolen objects. Much less danger."

"If you say so."

Bending down, he kissed the hollow between her collarbones. "I say so." He raised his head. "There's no need to worry."

Amanda didn't believe that, but she knew Julius was as safe as he could be. He was smart and strong, and she would just have to trust him.

He cupped her cheek. "Now. We need to discuss our marriage."

Her body jerked. Every time he said that word, it felt as though a thousand tiny needles jabbed into her heart. It would be so easy to take what she wanted. Pretend circumstances had forced them both into it.

But she owed Julius too much. His freedom was the least she could give him.

Rolling up to her toes, she drew his lower lip into her mouth. She slid her hand down his flat belly and cupped the bulge behind his pants. "There's nothing to talk about. Now come up to bed." Grasping his hand, she turned to lead him upstairs.

He tugged on her hand, stopping her. "You can distract me for a while, but we will have that conversation."

She nodded. She couldn't avoid it forever. But at the end of that conversation, neither one of them would be happy. Julius would feel as though he'd betrayed his honor. And Amanda would have to end the affair. If they continued, he would eventually wear her down, leaving him miserable and her hopeless in their marriage.

After that conversation, there was no more future for them.

Chapter Twenty-One

Clutching her slippers to her stomach, Amanda pressed her ear against the seam of the double door. She shouldn't be here, eavesdropping like a child, but ever since she'd heard that several of Julius's friends had gathered in the library, she'd been desperate to know what was discussed. Were they plotting against Lord Hanford? Had the other men received blackmail notes? She didn't think they'd invite her into their discussions, so she lurked. And listened.

A deep booming laugh vibrated the door. Not Julius's. Although he seemed as excited by the prospect of breaking into Hanford's home as the rest of them. Almost as though it were a schoolboy prank.

She would never understand men.

A floorboard creaked down the hall, and Amanda threw herself against the wall by the door, fiddling with the small heel on her slipper. Whoever it was turned down another corridor, and she eased back into position.

With one cheek pressed against the wood, she kept her eyes trained at the far end of the hall. A disagreement had broken out of how best to remove Hanford from his house that night. Amanda narrowed her eyes. It sounded as though Julius was telling someone he couldn't start a fire and smoke him out. Though why anyone would need to be told that, Amanda didn't know.

Someone tapped her on the shoulder. Spinning, Amanda's slippers went flying. She clamped a hand over her mouth to muffle her shriek.

Lady Mary tilted her head. "Whatever are you doing, dear?"

"How did you ... where did you ...?" Pressing a hand to her chest, Amanda tried to slow the beating of her heart.

"I came down the back stairs."

A draught of air shifted Amanda's skirts. Biting her lip, she turned again. Julius held open the door, an eyebrow disappearing under his hair. Her shriek hadn't been as muffled as she'd hoped.

Amanda patted her bun. This one had turned out rather neatly. Julius had improved in his duties as lady's maid. "Good morning." She tried to look around him. "We were just walking past and I saw, uh, a mouse."

"A mouse," Julius drawled.

Amanda lifted her chin. "Yes. And in the home of a duke it was all the more shocking." She clasped her hands together in front of her. "Do you have company? Shall I call for some tea?"

The other side of the door swung inward. "Some tea would be lovely," said the man holding the handle. Amanda fell back a step. Julius's friend was stunning in his beauty, his face a study in symmetry. Cobalt blue eyes assessed her from under a crop of artfully-mussed blond curls. But it was his clothes that Amanda couldn't drag her gaze from. They were as colorful as a field of wildflowers. He stood out like a peacock.

The man looked behind her, and his eyes lit up. "Auntie May! How marvelous to see you."

Two other men crowded forwards. One, Amanda knew. The Baron of Sutton nodded at her, his thick bush of a beard as unruly as it had been at The Black Rose. The other man could only be the Marquess of Dunkeld. His long auburn hair whispered of the Highlands. It was longer than fashionable and tied back with a black ribbon. But it was his massive size that gave him away. Julius had done a fair job of describing his friends. Which meant the peacock was—

"Johnnie, how many times have I told you not to call me Auntie?" Lady Mary shook her head, but her cheeks pinkened with delight. "I have enough problems with my real nephew. I don't need to add the Earl of Summerset onto my list."

Summerset took the older woman's hand and kissed her cheek. "When you stop calling me Johnnie, I'll quit calling you Auntie."

Lady Mary sniffed. "Impertinent boy."

Summerset led her into the library. "Besides, I spent more time at your house in London with Marcus when I was just a young lad than I did with any of my own family members."

"You weren't so young, and if I remember, you were nothing but trouble." Lady Mary dipped a polite curtsy to Dunkeld and Sutton, and Summerset made the introductions.

Julius quirked one edge of his mouth up and swept his arm towards the room. Amanda minced in. Her skirts were long enough to cover her feet, but only if she stood still. Each step revealed her stockinged toes, and she didn't know how to explain why she wore no slippers.

Lady Mary took a seat and smoothed her skirts. "What are you boys up to? With Johnnie involved, it must mean trouble."

The man in question clutched a hand to his lavender silk coat. "I am all that is hurt."

Dunkeld moved behind him. "You will be if you don't show me that letter my mother wrote to you."

"I told you she wrote no letter."

"And I told you I recognize her handwriting." The bear of a man flexed his hands, knuckles cracking. "If you and my mother have joined forces to plot against me, I'll—"

"Not now." Julius rubbed the back of his neck. He turned to Amanda. "Dunkeld is convinced Summerset is in league with his mother to marry him off. But they can argue about that later." He pinned the men with glares. "Isn't that right?"

Dunkeld landed a meaty palm on Summerset's shoulder, and the poor man staggered. "Fine," the big man said, his voice as icy as a Scottish moor. He bared his teeth at Summerset.

Lady Mary clapped her hands together. "Well, now that it's settled that Johnnie shall be murdered later rather than sooner, you can tell us what it is you boys are up to."

The sound of a mantle clock ticking became very loud.

Julius cleared his throat. "It's nothing for you to concern yourself over, My Lady. Now how about a nice glass of sherry. You can show us all the lovely needlepoint designs you've been working on."

Summerset hooted and flung himself into the chair next to the older woman. He draped one lilac-clad leg over the arm. "You've duped another one, May. I thought you were going to drop your act?"

She sniffed. "It isn't all an act. I'm allowed to express different aspects of my psyche."

Julius scratched his jaw. "What are you talking about, John?"

"Just that crazy Aunt May isn't nearly so vapid as she likes to appear." Summerset shook his head. "I had you figured out the first five minutes we met."

"Yes, well, luckily for me dear Marcus wasn't nearly so discerning." A tiny smile crinkled the paper-thin skin of her cheeks. "He might have wondered more over my nightly comings and goings."

Readjusting the diamond pin in his cravat, Summerset said, "He knows more than you think. He just chose to turn a blind eye on your eccentricities."

"But ..." Julius placed his hands on his hips. "Why the deuce would anyone do that? And to fool the woman in your charge ..." He looked at Amanda.

Holding her hands behind her back, Amanda toed a circle on the floor.

"You knew." Julius rolled his eyes. "Why am I not

surprised?" He sank onto a wide settee.

Lady Mary tugged at the end of her sleeve. "You men think we're blind as well as dumb. Did you really believe you could hide the fact that you're doing a job for the government?" She held up a blue-veined hand and uncurled her index finger. "One, you've come home bloodied and bruised on more than one occasion. Not typical for a man of your station. Two"—she raised another finger—"there have been some very nice gentlemen watching this house. During my daily constitutionals, I would chat them up. After I got one of them talking about his wife and new baby daughter, he let slip a few details." She glanced over at Summerset. "Your men, I presume."

The dandy opened and closed his mouth. "Bloody hell. Dunkeld's men, actually. But they were supposed to be professionals. They shouldn't have let anyone see them, much less speak to them."

She patted his hand. "He didn't reveal specifics. But he did enough dancing around that I could identify the waltz he was in. Besides, you know I can get people to open up."

"Liverpool has been employing the wrong Montague." Sutton snorted in disgust.

Julius rubbed his temples. "I should be horsewhipped. I didn't think I'd need to employ subterfuge."

"In your defense, I did have an advantage knowing that Marcus was involved with Liverpool." Lady Mary bestowed a kindly smile on him. "Don't be too hard on yourself."

Sutton stroked his beard. "Interesting as all this is, we do have a plan we need to devise."

Dunkeld cleared his throat and pulled a chair from along the wall. "Ladies present," he said in a low, warning voice. He flopped down, and the chair's legs creaked in protest.

"Yes." Julius lounged back. "Amanda. Lady Mary. If you would excuse us for a couple minutes more then I'll send for some tea and we can all have a visit."

"But Julius"—Amanda plopped down next to him—"I

can help. You want Lord Hanford out of his home. Perhaps if I write to him and invite him here to discuss our disagreement ..."

Amanda bit her lip and looked at the surrounding faces. She wasn't supposed to know that. She didn't know if she felt honored or insulted that Julius didn't look surprised by her admission.

"It won't work," Julius said. "He may debate you in the papers, but he won't deign to meet you here, one on one."

"It would be beneath him," Dunkeld agreed.

Julius glared at him.

"Is how he would feel," the Scotsman amended. "I, of course, am not saying that visiting Miss Wilcox would be anything but delightful."

Amanda flapped her hand in reassurance. "But there must be some way he would agree to come. Perhaps if I imply I have something scandalous to write to the papers about him?"

Summerset crossed one leg over the other and bobbed his foot. The diamond-studded broach pinned to the top of his shoe winked in the sunlight. "And set yourself up as his next victim? Hardly smart."

"And never going to happen." Julius growled, and the gazes of his three friends swung their way. The men eyed Julius and Amanda like they were the catch of the day, trying to decipher if the smell they'd caught wind of meant something was off. Dunkeld raised an auburn eyebrow, looking contemplative.

Amanda leaned back over the armrest, trying to put space between her and Julius. The men all must know she and Julius were intimate. But she didn't need them suspecting Julius might actually care for her more than a lord should. It would be most awkward for him later.

"But what if she set herself up as another type of victim?" Lady Mary scooted to the edge of her seat. "Lord Hanford loves to take someone down in print and I'd bet he'd jump at the chance to humiliate her verbally, as well."

"But they just said he wouldn't come." A pinprick of dread flared in Amanda's stomach. Lady Mary was shrewd. And Amanda had a feeling she wouldn't like the direction she was heading.

"He won't pay a visit to you personally, no." The older woman's eyes flared with excitement. "But I bet he wouldn't be able to say no to debating you on the public stage. He has too much invested in this quarrel with you. If you went to Simon's like Rothchild's friend asked, I'd lay odds Hanford would show, too. He couldn't let you have an uncontested platform."

"No," Amanda and Julius said at the same time.

"The idea has merit." Sutton pursed his lips. "We know he'd be away from his house for at least two hours."

Dunkeld grunted. "The way politicians talk? I'd say more like four."

Summerset lifted Lady Mary's hand and pressed a kiss to the back of it. "If I were a younger man, I'd ask you to marry me. Brilliant."

Lady Mary slapped his hand away, her translucent skin blushing a delicate pink. "Such brass."

Her shoulders rounding inward, Amanda pressed her body into the settee's back cushion. "Brilliant or not, I can't do it."

"Of course, you can," Lady Mary said stoutly. "It's just a question of whether you will or not."

Amanda glared at the woman, feeling betrayed. Why she told her companion about the invitation to Simon's, she didn't know. Temporary insanity. She never expected the woman to use it against her.

"Whether she can or not is beside the point." Julius patted her knee. "Since I won't allow it, the issue is moot."

Amanda slowly sat up until her spine was ramrod straight. "I beg your pardon? You won't allow it."

"Uh ... that didn't come out right." Easing his hand off her leg, Julius gave her a wary look. "I only meant that as your temporary protector, it would be ill-advised of me to let a woman like you out in public."

Dunkeld whistled, long and low.

Summerset gave Julius a pitying look. "Poor sod doesn't know when to shut up."

Amanda uncurled from the settee until she stood tall before Julius. She clenched her fists at her sides. "A woman like me?"

He jumped to his feet and grabbed her hands. She pulled them back.

"I meant a woman who has been a thorn in the side of a man I now suspect of grave wrongdoing." Running a hand through his dark hair, Julius looked around the room for support.

His friends were wise enough to stay silent.

"It seems like the intelligence of Marcus's friends has declined since you," Lady Mary said, nudging Summerset with her elbow. "Since we can all ignore Rothchild's rubbish, the question still remains: will you debate Lord Hanford?" She turned wide, faded-blue eyes on Amanda.

Amanda faltered back. They all awaited her response. She swallowed, trying to bring moisture to her bone-dry mouth. Could she? Taking a walk around the block had nearly sent her into a fit. Standing in front of a group of men, being heckled ...

The last time that had happened she'd been standing before the Tyburn tree. That crowd had been men, women, and children, laughing and jeering, excited for their coming entertainment. She'd been numb, long ago resigned to her fate. After a year alone in her squalid cell, death had seemed more a welcoming respite rather than something to fear.

She'd been numb until Julius had rescued her. She owed him so much more than her life. She owed him the joy she'd rediscovered. The strength she'd begun to find deep within. And she owed all those innocents, the children and adults who didn't deserve death for their mild crimes. They didn't have a Julius to save them.

But they would have her.

She nodded, the smallest of jerks. Letting out a long, quavering breath, she nodded again, slow and deep. "Yes. I'll do it."

Lady Mary beamed. "I never had any doubt."

That made one of them.

Julius gripped her shoulders and turned her to face him. "This isn't like your afternoon constitutional. People won't be ignoring you. They'll be cruel, say hurtful things." His Adam's apple bobbed up and down. "And I won't be there to stand next to you."

She swayed towards him, her body tingling with warmth. "Even if you aren't holding my hand, I'll still feel you there. You're always with me." And for the first time, Amanda believed she could do this. The idea still terrified, but she would muddle her way through.

Dunkeld cleared this throat. "We could go without you, Rothchild. You take Miss Wilcox to the club."

"And me." Lady Mary sprung to her feet. "I want to go to the club, too."

Dunkeld nodded.

"That's all very well and good," Summerset said, "but Julius has skills we don't. We'll need him if Hanford has a safe."

Dunkeld ground a fist into his broad palm. "Finesse isn't everything."

"It is if we want our activities to go unnoticed." Julius sighed. "No, I need to go to Hanford's. I'll write the letter to Bertie telling him to let the word out. The scandalous Miss Wilcox will be speaking at Simon's tonight."

Lady Mary bustled to the desk and pulled a sheet of paper from the top drawer. "And I'll write Lord Hanford, tell him how exciting it is that Miss Wilcox will be arguing for reform at your club. That should draw him in. And I'll contact the Ladies' Society for Prison Reform. Mrs. Fry should be able to bring in a supportive crowd."

"I'm sorry I'm going to miss it." Dunkeld looked

forlorn. "Sounds like a right entertaining row."

Julius strode to the wall and pulled the servant's bell. A moment later, a footman scratched at the door.

"Tea all around," Julius said. "And send Carter up, please." He followed the servant out and returned moments later with Amanda's slippers. He handed them to her. "You might want to put these on. You know, so you don't step on any of those mice with big ears running around."

Biting the inside of her cheek, Amanda slipped them on, a hand on Julius's arm for balance. "I suppose neither of us is as stealthy as we thought."

He trailed his thumb over her hand and smiled. "I'll go write that letter."

Julius joined Lady Mary at the desk, standing next to her seated form and bending over to write. Dunkeld and Summerset immediately invaded the space he'd vacated. "Miss Wilcox," the large Scotsman said, "what are your intentions?"

Summerset planted a silk elbow in his friend's gut. "You can't ask a lady a question like that."

"But we all know I'm no lady." Amanda folded her arms over her chest. "I appreciate the marquess's directness."

Summerset mirrored her pose. "Fine. Then care to tell us your objective? Are you hoping to trap Julius into marriage? Because I'll warn you now, that is an institution he will never enter into."

"I've already refused him." Amanda ignored the shocked expressions of the two men and gazed at Julius, a soft smile at her lips. He'd been willing to give up his freedom to do the right thing by her. Her decision to debate Hanford felt better every second. Turning back to the two men, she tried to put them at ease. "You don't need to worry about your friend's reputation. He's safe from a permanent association with me."

"We mean no disrespect, miss." Dunkeld leaned in awkwardly, his hands shoved in his coat pockets. "We're only concerned about Julius."

Summerset eyed her with grudging respect. "He actually proposed to you?"

"After what Hanford wrote in the paper about us, of course he did." Amanda shrugged. "He felt it was his duty. Did you expect less of him?"

"Well ..." Summerset pursed his lips.

The door opened, and a footman pushed a rolling cart in front of him, stacked high with plates of pastries, a tea pot, and cups. Carter was a step behind. He dipped his head. "Your tea, m'lord."

Julius straightened from the desk and replaced the quill in the inkwell. "Thank you." He crossed to Amanda's side. "After you apologize to Miss Wilcox, you can collect your things and leave this house."

Carter snapped his head up. "Excuse me, my lord?"

"As the duke's representative, I won't tolerate disloyalty to the house you work for." Julius flicked a bit of lint off his sleeve. "I know you have been feeding Lord Hanford information about Miss Wilcox. It was quite careless of you to deposit the money you received from him into your own accounts."

Amanda kept her features even, but inside she seethed. She'd known Marcus's butler disliked her, but she hadn't imagined he'd been feeding Hanford stories. A sliver of shame slipped behind her breastbone, cooling her anger. That she'd even for a moment suspected Julius had been the one to let something slip to the marquess had been grossly unfair.

Carter wasn't so adept at hiding his emotions. His cheeks turned ruddy and his jowls quivered. "You speak of loyalty to this house? How dare you. I wasn't the one who savaged the name of Montague by letting this, this ..."

"Be very careful what words leave your mouth next." Julius's voice was silky, but every muscle had tensed to rock hardness. Amanda laid a hand on his forearm and squeezed.

"The duke marrying her harlot of a sister was bad

enough." Carter smoothed his hands down the front of his coat. "But allowing shelter to this piece of trash went beyond the pale. She deserved the noose, and she landed in the lap of luxury instead." Nostrils flaring, he shook his head. "I feel no shame in my actions. I would have done my part to expose her true nature regardless of coin."

"Right, then." Dunkeld laced his fingers together and extended his arms, palms out, knuckles cracking. His shoulders bunched into small boulders with the movement. "I'll just show this man to the streets." He took a step towards the butler, and Carter stumbled back.

"Julius?" Amanda whispered.

"We don't want Montague to receive any bills from the bone-mender." Julius cocked an eyebrow at the Scotsman. "Just pointing him to the door will suffice."

Dunkeld grumbled, sounding a bit like Reggie when told to do something he'd rather not. But he nodded and pointed a thick finger at the door. Carter fled through it. Dunkeld followed at a more sedate pace.

"Another one of Marcus's servants fired." Amanda sighed.

Julius shrugged. "It couldn't be helped."

"How long have you known he was working for Hanford?" Amanda asked.

"I received confirmation earlier this morning." He clenched his jaw. "I should have seen it sooner."

Lady Mary tossed her pen down on the desk. "I wish you had. I just gave that man a pound and five shillings to buy a dress for his granddaughter."

"It isn't the chit's fault that her grandfather is a lout." Summerset winked at the older woman. "And money dedicated to fashion is never wasted."

Sutton rolled his eyes. "You would think that."

"Gentleman, we have a lot of work ahead of us if we are to pull this off tonight." Julius strode to the desk and folded his letter. "Now isn't the time to debate the height of Summerset's boot heel."

Amanda sank back onto the settee, feeling for the seat back behind her. The room burst into activity around her, the men discussing strategy, and Lady Mary penning ever more letters and ringing for footmen to deliver them.

Everyone knew their roles, Amanda included. She had convinced Julius to trust her to draw out Lord Hanford. That she could stand before a crowd, in public, and not break.

It only remained to convince herself.

Chapter Twenty-Two

Julius crouched in the shadow of a hedge by the side of Hanford's townhouse. The skies had cleared, and the light from the full moon created strange and disquieting shadows in the side garden. Sutton knelt next to him, and on his other side a rose bush cast the shape of a hunched goblin.

Julius worried the inside of his cheek. Amanda should be leaving Montague's house about now. With Lady Mary at her side, Amanda would make it into the carriage. But would she have the nerve to step out when they reached the club? Their plan depended upon Amanda distracting Hanford for the several hours it would take to search his home. And if she did manage to stand up in front of the club, what sort of condition would that leave her in?

"What is taking them so long?" A cloud of vapor burst from Sutton's mouth.

"It takes time to evacuate a marquess's house." Julius had decided that the best way to safely empty the house of all servants would be for Liverpool's men, posing as city workers, to pound on the doors of all the homes on this block to inform the residents of a dangerous gas leak. The recent installation of the new lamps along the street provided a perfect story. And by evacuating several households, there was less of a chance of Hanford becoming suspicious.

Sutton shifted. "Smoke filling a room empties a house much more quickly."

Julius didn't bother rearguing the point.

The door to the kitchen swung open. Summerset poked

his head out and waved.

Julius stood, ignoring the twinge in his knee. Each year that passed made his recovery missions a little harder. He slipped inside the door, Sutton breathing down his neck.

Dunkeld walked into the kitchen carrying a lantern. "After Liverpool's men let us in the side entrance, they left out the front. They're doing a lot of head-scratching and pointing at the street lamps. I'm not sure how much time they'll buy us." He passed out candles and lifted the glass cover of his lamp. "I closed the drapes at the front windows, but still be careful about creating shadows."

Julius dipped his candle's wick in the lamp's flame. His candle hissed to life. "Let's start with the obvious places. His office, then his bedroom."

The men nodded and they padded down the hall, poking their heads in doors, before they found the office. Julius headed for the desk.

Dunkeld pulled books from a case built into the wall. He flipped through the pages before replacing the book and removing another. "Anything in particular we're looking for?"

"It always comes down to money," Julius said. He tugged on the middle drawer, but it didn't budge. He knelt beside it and held the candle up, examining the lock. "Foreign bank accounts, land holdings, the usual suspects." Placing the candlestick on the desk, he removed a leather case from his breast pocket and untied the cord wound around the front cover button. He opened the case and pulled out a small tool.

Summerset stood on a chair and ran a hand along the head of a window. "If Hanford is the ringleader of a major criminal organization, would he leave incriminating evidence laying around his house?"

"You'd be surprised how safe men believe themselves to be in their own homes." Sutton replaced a painting on the wall, his mouth a grim line. "They rarely take the proper precautions."

Summerset sneezed loudly.

"Quiet," Dunkeld growled.

"It's dusty up here." Flicking out his pocket square, Summerset dabbed beneath his eyes. "Hanford's housekeeper is slack in her duties."

Julius blocked out the prattle of his friends, focusing on the lock. The tumbler was being a coy bitch, and Julius had to persuade it to release without its key. He could feel the resistance, but if he applied too much force he would break the lock. A sure sign to Hanford that his security had been breached.

Had Hanford arrived at the club yet? Met with Amanda? If Hanford made her cry, Julius swore he was going to break more than just this lock.

A lever in the tumbler shifted, and his tool slipped, letting it pop back into place. Julius cursed. He was three miles away from Amanda and could do nothing to help ease her fears. He needed to stop worrying about her and focus on his task at hand.

Pushing Amanda from his mind proved impossible. Nevertheless, he managed to open the lock. Putting his tools away, he shook his head, disgusted at the length of time it had taken to open a simple desk drawer. A metal box squatted at the bottom. Julius pulled it out, and faced a small padlock attaching the lid to the base.

Sighing, he drew his tools out again and set to work.

Three clicks of the lock and several minutes later, and Julius was able to open the box.

Sutton stepped up beside him. "What did you find?"

"I don't know yet." Julius removed a bundle of correspondence and passed it to his friend. "You take this pile. I'll start on this end." Lifting the remaining batch of folded letters, Julius started from the bottom, at the oldest, and began to read.

As he and Sutton discarded the letters they'd read, Dunkeld and Summerset picked them up. When Julius had finished his pile, he placed the last letter down and looked at his friends. A ball of iron settled in his gut.

Summerset stared back at him incredulously. "They're not just a criminal organization. They've insinuated themselves in legal businesses. Big businesses. If we take them down, there will be huge repercussions."

Dunkeld loosed a bark of laughter. "Hell, I'm on the board of one of their companies. My holdings will take a hit." He rubbed his jaw. "The effects of this will ripple all throughout society."

"It's smart." Julius rolled his head, trying to ease the stiffness of his neck. "By placing people on the boards of London's major companies, they know there will be intense pressure to cover this up. How much political will do you think will be behind their prosecutions if it means certain men will lose their fortunes?" He held up a letter. "This is the one that really boils my fucking blood. Hanford and his accomplices are majority stakeholders in the Chesseworth Corporation, the company that owns London's prisons. Does his anti-reform stance have anything to do with his political beliefs, or was it always about lining his pocket?"

Dunkeld rocked back on his heels. "In addition to the jail fees every prisoner must pay before being freed, Chesseworth gets a stipend from the local magistrate based on a percentage of the prison population. It would do him no good if England went soft on crime." He tilted his head. "On the other hand, hanging the prisoners would seem to deprive him of a population base. Maybe he is sincere in his belief that capital punishment deters bad behavior."

"Yes, the ten-year-old who's had his neck broken can't ever steal another loaf of bread," Summerset said. Dunkeld glowered and opened his mouth, but Summerset waved him silent. "But I don't think you're remembering that spending bill we passed two years ago. The one put forward by Lord Wallace."

"There were over three hundred provisions in it." Resting his hands on his hips, Dunkeld glared at Summerset. "How the hell am I supposed to—"

"What was in the bill?" Julius glanced at the grandfather clock that stood next to the doorway. The second hand ticked loudly.

Summerset pressed his palms flat on the desk. "Because of Sir Romilly's speeches in the House of Commons, a push was made for basic prison reform, including providing basic sustenance to those who can't afford to purchase their own food."

"So?" Dunkeld asked.

"So, the prison population is counted once a month, with those numbers determining how much the prisons gets paid for each prisoner's upkeep," Summerset said. "The count is made the last day of the month, but the count is prospective. Meaning the number of prisoners counted at the end of January determines how much Chesseworth is paid for the month of February."

A divot appeared in between Dunkeld's eyebrows. "Why?"

Julius swallowed. "Because the executions typically happen the first of the month."

Summerset nodded, his nostrils flaring.

"If one thousand people are counted at the end of the month, and the next day one hundred of them are executed, the prison gets paid for the thousand even though they're only supplying nine hundred people with food and guard." Julius ran a hand through his hair. It was diabolical. If he ran the numbers, he could calculate exactly how much a human life was worth to these monsters.

Dunkeld crossed his arms over his thick chest. "But the prisons will start to fill up again. There wouldn't be just those nine hundred for the entire month."

"No." Summerset sighed, his face going slack, looking exhausted. "But it could take several days up to half a month before the numbers evened out. It's enough at the margins to turn a tidy profit."

Julius pulled a small notebook from his pocket. "We need to copy down names, dates, companies, and get the information to Liverpool. With how deep the tentacles of this crime ring stretch, he might not directly prosecute the members. But I have no doubt with the information here that he'll find a way to make the bastards slowly disappear."

"That's a project I wouldn't mind lending a hand to," Dunkeld said, his voice as rough as crushed gravel.

"Before you start busting heads," Sutton interrupted, "we have a more immediate problem." He looked up from the letter he'd been studying. "The most recent letter to Hanford, from someone who only signs his name with a zed, mentions Miss Wilcox by name."

Julius tore the letter from his friend's hand and scanned the document.

Sutton frowned at Julius. "This Zed had become most concerned about the support your Miss Wilcox is raising among the Cits with her pieces in *The Times*. He wanted Hanford to shut her up."

"'By any means necessary.'" The pounding of Julius's pulse slowed to match the ticking of the clock. Or perhaps time was slowing to match his stalled heart. If this Zed and Hanford were determined to stop her letters, what would they do to stop her from publicly speaking? His mind emptied of thought, leaving only grim determination. "I have to go."

"We'll all go," Dunkeld said.

Summerset spread his hands out, encompassing the office that was littered with evidence of their visit. "This is supposed to be a stealth operation. Hanford isn't to know we've been here."

"I don't care, I'm going." Julius turned for the door. Calm enveloped him like a warm blanket. He'd become an expert during his time in the East at tamping out emotion. Fear and panic were useless when it came time to fight. And he had no doubt that time had come. Amanda was out there alone, unprotected ... He ground his jaw so hard the back of his neck ached. No, he couldn't think of that. Of her. He needed to concentrate on the fight ahead. "The rest of you stay and clean up. Take down what information you can. I'm going to get Amanda." He strode through the door.

Someone cursed behind him. Sutton's voice reached him as though through a tunnel. "Dunkeld, go with him. Summerset and I will stay and join you later."

A heavy hand landed on Julius's shoulder bringing him up short. Julius blinked up at Dunkeld.

"We can't use the front door. This way." Dunkeld led him out the side, across the yard, and down an alley to where their carriage was waiting. He pushed Julius inside and told their driver where to go.

Climbing inside, Dunkeld pounded on the roof, and the carriage jerked into motion. "She's at Simon's. Nothing bad ever happens under that roof. The club is filled with adolescent, self-satisfied twats, but they wouldn't let a woman come to harm."

Julius nodded. He sat very still, and willed the carriage to move faster. In his mind, he could still hear the ticking of that damn clock.

In the dark part of him, the part that had never truly left his prison, he knew that time had run out for him and Amanda.

* * *

Lady Mary pulled open the bottom door on a mahogany bureau and peered inside. "I've always wondered what went on in these gentlemen's clubs. What they were doing that was so illicit that women couldn't be allowed to see."

"Have you found anything?" Rubbing her damp palms along the front of her skirts, Amanda ignored the quaver in her voice. As long as she was able to make the words she wanted come out of her mouth, she was fine. A tremor here or there was of no matter.

Because people won debates all the time whilst sounding like scared little mice.

Amanda sagged into her brocade chair. This was a

doomed endeavor. Except, she didn't have to win. She placed both hands on her stomach and took a deep breath. She only needed to delay Hanford.

"Are you certain Mrs. Fry said she'd come?"

Dropping a cigar back in a drawer, Lady Mary pushed it shut with her hip and sauntered to the bookcase. "That's what she wrote. Did you really think she'd miss this?"

No. That was too much to hope for. Amanda didn't mind losing the debate if it meant she'd helped Julius. But failing miserably in front of the earnest reformer— "And the rest of the Ladies' Society?"

"Mrs. Fry is rounding all of them up." Lady Mary shot her a warm smile. "You will have much support from the crowd."

She would fail in front of the lot of them. "Oh. Good." Perhaps, Amanda consoled herself, the women would be denied entrance. Stomach quivering, Amanda focused on keeping her tea down and stared at the closed door. Julius's acquaintance, Lord Bertrand Waverly, had seated them in a back room and told them he'd return when it was time to speak. The look of glee on his face as he anticipated the debacle to come had almost sent Amanda fleeing back into the carriage.

The room at least was small and windowless, an interior chamber with two doors. The one they'd entered opened onto the hallway. The other, Amanda didn't know. But the cloistered space helped to calm her nerves.

Lady Mary finished her perambulation of the room and stood in the center. She planted her fists on her wide hips. "Cigars and liquor. No different than any drawing room. I don't understand the great appeal."

Amanda shrugged. "A place where gentlemen don't have to worry about offending the fairer sex, where they can say, or behave, in any manner they wish. Everyone deserves such freedom."

"Except for women, apparently." Perching on the armrest of a chair, Lady Mary fluffed out the skirt of her lavender gown. "We don't have such clubs."

"You could always start one."

Pursing her mouth, Lady Mary tapped a finger to her lips. "That is an interesting idea."

Amanda opened her mouth. She hadn't been serious. But the door swung inward, and she fell silent.

The Marquess of Hanford stood in the opening, the black silk of his coat glimmering in the lamplight. The pointed tips of his collar were so starched they left little red imprints in the soft skin of his neck. His valet had spared no expense in dressing his master for the debate.

Amanda looked down at her own dress. The preparations for the night had been rushed, and she hadn't bothered changing from her day gown. The faded Mornine fabric was neat and serviceable, and looked like pauper's rags next to the marquess.

He clapped his hands together. "My dear, here you are! I wanted to advise you before you spoke. I'm certain public discourse is unfamiliar to you, and I thought you could benefit from my many years of oration."

Amanda narrowed her eyes. If she hadn't seen the evidence with her own eyes, she would still believe him a sweet old man dedicated to his cause. But like many politicians, he spoke with a serpent's tongue.

"You are Miss Wilcox, I presume? Come, come, you must be."

Amanda nodded.

"And who is this charming lady?" he asked.

Amanda and Lady Mary stood, and Amanda made the introductions.

Hanford clicked his heels together and bowed deeply. "Charming. Simply charming. Cavindish." His bushy grey eyebrows drew together. "Did we meet at the prince's annual Michaelmas ball?"

Lady Mary patted her bun. "I think I'd remember meeting a gentleman such as yourself. Also, I make it a point not to celebrate Michaelmas. I have a bone to pick with that particular archangel. As an administrator of cosmic intelligence, he has been much too lax when it comes to informing the populace in the recklessness of the unadulterated slaughter of geese."

"Uh ..." Hanford blew out his cheeks and slid a glance at Amanda.

She frowned at her chaperone. Now really wasn't the time to act the mental incompetent. Between her and Hanford, it was like watching a joust of who could act the biggest idiot. She cleared her throat. "I'm glad you decided to come tonight. I wasn't certain you would."

He flashed his incisors at her. "Oh, I wouldn't miss it. I think the public deserves an informed debate."

Amanda's body tensed. Informed debate, her foot. But now wasn't the time to antagonize the marquess. She'd save her anger for the stage. Perhaps it would help her to find her voice.

Lady Mary glided to a side table and adjusted the mirror hanging above it. "What is it exactly that you gentlemen do here at Simon's? I'm thinking of opening a ladies' club, and am curious about your activities."

"A ladies' club?" Hanford tossed his head back and loosed peals of laughter. "What on earth would a group of women do at a club?"

Lady Mary tapped her fingers along the marble top of the table and plastered a wide smile on her face. "That's why I asked you about your club's activities. To determine our options."

"It is a sound idea." If it had sounded foolish to Amanda before, the marquess's mockery had transformed it to an outstanding proposition. "Women want the freedom to act without the strictures imposed by male society."

"Isn't that what your sitting rooms are for?" he asked.

Lady Mary and Amanda stared at him, unblinking.

He straightened his cravat. "Yes. Well, if you are that interested, I'm more than happy to show you around the club. I'm not a member here, but many of my friends are.

I'll introduce you, and you can see what we're all about."

Lady Mary rolled up onto her toes. "That would be lovely." She glanced at Amanda and her smile faltered. "But I'm here to support Miss Wilcox. I don't suppose you'd like to go on the tour, dear?"

Mingle among the crowds, people who would love to jeer at her, snub her? No, that wasn't at the top of her list. She shook her head. "But you go if you want the tour. I'm happy to wait here." She nibbled on her bottom lip. A public tour in a well-respected club couldn't be dangerous to Lady Mary, could it? Even if the tour was led by a criminal.

Maybe she should go along.

"Wonderful." Lady Mary bustled to the door and waited for Hanford to open it. "I'll be back soon, and I'm sure the Ladies' Society will be here at any moment."

With a swish of satin, Lady Mary swept from the room. Hanford dipped his head, a slight smile dancing around his lips. "Goodbye, Miss Wilcox." He tapped the wall three times in quick succession, then left the room, closing the door with a decided snick behind him.

Amanda's scalp prickled. She stepped forward, hesitated. Lady Mary really should be safe with the marquess in public, and it wasn't as though she was a helpless, old lady. But Hanford's behavior had been decidedly odd.

A slight whisper of air on the back of her neck sent a shiver racing down her spine. She rubbed her arms, trying to chase away the chill.

Another set of arms wrapped around her from behind. Large, strong, and tight as a python. She opened her mouth to scream, and a meaty palm slapped across her mouth. The man easily lifted her off the ground and turned to the open door in the back of the room. Amanda kicked at him and struggled to pull her arms loose from his hold, to no avail.

Her head started to swim, pinpricks of light dancing

before her eyes. She managed to suck down the barest amount of air between his fingers, but it wasn't enough.

As he carried her through the door and kicked it closed behind them, she realized it wasn't Lady Mary she should have been worried about.

Chapter Twenty-Three

Julius leapt from the carriage before it stopped rolling. The moon had emerged from the clouds, and the shadow of St. Katherine's bell tower slanted across the front of Simon's. The footman at the front of the club hurried to open the door but wasn't fast enough. Julius ran into it, leading with his shoulder, and burst through.

He ignored the flare of pain that shot through his arm and raced to the meeting hall where the debate would be held. A crush of men formed a barrier. Pushing his way through, Julius kept his eye out for any flash of muslin. An untidy bun of mahogany hair. Anything feminine.

Men joked and jostled each other, obviously growing impatient for their night's entertainment. Julius cursed. Amanda could be five feet from him and he wouldn't see her. He forced his way to the raised stage, pushing men aside, ignoring their shouts of displeasure.

Jumping onto the wood planks, he searched the crowd. No Amanda. No Lady Mary. He breathed deeply through his nose. He needed to think. Amanda was most likely in a waiting room, and there was nothing for him to worry over.

Dunkeld entered the room and made his way to the stage. The throng of men parted before him like waves before a frigate. Size had its advantages.

Climbing the stairs at the side of the stage, Dunkeld asked, "Do you see them?"

A boyish face Julius recognized jogged after Dunkeld. Bertie beamed and stuck a hand out to Julius. "I'm glad you could make it. We're just about to get started, just as soon as we find our debaters."

Julius's fist involuntarily clenched, and Bertie winced. Releasing the young man's hand, Julius took a step closer. "What do you mean? Where's Miss Wilcox?"

Bertie flexed his fingers. "Well, I'd left the women in the back study, but they must have wandered away." His eyes lit up. "Oh, look, there they are now."

Julius spun and saw Lady Mary holding the arm of Hanford as he led her into the room. The marquess stopped and said a few words with one man, slapped the back of another.

Julius leapt off the stage. He hit the back of a squat man in garish orange pantaloons and bounced off.

Dunkeld steadied him with a hand at his shoulder. "Allow me." The Scotsman started forward, and bodies either jumped out of the way or were tossed aside like yesterday's newspaper.

Julius followed in the path his friend created. But when they reached Hanford, Julius stepped around Dunkeld and into Hanford's space. "Where is she?"

Hanford rounded his pale blue eyes. "I don't know what you mean."

"Miss Amanda Wilcox." Planting his feet wide, Julius gripped the lapels of Hanford's coat. "You will tell me where she is right now."

Lady Mary's gaze darted between the two men. "We left her in the back room."

"She isn't there now." Julius shook the man, and was pleased when Hanford let out an unmanly squawk. "Where. Is. She?"

Bertie rushed up to them. "Julius! You can't manhandle the marquess in the middle of our club."

Dunkeld placed a palm on the young man's chest. He glanced back at Julius. "He's right, you know."

Smiling grimly, Julius said, "Then you'll have to excuse us. Lady Mary, please stay here." Pulling Hanford on to the tips of his booted toes, Julius strode from the room, dragging the flailing man behind him. He headed down the hall to one of the smaller smoking rooms and kicked the door open. He flung Hanford onto a low-lying settee.

Dunkeld closed the door behind them. He jiggled the handle and frowned. "You broke the lock."

Someone pounded on the door. "This is supposed to be a friendly debate," Bertie yelled through the wood.

With one hand pressing the door shut, Dunkeld grabbed a low bureau and dragged it to block the frame. "That should give us plenty of time."

"Time for what?" Hanford jerked on his cravat and pushed to his feet. Julius shoved him back down. Bright red blotches darkened the marquess's face. "I demand you tell me the reason for this impertinence."

Julius cracked his neck. "You already know the reason. I've asked you twice. Don't make me ask a third time."

"This is about Miss Wilcox?" Hanford pinched his bottom lip between his thumb and forefinger. "Lady Mary and I left her in the sitting room. I know nothing further."

"Horse shit." Dunkeld crossed his arms over his chest, the wool of his jacket's sleeves pulling taut across the biceps.

"I agree." Julius bent over Hanford, placing one hand on the man's knee, the other on his shoulder. The thin silk of the man's pantaloons provided no protection. Julius dug his thumb into the nerve on the inside of his leg.

Hanford yelped and tried to jump off the settee.

Julius held him down. "That's usually a man's first response. To try to escape the source of pain. It gets worse when you realize there is no escape."

Hanford's broad forehead glistened in the light. "Sod off, Rothchild. I've done nothing wrong."

Dunkeld sighed heavily. He turned sad eyes on Julius. "Can I assume that our order to keep this a stealth mission has been nullified?"

"That would be correct." Julius dug his thumb in again and tucked his head against one of Hanford's flailing arms. Liverpool could kiss his arse if he thought he was going to put his investigation over Amanda. Gripping Hanford's collar, he throttled the man back against the settee. "We know about your crime ring. The businesses you've infiltrated. All the men you've blackmailed." Julius doubted they knew a tenth of the people this man had victimized. But it never hurt to bluff.

"You don't know what you're talking about," Hanford spat out.

Julius gripped Hanford high up on his shoulder. With his fingers digging into the man's back, he tucked his thumb under Hanford's coat, found the spot right under the man's collarbone and squeezed.

He kept the pressure on, even as Hanford shrieked and writhed beneath him. He kept it on until Dunkeld pulled him away.

"I think he's ready to talk," Dunkeld said mildly.

"All of you can go to hell." Hanford wheezed, spittle rolling down his chin.

Julius stepped towards him, and the older man shied away.

"Wait." Hanford raised a hand, and slumped against the brocade back. "Just wait."

Bile rose to the back of Julius's throat. Every second he wasted with this scum could be the second Amanda needed him most. "I don't have time to wait."

Hanford shook his head. "I'm not admitting to anything. But if you want to find your woman, I have an idea where she might be."

Dunkeld slapped a hand around Hanford's neck. "Did you not understand the man when he said time was of the essence? Stop dancing around the answer."

"The catacombs!" Clawing at the fingers around his neck, Hanford's gaze darted between Dunkeld and Julius. "There's an entrance into them from the basement of this building. It's a web of pathways. There are entrances to the catacombs from all the buildings on this block. St. Katherine's used to have an abbey. It's been torn down and built over by this club and others, but the foundations remain. And the basement entrances. Most of them had been bricked over, but not this one." He bobbed his head up and down. "I'll bet Miss Wilcox was taken down there."

Julius stumbled back. He gripped the back of a chair as chills swamped his body. He locked his knees and prayed he wouldn't collapse. It had to be the damn catacombs.

Without looking at Dunkeld, Julius said, "Send a message to Liverpool. Tell him what's happened." Slowly, he straightened and plodded to the door.

"I can't leave him until one of Liverpool's men arrives." Dunkeld looked from Julius to Hanford, and back again. "If we want to keep this under wraps, we can't give him time to communicate with his accomplices."

"I know." Grabbing the end of the bureau, Julius pushed it aside and jerked the door open. The hallway was empty. "Stay here with him. I need to find Amanda."

"But ..." Dunkeld grabbed his hair and cursed at the ceiling. Gathering himself, he put his fists on his hips and took a deep breath. "I'll go into the catacombs. You stay here."

"The woman I'm going to marry is down there. I can't stay." Julius ignored his friend's dropped jaw and ran from the room. He'd never been to the club's basement before, but it wasn't hard to find the staircase. He grabbed a candle from a wall sconce and took each step down on shaking legs. He told his body to hurry, but his legs refused, each step closer to the labyrinth of passageways a battle.

He crossed the basement and stood at the entrance to a small archway that had long ago lost its door. The stone steps down were narrow, uneven. Dank air washed over him, and he knew he'd found the catacombs. Sweat ran down his spine. He tried to focus on marshaling his nerve, pushing out the fear.

The fear fought back. With a groan, he descended into the darkness. Of course, there was no question he'd go down and find her, claustrophobia be damned. Because of

Amanda, there were some things he feared more than being trapped. A life without Amanda was right there at the top.

He'd been a right arse. Thinking that a woman could trap him. That marriage was another prison. Amanda had shown him just how liberating loving a woman could be. He'd built his own walls, never letting a woman get too close, trying to safeguard his heart. She'd blasted right through them. She was his light guiding him out of the darkness.

And if he didn't find Amanda alive and in one piece, Julius knew he'd be lost in the dark forever.

* * *

The skin around Amanda's wrists burned, but she kept trying to wriggle her hands free from their bindings. The rope her kidnapper had used wasn't the soft silk or hemp that she was used to. Nor was she accustomed to the panic she'd felt in the ropes when she'd awoken, face down on cold stone, with her arms bound behind her. The feeling of safety Julius created with his knotwork was gone, transformed into terror and pain.

If she survived this, Amanda vowed not to let this piece of filth ruin what she and Julius had found together.

No, she corrected herself, *when* she survived this. When she got out of here, she would take Julius's hand, slip a length of rope into it, and let him choose what to do with her. The sense of freedom she had when bound to his bed was something she cherished and would fight for.

Laying on her right side, her back to the wall, she let her head sag to the floor. Everything ached. She rolled her shoulders and peeked at the man who'd taken her. The torch by the door sent flickering shadows over his face. He leaned against the wall of the small chamber they were in, arms crossed, tracing patterns in the dirt with his toe.

Bastard didn't even have the decency to look abashed. He looked bored as he waited for the partner he'd said was coming. Amanda had asked what would happen to her then, but the man had smiled, told her not to worry.

She worried.

The pain in her upper arms started to dull as numbness crept into its place. Amanda closed her eyes and tried to collect herself. She was incapacitated and defenseless. There had been a time when she hadn't wanted to be responsible. Now she wasn't. Her fate laid in someone else's hands. She should be ecstatic.

Tucking her knees into her chest, she curled into a ball. She was an idiot. Of course, she was responsible for herself. Just as she'd been responsible for her little sister. Every second that she'd questioned her actions, relived the moment when she'd fought off her father and plunged a knife into his side, all those recriminations were over.

She'd made a decision to protect herself and Liz. She'd taken the responsibility of stopping their father, and she wouldn't regret it.

She would even repeat it if given the chance. Amanda opened her eyes and pressed her lips together. She would get out of here, even if she had to kill her captor to do so. She circled her wrists as much as the ropes allowed, not stopping when she felt blood trickle down her palms.

Her kidnapper tossed a glance over at her, and Amanda froze. He cleared his throat and spat something Amanda didn't want to identify onto the floor. Sighing, he peered back down the narrow hallway.

Amanda tugged on her left hand. It shifted an inch. Her blood slickened her wrists, easing the way. She tugged again and bit back a whimper. She was sure she'd lost some skin, but her hand had moved another inch.

Something soft echoed in the distance, a steady beat growing louder. Her abductor pushed off the wall, coming to attention.

Amanda twisted harder. She might, *might*, have a chance against one man. Against two there was no hope.

Her hand popped free as a second man filled the small doorway. She swallowed back tears, her chest burning. Life just wasn't fair. It was as though the fates were telling her not to even bother fighting back.

She was going to miss so much. Laughing with her sister. Being a doting aunt to Liz's children. Enjoying whatever time was left of Julius's touches.

Her heart squeezed. It was that last one that would be her final living thought. It would keep her warm as the darkness crept in.

The two men talked in low tones before turning towards her. They filled the small chamber, looming over her as they stepped close. A blade glittered in her abductor's hand.

Yes, she would think of Julius in her last moments, not of pain or fear. She closed her eyes and put a picture of him in her mind.

Someone cursed, and something heavy hit the ground.

Amanda snapped her eyes open, and her image of Julius came to life. He stepped over her kidnapper's body, grabbed the other man by the hand and twisted his wrist. The ruffian dropped to his knees with a shriek, grabbing for the hand contorted beyond any reasonable angle.

Julius turned ravaged eyes on Amanda. He was as pale as moonlight and looked as though he might cast up his accounts at any moment. He was the most beautiful thing she'd ever seen.

She scrambled into a seated position. She tried to push to her feet, but her arms weren't cooperating. "Julius! How did you—"

"Are you all right?" Julius kneed the man in the face and dropped him. He took two steps and lifted Amanda by her shoulders. "Did they hurt you?"

Amanda opened her mouth and caught a flash of silver flying at Julius. She threw herself to the side, pulling Julius with her, and the blade of her kidnapper's knife scraped off the stone wall.

"Close your eyes." Julius pushed her into the corner and faced the attacker.

The kidnapper slowly approached, swinging his arm

back and forth, his blade in constant motion. The other man stumbled to his feet, cradling his arm.

"What?" Why would she close her eyes? Not with two men intent on doing them harm in the room.

"Please." Julius's voice was hoarse, desperate. He kicked the kidnapper in the stomach, and the man fell back a step. "I don't want you to see me do this. I don't want the image of the next few moments anywhere in your head."

She wanted to argue. Tell him that nothing he did would ever frighten her. Or disgust her. But there was no time. So, she nodded and closed her eyes.

And wished she had blocked her ears, as well. The sounds were horrific. The cracks echoing off the stone, noises that could only be bones snapping. The howls of pain. And finally, the silence.

A thumb brushed her cheek, and she threw herself at Julius. He wrapped his arms tightly around her waist, burying his face in the crook of her neck. "Keep your eyes closed," he said and stroked her hair. "Will you keep them closed until I say?"

She nodded.

Julius lifted her into his arms and started walking. Amanda rested her head against his chest, felt the rapid pounding of his heart beneath her cheek. His arms trembled beneath her legs and back. She couldn't imagine what this had cost him.

"You came down into a dungeon for me." She burrowed deeper into his coat, inhaled his musk.

"I'd do anything for you." Gently, Julius set her down on her feet. "You can open your eyes now."

She blinked. They stood at the bottom of a stairwell. A row of skulls had been cemented into the walls around them, a macabre mosaic.

Julius tipped up her chin. "Haven't you figured it out yet? I love you." He pressed his forehead against hers. "I realized as I was searching for you that had Hanford's letter to the paper about us not been published, I still would want to marry you. You are the only woman who will make me happy. I choose you." His breath brushed her lips. "Please, choose me back."

"But the disgrace ..."

"Doesn't matter to me in the least." He ran his hands up her arms and down her back, as though checking that all her parts were still in the right place. "We will live quite happily at my country estate, away from the censure of society. Away from a bevy of interfering servants. Just the two of us, and whatever family we create."

It sounded wonderful. A peaceful life, loving the man of her dreams. Being loved by him in return.

Yet she hesitated. "A lord needs heirs. What if I can't have children?"

"You know I don't care about that." He cupped her cheek. "Besides, every couple will face problems. It comes down to who you want to face those problems with. We'll face them together." A sly smile tugged at his lips. "Though we'll have a devil of a good time trying for those heirs."

She nodded, warmth radiating through her body.

"That's a yes?" Julius asked.

She nodded again.

Julius whooped and planted a kiss on her lips. He broke away smiling. "First, let's get the hell out of here." With a hand at her elbow, he pulled her up the stairs. "Second, I'm going to see the archbishop for a special license as soon as I apprise Liverpool of what I've learned."

Amanda flew up the stairs beside him, her feet barely touching the ground. "We don't need a special license."

"I don't want to wait." He pushed through a wood door and dragged her through a storage room. "I think three days should be enough time to get you an adequate dress."

Amanda pulled to a stop in an empty kitchen. "I don't care about a dress. But I do want my sister to be there."

Julius frowned. "Damn Marcus and his continental tour." He blew out a breath. "Fine. I will wait. And I'll write to Marcus and tell him to get his arse home." He took her hands, and his eyebrows drew together. Julius looked down. Cursing, he whipped his handkerchief out of his coat pocket. "Why didn't you say you were hurt?"

Amanda examined her wrists. The right one was red and inflamed, a thin streak of dried blood stretched from the palm of her hand to her thumb. The wounds on her left wrist were worse. The bleeding had slowed, but dark red beads still oozed from the deep gashes left by the rope.

Julius folded the white linen into a long rectangle and wrapped it around her left wrist. He tied a neat knot with the two tails and clamped his hand around it, providing pressure. He glared back the way they'd come.

Amanda patted his chest with her right hand. "You can't kill them twice." Her hand paused. "They are dead, right?"

"They're dead," Julius said grimly.

"Then let's get out of here." Amanda led him to the staircase. "I want a hot—" She sucked in a breath. "Lady Mary! She's with Hanford."

"She's fine. And Dunkeld is with Hanford." Julius rubbed small circles on her lower back.

Amanda released her breath and nodded. They continued up the stairs and stepped into the hall. Fine paper covered the walls and an oriental rug ran the length. They were back in the club's public space. A muted roar met their ears, followed by some boos.

"Bertie must have found someone to replace you and Hanford." Julius peeked under the handkerchief, checking her wrist. He applied more pressure. "It sounds like the club's members are getting their entertainment."

Tiptoeing down the hall, Amanda peered through open doors into the empty rooms they passed. She stopped in front of a set of closed double doors, just as another chorus of boos erupted from behind it. "That's the members being entertained?" She swallowed. "I'd hate to hear them when they don't find something diverting."

"It's just how this lot are." Peeling the door open an inch, Julius looked through. "At least this crowd won't pelt you with rotten tomatoes if they don't like what you have to say." He waved at her to come close.

Amanda pressed her eye to the opening. And gasped. "It's Mrs. Fry. They've let her speak."

"Yes, but they wanted to hear from you. She's a poor substitute." Julius smiled down at her. "Then again, I am biased."

Amanda looked from his dear face, to her bandaged wrist, to the crowd jeering behind the door. Mrs. Fry beamed at the club members, obviously unperturbed by her reception. She smiled, and argued, and stood her ground. And the men didn't look so scary anymore.

Smoothing down her skirts, Amanda nodded. She could do this.

Julius's brow knotted together. "What ...?" His forehead cleared. "You don't have to go up there. After what you've been through tonight, no one could expect it."

"I want to." Amanda pulled her sleeve over her bandage and scraped at the dried blood on her skin with her nail. *Want* might be a step too far. But it was something she felt she needed to do. For herself. For Mrs. Fry. And for the thousands of people out there who screamed and shouted over the injustice in the world but had nobody to hear them.

Julius tidied her hair, pinning loose strands back into her bun. He brushed dirt from her gown. "I'll be in the front row. If you need anything, or just a friendly face to look at, I'll be there."

"I know." Amanda squeezed his hand and took a deep breath. Pulling open the door, she stepped into the meeting room and headed for the stage. She could feel Julius behind her, and it was enough.

Mrs. Fry saw her coming and her eyes lit up. She waved for Amanda to climb the steps. "Gentlemen, I have a friend here who can tell you her own experiences with the English penal system. A first-hand account of how we, as a nation, allow the mistreatment of the young and innocent. Please welcome Miss Amanda Wilcox."

A flood of cheers and boos crashed into Amanda. Heart in her throat, her gaze fled to Julius. The steady look in his eyes soothed her and her pulse rate evened out. She could do this.

With her head held high, Amanda climbed onto the stage and faced her fears.

Chapter Twenty-Four

Julius blotted her wet hair with a towel, squeezing out the drops of water from her bath. They sat on the thick carpet of Julius's room, before the fireplace. Amanda had never felt so pampered and relaxed in her life.

And after the stresses of the evening, she felt like she deserved it. That was the second time in her life when she'd been minutes away from death. The knowledge caused her insides to clench and twist. But facing death had a way of wiping your mind of irrelevancies, leaving only what was truly important.

She leaned against Julius's chest, his skin warm against her bare back. She sat in the vee of his legs and idly ran her fingers up and down his thigh.

Her speech hadn't gone as she'd anticipated. Although still receiving her share of boos, the evening had turned more into a question and answer session with the club's members, not the lecture she'd planned. The men had been curious about her experiences, and seemed genuinely shocked by the conditions she'd revealed. Mrs. Fry had an idea for a series of speaking engagements with the two of them, but Amanda hadn't decided. Although she'd confronted her fear, she didn't know if it was something she'd want to do on a weekly basis. Besides, she wanted her nights to belong to Julius.

He shook her hair out before the fire, combing his fingers through the locks. Reggie rolled over, bumping her foot, and fell back asleep. Amanda understood why the dog offered up his belly so quickly. It really was a lovely feeling to be petted so.

"I'm going to miss Reggie after we're married." She scratched his furry leg with her toe.

"Oh, he's coming with us." Julius brought the towel to her stomach and slowly dried it. "He's more ours than Marcus's and your sister's now, anyway. I'll dognap him if I have to."

Amanda laughed. "He'll be my perfect wedding gift." She held up her hand. The sapphire in the ring Julius had given her looked as dark as the sky right after the sun set. She still couldn't believe she was betrothed.

After the club, Julius had taken her and Lady Mary home and left immediately to talk with Liverpool. After his meeting, Julius had stopped at his own townhouse to retrieve his mother's ring from his safe. He'd wasted no time sliding it on her finger when he'd returned.

Sleep tugged at her eyelids, but Amanda didn't want the night to end. "What will happen with your investigation? With Hanford?"

"Hanford will be joining Madame Sable in a safe house until the time Liverpool deems it acceptable to try them. He can't let it be known they're under arrest until we clean up the rest of the crime ring." Julius swiped the soft terry cloth across one breast, then the other.

Amanda was quite dry, but she didn't feel the need to point that out. She arched her back into the caress. "And will you find everyone involved."

"Nearly." Dropping a row of kisses down her neck, Julius squeezed her breast through the cloth. "It may take Liverpool and his men awhile to analyze all the information we found, to go through all the business filings, but he'll find the center of the web eventually. Now"—he trailed the towel down her stomach and lower—"the time to talk business is over. I won't be able to bind your hands until you heal, but I can do a lot with just your lower body."

She believed him. Letting her knees drop open, she rocked into his hand. The terry cloth scraped and soothed.

Made her wet and then dried her up. She clasped the back of his neck. "I understand now. Why I love being tied up by you."

Julius tossed the towel to the side and slid his fingers between her lower lips. He dipped the tip of his index finger into her opening before drawing back and gliding it over her seam. "Why?"

She dug her nails into his skin and willed him to increase the pressure. The feather-light touches drove her mad and offered no relief. But she knew he had his reasons, and that she would benefit from his patience.

"By letting you bind me, I was giving you responsibility over my body. My welfare." Turning her head, she nipped at his stubbled jaw. "I was so tired of looking after myself, after Liz, and I hadn't done a very good job of taking care of us."

Amanda felt the rumble in his chest and cut him off before he could argue. "That's in the past." She rubbed his hard thigh and blinked back the sudden rush of tears. It was true. She could box up that part of her life and put it away forever. "But I could only enjoy making myself helpless because it was *you* tying the knots. I trust you. And letting you bind my body connected me to you in a way I never thought possible."

His fingers stilled. "I'll never betray that trust."

That vow meant more to her than the ones he'd say on their wedding day. The back of her throat burned. But this wasn't the time for mawkish sentiment. She and Julius were entangled naked before the fire, and her emotions could be channeled to a much better use.

She rolled to her knees and faced him. Brushing the back of her fingers up his inner thigh, she lowered her head and took his mouth. He groaned when she wrapped her fist around his length, and Amanda swallowed the sound.

"I won't always want to give you the power," she whispered. She licked around the rim of his ear and bit the lobe. "Sometimes I'll want to take it. Or share it."

He slapped her behind, and the shot made her core tingle. "And I won't always want it." Taking her hand off of him, Julius rolled to his feet, pulling her up. He led her to the bed and nudged her to lay down. "You're a damned difficult woman to keep an eye on all the time." He bent and removed his chest of toys from the bedside bureau. Firelight flickered over the muscled planes of his thighs and arse.

Amanda bit her lip.

Julius opened the lid and pulled out a length of red rope. He tossed it on her ankles. "Prison escapes, kidnappings," he grumbled. "It's a good thing you're in love with a retrieval expert."

Amanda lifted a leg, pointing her toes at the canopy. The rope slid down into her lap. She picked it up and dragged the end of it across her abdomen. She circled her navel and drew a line down to her aching bundle of nerves. The first scrape of silk against her nub was almost more than she could take.

Julius's eyes flared and went dark as midnight. Climbing onto the bed, he prowled over her body. Bending down to kiss her stomach, he took the rope from her hand. He wound it around her thigh and tugged her leg wide. He wrapped the other end of the rope around his palm.

"Did you forget something from that chest?" she asked.

He arched an eyebrow in question.

"The linen pocket." She chewed on her lower lip, feeling a small pang of regret for the words she knew she must speak. "I won't mind if you wish to wait to try for children." Julius had come so far for her. Had expanded his limits more than she could ever have dreamed. When it came to something so important as fatherhood, she didn't want to rush him if he was not yet ready.

"I haven't forgotten." He lowered his head, and the first velvety swipe of his tongue made her back bow. "The linens shall remain in the box until I find a moment to burn them."

Julius climbed up her body and kept his eyes locked with hers as he sank into her channel.

She dug her fingers into the counterpane and strangled back a moan at the silky glide. Bare, he was everything she'd imagined. Hard and smooth. Hot and throbbing. Pure heaven.

He cupped her jaw and ran his thumb along her cheek. He lowered his mouth to hers, teasing and taking, giving and demanding. When he broke away, they were both breathless.

Julius whispered against her lips, "Nothing is ever coming between us again."

Amanda wrapped her arms around his back. She was going to hold him to that promise. Their future would hold highs and lows, joys and heartbreak. Such was the reality of life. But as long as she and Julius walked through it together, with no walls between them, Amanda would face it, unafraid.

And relishing every moment.

* * * *

About the Author

Like almost one-third of all romance writers, Alyson Chase is a former attorney (okay, maybe a slight exaggeration, but not by much). She happily ditched those suits and now works in her pajamas writing about men's briefs instead of legal briefs. When she's not writing, she's probably engaged in one of her favorite hobbies: napping, eating, or martial arts (That last one almost makes up for the first two, right?) She also writes humorous, small-town, contemporary romance novels under the name Allyson Charles.

Connect with Alyson at:

www.alysonchase.com
www.facebook.com/AlysonChaseAuthor
Twitter: @1alysonchase
Email: alysonchaseauthor@gmail.com

30290943R00179

Printed in Poland
by Amazon Fulfillment
Poland Sp. z o.o., Wrocław